Miguel de Cervantes Saavedra, Peter Anthony Motteau

The History of the Ingenious Gentleman Don Quixote of la Mancha

Vol. 1

Miguel de Cervantes Saavedra, Peter Anthony Motteau

The History of the Ingenious Gentleman Don Quixote of la Mancha
Vol. 1

ISBN/EAN: 9783337338534

Printed in Europe, USA, Canada, Australia, Japan

Cover: Foto ©Andreas Hilbeck / pixelio.de

More available books at **www.hansebooks.com**

THE HISTORY

OF THE INGENIOUS GENTLEMAN

DON QUIXOTE

OF

LA MANCHA;

TRANSLATED FROM THE SPANISH

By MOTTEUX.

WITH COPIOUS NOTES; AND AN ESSAY ON THE LIFE
AND WRITINGS OF CERVANTES,

By JOHN G. LOCKHART, Esq.

IN FOUR VOLUMES.

VOL. I.

BOSTON:
LITTLE, BROWN AND COMPANY,
1865.

PUBLISHERS' ADVERTISEMENT.

THIS edition of Don Quixote is an exact reprint of that edited by Mr. LOCKHART, and published in five volumes at Edinburgh, in 1822. It was then that the translations of the Spanish Ballads first appeared, and although Mr. Lockhart did not place his name in the title-page, he is well known to be the translator of the Ballads, and to have edited the edition. We give from Blackwood's Magazine of June, 1822, by way of preface, a notice of Mr. Lockhart's notes and criticisms, and of the character of Motteux's translation:

" We have had in England no less than four distinct translations of the best of all romances, and none of them bad ones; but it strikes us as something very strange, that until now we should never have had any edition whatever of any one of these translations, containing *notes*, to render the text intelligible. The few miserable scraps, commonly found at the foot of the page, in the editions either of Smollett or Motteux, are not worth mentioning. The text of Don Quixote, full as it is of allusions to history and romance, remained, to all intents and purposes, without annotation, comment, or explanation; and of course, of the readers of Don Quixote, very few ever understood the meaning of Cervantes. A thousand of his happiest *hits*

went for nothing; and a Spanish reader, with a translation of the bare text of Shakspeare in his hands, had just
as good a chance to understand Shakspeare, as the English
reader had to understand the author, who, though writing
in a different form, is, perhaps more than any other the
world has produced, entitled to be classed with Shakspeare.

"This great blank has now been ably and fully supplied;
and the English reader is in possession of an edition of
Don Quixote, not only infinitely superior to any that ever
before appeared in England, but, so far as we are able to
judge, much more complete and satisfactory than any one
which exists in the literature of Spain herself.

"The text used is that of MOTTEUX, and this is, we
think, out of all sight, the richest and best — although the
editor himself seems to hint, now and then, something not
unlike a partiality for the much older version of Shelton.
Shelton's Quixote is undoubtedly well worthy of being
studied by the English scholar; but it is far too antiquated
an affair to serve the purposes of the English reader.
That of Motteux is, if not so literally accurate, quite as
essentially and substantially so; and Motteux, the translator of Cervantes and Rabelais, ·possesses a native humour
which no other translator that we ever met with has approached.

"The notes, read continuously, and without reference to
the text they so admirably illustrate, would form a most
delightful book. Indeed, what can be more interesting than
such a collection of rare anecdotes, curious quotations from
forgotten books, and beautiful versions of most beautiful
ballads? Printed in a volume by themselves, these notes

to Don Quixote would constitute one of the most entertaining *Ana* in our language, or in any other that we are acquainted with. But, above all, to the student of *Spanish*, who attacks the Don in the original, they must be altogether invaluable, for Cervantes' allusions to the works of Spanish authors, particularly his own contemporaries, are so numerous, that when Don Quixote appeared, it was regarded by the literati of Madrid almost as a sort of Spanish *Dunciad*."

CONTENTS

OF

VOLUME FIRST.

PART I.—BOOK II.

PART I.—BOOK III.

LIFE OF CERVANTES.

ALTHOUGH Miguel de Cervantes Saavedra was
not only the brightest genius of his age and
country, but a man of active life and open manners, and engaged personally in many interesting
transactions of his time, there are, nevertheless,
few distinguished men of letters who have left
behind them more scanty materials of biogra-
phy. His literary reputation was not of the
highest order till *Don Quixote* made it so ; and
ere then he had outlived the friends and companions of his youthful adventures, and withdrawn into a life of comparative privacy and
retirement. In the age immediately succeeding
his own, abundant exertions were made to discover the scattered and faded traces of his
career; but with what very indifferent success
is well known to all acquainted with the literary
history of Spain. More recently, the life of
Cervantes has been elaborately written, both by
the best of his commentators, Don Juan Pellicer,

and by Don Vincente de los Rios, editor of the
Spanish Academy's superb edition of Don Quixote; but neither of these has, after all, been able
to add much to the original naked outline which
guided their researches.

Cervantes was by birth a gentleman, being
descended from an ancient family, originally of
Galicia, many branches of which were, at the
beginning of the sixteenth century, honorably
settled in Toledo, Seville, and Alcarria. Rod-.
rigo de Cervantes, his father, seems to have resided, for the most part, at Alcala de Henares,
where, thirty years before the birth of his son,
the second university of Spain was founded by
the munificent Cardinal Ximenes. His mother,
Donna Leonora de Corteñas, was also a lady of
gentle birth. The parish register shows that he
was baptized on the 9th of October, 1547.

His parents, whose circumstances were the
reverse of affluent, designed their son for one
of the learned professions; and being most probably of opinion that his education would proceed better were it conducted at some distance
from their own residence, they sent him early
to Madrid, where he spent several years under
the direction of a philologer and theologian,
(famous in his day,) by name Juan Lopez de
Hoyos. This erudite person superintended, early
in 1569, the publication of certain academical

Luctus, on occasion of the death of the queen ;
and, among the rest, there appear an elegy and
a ballad, both written, as the editor expresses it,
by his " dear and beloved disciple Miguel de Cervantes." Doctor Lopez de Hoyos seems to have
been in the custom of putting forth, now and
then, little volumes of poetical miscellanies,
chiefly composed by himself ; and we have Cervantes' own authority * for the fact, that the
doctor's " dear disciple " contributed to these
publications *Filena,* a pastoral poem of some
length, besides a great variety of sonnets, canzonets, ballads, and other juvenile essays of ver-
sification.

These attempts, in themselves sufficiently
trifling, had probably excited some little attention ; for Cervantes, in the summer of 1569, accompanied the Cardinal Julio Aquaviva from
Madrid to Rome, where he resided for more than
twelve months as chamberlain to his eminence.
This situation, which, according to the manners
of those days, would have been coveted by persons much his superiors both in birth and in fortune, may in reality have been serviceable to the
development of young Cervantes' genius, as af-
fording him early and easy introduction to the
company both of the polite and of the learned ;
for among the first of both of these classes the

* In the Viage de Parnasso.

Cardinal Aquaviva lived. But the uniformity
and stately repose of a great ecclesiastic's establishment was probably little suited to the inclinations of the young and ardent Spaniard, for.
he seems to have embraced, without hesitation,
the first opportunity of quitting the cardinal's
mansion for scenes of a more stirring character.

On the 29th of May, 1571, there was signed
at Rome the famous treaty between Philip II.,
the Papal See, and the Venetian Senate, in consequence of which the naval forces of those three
powers were immediately combined into one
fleet, for the purpose of checking the progress
of the Turkish navies in the Mediterranean.
Don Juan of Austria, natural son of Charles V.
and brother to the reigning King of Spain, was
intrusted with the supreme command of the
Christian armament, and the young gentlemen
both of Spain and Italy flocked in multitudes
to act as volunteers under his already famous
standard. Cervantes quitted Rome amidst the
first enthusiasm of the universal preparation ;
and having enlisted under Colonna, the General
of the Papal galleys, joined with him the fleet
of Don Juan ere it commenced the cruise which
terminated in the battle of Lepanto. He was
present on that eventful day ; and as he himself
says, (in the preface to the *Second Part of Don
Quixote*,) considered the loss of his left hand,

(which was struck off in the course of the action by a blow of a scymetar,) as a " trifling price to pay for the honor of partaking in the first great action in which the naval supremacy of the Ottoman was successfully disputed by Christian arms." The season being far advanced, the victorious fleet withdrew immediately after this action to Messina, where Cervantes' wound compelled him to spend some weeks in the hospital. Although his hand had been cut off close by the wrist, the whole of that arm remained ever after quite stiff and useless; partly, it is most probable, in consequence of the unskilfulness of the surgeons who attended on him.

This very serious misfortune did not, however, extinguish his military ardor, for he sailed with the same fleet in the following summer, and was present at several descents, on the coast of the Morea; one of which he has described in *Don Quixote* in the person of the Captain De Viedma. At the end of 1572, when the great naval armament in which he had hitherto served was dissolved, he passed into the regular service of his own sovereign. The company he joined was stationed at Naples, and there he remained with it for three years; without rising, or perhaps hoping to rise, above the condition of a private soldier. It must be had in mind, however, that this rank was in those days so far from being held dishonorable or degrading, that men of the very highest birth and fortune were, almost without exception, accustomed to spend some time in it ere they presumed to expect any situation of authority. Thus, for example, the Anne de Montmorencies, the Lantrecs, the Tremouilles, and the Chabannes, had all distinguished themselves as simple men-at-arms ere they rose to any office of command in the army of France; and in that of Spain, it is well known that the wise policy of Charles V. had, long before Cervantes' time, elevated the halberdier and musketeer to be nearly on the same footing with the mounted soldier. It is, therefore, a matter of no great importance that we are left altogether ignorant whether Cervantes served in the infantry or the cavalry during his residence at Naples.

In the autumn of 1575, he was on his way from Italy to Spain; it is not known what was the motive of his journey; when the galley in which he sailed was surrounded by some Moorish corsairs, and he, with all the rest of the Christian crew, had the misfortune to be carried immediately to Algiers. He fell to the share of the corsair captain who had taken him, an Albanian, or Arnaut renegade, known by the name of *Dali Mami the lame;* a mean and cruel creature, who seems to have used Cervantes with the utmost possible harshness. Having a great number of slaves in his possession, he employed the most of them in his galleys, but kept always on shore such as were likely to be ransomed by their friends in Europe ; confining them within the walls of his baths,* and occasionally compelling them to labor in his gardens. Cervantes, whose birth and condition gave hopes of a considerable ransom, spent the greater part of five years of servitude among this latter class of the slaves of Mami, undergoing, however, as he himself intimates, even greater hardships than fell to the lot of his companions, on account of the pertinacity and skill with which he was continually forming schemes of evasion. The last of these, at once the boldest and most deliberate of them all, was deficient of complete success, only because Cervantes had admitted a traitor to his counsels.

Dali Mami, the Arnaut, had for his friend a brother renegade, by birth a Venetian, who had risen high in the favor of the king, and was now a man of considerable importance in the government of Algiers : the same Hassan Aga,

---

* In the notes to this edition of Don Quixote may be found some curious particulars concerning these *Baths* and the manner in which the Christian captives of Cervantes' age were treated at Algiers and Tunis. See the Notes on the story of Viedma.

of whose ferocious character a full picture is drawn in *Don Quixote* by the Captain de Viedma. Mami sometimes made Cervantes the bearer of messages to this man's villa, which was situated on the sea-shore, about three miles from Algiers. The gardens of this villa were under the management of one of Hassan's Christian slaves, a native of Navarre, with whom Cervantes speedily formed acquaintance, and whom he ere long persuaded to undertake the formation of a secret cave beneath the garden, capable of sheltering himself, and as many as fifteen of his brother captives, on whose patience and resolution he had every reason to place perfect reliance. The excavation being completed in the utmost secrecy, Cervantes and his associates made their escape by night from Algiers, and took possession of their retreat, where, being supplied with provisions by the gardener and another Christian slave of Hassan Aga, named or nick-named *El Dorador*, they remained for several months undiscovered, in spite of the most minute and anxious researches, both on the part of their own masters, and of the celebrated Ochali, then tyrant of Algiers.

They had, in the mean time, used all their exertions to procure a sum of money sufficient for purchasing the freedom of one of their companions, who had staid behind them in the city, a

gentleman of Minorca, by name Niana. This
gentleman at length obtained his liberty in the
month of September, 1577, and embarked for
his native island, from whence, according to the
plan concerted, he was to return immediately
with a Spanish brigantine, and so coming close
under shore, at a certain hour of a certain night,
furnish Cervantes and his friends (including the
gardener and *El Dorador*) with the means of
completing their escape. Viana reached Minorca in safety, procured without difficulty a sufficient vessel from the Spanish viceroy, and came
off the coast of Barbary, according to his agreement; but ere he could effect his landing, the
alarm was given by a Moorish sentinel, and he
wisely put out to sea again, being afraid of at-
tracting any more particular attention to the
place of Cervantes' concealment. He and the
unfortunate gentlemen, his companions, were
aware of Viana's attempt, and of the cause of
its failure; but they knew Viana would not be
altogether discouraged by one such accident,
and had good hope of ere long seeing his brigantine again under more happy auspices. But
Hassan's slave *El Dorador*, who had hitherto
been, next to the gardener, the most effectual instrument of their safety, happened, just at this
juncture, to think proper to renounce his Christianity, and it not unnaturally occurred to him,

he could not better commence the career of a
renegade, than by betraying the retreat of Cervantes and his companions. Hassan Aga consequently surrounded the entrance to their cave,
with such a force as put all resistance out of the
question, and the whole fifteen were conducted
in fetters to Algiers. The others were immediately delivered into the possession of their
former masters; but Cervantes, whose previous
attempts at once fixed on him the suspicion of
having headed the whole enterprise, was retain-
ed by the king, in the hope of extracting information, and perhaps of discovering some accom-
plices among the wealthier renegades. It is
probable that Cervantes had no such information to give; but, at all events, he was one of
the last men in the world to give it, had he had
it in his power. He underwent various examinations, declared himself on every occasion the sole
author and contriver of the discovered plot;
and, at last, effectually exhausted the patience
of Ochali, by the firmness of his behavior. The
savage Hassan Aga, himself one of the most extensive slave proprietors in Barbary, exerted all
his influence to have Cervantes strangled *in ter-
rorem;* but, although Ochali was not without
some inclination to gratify Hassan in this particular, the representations of Dali Mami, concerning the value of his private property, could

not be altogether disregarded; and the future author of *Don Quixote* escaped the bowstring, because an Arnaut renegade told an Algerine pirate, that he considered him to be worth something better than two hundred crowns. The whole of these particulars, let it be observed, are not gathered from Cervantes himself,* but from the contemporary author of a history of Barbary, Father Heado. The words in which this ecclesiastic concludes his narrative, are worthy of being given as they stand. "Most marvellous thing!" says he, "that some of these gentlemen remained shut up in the cave for five, six, even for seven months, without even so much as beholding the light of day, sustained all that time by Miguel de Cervantes, and this at the great and continual risk of his own life ; for no less than four times did he incur the nearest peril of being strangled, impaled, or burnt alive, by reason of the bold things on which he adventured, in the hope of bestowing liberty upon many. Had fortune been correspondent to his spirit, industry,

* It has been very commonly supposed, that Cervantes tells his own Algerine history in the person of the captive in Don Quixote. But the reader will find, in the notes to this edition, sufficient reasons for discrediting this notion, in itself certainly a very natural one. There can be no doubt, however, that Cervantes' own experience furnished him with all that knowledge of Algerine affairs and manners, which he has displayed in the story of the Captive, as well as in his less known pieces, the *Trato de Argel*, and the *Española Inglesa*.

B

and skill, at this day Algiers would have been
in the safe possession of the Christians, for to no
less lofty consummation did his designs aspire.
In the end, the whole was treasonously discovered, and the gardener, after being tortured and
picketed, perished miserably. But, indeed, of
the things which happened in that cave, during
the seven months that it was inhabited by those
Christians, and altogether of the captivity and
various enterprises of Miguel de Cervantes, a
particular history might easily be formed. Hassan Aga was accustomed to say, that he should
consider captives, and barks, and the whole city
of Algiers in perfect safety, *could he but be sure
of that handless Spaniard.*"

In effect it appears, that the King of Algiers
did not consider it possible to make sure of Cervantes, so long as he remained in the possession
of a private individual; for shortly after he purchased him from Dali Mami, and kept him shut
up with the utmost severity in the dungeon of
his own palace. The hardships thus inflicted
on Cervantes were, however, in all probability,
the means of restoring to him his liberty much
sooner than he would otherwise have obtained
it. The noble exertions he had made, and the
brilliant talents he had exhibited, had excited
the strongest interest in his favor; and the
knowledge of his harsh treatment in the Haram,

determined the public functionary for ·the redemption of Spanish captives, then resident at
Algiers, to make an extraordinary effort in his
behalf. In fine, this person, by name Father
Juan Gil, declared his willingness to advance
whatever might be necessary, along with the con-
tributions already received from his family in
Spain, to procure the liberty of Cervantes ;· and
although the king forthwith raised his demand
to five hundred crowns, the ransom was paid, and
Cervantes recovered his freedom. The records
of the Redeeming Commission show, that Cervantes' mother (now a widow) contributed two
hundred and fifty crowns ; his sister (married to
a Florentine gentleman, Ambrosio,) fifty ; and a
friend of the family, one Franciso Caramamble,
a similar sum. It was thus that Cervantes at
length returned to Spain in the spring of 1581.

He returned at the age of thirty-four, after
having spent more than ten years of .manhood
amidst such varieties of travel, adventure, enterprise, and suffering, as must have sufficed to sober
very considerably the lively temperament, and at
the same time to mature, enlarge, and strength-
en the powerful understanding, with which he
had been gifted by nature. He returned, however, under circumstances of but little promise,
so far as his personal fortune and advancement
were concerned. His wound had disabled him

as a soldier, and, besides, the long period of his captivity had thrown him out in the course of his military profession. With all his variety of . accomplishments, and all his brilliancy of talents, there was no other profession for the exercise of which he felt himself prepared. His family was poor, his friends few and powerless; and, after some months spent in fruitless solicitation, Cervantes seems to have made up his mind that no path remained open for him but that of literature; in one point of view, indeed, the path most worthy of his genius, and therefore the best he could have selected, had greater choice been afforded; but one which, according to the then manners and customs of Spain, was not likely to prove, in any remarkable degree, conducive to the improvement of his worldly fortunes. He shut himself up, however, and proceeded to labor in his new vocation at once with all the natural fervor of his disposition, and with all the seriousness of a man sensible how much the whole career of life is often affected by the good or ill success of a first effort. As such, he, without doubt, regarded the work in which he had now engaged himself; for he could not, after the lapse of so many years, attach any importance to the juvenile and by this time forgotten productions, which had gone forth under his name, ere he quitted Spain in the suite of

Cardinal Acquaviva. The reader, who has compared the different Lives of Cervantes written by Spanish authors, will, from what I have now said, perceive that I am inclined to follow the opinion of those who think the pastoral romance of *Galatea* was the first work published by him after his return from captivity. The authority of Pellicer, indeed, favors the contrary opinion ; but although he says that Cervantes *immediately* commenced writing for the stage, I can find no authentic record of any dramatic effort of his, until some time after the appearance of the *Galatea*, or indeed until after his marriage, which took place in 1584.

The *Galatea*, like all the lesser works of Cervantes, has been thrown into the shade by the preëminent merit and success of his Don Quixote. Yet there can be no question, that, had Cervantes never written any thing but the *Galatea*, it must have sufficed to give him a high and a permanent place in the literary history of Spain. The grace and beauty of its composition entitle the romance to be talked of in this manner ; but it must be confessed, that it exhibits very few traces of that originality of invention, and none at all of that felicitous exposition of human character, in which the genius of Cervantes afterwards shone forth with its brightest and most peculiar lustre. It is, at the best, a happy imitation of the *Diana* of Montemayor, and of the continuation of that performance by Gil Polo. Like these works, it is deficient in fable, (but indeed the fable of *Galatea,* such as it is, was never completed); like them, it abounds in beautiful description and graceful declamation; and like them, it is continually diversified with the introduction of lyrical pieces, sonnets canzonets, and ballads — some of these exquisite in merit. The metrical effusions of the *Galatea* are, indeed, so numerous, that Bouterweck * says he has little doubt Cervantes wrote the prose narrative expressly for the purpose of embodying the miscellaneous contents of a poetical commonplace book, to whose stores he had probably been making continual additions throughout the whole period of his absence from Spain ; and, above all, during the many weary and idle hours of his captivity. It is certain that many of the poems introduced in the *Galatea* have little apparent relation to the story of the romance ; and, therefore, there may be some foundation for Bouterweck's conjecture. But, on the other hand, it cannot be denied, that the finest strains in the book are filled with allusions, which imply their having been composed subsequent to the termination of the author's residence in Barbary. On

* Geschichte der Spanisches Literatur, B. II.

the whole, the *Galatea* exhibited abundantly the defects of the false and unnatural species of composition to which it belongs ; but it displayed, at the same time, a masterly command of Spanish style, and in general a richness and energy both of thought and of language, enough at the least to excite the highest expectations in regard to the future literary career of Cervantes. It might have been fortunate had he gone on to exert himself in the walk of fiction, in which this first, and, on the whole, successful effort had been made, and by returning to which, long afterwards, he secured his literary immortality, instead of betaking himself, as he soon did, to the dramatic field, in which he had to contend with the most formidable competitors, and for which the event has shown his own talents were less splendidly adapted.

Very shortly after the *Galatea* was published, Cervantes married a young lady, whose charms were supposed to have furnished the chief inspiration of its numerous amatory effusions ; Donna Catalina de Palacios y Salazar y Vozmediano. This lady's dowry was not indeed quite so ample as might be augured from the magnificence of her style ; but she brought Cervantes enough to furnish him with the means of subsistence, and it is probable of idleness, for a considerable number of months. After the lady's portion was exhausted, he seems to have plunged himself at once into the full career of dramatic composition. In this he labored incessantly, but with little success, for about three years. His plays, as was the fashion of the day, he sold, as fast as they were written, to the managers of different theatres in Madrid and elsewhere, receiving, it is probable, but very trifling and inadequate remuneration. For Lope de Vega received at the highest about eighty reals for a comedy; and we may be sure his unsuccessful rival was obliged to be content with very inferior payment.

That the author of Don Quixote should have been unsuccessful in writing for the stage, is a circumstance which cannot but excite considerable astonishment at first sight; nor has all the ingenuity of the celebrated historian of Spanish literature been able to throw much light upon the causes of his failure. " That mass of intrigues, adventures, and prodigies," says he,* " of which the Spanish drama was chiefly composed, was altogether in opposition to the particular character of Cervantes' genius. His manner of thinking and of writing was too nervous and accurate to be accommodated to a species of composition, fantastic, destitute of any plain purpose, and of any durable interest. As

* Bouterwock, Sect. II. Chap. I.

a spectator, he enjoyed pieces, which, as a poet, he could not imitate; and he believed himself to be capable of imitating the Spanish dramatists, because he felt within himself the power and the capacity of doing better things." But when we reflect that the very best of Cervantes' followers and imitators in the field of comic romance, Le Sage, Fielding, and Smollett, attempted, like him, the drama, and, like him, attempted it with indifferent success, we shall most probably be constrained to conclude, that the two kinds of composition, which we might at first sight imagine to require very much the same sort of talents, do in fact require talents of totally different kinds; and so, to attribute the ill-success of Cervantes to causes much more general than are to be deduced from any examination of the particular system of the Spanish stage. Had Calderon, or Shakspeare, or Moliere, written admirable romances, it certainly would have been much more difficult to account for the dramatic failures of Cervantes; but even then it would not have followed that, because great dramatists could write excellent romances, great romance-writers should also be able to write excellent dramas. In a word, there is no doubt that powers may be exhibited in a romance as high and as varied as ever adorned either a tragedy or a comedy; but it seems no less certain, ⸶

that a man may possess all the talents requisite for giving interest and beauty to a romance, in the total absence of those faculties of concentrating interest and condensing expression, without a perfect command of which, neither in Spain nor any other country, has the Genius of the Drama ever achieved any of its wonders.

Cervantes himself informs us, that he wrote during this period of his life between twenty and thirty plays ; but not more than a third part of these have ever been published, although says Bouterweck, there might yet be some hope of recovering the whole, were the theatrical records of Spain sufficiently examined. Of those which have been given to the world, the *Numancia Vengada*, a tragedy in four acts, is universally esteemed the most favorable specimen. The mixture in the fable, and even in the dialogue, of such personages as the Genius of Spain, the God of the river Douro, &c., along with Roman soldiers and Spanish ladies, is a defect too gross and palpable either to admit excuse or to require commentary. But, even in spite of this and of other scarcely less glaring defects, the fine story of Numantian heroism and devotion is certainly told in this drama with a power quite worthy of the genius of its author. The dark superstitions of heathenism are introduced with masterly and chastened skill ; and the whole

of the last act in particular is worked up with
a sustained and fearless vigor both of imagination and of diction, such as no one can survey
without saying to himself, *si sic omnia!* The
comic humor of Cervantes, again, rarely appears
in his comedies, but shines out with infinite ease
and effect in several of his little interludes and
afterpieces; more than one of which have been
of late years translated, and represented with
much success upon the German stage. And
here, by the way, is another coincidence that
may be worth remarking; for Fielding, whose
regular plays were all damned, still lives upon
our own theatre as the author of TOM THUMB.

On the whole, imperfect as are even the best
of Cervantes' theatrical pieces, there occur, nevertheless, in the very worst of them, continual
indications of the fervid genius of the author.
The circumstance which, in all probability, will
be most immediately remarked, and most feel-
ingly regretted by the reader who turns from
Don Quixote to the comedies of Cervantes, is the
absence of that joyous and easy vein which con-
stitutes, throughout the whole of the first of romances, the principal charm of its composition.
I have little doubt that Cervantes began to write
for the stage in the hope of rivalling Lope de
Vega; and that, after the first failure, he was
continually depressed with the more and more

forcible conviction of his own inferiority to that
great and inexhaustible master of the dramatic
art.   He might afterwards derive some conso-
lation from reading Lope de Vega's two very ordinary romances, and his still more ordinary novels.

While Cervantes was occupied in this way, his
residence seems to have been chiefly at Madrid,
but occasionally at Esquivias, where the family
of his wife were settled.   He removed in 1588
to Seville, " having," as he himself expresses it,
"found something better to do than writing comedies."   What this *something* was we have no
means of ascertaining; but we know that one
of the principal branches of his own family had
long been established at Seville in great mercantile opulence, and it is therefore highly probable
that through their means he had procured some
office or appointment which furnished him with
means of subsistence less precarious than could
be afforded by the feverish drudgery in which he
had spent the last three or four years of his life.
Not less than two of the Cervantes-Saavedras of
Seville had written and published poems; so
that we may easily imagine some interest to
have been excited among this wealthy family in
behalf of their poor cousin of Alcala de Henares; and it is far from being unlikely that they
intrusted to his management some subordinate
department of their own mercantile concerns.

In 1595, the Dominicans of Zaragoza proposed
certain prizes for poems to be recited at the festival of St. Hyacinthus ; and one of these was
adjudged to " Miguel Cervantes Saavedra of Seville." In 1596, the Earl of Essex made the
second of his famous descents upon the Spanish
coast, and having surprised Cadiz, rifled the town
and destroyed the shipping of the harbor, including the whole of a second armada, designed, like
that of 1588, for the invasion of England. While
the earl kept possession of Cadiz, the gentlemen
of Seville hastened to take arms, and prepare
themselves to assist in delivering that city from
the English yoke; and amidst other memorials
of their zeal, there are preserved two short poetical effusions of Cervantes. In 1598, Philip
the Second died at Seville ; and Cervantes' name
appears among the list of poets who wrote verses
on occasion of the royal obsequies. A serious
quarrel took place, on the day of the funeral,
between the civil and ecclesiastical authorities
of Seville, and Cervantes was exposed to some
trouble for having ventured to hiss at some part,
we know not what, of their proceedings. Such
are all the traces that have been discovered of
Cervantes' occupations and amusements during
his residence at Seville, which extended from
1588 to 1603, or perhaps the beginning of
1604. The name of the branch of his family

settled there being well known, it is not wonderful, that, after a residence of so many years,
Cervantes should have been often talked of by
his contemporaries as " one of the Saavedras of
Seville."

" It cannot be doubted," says Bouterweck, " although no Spanish author has said so, that the
death of Philip II. must have had a favorable
effect on the genius of Cervantes. When the
indolent Philip III. ascended the throne, the
Spanish people began to breathe more freely.
The nation recovered at least the courage to
sport with those chains which they could not
break, and satire was winked at, provided only
it were delicate." I know not how much foundation of truth there may be for this conjecture,
but it is certainly not the less likely, because
we find Cervantes so soon after the accession of
the new king transferring his habitation to Valladolid, where, during the first years of his reign,
Philip III. was chiefly accustomed to hold his
court. We are almost entirely without information how Cervantes spent the two or three years
immediately preceding his appearance at Valladolid; and this is the more to be regretted
because it is certain that the First Part of *Don
Quixote* was written during this period. A
vague tradition has always prevailed that Cervantes had been sent into La Mancha for the pur-

pose of recovering some debts due to a mercantile house in Seville; that he was maltreated by
the people of La Mancha, and on some pretence
confined for several months in the jail of Argasamilla, and that during this imprisonment the
First Part of *Don Quixote* was both planned and
executed. We know from Cervantes himself,[*]
that the First Part of *Don Quixote* was written in
a *prison;* but have no means of ascertaining in
how far the circumstances of Cervantes' confinement actually corresponded with those of the
tradition.

It is, however, extremely probable, that Cervantes employed a considerable part of the time
during which his family were settled in Seville,
in travelling, for purposes of business, over various districts of Spain, which, in the earlier periods of his life, he could have had small opportunities of examining. The minute knowledge displayed in *Don Quixote,* not only of the soil, but
of the provincial manners of La Mancha, can
scarcely be supposed to have been gathered otherwise than from personal inspection, and that
none of the most hasty. In his novels, most of
which are generally supposed to have been composed about the same period, although they were
not published for several years afterwards, a similar acquaintance is manifested with the manners

* See the Prologue to *Don Quixote.*

of Cordova, Toledo, and many other cities and districts of Spain. Whatever the nature of Cervantes' occupation at Seville might have been, there is, therefore, every reason to believe that excursions, of considerable extent, formed a part either of his duty, or his relaxation.

However all these things might be, it is certain that Cervantes was resident in Valladolid in the summer of 1604, and there is reason to think he had removed to that city at least a year earlier. *Don Quixote* was published at Madrid either in the end of 1604, or at latest in 1605. Some curious particulars of his mode of life, about the time of its appearance, have been gathered from the records of the magistracy of Valladolid, before whom he was brought in the month of June, 1605, on suspicion of having been concerned in a nocturnal brawl and homicide, with which, in reality, he had no manner of concern. A gentleman, by name Don Gaspar Garibay, was assassinated about midnight, close to the house where Cervantes lived. The alarm being given, Cervantes was the first to run out and offer every assistance to the wounded man. It is clear, that the neighborhood was none of the most respectable, for it was instantly suspected that the women of Cervantes' family were ladies of easy virtue, and that he himself having acted as their bully, had, in the course of some infamous scuffle, dealt the deadly blow with his own hand. He and all his household were forthwith arrested, and did not recover their liberty until they had undergone very strict and minute examinations. From the records of the court we gather, that Cervantes professed himself to be resident at Valladolid, for purposes of *business ;* that, on account of his literary reputation, he was in the custom of receiving frequent visits both from gentlemen of the court, and the learned men of the university ; and, lastly, that he was living in a style of great penury ; for he, his wife, his two sisters, (one of them a nun) and his niece, are represented as occupying a scanty lodging, on the fourth floor of a mean-looking house, and as entertaining among them all no domestic but a single girl. Cervantes, in his declaration, states his own age at *upwards of fifty,* but he had, in fact, completed his fifty-seventh year before this transaction took place. With such obscurity were both the person and the character of Cervantes surrounded, according to some, immediately *before,* according to others, immediately *after,* the publication of the First Part of *Don Quixote.* But from these very circumstances, I am inclined to agree with those who deny that *Don Quixote* appeared before the summer of 1605.

c

It was dedicated to Don Alonzo Lopez de Zuniga, seventh Duke of Bexar, a nobleman who much affected the character of a Mecænas, but who does not appear to have requited the homage of Cervantes by any very useful marks of his favor. The book, however, stood in no need of patronage, whatever might be the necessities of its author; it was read immediately in court and city, by young and old, learned and unlearned, with equal delight; or, as the Duchess in the second part expresses it, "went forth into the world with the universal applause of the nations." Four editions, published and sold within the year, furnish the best proof of its wide and instant popularity; and if any further proof be wanting, the well-known story (first told by Barrano Porreno, in his *Life and Deeds of Philip III.*) may supply it. "The king standing one day," says this chronicler, "on the balcony of the palace of Madrid, observed a certain student, with a book in his hand, on the opposite banks of the Manzanares. He was reading, but every now and then he interrupted his reading, and gave himself violent blows upon the forehead, accompanied with innumerable motions of ecstasy and mirthfulness. That student, said the king, is either out of his wits, or reading the history of *Don Quixote.*" This must have happened in the beginning of

1606, after the court had removed from Valladolid to the capital. Cervantes himself followed
the court, and resided in Madrid almost all the
rest of his life.

In the midst of general approbation, the author of *Don Quixote* was assailed, on his arrival
in the capital, by all the unwearied arts of individual spleen, envy, and detraction. He had
irritated, by his inimitable satire, a great number of contemporary authors, some of them men
of high rank, whose fame depended on books of
the very species which he had for ever destroyed. Another numerous and active class, the
writers for the theatre, were not less seriously
offended by the freedom with which Cervantes
had criticized, in the person of the Canon of
Toledo, many of the most popular pieces which
had at that time possession of the Spanish
stage. Among the rest, it is said, and probably
not without some foundation, that the great Lope
de Vega himself was excessively displeased with
the terms in which his plays were talked of;
and a sonnet against Cervantes and his book,
still extant, is generally attributed to his pen.
Cervantes endured all this very calmly; and
with that noble retention of the thirst for fame,
which he had already so well exemplified, shut
himself up in his study to compose works worthy
of himself, instead of hastening to take the more

vulgar revenge he might so easily have obtained against his adversaries. The two brothers, Lupercio and Bartholomeo D'Argensola,
after himself and Lope de Vega, the first men
of letters in Spain, lived with him on terms of
intimacy, which might easily console him under
the assaults of his inferiors; and through them
he was introduced to the Conde de Lemos, and
the Cardinal of Toledo, two enlightened and
high-spirited noblemen, who, throughout all the
rest of his life, never failed to afford him their
protection and support. Count Lemos being
appointed Viceroy of Naples shortly after, Cervantes solicited and expected some appointment
in his suite; but it is painful to add, that he
seems to have been disappointed in this particular, in consequence of the coldness, or perhaps
the jealousy, of the very friends by whom he
had been first introduced to that nobleman's notice. He resented, it is certain, the behavior of
the Argensolas, but the dedications of almost
all the works he subsequently put forth, attest
that he acquitted Lemos himself of any unkindness to his person, or coldness to his interests.

The remains of his patrimony, with the pro-
fits of *Don Quixote*, and, it is probable, some al-
lowances from Lemos and the Cardinal, were
sufficient to support Cervantes in the humble
style of life to which his habits were formed;

for he allowed nearly ten years to elapse before he sent any new work to the press. In 1613, he published his *Novelas Exemplares*, most of which had been written many years before, and of which he had already given a specimen in the story of *The Curious Impertinent*, introduced in *Don Quixote*. These tales were received with great and deserved applause, although they have never been placed on a level with the great work which had preceded them. They have been translated into English, and are well known to most readers, so that it were needless to enlarge upon their character and merits. They are, for the most part, felicitous imitations of the manner of Boccacio, whose Italian popularity, as a writer of short romances and anecdotes, it was no doubt Cervantes' ambition to rival in his own country. They are written in a style of manly ease and simplicity ; and when compared with the Galatea, (for, as I have already said, they were chiefly written before *Don Quixote*,) afford abundant evidence of the progressive enlargement of the author's powers, and improvement of his taste. Their morality is uniformly pure, and many of them are full of interest; so that it is no wonder the novels of Cervantes should to this hour keep their place among the favorite reading of the Spanish youth. In 1614, Cervantes published another work highly credit-

able to his genius, but of a very different description.   This is the *Viage de Parnasso*, his
celebrated poetical picture of the state of Spanish literature in his time; and, without question,
the most original and energetic of his own poetical performances.   It is, as might be expected, full of satire; but the satire of Cervantes
was always gentle and playful; and among the
men of true genius, then alive in Spain, there was
not one (not even of those that had shown personal hostility to Cervantes) who had the smallest reason to complain of his treatment.   Cervantes introduces himself as " the oldest and
the poorest " of all the brotherhood; " the naked
Adam of Spanish poets;" but he describes his
poverty without complaining of it; and, indeed
throughout the whole work, never for a moment
loses sight of that high feeling of self-respect,
which became him both as an author and as a
gentleman.   The vessel, in which the imaginary
voyage of Parnassus is performed, is described
in a strain worthy of Cervantes.   " From the
keel to the topmast," says he, " it was all of
verse; there was not a single foot of prose in it.
The deck was all fenced with an airy railing-work
of double-rhymes.   The rowing benches were
chiefly occupied by Ballads, an impudent but
necessary race; for there is nothing to which
they cannot be turned.   The poop was grand and

gay, but a little outlandish in its style, being stuck all over with sonnets of the richest workmanship. Two vigorous Triplets had the stroke-oars on either side, and regulated the motion of the vessel in a manner at once easy and powerful. The gangway appeared to be one long and most melancholy elegy, from which tears were continually distilling," &c.

During the same year, while Cervantes was preparing for the press the Second Part of *Don Quixote*, there was published at Tarragona a continuation of the same story, written chiefly for the purpose of abusing Cervantes, by a person who assumed the name of Avellenada, and who appears to have been successful in keeping his true name entirely concealed. The greater part of this Continuation is made up of very humble imitation, or rather of very open plagiarism from the First Part of *Don Quixote;* and towards its conclusion, it contains some incidents which leave little doubt, but that its writer must have found access to the MS. of Cervantes' Second Part. In the Notes to this edition, (vol. iii.) the reader will find such farther particulars as have appeared worthy of being preserved. Cervantes, whose own Continuation had already in all probability begun to be printed, took his revenge by interweaving in the thread of his story a variety of the most bitter sarcasms upon the

vulgarity, obscenity, and coarseness of his anonymous enemy; a revenge, but for which, in
all likelihood, the memory of Avellenada's performance would not have survived the year in
which it was published. The Second Part of
Don Quixote made its appearance in the beginning of 1615; and it is inscribed to the Conde
de Lemos, in a strain well worthy of the imitation
of all future dedicators. It was received with
applause not inferior to that with which the
First Part had been greeted ten years before;
and no doubt lightened the pecuniary circumstances of the author during the few remaining
months of his life. His fame was now established
far above the reach of all calumny and detraction.
Lope de Vega was dead, and there was no one
to divide with Cervantes the literary empire of
his country. He was caressed by the great;
strangers, who came to Madrid, made the author
of *Don Quixote* the first object of their researches;
he enjoyed all his honors in the midst of his
family; and was continually exercising his mind
in labors worthy of himself. In short, Cervantes had at last obtained all the objects of
his honorable ambition, when his health began
to fail, and he felt within himself the daily
strengthening conviction that his career drew
near its close.

In the beginning of the year 1616, he super-

intended the publication of eight of his comedies, and as many of his interludes, and prefixed
to them a dissertation, which is extremely valuable and curious, as containing the only authentic account of the early history of the Spanish
drama. He also finished and prepared for the
press his romance of *Persiles and Sigismunda.*
This performance is an elegant and elaborate
imitation of the style and manner of Heliodo-
rus. It displays felicity of invention and power
of description, and has always been considered
as one of the purest specimens of Castilian
writing; nevertheless, it has not preserved any
very distinguished popularity, nor been classed
(except in regard to style) by any intelligent
critic of more recent times with the best of
Cervantes' works.

The prologue and dedication of the *Persiles*
must always be read with attention, on account
of the interesting circumstances under which
they were composed, and of which they themselves furnish some account.

Cervantes, after concluding his romance, had
gone for a few days to Esquivias for the benefit
of country air. He tells us, that, as he was riding back to Madrid, in company with two of his
friends, they were overtaken by a young student on horseback, who came on pricking violently, and complaining that they went at such a

pace as gave him little chance of keeping up
with them. One of the party made answer that
the blame lay with the horse of Señor Miguel
de Cervantes, whose trot was of the speediest.
He had scarcely pronounced the name, when the
student dismounted, and touching the hem of
Cervantes' left sleeve, said, " Yes, yes, it is indeed the maimed perfection, the all-famous, the
delightful writer, the joy and darling of the
Muses."   Cervantes returned the young man's
academic salutation with his natural modesty,
and they performed the rest of the journey in
company with the student. " We drew up a
little," says he, " and rode on at a measured
pace ; and as we rode, there was much talk
about my illness. The good student knocked
away all my hopes, by telling me my disease
was the dropsy, and that I could not cure it by
drinking all the water of the ocean.   'Be chary
of drinking, Señor Cervantes,' said he ; 'but eat,
and eat plentifully, for that is the only medicine
that will do you any good.'   I replied, that many
had told me the same story ; but that, as for
giving over drinking, they might as well desire
a man to give up the sole purpose of his being.
My pulse, I said, was becoming daily more and
more feeble, and that if it continued to decline
as it had been doing, I scarcely expected to out-
live next Sunday ; so that I feared there was but

little chance of my being able to profit much further by the acquaintance that had so fortunately been made. With that we found ourselves at the bridge of Toledo, by which we entered the city; and the student took leave of us, having to go round by the bridge of Segovia." This is the only notice we have of the nature of Cervantes' malady. It proceeded so rapidly, that a very few days after, (on the 18th April,) it was thought proper for him to receive extreme unction, which he did with all the devotion of a true Catholic. The day following he dictated the dedication of *Persiles* to the Conde de Lemos, one of the most graceful pieces of writing he ever produced; and wasting gradually away, expired on the 23d of the same month. He had made his will a day or two before, in which he appointed his wife, and his friend the licentiate Francisco Numer his executors; and desired that he might be buried in the Monastery of the Holy Trinity at Madrid. Some time before his death, he had, after a fashion not unfrequent in these times, enrolled himself in the third class of the Franciscans. He was, therefore, carried forth in the sanctified dress, and interred with all the simplicity prescribed by the statutes of this order. It has not been thought unworthy of notice, that the mortal career of CERVANTES terminated on the same day with that of SHAKSPEARE.

Cervantes was a man of ordinary stature, and of a complexion unusually fair in his country; for his eyes were bright blue, and his hair auburn. His countenance was, in his youth, handsome and spirited, and his frame capable of undergoing every species of fatigue. His manners were light and cheerful; and there seems to be not the lest reason for doubting, that, in every relation of life, he exhibited all the virtues of an amiable, upright, and manly character. Loyalty, bravery, and religion were in those days supposed to be inherent in the breast of every Castilian gentleman; and Cervantes was in these, as in all other particulars, an honor and an ornament to the generous race from which he sprung.

In regard to the literary character and merits of Cervantes, the first thing which must strike every one acquainted with Spanish literature is, that the genius, whose appearance forms an epoch so very remarkable in the general history of European intellect, can scarcely be said to have formed any epoch in the literature of his own country. In Spain, the age in which *Don Quixote* was written is not the age of Cervantes, but the age of Lope de Vega. Out of Spain, the writings of Lope de Vega have scarcely been known, and certainly have never been popular; while the masterpiece of Cervantes, under all the disadvantages of translation, has taken, and preserved, in every country of Europe, a place hardly inferior to the most admired productions of native talent. Had Cervantes written nothing but his plays there could have been nothing to excite wonder in the superior Spanish popularity of Lope de Vega ; for, in spite of greater correctness of execution, and perhaps even of greater felicity in delineating human character, it is not to be questioned, that Cervantes, as a dramatist, is quite inferior to his contemporary. But when *Don Quixote* is thrown into the scale, the result must, indeed, appear as difficult to be accounted for, as it is incapable of being denied. The stage, no doubt, was in those days the delight and the study of the Spanish public throughout all its classes ; but even the universal predilection, or rather passion, for a particular form of composition, will scarcely be sufficient to explain the comparative neglect of genius at least equal, exerted with infinitely more perfect skill, in a form which possessed at that period, in addition to all its essential merits, the great merit of originality, and charm of novelty.

Even had Cervantes died without writing *Don Quixote*, his plays, (above all, his *Interludes* and his *Numancia*) ; his *Galatea*, the beautiful dream of his youth ; his *Persiles*, the last effort of his chastened and purified taste; and his fine poem of the *Voyage of Parnassus*, must have given him at least the second place in the most productive age of Spanish genius. In regard to all the graces of Castilian composition, even these must have left him without a rival, either in that or in any other age of the literature of his country. For, while all the other great Spanish authors of the brilliant CENTURY of Spain, (from 1560 to 1656,) either deformed their writings by utter carelessness, or weakened them by a too studious imitation of foreign models, Cervantes alone seized the happy medium, and was almost from the beginning of his career, Spanish without rudeness, and graceful without stiffness of affectation. As a master of Spanish style, he is *now*, both in and out of Spain, acknowledged to be first without a second; but this, which might have secured the immortality and satisfied the ambition of any man, is, after all, scarcely worthy of being mentioned in regard to the great creator of the only species of writing which can be considered as the peculiar property of modern genius. In that spacious field, of which Cervantes must be honored as the first discoverer, the finest spirits of his own, and of every other European country, have since been happily and successfully employed. The whole body of modern romance

and novel writers must be considered as his followers and imitators ; but among them all, so
varied and so splendid soever as have been their
merits, it is, perhaps, not going too far to say,
that, as yet, Cervantes has found but one *rival.*

The learned editor of the Spanish Academy's
edition of 1781 has thought fit to occupy the
space of a very considerable volume with an inquiry into the particular merits of *Don Quixote.*
I refer to his laborious dissertation all those who
are unwilling to admire any thing without knowing why they admire it, or rather why an erudite
Doctor of Madrid deemed it worthy of his admiration.*   In our own country, almost every
thing that any sensible man would wish to hear
said about *Don Quixote* has been said over and
over again by writers, whose sentiments I should
be sorry to repeat without their words, and
whose words I should scarcely be pardoned for
repeating.

Mr. Spence, the author of a late ingenious
tour in Spain, seems to believe, what I should
have supposed was entirely exploded, that Cer-

---

* As a specimen of the style of his criticisms take this : he
approves of the introduction of a *Roque Guinart* in Don Quixote, because in the Odyssey there is a *Polyphemus*, and in the
Æneid there is a *Cacus*.   And yet this man must have at least
read Cervantes' own preface to his work, in which that pedantic
species of criticism is so powerfully ridiculed.   " If thou namest
any giant in the book, forget not Goliah of Gath," &c.

vantes wrote his books for the purpose of ridi-
culing knight-errantry; and that, unfortunately
for his country, his satire put out of fashion, not
merely the absurd misdirection of the spirit of
heroism, but that sacred spirit itself. But the
practice of knight-errantry, if ever there was
such a thing, had, it is well known, been out of
date long before the age in which Don Quixote
appeared; and as for the spirit of heroism, I
think few will sympathize with the critic who
deems it possible that an individual, to say nothing of a nation, should have imbibed any contempt, either for that or any other elevating prin-
ciple of our nature, from the manly page of Cervantes. One of the greatest triumphs of his skill
is the success with which he continually pre-
vents us from confounding the absurdities of the
knight-errant with the generous aspirations of
the cavalier. For the last, even in the midst of
madness, we respect Don Quixote himself. We
pity the delusion, we laugh at the situation, but
we revere, in spite of every ludicrous accompa-
niment, and of every insane exertion, the noble
spirit of the Castilian gentleman; and we feel,
in every page, that we are perusing the work,
not of a heartless scoffer, a cold-blooded satirist,
but of a calm and enlightened mind, in which
true wisdom had grown up by the side of true
experience; of one whose genius moved in a

sphere too lofty for mere derision; of one who knew human nature too well not to respect it; of one, finally, who, beneath a mask of apparent levity, aspired to commune with the noblest principles of humanity; and above all, to give form of expression to the noblest feelings of the national character of Spain. The idea of giving a ludicrous picture of an imaginary personage, conceiving himself to be called upon, in the midst of modern manners and institutions, to exercise the perilous vocation of an Amadis or a Belianis, might perhaps have occurred to a hundred men as easily as to Cervantes. The same general idea has been at the root of many subsequent works, written in derision of real or imaginary follies; but Cervantes is distinguished from the authors of all these works, not merely by the originality of his general conception and plan, but as strongly, and far more admirably, by the nature of the superstructure he has reared upon the basis of his initiatory fiction.

Others have been content with the display of wit, satire, eloquence; and some of them have displayed all these with the most admirable skill and power; but he who rises from the perusal of Don Quixote, thinks of the wit, the satire, the eloquence of Cervantes, but as the accessories and lesser ornaments of a picture of national life and manners, by far the most perfect

and glowing that was ever embodied in one
piece of composition, a picture, the possession
of which alone will be sufficient to preserve, in
freshness and honor, the Spanish name and character, even after the last traces of that once noble character may have been obliterated, and
perhaps that name itself forgotten among the
fantastic innovations of a degenerated people.
Don Quixote is thus the peculiar property, as
well as the peculiar pride of the Spaniards. In
another, and in a yet larger point of view, it is
the property and pride of the whole cultivated
world; for *Don Quixote* is not merely to be regarded as a Spanish cavalier, filled with a Spanish madness, and exhibiting that madness in the
eyes of Spaniards of every condition and rank
of life, from the peasant to the grandee, he is
also the type of a more universal madness; he
is the symbol of Imagination, continually struggling and contrasted with Reality; he repre-
sents the eternal warfare between Enthusiasm
and Necessity; the eternal discrepancy between
the aspirations and the occupations of man; the
omnipotence and the vanity of human dreams.
And thus, perhaps, it is not too much to say, that
Don Quixote, the wittiest and the most laugh-
able of all books — a book which has made many
a one, besides the young student on the banks
of the Manzanares, look as if he were *out of him-*

self — is a book, upon the whole, calculated to produce something very different from a merely mirthful impression.

The serious style of *Don Quixote*, in the original language, preserves the most perfect harmony with this seriousness of purpose. The solemn, eloquent, impassioned Don Quixote, the shrewd, earth-seeking, yet affectionate Sancho, do not fill us with mirth, because they seem to be mirthful themselves. From the beginning of the book to the end, they are both intensely serious characters; the one never loses sight of the high destinies to which he has devoted himself; the other wanders amidst sierras and moonlight forests, and glides on the beautiful stream of the Ebro, without forgetting for a moment the hope of pelf that has drawn him from his native village; the *insula** which has been promised by his master to him, and which he does not think of the less, because he does not know what it is, and because he does know that it has been promised by a madman. The contrasts perpetually afforded by the characters of Quixote and Sancho, the contrasts not less remarkable between the secondary objects and individuals introduced — as these are in reality, and as they appear to the hero, all the contrasts in a

---

* See Notes, Vol. II. p. 3.

work where, more successfully than in any other, the art of contrast has been exhibited, would be comparatively feeble and ineffectual, but for the never-failing contrast between the *idea* of the book, and the *style* in which it is written. Never was the fleeting essence of wit so richly embalmed for eternity.

In our time, it is certain, almost all readers must be contented to lose a great part of the delight with which *Don Quixote* was read on its first appearance. The class of works, to parody and ridicule which it was Cervantes' first and most evident purpose, has long since passed into almost total oblivion; and therefore a thousand traits of felicitous satire must needs escape the notice even of those best able to seize the general scope and appreciate the general merits of the history of The Ingenious Hidalgo. Mr. Southey's admirable editions of *Amadis de Gaul*, and *Palmerin of England*, have indeed revived among us something of the once universal taste for the old and stately prose romance of chivalry; but it must be had in mind that Cervantes wrote his book for the purpose not of satirizing these works, which are among the most interesting relics of the rich, fanciful, and lofty genius of the middle ages; but of extirpating the race of slavish imitators, who, in his day, were deluging all Europe, and more particularly Spain, with eternal caricatures of the venerable old romance. Of the *Amadis*, (the plan and outline of which he for the most part parodied merely because it was the best known work of its order,) Cervantes has been especially careful to record his own high admiration; and if the Canon of Toledo be introduced, as is generally supposed, to express the opinions of Cervantes himself, the author of *Don Quixote* had certainly, at one period of his life, entertained some thoughts of writing, not a humorous parody, but a serious imitation, of the *Amadis*.

I shall conclude what I have to say of the author of *Don Quixote* with one remark, namely, That Cervantes was an old man when he wrote his masterpiece of comic romance; that nobody has ever written successful novels, when young, but Smollett; and that *Humphrey Clinker*, written in the last year of Smollett's life, is, in every particular of conception, execution, and purpose, as much superior to *Roderick Random*, as *Don Quixote* is to the *Galatea*.

It remains to say a few words concerning this new edition of the first of modern romances. The translation is that of Motteux; and this has been preferred, simply because, in spite of many defects and inaccuracies, it is by far the most spirited. Shelton, the oldest of all our

translators, is the only one entitled to be compared with Motteux. Perhaps he is even more
successful in imitating the "serious air" of Cervantes; but it is much to be doubted, whether
the English reader of our time would not be
more wearied with the obsolete turns of his
phraseology, than delighted with its occasional
felicities.

In the Notes appended to these volumes, an
attempt has been made to furnish a complete
explanation of the numerous historical allusions
in *Don Quixote*, as well as of the particular traits
in romantic writing, which it was Cervantes'
purpose to ridicule in the person of his hero.
Without having access to such information, as
has now been thrown together, it may be doubted whether any English reader has ever been
able thoroughly to seize and command the meaning of Cervantes throughout his inimitable fiction. From the Spanish editions of Bowle, Pellicer, and the Academy, the greater part of the
materials has been extracted; but a very considerable portion, and perhaps not the least interesting, has been sought for in the old histories and chronicles, with which the Spaniards of
the 16th century were familiar. Of the many
old Spanish ballads, quoted or alluded to by Don
Quixote and Sancho Panza, metrical translations
have uniformly been inserted in the Notes; and

as by far the greater part of these compositions are altogether new to the English public, it is hoped this part of the work may afford some pleasure to those who delight in comparing the early literatures of the different nations of Christendom.

THE

AUTHOR'S PREFACE

TO

THE READER.

You may depend upon my bare word, reader, without any farther security, that I could wish this offspring of my brain were as ingenious, sprightly, and accomplished, as yourself could desire; but the mischief on't is, nature will have its course. Every production must resemble its author, and my barren and unpolished understanding can produce nothing but what is very dull, very impertinent, and extravagant beyond imagination. You may suppose it the child of disturbance, engendered in some dismal prison,* where wretchedness keeps its residence, and every dismal sound its habitation. Rest and

* The Author is said to have wrote this satirical romance in a prison.

ease, a convenient place, pleasant fields and
groves, murmuring springs, and a sweet repose
of mind, are helps that raise the fancy, and im-
pregnates even the most barren muses with
conceptions that fill the world with admiration
and delight. Some parents are so blinded by
a fatherly fondness, that they mistake the very
imperfections of their children for so many beauties; and the folly and impertinence of the brave
boy must pass upon their friends and acquaintance for wit and sense. But I, who am only a
stepfather, disavow the authority of this modern
and prevalent custom; nor will I earnestly beseech you, with tears in my eyes, which is many
a poor author's case, dear reader, to pardon or
dissemble my child's faults; for what favor can
I expect from you, who are neither his friend
nor relation? You have a soul of your own,
and the privilege of free-will, whoever you be,
as well as the proudest he that struts in a gaudy
outside; you are a king by your own fireside,
as much as any monarch on his throne; you
have liberty and property, which set you above
favor or affection, and may therefore freely like
or dislike this history, according to your humor.

I had a great mind to have exposed it as
naked as it was born, without the addition of a
preface, or the numberless trumpery of commendatory sonnets, epigrams, and other poems

that usually usher in the conceptions of authors;
for I dare boldly say, that though I bestowed
some time in writing the book, yet it cost me
not half so much labor as this very preface. I
very often took up my pen, and as often laid it
down, and could not for my life think of any
thing to the purpose. Sitting once in a very
studious posture, with my paper before me, my
pen in my ear, my elbow on the table, and my
cheek on my hand, considering how I should begin, a certain friend of mine, an ingenious gentleman, and of a merry disposition, came in and
surprised me. He asked me what I was so very
intent and thoughtful upon? I was so free
with him as not to mince the matter, but told
him plainly I had been puzzling my brain for a
preface to Don Quixote, and had made myself
so uneasy about it, that I was now resolved to
trouble my head no further either with preface
or book, and even to let the achievements of
that noble knight remain unpublished; for, continued I, why should I expose myself to the
lash of the old legislator, the vulgar? They
will say, I have spent my youthful days very
finely to have nothing to recommend my gray
hairs to the world, but a dry, insipid legend,
not worth a rush, wanting good language as
well as invention, barren of conceits or pointed
wit, and without either quotations in the mar-

gin, or annotations at the end, which other
books, though never so fabulous or profane, have
to set them off.   Other authors can pass upon
the public by stuffing their books from Aristotle, Plato, and the whole company of ancient
philosophers, thus amusing their readers into a
great opinion of their prodigious reading.   Plutarch and Cicero are slurred on the public for as
orthodox doctors as St. Thomas, or any of the
fathers.   And then the method of these moderns
is so wonderfully agreeable and full of variety,
that they cannot fail to please.   In one line,
they will describe you a whining amorous cox-
comb, and the next shall be some dry scrap of
a homily, with such ingenious turns as cannot
choose but ravish the reader.   Now I want all
these embellishments and graces; I have neither
marginal notes nor critical remarks; I do not
so much as know what authors I follow, and
consequently can have no formal index, as it is
the fashion now, methodically strung on the letters of the alphabet, beginning with Aristotle,
and ending with Xenophon, or Zoilus, or Zeuxis,
which last two are commonly crammed into the
same piece, though one of them was a famous
painter, and the other a saucy critic.   I shall
want also the pompous preliminaries of commendatory verses sent to me by the right honorable my Lord such a one, by the honorable the

Lady such a one, or the most ingenious Master
such a one; though I know I might have them
at an easy rate from two or three brothers of
the quill of my acquaintance, and better, I am
sure, than the best quality in Spain can compose.

In short, my friend, said I, the great Don
Quixote may lie buried in the musty records of
La Mancha, until providence has ordered some
better hand to fit him out as he ought to be;
for I must own myself altogether incapable of
the task. Besides, I am naturally lazy, and
love my ease too well to take the pains of turning over authors for those things which I can
express as well without it. And these are the
considerations that made me so thoughtful when
you came in. The gentleman, after a long and
loud fit of laughing, rubbing his forehead, O'
my conscience, friend, said he, your discourse
has freed me from a mistake that has a great
while imposed upon me. I always took you for
a man of sense, but now I am sufficiently convinced to the contrary. What! puzzled at so
inconsiderable a trifle! a business of so little
difficulty confound a man of such deep sense
and searching thought, as once you seemed
to be!

I am sorry, sir, that your lazy humor and
poor understanding should need the advice I am

about to give you, which will presently solve all your objections and fears concerning the publishing of the renowned Don Quixote, the luminary and mirror of all knight-errantry. Pray, sir, said I, be pleased to instruct me in whatever you think may remove my fears, or solve my doubts. The first thing you object, replied he, is your want of commendatory copies from persons of figure and quality. There is nothing sooner helped; it is but taking a little pains in writing them yourself, and clapping whose name you please to them. You may father them on Prester John of the Indies, or on the emperor of Trapizonde, whom I know to be most celebrated poets. But suppose they were not. and that some presuming pedantic critics might snarl, and deny this notorious truth, value it not two farthings; and though they should convict you of forgery, you are in no danger of losing the hand with which you wrote* them.

As to marginal notes and quotations from authors for your history, it is but dropping here and there some scattered Latin sentences that you have already by rote, or may have with little or no pains. For example, in treating of liberty and slavery, clap me in,

" *Non bene pro toto libertas venditur auro;*"

* He lost his left hand (*izquierda*) in the sea-fight at Lepanto against the Turks.

and, at the same time, make Horace, or some
other author, vouch it in the margin. If you
treat of the power of death, come round with
this close,

> " *Pallida mors æquo pulsat pede pauperum tabernas,*
> *Regumque turres.*"

If of loving our enemies, as heaven enjoins, you
may, if you have the least curiosity, presently
turn to the divine precept, and say, *Ego autem
dico vobis, diligite inimicos vestros;* or, if you discourse of bad thoughts, bring in this passage,
De corde exeunt cogitationes malæ. If the uncertainty of friendship be your theme, Cato offers
you his old couplet with all his heart,

> " *Donec eris felix multos, numerabis amicos,*
> *Tempora si fuerint nubila, solus eris.*"

And so proceed. These scraps of Latin will at
least gain you the credit of a great grammarian,
which, I'll assure you, is no small accomplish-
ment in this age. As to annotations or remarks
at the end of your book, you may safely take
this course. If you have occasion for a giant
in your piece, be sure you bring in Goliah, and
on this very Goliah (who will not cost you one
farthing) you may spin out a swingeing annotation. You may say, The Giant Goliah, or
Goliat, was a Philistine, whom David the shep-

herd slew with the thundering stroke of a pebble in the valley of Terebinthus; *vide* Kings, in such a chapter, and such a verse, where you may find it written. If not satisfied with this, you would appear a great humanist, and would show your knowledge in geography, take some occasion to draw the river Tagus into your discourse, out of which you may fish a most notable remark. The river Tagus, say you, was so called from a certain king of Spain. It takes its rise from such a place, and buries its waters in the ocean, kissing first the walls of the famous city of Lisbon; and some are of opinion that the sands of this river are gold, &c. If you have occasion to talk of robbers, I can presently give you the history of Cacus, for I have it by heart. If you would descant upon whores, or women of the town, there is the Bishop* of Mondonedo, who can furnish you with Lamia, Lais, and Flora, courtesans, whose acquaintance will be very much to your reputation. Ovid's Medea can afford you a good example of cruelty. Calypso from Homer, and Circe out of Virgil, are famous instances of witchcraft or enchantment. Would you treat of valiant commanders? Julius Cæsar has writ his commentaries on purpose; and Plutarch can

* Guevara.

furnish you with a thousand Alexanders. If
you would mention love, and have but three
grains of Italian, you may find Leon the Jew
ready to serve you most abundantly. But if
you would keep nearer home, it is but examining Fonseca of divine love, which you have here
in your study, and you need go no farther for
all that can be said on that copious subject. In
short, it is but quoting these authors in your
book, and let me alone to make large annotations. I'll engage to crowd your margin sufficiently, and scribble you four or five sheets to
boot at the end of your book; and for the cita-
tions of so many authors, it is the easiest thing
in nature. Find out one of these books with
an alphabetical index, and without any farther
ceremony, remove it *verbatim* into your own;
and though the world won't believe that you
have occasion for such lumber, yet there are fools
enough to be thus drawn into an opinion of the
work; at least, such a flourishing train of attendants will give your book a fashionable air,
and recommend it to sale; for few chapmen will
stand to examine it, and compare the authorities'
upon the counter, since they can expect nothing
but their labor for their pains. But, after all,
sir, if I know any thing of the matter, you have
no occasion for any of these things; for your
subject being a satire on knight-errantry, is

so absolutely new, that neither Aristotle, St.
Basil, nor Cicero, ever dreamt or heard of it.
Those fabulous extravagances have nothing to
do with the impartial punctuality of true history; nor do I find any business you can have
either with astrology, geometry, or logic, and I
hope you are too good a man to mix sacred
things with profane. Nothing but pure nature
is your business; her you must consult, and the
closer you can imitate, your picture is the better. And since this writing of your's aims at
no more than to destroy the authority and ac-
ceptance the books of chivalry have had in the
world, and among the vulgar, you have no need
to go begging sentences of philosophers, passages out of holy writ, poetical fables, rhetorical
orations, or miracles of saints. Do but take
care to express yourself in a plain, easy manner,
in well chosen, significant, and decent terms,
and to give an harmonious and pleasing turn to
your periods; study to explain your thoughts,
and set them in the truest light, laboring, as
much as possible, not to leave them dark nor
intricate, but clear and intelligible. Let your
diverting stories be expressed in diverting
terms, to kindle mirth in the melancholic, and
heighten it in the gay. Let mirth and humor
be your superficial design, though laid on a solid
foundation, to challenge attention from the ig-

norant, and admiration from the judicious; to
secure your work from the contempt of the
graver sort, and deserve the praises of men of
sense ; keeping your eye still fixed on the principal end of your project, the fall and destruction of that monstrous heap of ill-contrived
romances, which, though abhorred by many,
have so strangely infatuated the greater part
of mankind. Mind this, and your business is
done.

I listened very attentively to my friend's discourse, and found it so reasonable and convincing, that, without any reply, I took his advice,
and have told you the story by way of preface;
wherein you may see, gentlemen, how happy I
am in so ingenious a friend, to whose season-
able counsel you are all obliged for the omission
of all this pedantic garniture in the history of
the renowned Don Quixote de la Mancha,
whose character among all the neighbors about
Montiel is, that he was the most chaste lover,
and the most valiant knight, that has been
known in those parts these many years. I will
not urge the service I have done you by intro-
ducing you into so considerable and noble a
knight's acquaintance, but only beg the favor
of some small acknowledgment for recommending you to the familiarity of the famous Sancho
Pança, his squire, in whom, in my opinion, you

will find united and described all the squire-like
graces, which are scattered up and down in the
whole bead-roll of books of chivalry. And
now I take my leave, entreating you not to forget your humble servant.

LIFE AND ACHIEVEMENTS

DON QUIXOTE DE LA MANCHA.

PART I. BOOK I.

CHAPTER I.

THE QUALITY AND WAY OF LIVING OF THE RENOWNED DON QUIXOTE DE LA MANCHA.

AT a certain village in La Mancha,* of which I cannot remember the name, there lived not long ago one of those old-fashioned gentlemen, who are never without a lance upon a rack, an old target, a lean horse, and a greyhound. His diet consisted more of beef than mutton; and with minced meat on most nights, lentiles on Fridays, griefs and groans on Saturdays, and a pigeon extraordinary on Sun-

---

* A small territory, partly in the kingdom of Arragon, and partly in Castile; it is a liberty within itself, distinct from all the country about.

days, he consumed three quarters of his revenue; the rest was laid out in a plush coat, velvet breeches, with slippers of the same, for holidays; and a suit of the very best home-spun cloth, which he bestowed on himself for working days. His whole family was a housekeeper something turned of forty, a niece not twenty, and a man that served him in the house and in the field, and could saddle a horse and handle the pruning-hook. The master himself was nigh fifty years of age, of a hale and strong complexion, lean-bodied, and thin-faced, an early riser, and a lover of hunting. Some say his surname was Quixada or Quesada, (for authors differ in this particular;) however, we may reasonably conjecture, he was called Quixada, (that is, lantern-jaws,) though this concerns us but little, provided we keep strictly to the truth in every point of this history.

You must know, then, that when our gentleman had nothing to do, (which was almost all the year round,) he past his time in reading books of knight-errantry, which he did with that application and delight, that at last he in a manner wholly left off his country sports, and even the care of his estate; nay, he grew so strangely besotted with these amusements, that he sold many acres of arable land to purchase books of that kind, by which means he collected as many of them as were to be had; but, among them all, none pleased him like the works of the famous Feliciano de Sylva; for the clearness of his prose, and those intricate expressions with which it is interlaced, seemed to him so many pearls of eloquence, especially when he came to read the

challenges, and the amorous addresses, many of
them in this extraordinary style: " The reason of
your unreasonable usage of my reason, does so en-
feeble my reason, that I have reason to expostulate
with your beauty." And this, " The sublime heavens, which with your divinity divinely fortify you
with the stars, and fix you the deserver of the desert
that is deserved by your grandeur." These, and
such like expressions, strangely puzzled the poor
gentleman's understanding, while he was breaking
his brain to unravel their meaning, which Aristotle
himself could never have found, though he should
have been raised from the dead for that very purpose.

He did not so well like those dreadful wounds
which Don Belianis gave and received; for he considered that all the art of surgery could never secure
his face and body from being strangely disfigured
with scars. However, he highly commended the
author for concluding his book with a promise to
finish that unfinishable adventure; and many times
he had a desire to put pen to paper, and faithfully
and literally finish it himself; which he had certainly done, and doubtless with good success, had
not his thoughts been wholly engrossed in much
more important designs.

He would often dispute with the curate * of the
parish, a man of learning, that had taken his degrees at Giguenza, who was the better knight, Palmerin of England, or Amadis de Gaul; but Master

* In Spain, the curate is the head priest in the parish, and he
that has the cure of souls.

Nicholas, the barber of the same town, would say,
that none of them could compare with the Knight
of the Sun; and that if any one came near him,
it was certainly Don Galaor, the brother of Amadis
de Gaul; for he was a man of a most commodious
temper, neither was he so finical, nor such a puling
whining lover as his brother; and as for courage,
he was not a jot behind him.

In fine, he gave himself up so wholly to the
reading of romances, that a-nights he would pore
on until it was day, and a-days he would read on
until it was night; and thus by sleeping little, and
reading much, the moisture of his brain was exhausted to that degree, that at last he lost the
use of his reason. A world of disorderly notions,
picked out of his books, crowded into his imagination; and now his head was full of nothing but
enchantments, quarrels, battles, challenges, wounds,
complaints, amours, torments, and abundance of
stuff and impossibilities; insomuch, that all the
fables and fantastical tales which he read, seemed
to him now as true as the most authentic histories.
He would say, that the Cid Ruydiaz was a very
brave knight, but not worthy to stand in compe-
tition with the Knight of the Burning-sword, who,
with a single back-stroke, had cut in sunder two
fierce and mighty giants. He liked yet better Bernardo del Carpio, who, at Roncesvalles, deprived
of life the enchanted Orlando, having lifted him
from the ground, and choked him in the air, as
Hercules did Antæus, the son of the Earth.

As for the giant Morgante, he always spoke very
civil things of him; for though he was one of that

monstrous brood, who ever were intolerably proud
and brutish, he still behaved himself like a civil
and well-bred person.

But of all men in the world he admired Rinaldo
of Montalban, and particularly his sallying out of
his castle to rob all he met; and then again when
abroad he carried away the idol of Mahomet, which
·was all massy gold, as the history says; but he so
hated that traitor Galalon, that for the pleasure of
kicking him handsomely, he would have given up
his housekeeper; nay, and his niece into the bargain.

Having thus lost his understanding, he unluckily
stumbled upon the oddest fancy that ever entered
into a madman's brain; for now he thought it convenient and necessary, as well for the increase of
his own honor, as the service of the public, to turn
knight-errant, and roam through the whole world,
armed cap-a-pie, and mounted on his steed, in
quest of adventures ; that thus imitating those
knight-errants of whom he had read, and following their course of life, redressing all manner of
grievances, and exposing himself to danger on all
occasions, at last, after a happy conclusion of his
enterprises, he might purchase everlasting honor
and renown. Transported with these agreeable
delusions, the poor gentleman already grasped in
imagination the imperial sceptre of Trebizonde,
and, hurried away by his mighty expectations, he
prepares with all expedition to take the field.

The first thing he did was to scour a suit of
armor that had belonged to his great grandfather,
and had lain time out of mind carelessly rusting in

a corner; but when he had cleaned and repaired it
as well as he could, he perceived there was a material piece wanting; for, instead of a complete helmet, there was only a single head-piece. However,
his industry supplied that defect; for with some
pasteboard he made a kind of half-beaver or vizor,
which, being fitted to the head-piece, made it look
like an entire helmet. Then, to know whether it
were cutlass-proof, he drew his sword, and tried its
edge upon the pasteboard vizor; but with the very
first stroke he unluckily undid in a moment what
he had been a whole week a-doing. He did not
like its being broke with so much ease, and therefore, to secure it from the like accident, he made it
a-new, and fenced it with thin plates of iron, which
he fixed on the inside of it so artificially, that at
last he had reason to be satisfied with the solidity
of the work; and so, without any further experiment, he resolved it should pass to all intents and
purposes for a full and sufficient helmet.

The next moment he went to view his horse,
whose bones stuck out like the corners of a Spanish real, being a worse jade than Gonela's, *qui
tantum pellis et ossa fuit*, however, his master
thought, that neither Alexander's Bucephalus, nor
the Cid's Babieca, could be compared with him.
He was four days considering what name to give
him; for, as he argued with himself, there was no
reason that a horse bestrid by so famous a knight,
and withal so excellent in himself, should not be
distinguished by a particular name; and, therefore,
he studied to give him such a one as should de-
monstrate as well what kind of horse he had been

before his master was a knight-errant, as what he was now; thinking it but just, since the owner changed his profession, that the horse should also change his title, and be dignified with another; a good big word, such a one as should fill the mouth, and seem consonant with the quality and profession of his master. And thus after many names which he devised, rejected, changed, liked, disliked, and pitched upon again, he concluded to call him Rozinante; * a name, in his opinion, lofty, sounding, and significant of what he had been before, and also of what he was now; in a word, a horse before, or above, all the vulgar breed of horses in the world.

When he had thus given his horse a name so much to his satisfaction, he thought of choosing one for himself; and having seriously pondered on the matter eight whole days more, at last he determined to call himself Don Quixote. Whence the author of this most authentic history draws this inference, that his right name was Quixada, and not Quesada, as others obstinately pretend. And observing, that the valiant Amadis, not satisfied with the bare appellation of Amadis, added to it the name of his country, that it might grow more famous by his exploits, and so styled himself Amadis de Gaul; so he, like a true lover of his native soil, resolved to call himself Don Quixote de la

* *Rozin* commonly means an ordinary horse; *ante* signifies before and formerly. Thus the word Rozinante may imply, that he was formerly an ordinary horse, and also, that he is now a horse that claims the precedence from all other ordinary horses.

Mancha; which addition, to his thinking, denoted very plainly his parentage and country, and consequently would fix a lasting honor on that part of the world.

And now, his armor being scoured, his headpiece improved to a helmet, his horse and himself new named, he perceived he wanted nothing but a lady, on whom he might bestow the empire of his heart; for he was sensible that a knight-errant without a mistress, was a tree without either fruit or leaves, and a body without a soul. Should I, said he to himself, by good or ill fortune, chance to encounter some giant, as it is common in knight-errantry, and happen to lay him prostrate on the ground, transfixed with my lance, or cleft in two, or, in short, overcome him, and have him at my mercy, would it not be proper to have some lady, to whom I may send him as a trophy of my valor? Then when he comes into her presence, throwing himself at her feet, he may thus make his humble submission: "Lady, I am the giant Caraculiambro, lord of the island of Malindrania, vanquished in single combat by that never-deservedly-enough-extolled knight-errant Don Quixote de la Mancha, who has commanded me to cast myself most humbly at your feet, that it may please your honor to dispose of me according to your will." Oh! how elevated was the knight with the conceit of this imaginary submission of the giant; especially having withal bethought himself of a person, on whom he might confer the title of his mistress! which, it is believed, happened thus: Near the place where he lived, dwelt a good likely country lass, for whom he had formerly had a sort of an inclination, though, it is believed, she never heard of it, nor regarded it in the least. Her name was Aldonza Lorenzo, and this was she whom he thought he might entitle to the sovereignty of his heart ; upon which he studied to find her out a new name, that might have some affinity with her old one, and yet at the same time sound somewhat like that of a princess, or lady of quality ; so at last he resolved to call her Dulcinea, with the addition of del Toboso, from the place where she was born ; a name, in his opinion, sweet, harmonious, extraordinary, and no less significative than the others which he had devised. .

CHAPTER II.

OF DON QUIXOTE'S FIRST SALLY.

THESE preparations being made, he found his designs ripe for action, and thought it now a crime to deny himself any longer to the injured world, that wanted such a deliverer ; the more when he considered what grievances he was to redress, what wrongs and injuries to remove, what abuses to correct, and what duties to discharge. So one morning before day, in the greatest heat of July, without acquainting any one with his design, with all the secrecy imaginable, he armed himself cap-a-pie, laced on his ill-contrived helmet, braced on his target, grasped his lance, mounted Rozinante, and at the private door of his back-yard sallied out into the fields, wonderfully pleased to see with how much ease he had succeeded in the beginning of his enterprise. But he had not gone far ere a terrible thought alarmed him, a thought that had like to have made him renounce his great undertaking; for now it came into his mind, that the honor of knighthood had not yet been conferred upon him, and therefore, according to the laws of chivalry, he neither could, nor ought to appear in arms against any professed knight; nay, he also considered, that though he were already knighted, it would become him to wear white armor, and not to adorn his shield with any device, until he had deserved one by some extraordinary demonstration of his valor.

These thoughts staggered his resolution; but his folly prevailing more than any reason, he resolved to be dubbed a knight by the first he should meet, after the example of several others, who, as his distracting romances informed him, had formerly done the like. As for the other difficulty about wearing white armor, he proposed to overcome it, by scouring his own at leisure until it should look whiter than ermine. And having thus dismissed these busy scruples, he very calmly rode on, leaving it to his horse's discretion to go which way he pleased; firmly believing, that in this consisted the very being of adventures. And as he thus went on, I cannot but believe, said he to himself, that when the history of my famous achievements shall be given to the world, the learned author will begin it in this very manner, when he comes to give an account of this my early setting out: " Scarce had the ruddy-colored Phœbus begun to spread the golden tresses of his lovely hair over the vast surface of the earthly globe, and scarce had those feathered poets of the grove, the pretty painted birds, tuned their little pipes, to sing their early welcomes in soft melodious strains to the beautiful Aurora, who, having left her jealous husband's bed, displayed her rosy graces to mortal eyes from the gates and balconies of the Manchegan horizon, when the renowned knight Don Quixote de la Mancha, disdaining soft repose, forsook the voluptuous down, and, mounting his famous steed Rozinante, entered the ancient and celebrated plains of Montiel."* This was indeed the very road he took; and then proceeding, " O happy age! O fortunate times!" cried he, " decreed to usher into the world my famous achievements : achievements worthy to be engraven on brass, carved on marble, and delineated in some masterpiece of painting, as monuments of my glory, and examples for posterity! And thou, venerable sage, wise enchanter, whatever be thy name; thou whom fate has ordained to be the compiler of this rare history, forget not, I beseech thee, my trusty Rozinante, the eternal companion of all my adventures." After this, as if he had been really in love: " O Princess Dulcinea," cried he, " lady of this captive heart, much sorrow and woe you have doomed me to in banishing me thus, and imposing on me your rigorous commands, never to appear before your beauteous face! Remember, lady, that loyal heart your

* Montiel, a proper field to inspire courage, being the ground upon which Henry the Bastard slew his legitimate brother Don Pedro, whom our brave Black Prince Edward had set upon the throne of Spain.

slave, who for your love submits to so many mise-
ries." 'To these extravagant conceits, he added a
world of others, all in imitation, and in the very
style of those, which the reading of romances had
furnished him with; and all this while he rode so
softly, and the sun's heat increased so fast, and was
so violent, that it would have been sufficient to
have melted his brains, had he had · any left.

He travelled almost all that day without meeting
any adventure worth the trouble of relating, which
put him into a kind of despair; for he desired nothing more than to encounter immediately some
person on whom he might try the vigor of his arm.

Some authors say, that his first adventure was
that of the pass, called Puerto Lapice ; others, that
of the Wind-Mills ; but all that I could discover of
certainty in this matter, and that I meet with in the
annals of La Mancha, is, that he travelled all that
day ; and towards the evening, he and his horse
being heartily tired, and almost famished, Don
Quixote looking about him, in hopes to discover
some castle, or at least some shepherd's cottage,
there to repose and refresh himself, at last near the
road which he kept, he espied an inn, as welcome
a sight to his longing eyes as if he had discovered
a star directing him to the gate, nay, to the palace
of his redemption.   Thereupon hastening towards
the inn with all the speed he could, he got thither
just at the close of the evening.   There stood by
chance at the inn door two young female adventurers, alias common wenches, who were going to
Seville with some carriers, that happened to take
up their lodging there that very evening; and, as

whatever our knight-errant saw, thought, or imagined, was all of a romantic cast, and appeared to him altogether after the manner of the books that had perverted his imagination, he no sooner saw the inn, but he fancied it to be a castle fenced with four towers, and lofty pinnacles glittering with silver, together with a deep moat, draw-bridge, and all those other appurtenances peculiar to such kind of places.

Therefore when he came near it, he stopped a while at a distance from the gate, expecting that some dwarf would appear on the battlements, and sound his trumpet to give notice of the arrival of a knight; but finding that nobody came, and that Rozinante was for making the best of his way to the stable, he advanced to the inn door, where spying the two young doxies, they seemed to him two beautiful damsels, or graceful ladies, taking the benefit of the fresh air at the gate of the castle. It happened also at the very moment, that a swineherd getting together his hogs (for, without begging pardon, so they are called*) from the stubble-field, winded his horn; and Don Quixote presently imagined this was the wished-for signal, which some dwarf gave to notify his approach; therefore, with the greatest joy in the world, he rode up to the inn. The wenches, affrighted at the approach of a man cased in iron, and armed with a lance and target,

---

* In the original, (*que sin perdon assi se llaman.*) In this parenthesis the author ridicules the affected delicacy of the Spaniards and Italians, who look upon it as ill manners to name the word hog or swine, as too gross an image.

were for running into their lodging; but Don Quixote perceiving their fear by their flight, lifted up the
pasteboard beaver of his helmet, and discovering
his withered, dusty face, with comely grace and
grave delivery, accosted them in this manner: " I
beseech ye, ladies, do not fly, nor fear the least of-
fence; the order of knighthood, which I profess,
does not permit me to countenance or offer injuries
to any one in the universe, and, least of all, to virgins of such high rank as your presence denotes."
The wenches looked earnestly upon him, endeavoring to get a glimpse of his face, which his ill-contrived beaver partly hid; but when they heard
themselves styled virgins, a thing so out of the way
of their profession, they could not forbear laughing
outright, which Don Quixote resented as a great
affront. " Give me leave to tell ye, ladies," cried
he, " that modesty and civility are very becoming
in the fair sex; whereas laughter without ground
is the highest piece of indiscretion; however,"
added he, " I do not presume to say this to offend
you, or incur your displeasure; no, ladies, I assure
you, I have no other design but to do you service."
This uncommon way of expression, joined to the
knight's scurvy figure, increased their mirth, which
incensed him to that degree, that this might have
carried things to an extremity, had not the innkeeper luckily appeared at that juncture. He was
a man whose burden of fat inclined him to peace
and quietness, yet when he had observed such a
strange disguise of human shape in his old armor
and equipage, he could hardly forbear keeping the
wenches company in their laughter; but having the

fear of such a warlike appearance before his eyes,
he resolved to give him good words, and therefore
accosted him civilly: " Sir Knight," said he, " if
your worship be disposed to alight, you will fail of
nothing here but of a bed ; as for all other accom-
modations, you may be supplied to your mind."
Don Quixote observing the humility of the governor
of the castle, (for such the innkeeper and inn
seemed to him,) " Senior Castellano," said he, " the
least thing in the world suffices me ; for arms are
the only things I value, and combat is my bed of
repose."   The innkeeper thought he had called
him Castellano,* as taking him to be one of the
true Castilians, whereas he was indeed of Andalusia, nay, of the neighborhood of St. Lucar, no less
thievish than Cacus, or less mischievous than a
truant-scholar, or court-page, and therefore he made
him this reply : " At this rate, Sir Knight, your bed
might be a pavement, and your rest to be still
awake; you may then safely alight, and I dare assure you, you can hardly miss being kept awake all
the year long in this house, much less one single
night."   With that he went and held Don Quixote's stirrup, who, having not broke his fast that
day, dismounted with no small trouble or difficulty.
He immediately desired the governor (that is, the
innkeeper) to have special care of his steed, assuring him that there was not a better in the universe ;
upon which the innkeeper viewed him narrowly,
but could not think him to be half so good as Don

---

* Castellano signifies both a constable or governor of a castle,
and an inhabitant of the kingdom of Castile in Spain.

Quixote said. However, having set him up in the stable, he came back to the knight to see what he wanted, and found him pulling off his armor by the help of the good-natured wenches, who had already reconciled themselves to him; but though they had eased him of his corselet and back-plate, they could by no means undo his gorget, nor take off his ill-contrived beaver, which he had tied so fast with green ribbons, that it was impossible to get it off without cutting them; now he would by no means permit that, and so was forced to keep on his helmet all night, which was one of the most pleasant sights in the world; and while his armor was taking off by the two kind lasses, imagining them to be persons of quality, and ladies of that castle, he very gratefully made them the following compliment, (in imitation of an old romance,)

> " There never was on earth a knight
>   So waited on by ladies fair,
> As once was he, Don Quixote hight,
>   When first he left his village dear:
> Damsels to undress him ran with speed,
> And princesses to dress his steed."

O Rozinante! for that is my horse's name, ladies, and mine Don Quixote de la Mancha. I never thought to have discovered it, until some feats of arms, achieved by me in your service, had made me better known to your ladyships; but necessity forcing me to apply to present purpose that passage of the ancient romance of Sir Lancelot, which I now repeat, has extorted the secret from me before its time; yet a day will come, when you shall com-

mand, and I obey, and then the valor of my arm
shall evince the reality of my zeal to serve your
ladyships."

The two females, who were not used to such rhetorical speeches, could make no answer to this;
they only asked him whether he would eat any
thing? " That I will with all my heart," cried Don
Quixote, " whatever it be, for I am of opinion nothing can come to me more seasonably."   Now, as
ill-luck would have it, it happened to be Friday,
and there was nothing to be had at the inn but
some pieces of fish, which is called abadexo in Castile, bacallao in Andalusia, curadillo in some places,
and in others truchuela, or little trout, though after
all it is but poor Jack; so they asked him, whether
he could eat any of that truchuela, because they
had no other fish to give him.   Don Quixote imagining they meant a small trout, told them, " That,
provided there were more than one, it was the same
thing to him, they would serve him as well as a
great one; for," continued he, " it is all one to me
whether I am paid a piece of eight in one single
piece, or in eight small reals, which are worth as
much.   Besides, it is probable these small trouts
may be like veal, which is finer meat than beef; or
like the kid, which is better than the goat.   In
short, let it be what it will, so it comes quickly; for
the weight of armor and the fatigue of travel are
not to be supported without recruiting food."
Thereupon they laid the cloth at the inn door, for
the benefit of the fresh air, and the landlord brought
him a piece of that salt fish, but ill-watered, and as
ill-dressed; and as for the bread, it was as mouldy

and brown as the knight's armor. But it would
have made one laugh to have seen him eat; for,
having his helmet on, with his beaver lifted up, it
was impossible for him to feed himself without
help, so that one of those ladies had that office; but
there was no giving him drink that way, and he
must have gone without it, had not the innkeeper
bored a cane, and setting one end of it to his
mouth, poured the wine in at the other; all which
the knight suffered patiently, because he would not
cut the ribbons that fastened his helmet.

While he was at supper, a sow-gelder happened
to sound his cane-trumpet, or whistle of reeds, four
or five times as he came near the inn, which made
Don Quixote the more positive of his being in a
famous castle, where he was entertained with music
at supper, that the poor jack was young trout, the
bread of the finest flour, the wenches great ladies,
and the innkeeper the governor of the castle, which
made him applaud himself for his resolution, and
his setting out on such an account. The only thing
that vexed him was, that he was not yet dubbed a
knight; for he fancied he could not lawfully undertake any adventure till he had received the order of
knighthood.

CHAPTER III.

AN ACCOUNT OF THE PLEASANT METHOD TAKEN BY DON QUIXOTE TO BE DUBBED A KNIGHT.

Don Quixote's mind being disturbed with that thought, he abridged even his short supper; and as soon as he had done, he called his host, then shut him and himself up in the stable, and falling at his feet, "I will never rise from this place," cried he, "most valorous knight, till you have graciously vouchsafed to grant me a boon, which I will now beg of you, and which will redound to your honor and the good of mankind." The innkeeper, strangely at a loss to find his guest at his feet, and talking at this rate, endeavored to make him rise; but all in vain, till he had promised to grant him what he asked. "I expected no less from your great magnificence, noble sir," replied Don Quixote; "and therefore I make bold to tell you, that the boon which I beg, and you generously condescend to grant me, is, that to-morrow you will be pleased to bestow the honor of knighthood upon me. This night I will watch my armor in the chapel of your castle, and then in the morning you shall gratify me, as I passionately desire, that I may be duly qualified to seek out adventures in every corner of the universe, to relieve the distressed, according to the laws of chivalry, and the inclinations of knights-errant like myself." The innkeeper, who, as I said, was a sharp fellow, and had already a shrewd sus-

picion of the disorder in his guest's understanding,
was fully convinced of it, when he heard him talk
after this manner; and, to make sport that night,
resolved to humor him in his desires, telling him
he was highly to be commended for his choice of
such an employment, which was altogether worthy
a knight of the first order, such as his gallant deportment discovered him to be: that he himself had
in his youth followed that honorable profession,
ranging through many parts of the world in search
of adventures, without so much as forgetting to
visit the *Percheles of Malaga, the isles of Riaran,
the compass of Sevil, the quicksilver-house of Segovia, the olive field of Valencia, the circle of Granada, the wharf of St. Lucar, the potro of Cordova,†
the hedge-taverns of Toledo, and divers other
places, where he had exercised the nimbleness of
his feet, and the subtility of his hands, doing wrongs
in abundance, soliciting many widows, undoing
some damsels, bubbling young heirs, and in a word
making himself famous in most of the courts of
judicature in Spain, till at length he retired to this
castle, where he lived on his own estate and those
of others, entertaining all knights-errant of what
quality or condition soever, purely for the great
affection he bore them, and to partake of what they
got in recompense of his good will. He added,
that his castle at present had no chapel where the

* These are all places noted for rogueries and disorderly
doings. See Notes.
† A square in the city of Cordova, where a fountain gushes
out from the mouth of a horse, near which is also a whipping-
post. The Spanish word *Potro* signifies a colt or young horse.

knight might keep the vigil of his arms, it being pulled down in order to be new built; but that he knew they might lawfully be watched in any other place in a case of necessity, and therefore he might do it that night in the court-yard of the castle; and in the morning (God willing) all the necessary ceremonies should be performed, so that he might assure himself he should be dubbed a knight, nay, as much a knight as any one in the world could be. He then asked Don Quixote whether he had any money? " Not a cross," replied the knight, " for I never read in any history of chivalry that any knight-errant ever carried money about him." " You are mistaken," cried the innkeeper; " for, admit the histories are silent in this matter, the authors thinking it needless to mention things so evidently necessary as money and clean shirts, yet there is no reason to believe the knights went without either; and you may rest assured, that all the knights-errant, of whom so many histories are full, had their purses well lined to supply themselves with necessaries, and carried also with them some shirts, and a small box of salves to heal their wounds; for they had not the conveniency of surgeons to cure them every time they fought in fields and deserts, unless they were so happy as to have some sage or magician for their friend to give them present assistance, sending them some damsel or dwarf through the air in a cloud, with a small bottle of water of so great a virtue, that they no sooner tasted a drop of it, but their wounds were as perfectly cured as if they had never received any. But when they wanted such a friend in for-

mer ages, the knights thought themselves obliged
to take care that their squires should be provided
with money and other necessaries, as lint and salves
to dress their wounds; and if those knights ever
happened to have no squires, which was but very
seldom, then they carried those things behind them
in a little bag,* as if it had been something of
greater value, and so neatly fitted to their saddle,
that it was hardly seen; for had it not been upon
such an account, the carrying of wallets was not
much allowed among knights-errant. I must therefore advise you," continued he, " nay, I might even
charge and command you, as you are shortly to be
my son in chivalry, never from this time forwards
to ride without money, nor without the other necessaries of which I spoke to you, which you will find
very beneficial when you least expect it." Don
Quixote promised to perform very punctually all
his injunctions; and so they disposed every thing
in order to his watching his arms in a great yard
that adjoined to the inn. To which purpose the
knight, having got them all together, laid them in a
horse-trough close by a well in that yard; then
bracing his target, and grasping his lance, just as it
grew dark, he began to walk about by the horse-
trough with a graceful deportment. In the meanwhile the innkeeper acquainted all those that were
in the house with the extravagances of his guest,
his watching his arms, and his hopes of being made
a knight. They all admired very much at so strange

---

* Of striped stuff, which every one carries, in Spain, when
they are travelling.

a kind of folly, and went on to observe him at a distance; where they saw him sometimes walk about with a great deal of gravity, and sometimes lean on his lance, with his eyes all the while fixed upon his arms. It was now undoubted night, but yet the moon did shine with such a brightness, as might almost have vied with that of the luminary which lent it her; so that the knight was wholly exposed to the spectators' view. While he was thus employed, one of the carriers who lodged in the inn came out to water his mules, which he could not do without removing the arms out of the trough. With that, Don Quixote, who saw him make towards him, cried out to him aloud, "O thou, whoever thou art, rash knight, that prepares to lay thy hands on the arms of the most valorous knight-errant that ever wore a sword, take heed; do not audaciously attempt to profane them with a touch, lest instant death be the too sure reward of thy temerity." But the carrier never regarded these dreadful threats; and laying hold on the armor by the straps, without any more ado threw it a good way from him; though it had been better for him to have let it alone; for Don Quixote no sooner saw this, but lifting up his eyes to heaven, and addressing his thoughts, as it seemed, to his lady Dulcinea: "Assist me, lady," cried he, " in the first opportunity that offers itself to your faithful slave; nor let your favor and protection be denied me in this first trial of my valor!" Repeating such like ejaculations, he·let slip his target, and lifting up his lance with both his hands, he gave the carrier such a terrible knock on his inconsiderate head with his

lance, that he laid him at his feet in a woful condition; and had he backed that blow with another,
the fellow would certainly have had no need of a
surgeon.   This done, Don Quixote took up his armor, laid it again in the horse-trough, and then
walked on backwards and forwards with as great
unconcern as he did at first.

Soon after another carrier, not knowing what had
happened, came also to water his mules, while the
first yet lay on the ground in a trance; but as he
offered to clear the trough of the armor, Don Quixote, without speaking a word, or imploring any
one's assistance, once more dropped his target,
lifted up his lance, and then let it fall so heavily on
the fellow's pate, that without damaging his lance,
he broke the carrier's head in three or four places.
His outcry soon alarmed and brought thither all the
people in the inn, and the landlord among the rest;
which Don Quixote perceiving, " Thou Queen of
Beauty," cried he, bracing on his shield, and drawing his sword, " thou courage and vigor of my
weakened heart, now is the time when thou must
enliven thy adventurous slave with the beams of
thy greatness, while this moment he is engaging in
so terrible an adventure!" With this, in his opinion,
he found himself supplied with such an addition
of courage, that had all the carriers in the world at
once attacked him, he would undoubtedly have
faced them all.   On the other side, the carriers,
enraged to see their comrades thus used, though
they were afraid to come near, gave the knight
such a volley of stones, that he was forced to shelter himself as well as he could under the covert of

his target, without daring to go far from the horse-trough, lest he should seem to abandon his arms. The innkeeper called to the carriers as loud as he could to let him alone; that he had told them already he was mad, and consequently the law would acquit him, though he should kill them. Don Quixote also made yet more noise, calling them false and treacherous villains, and the lord of the castle base and unhospitable, and a ·discourteous knight, for suffering a knight-errant to be so abused. " I would make thee know," cried he, " what a per-fidious wretch thou art, had I but received the order of knighthood; but for you, base, ignominious rab-ble! fling on, do your worst; come on, draw nearer if you dare, and receive the reward of your indis-cretion and insolence." This he spoke with so much spirit and undauntedness, that he struck a terror into all his assailants; so that, partly through fear, and partly through the innkeeper's persuasions, they gave over flinging stones at him; and he, on his side, permitted the enemy to carry off their wounded, and then returned to the guard of his arms as calm and composed as before.

The innkeeper, who began somewhat to disrelish these mad tricks of his guest, resolved to despatch him forthwith, and bestow on him that unlucky knighthood, to prevent farther mischief; so coming to him, he excused himself for the insolence of those base scoundrels, as being done without his privity or consent; but their audaciousness, he said, was sufficiently punished. He added, that he had already told him there was no chapel in his castle; and that indeed there was no need of one to finish

the rest of the ceremony of knighthood, which consisted only in the application of the sword to the
neck and shoulders, as he had read in the register
of the ceremonies of the order; and that this might
be performed as well in a field as any where else;
that he had already fulfilled the obligation of watching his arms, which required no more than two
hours' watch, whereas he had been four hours upon
the guard. Don Quixote, who easily believed him,
told him he was ready to obey him, and desired
him to make an end of the business as soon as possible, for if he were but knighted, and should see
himself once attacked, he believed he should not
leave a man alive in the castle, except those whom
he should desire him to spare for his sake.

Upon this the innkeeper, lest the knight should
proceed to such extremities, fetched the book in
which he used to set down the carriers' accounts
for straw and barley; and having brought with him
the two kind females, already mentioned, and a boy
that held a piece of lighted candle in his hand, he
ordered Don Quixote to kneel; then reading in his
manual, as if he had been repeating some pious
oration, in the midst of his devotion he lifted up
his hand, and gave him a good blow on the neck,
and then a gentle slap on the back with the flat of
his sword, still mumbling some words between his
teeth in the tone of a prayer. After this, he ordered one of the wenches to gird the sword about the
knight's waist; which she did with much solemnity,
and, I may add, discretion, considering how hard a
thing it was to forbear laughing at every circumstance of the ceremony; it is true, the thoughts of

the knight's late prowess did not a little contribute
to the suppression of her mirth. As she girded on
his sword, " Heaven," cried the kind lady, " make
your worship a lucky knight, and prosper you
wherever you go." Don Quixote desired to know
her name, that he might understand to whom he
was indebted for the favor she had bestowed upon
him, and also make her partaker of the honor he
was to acquire by the strength of his arm. To
which the lady answered with all humility, that her
name was Tolosa, a cobbler's daughter, that kept a
stall among the little shops of Sanchobinaya at Toledo; and that whenever he pleased to command
her, she would be his humble servant. Don Quixote begged of her to do him the favor to add hereafter the title of lady to her name, and for his sake
to be called from that time the Lady Tolosa ; which
she promised to do. Her companion having buckled
on his spurs, occasioned a like conference between
them; and when he had asked her name, she told
him she went by the name of Miller, being the
daughter of an honest miller of Antequera. Our
new knight entreated her also to style herself the
Lady Miller, making her new offers of service.
These extraordinary ceremonies (the like never
seen before) being thus hurried over in a kind of
post-haste, Don Quixote could not rest till he had
taken the field in quest of adventures ; therefore,
having immediately saddled his Rozinante, and
being mounted, he embraced the innkeeper,.and returned him so many thanks at so extravagant a
rate, for the obligation he had laid upon him in
dubbing him a knight, that it is impossible to give

a true relation of them all: to which the innkeeper, in haste to get rid of him, returned as rhetorical though shorter answers; and without stopping his horse for the reckoning, was glad with all his heart to see him go.

CHAPTER IV.

WHAT BEFELL THE KNIGHT AFTER HE HAD LEFT THE INN.

Aurora began to usher in the morn, when Don Quixote sallied out of the inn, so well pleased, so gay, and so overjoyed to find himself knighted, that he infused the same satisfaction into his horse, who seemed ready to burst his girths for joy. But calling to mind the admonitions which the innkeeper had given him, concerning the provision of necessary accommodation in his travels, particularly money and clean shirts, he resolved to return home to furnish himself with them, and likewise get him a squire, designing to entertain as such a laboring man, his neighbor, who was poor, and had a charge of children, but yet very fit for the office. With this resolution, he took the road which led to his own village; and Rozinante, that seemed to know his will by instinct, began to carry him a round trot so briskly, that his heels seemed scarcely to touch the ground. The knight had not travelled far, when he fancied he heard an effeminate voice complaining in a thicket on his right hand. "I thank Heaven," said he, when he heard the cries, "for favoring me so soon with an opportunity to perform the duty of my profession, and reap the fruits of my desire! for these complaints are certainly the moans of some distressed creature who wants my present help." Then turning to that side with all the speed which Rozinante could make, he no sooner came into the wood, but he found a mare tied to an oak, and to another a young lad about fifteen years of age, naked from the waist upwards. This was he who made such a lamentable outcry; and not without cause, for a lusty country-fellow was strapping him soundly with a girdle, at every stripe putting him in mind of a proverb, *Keep your mouth shut, and your eyes open, sirrah.* " Good master," cried the boy, " I'll do so no more; as I hope to be saved, I'll never do so again! indeed, master, hereafter I'll take more care of your goods." Don Quixote seeing this, cried in an angry tone, " Discourteous knight, 'tis an unworthy act to strike a person who is not able to defend himself: come, bestride thy steed, and take thy lance," (for the farmer had something that looked like one leaning to the same tree to which his mare was tied,) " then I'll make thee know thou hast acted the part of a coward." The country-fellow, who gave himself for lost at the sight of an apparition in armor brandishing his lance at his face, answered him in mild and submissive words: " Sir knight," cried he, " this boy, whom I am chastising, is my servant, employed by me to look after a flock of sheep, which I have not far off; but he is so heedless, that I lose some of them every day. Now, because I correct him for his carelessness or his knavery, he says I do it out of covetousness, to defraud him of his wages; but

upon my life and soul he belies me." "What! the
lie in my presence, you saucy clown," cried Don
Quixote; "by the sun that shines, I have a good
mind to run thee through the body with my lance.
Pay the boy this instant, without any more words,
or, by the power that rules us all, I'll immediately
dispatch, and annihilate thee; come, unbind him
this moment." The countryman hung down his
head, and without any further reply, unbound the
boy; who being asked by Don Quixote what his
master owed him? told him it was nine months'
wages, at seven reals a month. The knight having
cast it up, found it came to sixty-three reals in all;
which he ordered the farmer to pay the fellow immediately, unless he intended to lose his life that
very moment. The poor countryman, trembling
for fear, told him, that, as he was on the brink of
death, by the oath he had sworn, (by the by he had
not sworn at all,) he did not owe the lad so much;
for there was to be deducted for three pair of shoes
which he had bought him, and a real for his being
let blood twice when he was sick. "That may be,"
replied Don Quixote; "but set the price of the
shoes and the bleeding against the stripes which
you have given him without cause; for if he has
used the shoe-leather which you paid for, you have
in return misused and impaired his skin sufficiently;
and if the surgeon let him blood when he was sick,
you have drawn blood from him now he is in health;
so that he owes you nothing on that account."
"The worst is, sir knight," cried the farmer, "that
I have no money about me; but let Andrew go
home with me, and I'll pay him every piece out of

hand." " What! I go home with him," cried the youngster; " the devil a-bit, sir! not I, truly, I know better things; for he'd no sooner have me by himself, but he'd flea me alive like another St. Bartho-. lomew." " He will never dare to do it," replied Don Quixote; " I command him, and that's sufficient to restrain him; therefore, provided he will swear by the order of knighthood which has been conferred upon him, that he will duly observe this regulation, I will freely let him go, and then thou art secure of thy money." " Good sir, take heed what you say," cried the boy; for my master is no knight, nor ever was of any order in his life; he's John Haldudo, the rich farmer of Quintinar." " This signifies little," answered Don Quixote, " for there may be knights among the Haldudo's; besides, the brave man carves out his fortune, and every man is the son of his own works." " That's true, sir," quoth Andrew; " but of what works can this master of mine be the son, who denies me my wages, which I have earned with the sweat of my brows?" " I do not deny to pay thee thy wages, honest Andrew," cried the master; " be but so kind as go along with me, and by all the orders of knighthood in the world, I swear, I'll pay thee every piece, as I said, nay, and perfumed to boot."* " You may spare your perfume," said Don Quixote; " do but pay him in reals, and I am satisfied; but be sure you perform

---

* To pay or return a thing perfumed, is a Spanish expression, signifying it shall be done to content or with advantage to the receiver. It is used here as a satire on the effeminate custom of wearing every thing perfumed, insomuch that the very money in their pockets was scented

your oath; for if you fail, I myself swear by the
same oath, to return and find you out, and punish
you, though you should hide yourself as close as a
lizard. And if you will be informed who it is that
lays these injunctions on you, that you may understand how highly it concerns you to observe them,
know, I am the valorous Don Quixote de la Man- ·
cha, the righter of wrongs, the revenger and redresser
of grievances; and so farewell; but remember what
you have promised and sworn, as you will answer
the contrary at your peril." This said, he clapped
spurs to Rozinante, and quickly left the master and
the man a good way behind him.

The countryman, who followed him with both
his eyes, no sooner perceived that he was passed
the woods, and quite out of sight, but he went back
to his boy Andrew. " Come, child," said he, " I will
pay thee what I owe thee, as that righter of wrongs,
and redresser of grievances has ordered me." "Ay,"
quoth Andrew, " on my word, you will do well to
fulfil the commands of that good knight, who Heaven grant long to live; for he is so brave a man,
and so just a judge, that adad if you don't pay me,
he'll come back and make his words good." " I
dare swear as much," answered the master; "and to
show thee how much I love thee, I am willing to
increase the debt, that I may enlarge the payment."
With that he caught the youngster by the arm, and
tied him again to the tree; where he handled him
so unmercifully, that scarce any signs of life were
left in him. " Now call your righter of wrongs, Mr.
Andrew," cried the farmer, " and you shall see he
will never be able to undo what I have done; though

I think it is but a part of what I ought to do, for I
have a good mind to flea you alive, as you said I
would, you rascal." However, he untied him at
last, and gave him leave to go and seek out his
judge, in order to have his decree put in execution.
Andrew went his ways, not very well pleased, you
may be sure, yet fully resolved to find out the valorous Don Quixote de la Mancha, and give him an
exact account of the whole transaction, that he
might pay the abuse with sevenfold usury; in
short, he crept off sobbing and weeping, while his
master staid behind laughing. And in this manner
was this wrong redressed by the valorous Don Quixote de la Mancha.

In the mean time, being highly pleased with himself and what had happened, imagining he had given
a most fortunate and noble beginning to his feats
of arms, as he went on towards his village, "O
most beautiful of beauties," said he, with a low
voice, "Dulcinea del Toboso! well may'st thou
deem thyself most happy, since it was thy good
fortune to captivate and hold a willing slave to thy
pleasure so valorous and renowned a knight as is,
and ever shall be, Don Quixote de la Mancha; who,
as all the world knows, had the honor of knighthood bestowed on him but yesterday, and this day
redressed the greatest wrong and grievance that
ever injustice could design, or cruelty commit; this
day has he wrested the scourge out of the hands of
that tormentor, who so unmercifully treated a tender infant without the least occasion given." Just
as he had said this, he found himself at a place
where four roads met; and this made him presently

bethink of those cross-ways which often use to put knights-errant to a stand, to consult with themselves which way they should take; and that he might follow their example, he stopped a while, and after he had seriously reflected on the matter, gave Rozinante the reins, subjecting his own will to that of his horse, who, pursuing his first intent, took the way that led to his own stable.

Don Quixote had not gone above two miles, but he discovered a company of people riding towards him, who proved to be merchants of Toledo, that were going to buy silks in Murcia. They were six in all, every one screened with an umbrella, besides four servants on horseback, and three muletcers on foot. The knight no sooner perceived them, but he imagined this to be some new adventure; and because he was resolved to imitate as much as possible the passages which he read in his books, he was pleased to represent this to himself as such a particular adventure as he had a singular desire to meet with; and so, with a dreadful grace and assurance, fixing himself in his stirrups, couching his lance, and covering his breast with his target, he posted himself in the middle of the road, expecting the coming up of the supposed knights-errant. As soon as they came within hearing, with a loud voice and haughty tone, " Hold," cried he, " let all mankind stand, nor hope to pass on further, unless all mankind acknowledge and confess, that there is not in the universe a more beautiful damsel than the empress of La Mancha, the peerless Dulcinea del Toboso." At those words the merchants made a halt, to view the unaccountable figure of their

opponent; and easily conjecturing, both by his expression and disguise, that the poor gentleman had
lost his senses, they were willing to understand the
meaning of that strange confession which he would
force from them; and therefore one of the company, who loved and understood raillery, having
discretion to manage it, undertook to talk to him.
" Signor cavalier," cried he, " we do not know this
worthy lady you talk of; but be pleased to let us
see her, and then if we find her possessed of those
matchless charms, of which you assert her to be the
mistress, we will freely, and without the least compulsion, own the truth which you would extort from
us." " Had I once shown you that beauty," replied
Don Quixote, " what wonder would it be to acknowledge so notorious a truth? the importance of
the thing lies in obliging you to believe it, confess
it, affirm it, swear it, and maintain it, without seeing her; and therefore make this acknowledgment
this very moment, or know, that it is with me you
must join in battle, ye proud and unreasonable
mortals. Come one by one, as the laws of chivalry
require, or all at once, according to the dishonorable
practice of men of your stamp; here I expect you
all my single self, and will stand the encounter, con-
fiding in the justice of my cause." " Sir knight,"
replied the merchant, " I beseech you in the name
of all the princes here present, that for the discharge of our consciences, which will not permit us
to affirm a thing we never heard or saw, and which,
besides, tends so much to the dishonor of the em-
presses and queens of Alcaria and Estramadura,
your worship will vouchsafe to let us see some por-

traiture of that lady, though it were no bigger than
a grain of wheat; for by a small sample we may
judge of the whole piece, and by that means rest
secure and satisfied, and you contented and ap-
peased. Nay, I verily believe, that we all find ourselves already so inclinable to comply with you,
that though her picture should represent her to be
blind of one eye, and distilling vermilion and brim-
stone at the other, yet to oblige you, we shall be
ready to say in her favor whatever your worship
desires." "Distil, ye infamous scoundrels," replied
Don Quixote in a burning rage, "distil, say you?
know, that nothing distils from her but amber and
civet: neither is she defective in her make or shape,
but more straight than a Guadaramian spindle.
But you shall all severely pay for the horrid blas-
phemy which thou hast uttered against the tran-
scendent beauty of my incomparable lady." Saying this, with his lance couched, he ran so furiously
at the merchant who thus provoked him, that, had
not good fortune so ordered it, that Rozinante
should stumble and fall in the midst of his career,
the audacious trifler had paid dear for his raillery;
but as Rozinante fell, he threw down his master,
who rolled and tumbled a good way on the ground;
without being able to get upon his legs, though he
used all his skill and strength to effect it, so encum-
bered he was with his lance, target, spurs, helmet,
and the weight of his rusty armor. However, in
this helpless condition, he played the hero with his
tongue: "Stay," cried he, "cowards, rascals, do not
fly! it is not through my fault that I lie here, but
through that of my horse, ye poltroons!"

One of the grooms, who was none of the best-natured creatures, hearing the overthrown knight thus insolently treat his master, could not bear it without returning him an answer on his ribs; and therefore coming up to him as he lay wallowing, he snatched his lance, and having broke it to pieces, he so belabored Don Quixote's sides with one of them, that, in spite of his arms, he thrashed him like a wheat sheaf. His master indeed called to him not to lay on him so vigorously, and to let him alone; but the fellow, whose hand was in, would not give over rib-roasting the knight, till he had tired out his passion and himself; and therefore running to the other pieces of the broken lance, he fell to it again without ceasing, till he had splinter-.ed them all on the knight's iron inclosure. He, on his side, notwithstanding all this storm of bastina-does, lay all the while bellowing, threatening hea-ven and earth, and those villanous ruffians, as he took them to be. At last the mule-driver was tired, and the merchants pursued their journey, suffi-ciently furnished with matter of discourse at the poor knight's expense. When he found himself alone, he tried once more to get on his feet; but if he could not do it when he had the use of his limbs, how should he do it now, bruised and battered as he was? But yet for all this, he esteemed himself a happy man, being still persuaded, that his misfor-tune was one of those accidents common in knight-errantry, and such a one as he could wholly attribute to the falling of his horse; nor could he possibly get up, so sore and mortified as his body was all over.

CHAPTER V.

A FURTHER ACCOUNT OF OUR KNIGHT'S MISFORTUNES.

DON QUIXOTE, perceiving that he was not able to stir, resolved to have recourse to his usual remedy, which was to bethink himself what passage in his books might afford him some comfort; and presently his folly brought to his remembrance the story of Baldwin and the Marquis of Mantua, when Charlot left the former wounded on the mountain; a story learned and known by little children, not unknown to young men and women, celebrated, and even believed by the old, and yet not a jot more authentic than the miracles of Mahomet. This seemed to him as if made on purpose for his present circumstances, and therefore he fell a rolling and tumbling up and down, expressing the greatest pain and resentment, and breathing out, with a languishing voice, the same complaints which the wounded Knight of the Wood is said to have made:

> " Alas! where are you, lady dear,
> " That for my woe you do not moan?
> " You little know what ails me here,
> " Or are to me disloyal grown!"

Thus he went on with the lamentations in that romance, till he came to these verses:

> " O thou, my uncle and my prince,
> " Marquis of Mantua, noble lord!"—

When kind fortune so ordered it, that a plough-

man, who lived in the same village, and near his
house, happened to pass by, as he came from the
mill with a sack of wheat. The fellow seeing a
man lie at his full length on the ground, asked him
who he was, and why he made such a sad complaint. Don Quixote, whose distempered brain presently represented to him the countryman for the
Marquis of Mantua, his imaginary uncle, made him
no answer, but went on with the romance, giving
him an account of his misfortunes, and of the loves
of his wife and the emperor's son, just as the book
relates them. The fellow stared, much amazed to
hear a man talk such unaccountable stuff; and taking off the vizor of his helmet, broken all to pieces
with blows bestowed upon it by the mule-driver, he
wiped off the dust that covered his face, and presently knew the gentleman. "Master Quixada!"
cried he, (for so he was properly called when he had
the right use of his senses, and had not yet from a
sober gentleman transformed himself into a wandering knight,) "how came you in this condition?"
But the other continued his romance, and made no
answers to all the questions the countryman put to
him, but what followed in course in the book; which
the good man perceiving, he took off the battered
adventurer's armor, as well as he could, and fell a
searching for his wounds; but finding no signs of
blood, or any other hurt, he endeavored to set him
upon his legs; and at last with a great deal of
trouble, he heaved him upon his own ass, as being
the more easy and gentle carriage; he also got all
the knight's arms together, not leaving behind so
much as the splinters of his lance; and having tied

them up, and laid them on Rozinante, which he
took by the bridle, and his ass by the halter, he led
them all towards the village, and trudged a-foot
himself, very pensive, while he reflected on the extravagances which he heard Don Quixote utter.
Nor was Don Quixote himself less melancholy; for
he felt himself so bruised and battered, that he
could hardly sit on the ass; and now and then he
breathed such grievous sighs, as seemed to pierce
the very skies, which moved his compassionate
neighbor once more to entreat him to declare to him
the cause of his grief; but one would have imagined the devil prompted him with stories, that had
some resemblance of his circumstances; for in that
instant, wholly forgetting Baldwin, he bethought
himself of the Moor Abindaraez, whom Rodrigo
de Narvaez, Alcayde of Antequera, took and carried prisoner to his castle; so that when the husbandman asked him how he did, and what ailed
him, he answered word for word as the prisoner
Abindaraez, replied to Rodrigo de Narvaez, in the
Diana of George di Monte Mayor, where that adventure is related; applying it so properly to his
purpose, that the countryman wished himself at the
devil rather than within the hearing of such strange
nonsense; and being now fully convinced that his
neighbor's brains were turned, he made all the haste
he could to the village, to be rid of his troublesome
impertinences. Don Quixote, in the mean time,
thus went on: " You must know, Don Rodrigo de
Narvaez, that this beautiful Xerifa, of whom I gave
you an account, is at present the most lovely Dulcinea del Toboso, for whose sake I have done, still

do, and will achieve the most famous deeds of chivalry that ever were, are, or ever shall be seen in the universe." "Good sir," replied the husbandman, "as I am a sinner, I am not Don Rodrigo de Narvaez, nor the Marquis of Mantua, but Pedro Alonzo by name, your worship's neighbor ; nor are you Baldwin, nor Abindaraez, but only that worthy gentleman Senior Quixada." "I know very well who I am," answered Don Quixote ; "and what's more, I know, that I may not only be the persons I have named, but also the twelve peers of France, nay, and the nine worthies all in one ; since my achievements will outrival not only the famous exploits which made any of them singly illustrious, but all their mighty deeds accumulated together."

· Thus discoursing, they at last got near their village about sunset; but the countryman staid at some distance till it was dark, that the distressed gentleman might not be seen so scurvily mounted ; and then he led him home to his own house, which he found in great confusion. The curate and the barber of the village, both of them Don Quixote's intimate acquaintance, happened to be there at that juncture, as also the house-keeper, who was arguing with them : " What do you think, pray, good doctor Perez," said she, (for this was the curate's name,) "what do you think of my master's mischance? neither he, nor his horse, nor his target, lance, nor armor, have been seen these six days. What shall I do, wretch that I am ! I dare lay my life, and it is as sure as I am a living creature, that those cursed books of errantry, which he used to be always poring upon, have set him besides his senses ; for now I remember, I have heard him often mutter to himself, that he had a mind to turn knight-errant, and jaunt up and down the world to find out adventures.   May Satan and Barabbas e'en take all such books that have thus cracked the best head-piece in all La Mancha!" His niece said as much, addressing herself to the barber ; " You must know, Mr. Nicholas," quoth she, (for that was his name,) " that many times my uncle would read you those unconscionable books of disventures for eight-and-forty hours together; then away he would throw you his book, and, drawing his sword, he would fall a fencing against the walls; and when he had tired himself with cutting and slashing, he would cry he had killed four giants as big as any steeples ; and the sweat which he put himself into, he would say was the blood of the wounds he had received in the fight; then would he swallow you a huge jug of cold water, and presently he would be as quiet and as well as ever he was in his life; and he said, that this same water was a sort of precious drink brought him by the sage Esquife, a great magician, and his special friend.   Now, it is I who am the cause of all this mischief, for not giving you timely notice of my uncle's raving, that you might have put a stop to it, ere it was too late, and have burnt all these excommunicated books ; for there are I do not know how many of them that deserve as much to be burned, as those of the rankest heretics." " I am of your mind," said the curate ; " and verily to-morrow shall not· pass over before I have fairly brought them to a trial, and condemned them to the flames, that they may not minister occasion to such as would read them, to be perverted after the example of my good friend."

The countryman, who, with Don Quixote, stood without, listening to all this discourse, now perfectly understood by this the cause of his neighbor's disorder; and therefore, without any more ado, he called out aloud, " Here! house; open the gates there, for the Lord Baldwin, and the Lord Marquis of Mantua, who is coming sadly wounded ; and for the Moorish Lord Abindaraez, whom the valorous Don Rodrigo de Narvaez, Alcayde of Antequera, brings prisoner." At which words they all got out of doors; and the one finding it to be her uncle, and the other to be her master, and the rest their friend, who had not yet alighted from the ass, because indeed he was not able, they all ran to embrace him; to whom Don Quixote: " Forbear," said he, " for I am sorely hurt, by reason that my horse failed me; carry me to bed, and if it be possible let the enchantress Urganda be sent for to cure my wounds." " Now, in the name of mischief," quoth the housekeeper, " see whether I did not guess .right, on which foot my master halted ? Come, get you to bed, I beseech you ; and, my life for yours, we will take care to cure you without sending for that same Urganda. A hearty curse, and the curse of curses, I say it again and again a hundred times, light upon those books of chivalry that have put you in this pickle." Thereupon they carried him to his bed, and searched for his wounds, but could find none ; and then he told them he was only bruised, having had a dreadful fall from his horse Rozinante, while he was fighting ten giants,

the most outrageous and audacious that ever could
be found upon the face of the earth. "How,"
cried the curate, " have we giants too in the dance?
nay then, by the holy sign of the cross, I will burn
them all by to-morrow night." Then did they ask
the Don a thousand questions, but to every one he
made no other answer, but that they should give
him something to eat, and then leave him to his repose, a thing which was to him of the greatest importance. They complied with his desires; and
then the curate informed himself at large in what
condition the countryman had found him; and having had a full account of every particular, as also
of the knight's extravagant talk, both when the fellow found him, and as he brought him home, this
increased the curate's desire of effecting what he
had resolved to do the next morning; at which time
he called upon his friend, Mr. Nicholas the barber,
and went with him to Don Quixote's house.

CHAPTER VI.

OF THE PLEASANT AND CURIOUS SCRUTINY WHICH THE CURATE AND THE BARBER MADE OF THE LIBRARY OF OUR INGENIOUS GENTLEMAN.

THE knight was yet asleep, when the curate
came attended by the barber, and desired his niece
to let him have the key of the room where her uncle
kept his books, the author of his woes; she readily
consented; and so in they went, and the housekeeper with them. There they found above an

hundred large volumes neatly bound, and a good number of small ones; as soon as the house-keeper had spied them out, she ran out of the study, and returned immediately with a holy-water pot and a sprinkler; " Here, doctor," cried she, " pray sprinkle every creek and corner in the room, lest there should lurk in it some one of the many sorcerers these books swarm with, who might chance to bewitch us, for the ill-will we bear them, in going about to send them out of the world." The curate could not forbear smiling at the good woman's simplicity; and desired the barber to reach him the books one by one, that he might peruse the title-pages, for perhaps he might find some among them that might not deserve to be committed to the flames. " Oh, by no means," cried the niece, " spare none of them; they all help, some how or other, to crack my uncle's brain. I fancy we had best throw them all out at the window in the yard, and lay them together in a heap, and then set them o' fire, or else carry them into the back-yard, and there make a pile of them, and burn them, and so the smoke will offend nobody." The housekeeper joined with her, so eagerly bent were both upon the destruction of those poor innocents; but the curate would not condescend to those irregular proceedings, and resolved first to read at least the title-page of every book.

The first that Mr. Nicholas put into his hands, was Amadis de Gaul, in four volumes.* " There

---

* Hence it appears, that only the first four books of Amadis were thought genuine by Cervantes. The subsequent volumes, to the number of twenty-one, are condemned hereby as spurious.

seems to be some mystery in this book's being the
first taken down," cried the curate, as soon as he
had looked upon it, "for I have heard it is the first
book of knight-errantry that ever was printed in
Spain, and the model of all the rest; and therefore
I am of opinion, that, as the first teacher and author
of so pernicious a sect, it ought to be condemned
to the fire without mercy." "I beg a reprieve for
him," cried the barber, "for I have been told 'tis the
best book that has been written in that kind; and
therefore, as the only good thing of that sort, it may
deserve a pardon." "Well, then," replied the curate, "for this time let him have it. Let's see that
other, which lies next to him." "These," said the
barber, "are the exploits of Esplandian, the lawful
begotten son of Amadis de Gaul." "Verily," said
the curate, "the father's goodness shall not excuse
the want of it in the son. Here, good mistress
housekeeper, open that window, and throw it into
the yard, and let it serve as a foundation to that
pile we are to set a blazing presently." She was
not slack in her obedience; and thus poor Don
Esplandian was sent headlong into the yard, there
patiently to wait the time of his fiery trial. "To
the next," cried the curate. "This," said the barber, "is Amadis of Greece; and I'm of opinion
that all those that stand on this side are of the same
family." "Then let them all be sent packing into
the yard," replied the curate; for rather than lose
the pleasure of burning Queen Pintiquiniestra, and
the shepherd Darinel with his eclogues, and the confounded unintelligible discourses of the author, I
think I should burn my own father along with them,

if I met him in the disguise of a knight-errant."
" I am of your mind," cried the barber. " And I
too," said the niece. " Nay, then," quoth the old
female, " let them come, and down with them all
into the yard." They were delivered to her accordingly, and many they were; so that to save herself
the labor of carrying them down stairs, she fairly
sent them flying out at the window.

" What overgrown piece of lumber have we
here ? " cried the curate. " Olivante de Laura," returned the barber. " The same author wrote the
Garden of Flowers; and, to deal ingenuously with
you, I cannot tell which of the two books has most
truth in it, or, to speak more properly, less lies ; but
this I know for certain, that he shall march into the
back-yard, like a nonsensical arrogant blockhead as
he is."

" The next," cried the barber, " is Florismart of
Hyrcania." " How! my Lord Florismart, is he
here ?" replied the curate; " nay then truly, he shall
e'en follow the rest to the yard, in spite of his wonderful birth and incredible adventures; for his
rough, dull, and insipid style deserves no better
usage. Come, toss him into the yard, and this other
too, good mistress." " With all my heart," quoth
the governess ; and straight she was as good as her
word.

" Here's the noble Don Platir," cried the barber.
" 'Tis an old book," replied the curate, " and I can
think of nothing in him that deserves a grain of
pity; away with him, without any more words ;"
and down he went accordingly.

Another book was opened, and it proved to be

the Knight of the Cross. " The holy title," cried
the curate, " might in some measure atone for the
badness of the book; but then, as the saying is,
The devil lurks behind the cross! To the flames
with him."

Then the barber taking down another book, cried,
" Here's the Mirror of Knighthood." " Oh! I have
the honor to know him," replied the curate. " There
you will find the Lord Rinaldo of Montalban, with
his friends and companions, all of them greater
thieves than Cacus, together with the Twelve Peers
of France, and that faithful historian Turpin.
Truly, I must needs say, I am only for condemning
them to perpetual banishment, at least because
their story contains something of the famous Boy-
ardo's invention, out of which the Christian poet
Ariosto also spun his web; yet, if I happened to
meet with him in this bad company, and speaking
in any other language than his own, I'll show him
no manner of favor; but if he talks in his own
native tongue, I'll treat him with all the respect
imaginable." " I have him at home in Italian,"
said the barber, " but I cannot understand him."
" Neither is it any great matter, whether you do or
not," replied the curate ; and I could willingly have
excused the good captain who translated it that
trouble of attempting to make him speak Spanish,
for he has deprived him of a great deal of his primitive graces; a misfortune incident to all those
who presume to translate verses, since their utmost
wit and industry can never enable them to preserve
the native beauties and genius that shine in the
original. For this reason I am for having not only

this book, but likewise all those which we shall find here, treating of French affairs,* laid up and deposited in some dry vault, till we have maturely determined what ought to be done with them; yet give me leave to except one Barnardo del Carpio, that must be somewhere here among the rest, and another called Roncesvalles; for whenever I meet with them, I will certainly deliver them up into the hands of the housekeeper, who shall toss them into the fire." The barber gave his approbation to every particular, well, knowing that the curate was so good a Christian, and so great a lover of truth, that he would not have uttered a falsity for all the world.

Then opening another volume, he found it to be Palmerin de Oliva, and the next to that Palmerin of England. "Ha! have I found you!" cried the curate. "Here, take that Oliva, let him be torn to pieces, then burnt, and his ashes scattered in the air; but let Palmerin of England be preserved as a singular relic of antiquity; and let such a costly box be made for him, as Alexander found among the spoils of Darius, which he devoted to inclose Homer's works: for I must tell you, neighbor, that book deserves particular respect for two things; first, for its own excellences; and, secondly, for the sake of its author, who is said to have been a learned king of Portugal; then all the adventures of the castle of Miraguarda are well and artfully managed, the dialogue very courtly and clear, and the decorum strictly observed in equal character,

---

* Meaning those romances, the scene of which lay in France, under Charlemagne and the Palatins.

with equal propriety and judgment. Therefore, Master Nicholas," continued he, " with submission to your better advice, this and Amadis de Gaul shall be exempted from the fire ; and let all the rest be condemned without any further inquiry or examination." " By no means, I beseech you," returned the barber, " for this which I have in my hands is the famous Don Bellianis." " Truly," cried the curate, " he, with his second, third, and fourth parts, had need of a dose of rhubarb to purge his excessive choler; besides, his Castle of Fame should be demolished, and a heap of other rubbish removed; in order to which I give my vote to grant them the benefit of a reprieve; and as they show signs of amendment, so shall mercy or justice be used towards them ; in the mean time, neighbor, take them into custody, and keep them safe at home ; but let none be permitted to converse with them." " Content," cried the barber; and to save himself the labor of looking on any more books of that kind, he bid the housekeeper take all the great volumes, and throw them into the yard. This was not spoken to one stupid or deaf, but to one who had a greater mind to be burning them, than weaving the finest and largest web ; so that laying hold of no less than eight volumes at once, she presently made them leap towards the place of execution; but as she went too eagerly to work, taking more books than she could conveniently carry, she happened to drop one at the barber's feet, which he took up out of curiosity to see what it was, and found it to be the History of the famous Knight Tirante the White. " Good lack-a-day," cried the curate, " is Tirante

the White here? oh! pray good neighbor give it
me by all means, for I promise myself to find in it
a treasure of delight, and a mine of recreation.
There we have that valorous knight Don Kyrie-
Eleison of Montalban, with his brother Thomas of
Montalban, and the knight Fonseca; the combat
between the valorous Detriante and Alano; the
dainty and witty conceits of the damsel Plazerde-
mivida, with the loves and guiles of the widow
Reposada; together with the lady empress, that
was in love with Hippolito her gentleman-usher.
I vow and protest to you, neighbor," continued he,
"that in its way there is not a better book in the
world; why here you have knights that eat and
drink, sleep, and die natural deaths in their beds,
nay, and make their last wills and testaments; with
a world of other things, of which all the rest of
these sort of books don't say one syllable. Yet
after all, I must tell you, that for wilfully taking
the pains to write so many foolish things, the worthy author fairly deserves to be sent to the galleys
for all the days of his life. Take it home with you
and read it, and then tell me whether I have told
you the truth or no." " I believe you," replied the
barber; " but what shall we do with all these
smaller books that are left?" " Certainly," replied
the curate, " these cannot be books of knight-errantry, they are too small; you'll find they are only
poets." And so opening one, it happened to be
the Diana of Montemayor; which made him say,
(believing all the rest to be of that stamp,) " These
do not deserve to be punished like the others, for
they neither have done, nor can do, that mischief

which those stories of chivalry have done, being generally ingenious books, that can do nobody any prejudice." "Oh! good sir," cried the niece, "burn them with the rest, I beseech you; for should my uncle get cured of his knight-errant frenzy, and betake himself to the reading of these books, we should have him turn shepherd, and so wander through the woods and fields; nay, and what would be worse yet, turn poet, which they say is a catching and an incurable disease." "The gentlewoman is in the right," said the curate, "and it . will not be amiss to remove that stumbling-block out of our friend's way; and since we began with the Diana of Montemayor, I am of opinion we ought not to burn it, but only take out that part of it which treats of the magician Felicia, and the enchanted water, as also all the longer poems; and let the work escape with its prose, and the honor of being the first of that kind." "Here's another Diana," quoth the barber, "the second of that name, by Salmantino, (of Salamanca,) nay, and a third too, by Gil Polo." "Pray," said the curate, "let Salmantino increase the number of the criminals in the yard; but as for that by Gil Polo, preserve it as charily as if Apollo himself had wrote it; and go on as fast as you can, I beseech you, good neighbor, for it grows late." "Here," quoth the barber, "I've a book called the Ten Books of the Fortunes of Love, by Anthony de Lofraco, a Sardinian poet." "Now, by my holy orders," cried the curate, "I do not think since Apollo was Apollo, the muses muses, and the poets poets, there ever was a more comical, more whimsical book! Of all the works of the kind, commend me to this, for in its way 'tis certainly the best and most singular that ever was published, and he that never read it, may safely think he never in his life read any thing that was pleasant. Give it me, neighbor," continued he, " for I am more glad to have found it, than if any one had given me a cassock of the best Florence serge." With that he laid it aside with extraordinary satisfaction, and the barber went on : " These that follow," cried he, " are the Shepherd of Iberia, the Nymphs of Enares, and the Cure of Jealousy." " Take them, jailer," quoth the curate, " and never ask me why, for then we shall ne'er have done." " The next," said the barber, " is the Shepherd of Filida." " He's no shepherd," returned the curate, " but a very discreet courtier ; keep him as a precious jewel." " Here's a bigger," cried the barber, " called The Treasure of Divers Poems." " Had there been fewer of them," said the curate, " they would have been more esteemed. 'Tis fit the book should be pruned and cleared of several trifles that disgrace the rest ; keep it, however, because the author is my friend, and for the sake of his other more heroic and lofty productions." " Here's a book of songs by Lopez Maldonardo," cried the barber. " He's also my particular friend," said the curate ; " his verses are very well liked when he reads them himself ; and his voice is so excellent, that they charm us whenever he sings them. He seems indeed to be somewhat too long in his eclogues ; but can we ever have too much of a good thing ? Let him be preserved among the best. What's the next book ?" " The Galatea of

Miguel de Cervantes," replied the barber. "That Cervantes has been my intimate acquaintance these many years," cried the curate; "and I know he has been more conversant with misfortunes than with poetry. His book indeed has I don't know what that looks like a good design; he aims at something, but concludes nothing; therefore we must stay for the second part, which he has promised us; * perhaps he may make us amends, and obtain a full pardon, which is denied him for the present; till that time, keep him close prisoner at your house." "I will," quoth the barber; "but see, I have here three more for you, the Araucana of Don Alonso de Ercilla, the Austirada of Juan Ruffo, a magistrate of Cordova, and the Monserrato of Christopher de Virves, a Valentian poet." "These," cried the curate, "are the best heroic poems we have in Spanish, and may vie with the most celebrated of Italy; reserve them as the most valuable performance which Spain has to boast of in poetry."

At last the curate grew so tired with prying into so many volumes, that he ordered all the rest to be burnt at a venture.† But the barber showed him one which he had opened by chance ere the dreadful sentence was past. "Truly," said the curate, who saw by the title it was the Tears of Angelica, "I should have wept myself, had I caused such a book to share the condemnation of the rest; for the

---

* Cervantes never performed this promise.

† In the original, à *Carga Cerrada*, (inside and contents unknown,) a mercantile phrase used in their bills of lading.

author was not only one of the best poets in Spain, but in the whole world, and translated some of Ovid's fables with extraordinary success."

.

CHAPTER VII.

DON QUIXOTE'S SECOND SALLY IN QUEST OF ADVENTURES.

WHILE they were thus employed, Don Quixote in a raving fit began to talk aloud to himself. " Here, here, valorous knights," cried he, " now's the time that you must exert the strength of your mighty arms; for lo, the courtiers bear away the honor of the tournament." This amazing outcry called away the inquisitors from any further examination of the library ; and therefore the housekeeper and the niece, being left to their own discretion, it is thought the Carolea and Leo of Spain, with the Deeds of the Emperor, written by Don Lewis d' Avila, which to be sure were part of the collection, were committed to the flames unseen and unheard, without any legal trial; a fate which perhaps they might have escaped, had the curate been there to have weighed what might have been urged in their defence.

When they came into Don Quixote's chamber, they found him risen out of his bed, as mad as ever he was, tearing his throat, and making a heavy bustle, laying about him with his sword, back-stroke and fore-stroke, as broad awake as if he had never slept. They ran in upon him, caught him in their arms, and carried him to bed again by main force ;

where, after he was somewhat quiet and settled, turning himself to the curate, "Certainly," cried he, " my Lord Archbishop Turpin, 'tis a great dishonor to us who are called the twelve peers, to suffer the knights of the court to bear away the honor of the tournament without any further opposition, after we the knight adventurers had carried it for three days before." "Be pacified, my good friend," replied the curate; fortune may have yet a better success in reserve for you, and they who lose to-day may win to-morrow; at present think on your health, for doubtless you must needs be now extremely tired, if not very much wounded." "Wounded!" replied Don Quixote, " no; but as for being bruised, I will not deny it, for that base-born knight Don Orlando has battered all my limbs with the trunk of an oak, out of mere envy, because he sees that I only dare rival his exploits: but may I no more be called Rinaldo of Montalban, if, in spite of his enchantments, I do not make him severely pay for this, as soon as I can leave my bed; and therefore let my dinner be brought in, for 'tis what I want most at this juncture, and then let me alone to revenge this abuse." Accordingly they brought him some victuals, which when he had eaten, he fell asleep again, and they left him, all of them strangely amazed at his uncommon madness. That night the housekeeper burnt all the books, not only those in the yard, but all those that were in the house; and several suffered in the general calamity, that deserved to have been treasured up in everlasting archives, had not their fate and the remissness of the inquisitors ordered it otherwise. And thus they verified the proverb, *That the good often fare the worse for the bad.*

One of the expedients which the curate and the barber thought themselves of, in order to their friend's recovery, was to stop up the door of the room where his books lay, that he might not find it, nor miss them when he rose; for they hoped the effect would cease when they had taken away the cause; and they ordered, that if he inquired about it, they should tell him, that a certain enchanter had carried away study, books, and all. Two days after, Don Quixote being got up, the first thing he did was to go visit his darling books; and as he could not find the study in the place where he had left it, he went up and down, and looked for it in every room. Sometimes he came to the place where the door used to stand, and then stood feeling and groping about a good while, then cast his eyes, and stared on every side, without speaking a word. At last, after a long deliberation, he thought fit to ask his housekeeper which was the way to his study. " What study," answered the woman, according to her instructions, " or rather, what nothing is it you look for? Alas! here's neither study nor books in the house now, for the devil is run away with them all." " No, 'twas not the devil," said the niece, " but a conjurer, or an enchanter, as they call them, who, since you went, came hither one night mounted on a dragon on the top of a cloud, and then alighting, went into your study, where what he did, he and the devil best can tell, for a while after, he flew out at the roof of the house, leaving it all full of smoke; and when we went to see what he had done, we

could neither find the books, nor so much as the
very study; only the housekeeper and I very well
remember, that when the old thief went away, he
cried out aloud, that out of a private grudge which
he bore in his mind to the owner of those books, he
had done the house a mischief, as we should soon
perceive; and then I think he called himself the
sage Muniaton." "Not Muniaton, but Freston,
you should have said," cried Don Quixote. "Truly,"
quoth the niece, "I can't tell whether it was Freston, or Friston, but sure I am that his name ended
with a ton." "It is so," returned Don Quixote,
"for he is a famous necromancer, and my mortal
enemy, and bears me a great deal of malice; for
seeing by his art, that in spite of all his spells, in
process of time I shall fight and vanquish in single
combat a knight whose interests he espouses, therefore he endeavors to do me all manner of mischief;
but I dare assure him, that he strives against the
stream, nor can his power reverse the first decrees
of fate." "Who doubts of that?" cried the niece;
" but, dear uncle, what makes you run yourself into
these quarrels? had not you better stay at home,
and live in peace and quietness, than go rambling
up and down like a vagabond, and seeking for better bread than is made of wheat, without once so
much as considering, that many go to seek wool,
and come home shorn themselves." "Oh, good
niece," replied Don Quixote, "how ill thou under-
standest these matters! know, that before I will suffer myself to be shorn, I will tear and pluck off the
beards of all those audacious mortals that shall attempt to profane the tip of one single hair within

the verge of these moustaches." To this neither the niece nor the governess thought fit to make any reply, for they perceived the knight to grow angry.

Full fifteen days did our knight remain quietly at home, without betraying the least sign of his desire to renew his rambling; during which time there passed a great deal of pleasant discourse between him and his two friends, the curate and the barber; while he maintained, that there was nothing the world stood so much in need of as knights-errant; wherefore he was resolved to revive the order; in which disputes, Mr. Curate sometimes contradicted him, and sometimes submitted; for had he not now and then given way to his fancies, there would have been no conversing with him.

In the mean time Don Quixote earnestly solicited one of his neighbors, a country laborer, and a good honest fellow, if we may call a poor man honest, for he was poor indeed, poor in purse, and poor in brains; and, in short, the knight talked so long to him, plied him with so many arguments, and made him so many fair promises, that at last the poor silly clown consented to go along with him, and become his squire. Among other inducements to entice him to do it willingly, Don Quixote forgot not to tell him, that it was likely such an adventure would present itself, as might secure him the conquest of some island in the time that he might be picking up a straw or two, and then the squire might promise himself to be made governor of the place. Allured with these large promises, and many others, Sancho Panza (for that was the name of the fellow) forsook his wife and children to be his neighbor's squire.

This done, Don Quixote made it his business to furnish himself with money; to which purpose, selling one house, mortgaging another, and losing by all, he at last got a pretty good sum together. He also borrowed a target of a friend, and having patched up his head-piece and beaver as well as he could, he gave his squire notice of the day and hour when he intended to set out, that he might also furnish himself with what he thought necessary; but above all, he charged him to provide himself with a wallet; which Sancho promised to do, telling him he would also take his ass along with him, which being a very good one, might be a great ease to him, for he was not used to travel much a-foot. The mentioning of the ass made the noble knight pause awhile; he mused and pondered whether he had ever read of any knight-errant whose squire used to ride upon an ass; but he could not remember any precedent for it; however, he gave him leave at last to bring his ass, hoping to mount him more honorably with the first opportunity, by unhorsing the next discourteous knight he should meet. He also furnished himself with shirts, and as many other necessaries as he could conveniently carry, according to the innkeeper's injunctions. Which being done, Sancho Panza, without bidding either his wife or children good-by; and Don Quixote, without taking any more notice of his housekeeper or of his niece, stole out of the village one night, nor so much as suspected by any body, and made such haste, that by break of day they thought themselves out of reach, should they happen to be pursued. As for Sancho Panza, he rode like a patriarch, with his canvas knapsack, or wallet, and his leathern bottle, having a huge desire to see himself governor of the island, which his master had promised him.

Don Quixote happened to strike into the same road which he took the time before, that is, the plains of Montiel, over which he travelled with less inconvenience than when he went alone, by reason it was yet early in the morning; at which time the sunbeams being almost parallel to the surface of the earth, and not directly darted down, as in the middle of the day, did not prove so offensive. As they jogged on, " I beseech your worship, Sir knight-errant," quoth Sancho to his master, " be sure you don't forget what you promised me about the island; for I dare say I shall make shift to govern it, let it be never so big." " You must know, friend Sancho," replied Don Quixote, " that it has been the constant practice of knights-errant in former ages, to make their squires governors of the islands or kingdoms they conquered; now I am not only resolved to keep up that laudable custom, but even to improve it, and outdo my predecessors in generosity; for whereas sometimes, or rather most commonly, other knights delayed rewarding their squires till they were grown old, and worn out with services, bad days, worse nights, and all manner of hard duty, and then put them off with some title, either of count, or at least marquis of some valley or province, of great or small extent; now, if thou and I do but live, it may happen, that before we have

passed six days together, I may conquer some kingdom, having many other kingdoms annexed to its
imperial crown; and this would fall out most luckily for thee; for then would I presently crown thee
king of one of them. Nor do thou imagine this to
be a mighty matter; for so strange accidents and
revolutions, so sudden and so unforeseen, attend the
profession of chivalry, that I might easily give thee
a great deal more than I have promised." "Why,
should this come to pass," quoth Sancho Panza,
"and I be made a king by some such miracle, as
your worship says, then happy be lucky, my
Whither d'ye-go Mary Gutierez would be at least
a queen, and my children infantas and princes, an't
like, your worship." "Who doubts of that?" cried
Don Quixote. "I doubt of it," replied Sancho
Panza; "for I cannot help believing, that though it
should rain kingdoms down upon the face of the
earth, not one of them would sit well upon Mary
Gutierez's head; for I must needs tell you, she's not
worth two brass jacks to make a queen of; no,
countess would be better for her, an't please you;
and that too, God help her, will be as much as she
can handsomely manage." "Recommend the matter to providence," returned Don Quixote, "'twill
be sure to give what is most expedient for thee; but
yet disdain to entertain inferior thoughts, and be
not tempted to accept less than the dignity of a
viceroy." "No more I won't, sir," quoth Sancho,
"especially since I have so rare a master as your
worship, who will take care to give me whatever
may be fit for me, and what I may be able to deal
with."

CHAPTER VIII.

As they were thus discoursing, they discovered
some thirty or forty wind-mills, that are in that
plain; and as soon as the knight had spied them,
" Fortune," cried he, " directs our affairs better than
we ourselves could have wished; look yonder, friend
Sancho, there are at least thirty outrageous giants,
whom I intend to encounter; and having deprived
them of life, we will begin to enrich ourselves with
their spoils; for they are lawful prize; and the ex-
tirpation of that cursed brood will be an acceptable
service to Heaven." " What giants?" quoth Sancho Panza. " Those whom thou see'st yonder,"
answered Don Quixote, "with their long extended
arms; some of that detested race have arms of so
immense a size, that sometimes they reach two
leagues in length." " Pray look better, sir," quoth
Sancho; "those things yonder are no giants, but
wind-mills, and the arms you fancy, are their sails,
which being whirled about by the wind, make the
mill go." " 'Tis a sign," cried Don Quixote, " thou
art but little acquainted with adventures! I tell
thee, they are giants; and therefore if thou art
afraid, go aside and say thy prayers, for I am resolved to engage in a dreadful unequal combat

against them all." This said, he clapt spurs to his horse Rozinante, without giving ear to his squire Sancho, who bawled out to him, and assured him, that they were wind-mills, and no giants. But he was so fully possessed with a strong conceit of the contrary, that he did not so much as hear his squire's outcry, nor was he sensible of what they were, although he was already very near them : far from that, " Stand, cowards," cried he, as loud as he could; " stand your ground, ignoble creatures, and fly not basely from a single knight, who dares encounter you all." At the same time the wind rising, the mill-sails began to move, which, when Don Quixote spied, " Base miscreants," cried he, " though you move more arms than the giant Briareus, you shall pay for your arrogance." He most devoutly recommended himself to his Lady Dulcinea, imploring her assistance in this perilous adventure ; and so covering himself with his shield, and couching his lance, he rushed with Rozinante's utmost speed upon the first wind-mill he could come at, and running his lance into the sail, the wind whirled it about with such swiftness, that the rapidity of the motion presently broke the lance into shivers, and hurled away both knight and horse along with it, till down he fell, rolling a good way off in the field. Sancho Panza ran as fast as his ass could drive, to help his master, whom he found lying, and not able to stir, such a blow he and Rozinante had received. " Mercy o' me!" cried Sancho, " did not I give your worship fair warning ? did not I tell you they were wind-mills, and that nobody could think otherwise, unless he

had also wind-mills in his head?" "Peace, friend
Sancho," replied Don Quixote; "there is nothing
so subject to the inconstancy of fortune as war. I
am verily persuaded, that cursed necromancer Freston, who carried away my study and my books, has
transformed these giants into wind-mills, to deprive
me of the honor of the victory, such is his inveterate malice against me; but in the end, all his pernicious wiles and stratagems shall prove ineffectual
against the prevailing edge of my sword." "Amen,
say I," replied Sancho. And so heaving him up
again upon his legs, once more the knight mounted
poor Rozinante, that was half shoulder-slipp'd with
his fall.

This adventure was the subject of their discourse,
as they made the best of their way towards the pass
of Lapice;* for Don Quixote took that road, believing he could not miss of adventures in one so
mightily frequented. However, the loss of his
lance was no small affliction to him; and as he was
making his complaint about it to his squire, "I
have read," said he, "friend Sancho, that a certain
Spanish knight, whose name was Diego Perez de
Vargas, having broken his sword in the heat of an
engagement, pulled up by the roots a huge oak tree,
or at least tore down a massy branch, and did such
wonderful execution, crushing and grinding so many
Moors with it that day, that he won himself and
his posterity the surname of † The Pounder, or

* A pass in the mountains, such as they call Puerto Seco, a
dry port, where the king's officers levy the tolls and customs
upon passengers and goods.
† *Machuca,* from *Machucar,* to pound in a mortar.

Bruiser. I tell thee this, because I intend to tear up the next oak, or holm-tree, we meet; with the trunk whereof I hope to perform such wondrous deeds, that thou wilt esteem thyself particularly happy in having had the honor to behold them, and been the ocular witness of achievements which posterity will scarce be able to believe." "Heaven grant you may," cried Sancho; "I believe it all, because your worship says it. But, an't please you, sit a little more upright in your saddle; you ride sideling, methinks; but that, I suppose, proceeds from your being bruised by the fall." "It does so," replied Don Quixote; "and if I do not complain of the pain, it is because a knight-errant must never complain of his wounds, though his bowels were dropping out through them." "Then I have no more to say," quoth Sancho; "and yet Heaven knows my heart, I should be glad to hear your worship hone a little now and then when something ails you; for my part, I shall not fail to bemoan myself when I suffer the smallest pain, unless indeed it can be proved, that the rule of not complaining extends to the squires as well as knights."

Don Quixote could not forbear smiling at the simplicity of his squire; and told him he gave him leave to complain not only when he pleased, but as much as he pleased, whether he had any cause or no; for he had never yet read any thing to the contrary in any books of chivalry. Sancho desired him, however, to consider, that it was high time to go to dinner; but his master answered him, that he might eat whenever he pleased; as for himself, he was not yet disposed to do it. Sancho having

thus obtained leave, fixed himself as orderly as he
could upon his ass; and taking some victuals out
of his wallet, fell to munching lustily as he rode behind his master; and ever and anon he lifted his
bottle to his nose, and fetched such hearty pulls,
that it would have made the best pampered vintner
in Malaga a-dry to have seen him. While he thus
went on stuffing and swilling, he did not think in
the least of all his master's great promises; and
was so far from esteeming it a trouble to travel in
quest of adventures, that he fancied it to be the
greatest pleasure in the world, though they were
never so dreadful.

In fine, they passed that night under some trees;
from one of which Don Quixote tore a withered
branch, which in some sort was able to serve him
for a lance, and to this he fixed the head or spear
of his broken lance. But he did not sleep all that
night, keeping his thoughts intent on his dear Dulcinea, in imitation of what he had read in books of
chivalry, where the knights pass their time, without
sleep, in forests and deserts, wholly taken up with
the entertaining thoughts of their absent mistresses.
As for Sancho, he did not spend the night at that
idle rate; for, having his paunch well stuffed with
something more substantial than dandelion-water,
he made but one nap of it; and had not his master
waked him, neither the sprightly beams which the
sun darted on his face, nor the melody of the birds,
that cheerfully on every branch welcomed the smiling morn, would have been able to have made him
stir. As he got up, to clear his eye-sight, he took
two or three long-winded swigs at his friendly bot-

tle for a morning's draught: but he found it somewhat lighter than it was the night before; which
misfortune went to his very heart, for he shrewdly
mistrusted that he was not in a way to cure it of
that distemper as soon as he could have wished.
On the other side, Don Quixote would not break
fast, having been feasting all night on the more delicate and savory thoughts of his mistress; and
therefore they went on directly towards the pass of
Lapice, which they discovered about three o'clock.
When they came near it, " Here it is, brother Sancho," said Don Quixote, " that we may wanton,
and, as it were, thrust our arms up to the very el-
bows, in that which we call adventures. But let
me give thee one necessary caution ; know, that
though thou should'st see me in the greatest extremity of danger, thou must not offer to draw thy
sword in my defence, unless thou findest me assaulted by base plebeians and vile scoundrels; for in
such a case thou may'st assist thy master: but if
those with whom I am fighting are knights, thou
must not do it, for the laws of chivalry do not allow thee to encounter a knight, till thou art one thyself." " Never fear," quoth Sancho; " I'll be sure
to obey your worship in that, I'll warrant you; for
I have ever loved peace and quietness, and never
cared to thrust myself into frays and quarrels ; and
yet I don't care to take blows at any one's hands
neither; and should any knight offer to set upon
me first, I fancy I should hardly mind your laws ;
for all laws, whether of God or man, allow one to
stand in his own defence, if any offer to do him a
mischief." " I agree to that," replied Don Quixote;

" but as for helping me against any knights, thou
must set bounds to thy natural impulses." " I'll
be sure to do it," quoth Sancho ; " never trust me if
I don't keep your commandments as well as I do
the Sabbath."

As they were talking, they spied coming towards
them two monks of the order of St. Benedict, mount‑
ed on two dromedaries, for the mules on which they
rode were so high and stately, that they seemed little
less.　They wore riding-masks, with glasses at the
eyes, against the dust, and umbrellas to shelter them
from the sun.　After them came a coach, with four
or five men on horseback, and two muleteers on foot.
There proved to be in the coach a Biscayan lady,
who was going to Seville to meet her husband, that
was there in order to embark for the Indies, to take
possession of a considerable post.　Scarce had Don
Quixote perceived the monks, who were not of the
same company, though they went the same way,
but he cried to his squire, " Either I am deceived,
or this will prove the most famous adventure that
ever was known ; for without all question those two
black things that move towards us must be some
necromancers, that are carrying away by force some
princess in that coach ; and 'tis my duty to prevent
so great an injury." " I fear me this will prove
a worse job than the wind-mills," quoth Sancho.
" 'Slife, sir, don't you-see these are Benedictine friars,
and 'tis likely the coach belongs to some travellers
that are in it : therefore once more take warning, and
don't you be led away by the devil." " I have
already told thee, Sancho," replied Don Quixote,
" thou art miserably ignorant in matters of adven‑

tures : what I say is true, and thou shalt find it so presently." This said, he spurred on his horse, and posted himself just in the midst of the road where the monks were to pass. And when they came within hearing, " Cursed implements of hell," cried he in a loud and haughty tone, " immediately release those high-born princesses whom you are violently conveying away in the coach, or else prepare to meet with instant death, as the just punishment of your pernicious deeds." The monks stopt their mules, no less astonished at the figure, than at the expressions of the speaker. " Sir Knight," cried they, " we are no such persons as you are pleased to term us, but religious men of the Order of St. Benedict, that travel about our affairs, and are wholly ignorant whether or no there are any princesses carried away by force in that coach." " I am not to be deceived with fair words," replied Don Quixote; " I know you well enough, perfidious caitiffs;" and immediately, without expecting their reply, he set spurs to Rozinante, and ran so furiously, with his lance couched, against the first monk, that if he had not prudently flung himself off to the ground, the knight would certainly have laid him either dead, or grievously wounded. The other, observing the discourteous usage of his companion, clapped his heels to his over-grown mule's flanks, and scoured over the plain as if he had been running a race with the wind. Sancho Panza no sooner saw the monk fall, but he nimbly skipt off his ass, and running to him, began to strip him immediately; but then the two muleteers, who waited on the monks, came up to him, and asked why he offered to strip him?

Sancho told them, that this belonged to him as lawful plunder, being the spoils won in battle by his lord and master Don Quixote. The fellows, with whom there was no jesting, not knowing what he meant by his spoils and battle, and seeing Don Quixote at a good distance in deep discourse by the side of the coach, fell both upon poor Sancho, threw him down, tore his beard from his chin, trampled on his guts, thumped and mauled him in every part of his carcass, and there left him sprawling without breath or motion. In the meanwhile the monk, scared out of his wits, and as pale as a ghost, got upon his mule again as fast as he could, and spurred after his friend, who staid for him at a distance, expecting the issue of this strange adventure; but being unwilling to stay to see the end of it, they made the best of their way, making more signs of the cross than if the devil had been posting after them.

Don Quixote, as I said, was all that while engaged with the lady in the coach. "Lady," cried he, "your discretion is now at liberty to dispose of your beautiful self as you please; for the presumptuous arrogance of those who attempted to enslave your person lies prostrate in the dust, overthrown by this my strenuous arm: and that you may not be at a loss for the name of your deliverer, know I am called Don Quixote de la Mancha, by profession a knight-errant and adventurer, captive to that peerless beauty Donna Dulcinea del Toboso: nor do I desire any other recompense for the service I have done you, but that you return to Toboso to present yourselves to that lady, and let her know what I have done to purchase your deliverance." To this strange talk, a certain Biscayan, the lady's squire, gentleman-usher, or what you will please to call him, who rode along with the coach, listened with great attention; and perceiving that Don Quixote not only stopped the coach, but would have it presently go back to Toboso, he bore briskly up to him, and laying hold of his lance, " Get gone," cried he to him in bad Spanish and worse Biscayan.* " Get gone, thou knight, and devil go with thou; or by he who me create, if thou do not leave the coach, me kill thee now so sure as me be a Biscayan." Don Quixote, who made shift to understand him well enough, very calmly made him this answer: " Wert thou a cavalier,† as thou art not, ere this I would have chastised thy insolence and temerity, thou inconsiderable mortal." " What! me no gentleman?" replied the Biscayan; " I swear thou be a liar, as me be Christian. If thou throw away lance, and draw sword, me will make no more of thee than cat does of mouse; me will show thee me be Biscayan, and gentleman by land, gentleman by sea, gentleman in spite of devil; and thou lie if thou say contrary." " I'll try titles with you, as the man said," replied Don Quixote; and with that, throwing away his lance, he drew his sword, grasped his target, and attacked the Biscayan, fully bent on his destruction. The Biscayan seeing him come

* The Biscayners generally speak broken Spanish, wherefore the English is rendered accordingly.

† Cavallero in Spanish signifies a gentleman as well as a knight; and used in these different senses by the knight-errant and the gentleman-usher, causes the difference between Don Quixote and the Biscayner.

on so furiously, would gladly have alighted, not
trusting to his mule, which was one of those scurvy
jades that are let out to hire; but all he had time
to-do was only to draw his sword, and snatch a
cushion out of the coach to serve him instead of a
shield; and immediately they assaulted one another
with all the fury of mortal enemies. The by-stand-
ers did all they could to prevent their fighting; but
it was in vain, for the Biscayan swore in his gibber-
ish he would kill his very lady, and all those who
presumed to hinder him, if they would not let him
fight. The lady in the coach being extremely affrighted at these passages, made her coachman
drive out of harm's way, and at a distance was an
eye-witness of the furious combat. At the same
time the Biscayan let fall such a mighty blow on
Don Quixote's shoulder over his target, that had not
his armor been sword-proof, he would have cleft
him down to the very waist. The knight feeling
the weight. of that unmeasurable blow, cried out
aloud, " Oh! lady of my soul, Dulcinea! flower of
all beauty, vouchsafe to succor your champion in
this dangerous combat, undertaken to set forth your
worth!" The breathing out of this short prayer,
the griping fast of his sword, the covering of himself with his shield, and the charging of his enemy,
was but the work of a moment; for Don Quixote
was resolved to venture the fortune of the combat
all upon one blow. The Biscayan, who read his
design in his dreadful countenance, resolved to face
him with equal bravery, and stand the terrible
shock, with uplifted sword, and covered with the
cushion, not being able to manage his jaded mule,

who, defying the spur, and not being cut out for such pranks, would move neither to the right nor to the left. While Don Quixote, with his sword aloft, was rushing upon the wary Biscayan, with a full resolution to cleave him asunder, all the spectators stood trembling with terror and amazement, expecting the dreadful event of those prodigious blows which threatened the two desperate combatants; the lady in the coach, with her women, were making a thousand vows and offerings to all the images and places of devotion in Spain, that Providence might deliver them and the squire out of the great danger that threatened them.

But here we must deplore the abrupt end of this history, which the author leaves off just at the very point when the fortune of the battle is going to be decided, pretending he could find nothing more recorded of Don Quixote's wondrous achievements, than what he had already related. However, the second undertaker of this work could not believe that so curious a history could lie forever inevitably buried in oblivion; or that the learned of La Mancha were so regardless of their country's glory, as not to preserve in their archives, or at least in their closets, some memoirs, as monuments of this famous knight; and therefore he would not give over inquiring after the continuation of this pleasant history, till at last he happily found it, as the next Book will inform the reader.

PART I. BOOK II.

CHAPTER I.

THE EVENT OF THE MOST STUPENDOUS COMBAT BETWEEN THE BRAVE BISCAYAN AND THE VALOROUS DON QUIXOTE.

In the First Book of this history, we left the valiant Biscayan and the renowned Don Quixote with their swords lifted up, and ready to discharge on each other two furious and most terrible blows, which, had they fallen directly, and met with no opposition, would have cut and divided the two combatants from head to heel, and have split them like a pomegranate; but, as I said before, the story remained imperfect; neither did the author inform us where we might find the remaining part of the relation. This vexed me extremely, and turned the pleasure, which the perusal of the beginning had afforded me, into disgust, when I had reason to despair of ever seeing the rest. Yet, after all, it seemed to me no less impossible than unjust, that so valiant a knight should have been destitute of some learned person to record his incomparable exploits; a misfortune which never attended any of his predecessors, I mean the knights-adventurers, each of whom was always provided with one or two learned men, who were always at hand to write not only their wondrous deeds, but also to set down their thoughts and childish petty actions, were they

never so hidden. Therefore, as I could not imagine
that so worthy a knight should be so unfortunate,
as to want that which has been so profusely lavish-
ed even on such a one as Platyr,* and others of
that stamp; I could not induce myself to believe,
that so admirable a history was ever left unfinished,
and rather choose to think that time, the devourer
of all things, had hid or consumed it. On the
other side, when I considered that several modern
books were found in his study, as the Cure of Jealousy, and the Nymphs and Shepherds of Henares,†
I had reason to think that the history of our knight
could be of no very ancient date; and that, had it
never been continued, yet his neighbors and friends
could not have forgot the most remarkable passages ·
of his life. Full of this imagination, I resolved to
make it my business to make a particular and exact inquiry into the life and miracles of our renowned Spaniard Don Quixote, that refulgent glory
and mirror of the knighthood of La Mancha, and
the first who, in these depraved and miserable
times, devoted himself to the neglected profession
of knight-errantry, to redress wrongs and injuries, to
relieve widows, and defend the honor of damsels;
such of them, I mean, who in former ages rode up
and down over hills and dales with whip in hand,
mounted on their palfreys, with all their virginity
about them, secure from all manner of danger, and
who, unless they happened to be ravished by some

* A second-rate knight in Palmerin of England.

† Henares runs by the university of Alcale (i. e. Complutum)
in Old Castile, and therefore much celebrated by Spanish poets
bred in that university. They call it Henarius in Latin.

boisterous villain or huge giant, were sure, at four
score years of age, (all which time they never slept
one night under a roof,) to be decently laid in their
graves, as pure virgins as the mothers that bore
them. For this reason and many others, I say, our
gallant Don Quixote is worthy everlasting and universal praise; nor ought I to be denied my due
commendation for my indefatigable care and dili-
gence, in seeking and finding out the continuation
of this delightful history; though, after all, I must
confess, that had not Providence, chance, or fortune,
as I will not inform you, assisted me in the discovery, the world had been deprived of two hours'
diversion and pleasure, which it is likely to afford
to those who will read it with attention. One day
being in the *Alcana at Toledo, I saw a young lad
offer to sell a parcel of old written papers to a
shopkeeper. Now I, being apt to take up the least
piece of written or printed papers that lies in my
way, though it were in the middle of the street,
I could not forbear laying my hands on one of the
manuscripts, to see what it was, and I found it to
be written in Arabic, which I could not read. This
made me look about to see whether I could find
e'er a Morisco † that understood Spanish, to read it
for me, and give me some account of it; nor was it
very difficult to meet with an interpreter there; for
had I wanted one for a better and more ancient
tongue, ‡ that place would have infallibly supplied

---

* An exchange; a place full of shops.
† Morisco is one of the race of the Moors.
‡ Meaning some Jew, to interpret the Hebrew or Chaldee.

me. It was my good fortune to find one immediately; and having informed him of my desire, he
no sooner read some lines, but he began to laugh.
I asked him what he laughed at? "At a certain
remark here in the margin of the book," said he.
I prayed him to explain it; whereupon still laughing, he did it in these words: " This Dulcinea del
Toboso, so often mentioned in this history, is said
to have had the best hand at salting pork of any
woman in all La Mancha." I was surprised when
I heard him name Dulcinea del Toboso, and presently imagined that those old papers contained the
history of Don Quixote. This made me press him
to read the title of the book; which he did, turning
it thus extemporary out of Arabic: THE HISTORY
OF DON QUIXOTE DE LA MANCHA; WRITTEN BY
CID HAMET BENENGELI, AN ARABIAN HISTORIO-
GRAPHER. I was so overjoyed when I heard the
title, that I had much ado to conceal it; and presently taking the bargain out of the shopkeeper's
hand, I agreed with the young man for the whole,
and bought that for half a real, which he might
have sold me for twenty times as much, had he but
guessed at the eagerness of his chapman. I immediately withdrew with my purchase to the cloister
of the great church, taking the Moor with me; and
desired him to translate me those papers that treated
of Don Quixote, without adding or omitting the
least word, offering him any reasonable satisfaction.
He asked me but two * arrobes of raisins, and two
bushels of wheat, and promised me to do it faith-

---

* An arroba is about 32 lb. weight.

fully with all expedition; in short, for the quicker despatch, and the greater security, being unwilling to let such a lucky prize go out of my hands, I took the Moor to my own house, where, in less than six weeks, he finished the whole translation.

Don Quixote's fight with the Biscayan was exactly drawn on one of the leaves of the first quire, in the same posture as we left them, with their swords lifted up over their heads, the one guarding himself with his shield, the other with his cushion. The Biscayan's mule was pictured so to the life, that with half an eye you might have known it to be an hired mule. Under the Biscayan was written Don Sancho de Aspetia, and under Rozinante Don Quixote. Rozinante was so admirably delineated, so slim, so stiff, so lean, so jaded, with so sharp a ridge-bone, and altogether so like one wasted with an incurable consumption, that any one must have owned at first sight, that no horse ever better deserved that name. Not far off stood Sancho * Panza holding his ass by the halter; at whose feet there was a scroll in which was written Sancho † Canzas; and if we may judge of him by his picture, he was thick and short, paunch-bellied, and long-haunched; so that in all likelihood for this reason he is sometimes called Panza and sometimes Canza, in the history. There were some other niceties to be seen in that piece, but hardly worth observation, as not giving any light into this true history, otherwise they had not passed unmentioned; for none can be amiss so they be authentic. I

* Paunch. † Haunches, or thigh-bones.

must only acquaint the reader, that if any objection is to be made as to the veracity of this, it is only the author is an Arabian, and those of that country are not a little addicted to lying; but yet, if we consider that they are our enemies, we should sooner imagine that the author has rather suppressed the truth, than added to the real worth of our knight; and I am the more inclinable to think so, because it is plain, that where he ought to have enlarged on his praises, he maliciously chooses to be silent; a proceeding unworthy of an historian, who ought to be exact, sincere, and impartial; free from passion, and not to be biased either by interest, fear, resentment, or affection, to deviate from truth, which is the mother of history, the preserver and eternizer of great actions, the professed enemy of oblivion, the witness of things past, and the director of future times. As for this history, I know it will afford you as great a variety as you could wish, in the most entertaining manner; and if in any point it falls short of your expectation, I am of opinion it is more the fault of the infidel its author, than the subject; and so let us come to the Second Book, which, according to our translation, began in this manner.

Such were the bold and formidable looks of the two enraged combatants, that with uplifted arms, and with destructive steel, they seemed to threaten heaven, earth, and the infernal mansions; while the spectators seemed wholly lost in fear and astonishment. The choleric Biscayan discharged the first blow, and that with such a force, and so desperate a fury, that had not his sword turned in his hand,

that single stroke had put an end to the dreadful
combat, and all our knight's adventures. But fate,
that reserved him for greater things, so ordered it,
that his enemy's sword turned in such a manner,
that though it struck him on the left shoulder, it
did him no other hurt than to disarm that side of
his head, carrying away with it a great part of his
helmet and one half of his ear, which like a dreadful ruin fell together to the ground. Assist me, ye
powers!——but it is in vain: the fury which then
engrossed the breast of our hero of La Mancha is
not to be expressed; words would but wrong it;
for what color of speech can be lively enough to
give but a slight sketch or faint image of his unutterable rage? Exerting all his valor, he raised himself upon his stirrups, and seemed even greater than
himself; and at the same instant griping his sword
fast with both hands, he discharged such a tremendous blow full on the Biscayan's cushion and his
head, that in spite of so good a defence, as if a
whole mountain had fallen upon him, the blood
gushed out at his mouth, nose, and ears, all at
once; and he tottered so in his saddle, that he had
fallen to the ground immediately, had he not caught
hold of the neck of his mule; but the dull beast
itself being roused out of its stupidity with that
terrible blow, began to run about the fields; and
the Biscayan, having lost his stirrups and his hold,
with two or three winces the mule shook him off,
and threw him on the ground. Don Quixote beheld the disaster of his foe with the greatest tranquillity and unconcern imaginable; and seeing him
down, slipped nimbly from his saddle, and running

to him, set the point of his sword to his throat, and
bid him yield, or he would cut off his head. The
Biscayan was so stunned, that he could make him
no reply; and Don Quixote had certainly made
good his threats, so provoked was he, had not the
ladies in the coach, who with great uneasiness and
fear beheld the sad transactions, hastened to beseech Don Quixote very earnestly to spare his life.
" Truly, beautiful ladies," said the victorious knight,
with a great deal of loftiness and gravity, " I am
willing to grant your request; but upon condition
that this same knight shall pass his word of honor
to go to Toboso, and there present himself in my
name before the peerless lady Donna Dulcinea, that
she may dispose of him as she shall see convenient."
The lady, who was frightened almost out of her
senses, without considering what Don Quixote enjoined, or inquiring who the lady Dulcinea was,
promised, in her squire's behalf, a punctual obedience to the knight's commands. " Let him live,
then," replied Don Quixote, " upon your word, and
owe to your intercession that pardon which I might
justly deny his arrogance."

CHAPTER II.

WHAT FARTHER BEFELL DON QUIXOTE WITH THE BIS-
CAYAN; AND OF THE DANGER HE RAN AMONG A PARCEL
OF YANGUESIANS.

SANCHO PANZA was got up again before this, not much better for the kicks and thumps bestowed on his carcass by the monks' grooms; and seeing his master engaged in fight, he went devoutly to prayers, beseeching heaven to grant him victory, that he might now win some island, in order to his being made governor of it, according to his promise. At last, perceiving the danger was over, the combat at an end, and his master ready to mount again, he ran in all haste to help him; but ere the knight put his foot in the stirrup, Sancho fell on his knees before him, and, kissing his hand, "An't please your worship," cried he, "my good lord Don Quixote, I beseech you make me governor of the island you have won in this dreadful and bloody fight; for though it were never so great, I find myself able to govern it as well as the best he that ever went about to govern an island in the world." "Brother Sancho," replied Don Quixote, "these are no adventures of islands; these are only rencounters on the road, where little is to be got besides a broken head or the loss of an ear; therefore have patience, and some adventure will offer itself, which will not only enable me to prefer thee to a government, but even to something more considerable." Sancho gave him a world of thanks; and having once more kissed his hand, and the skirts of his coat of armor, he helped him to get upon Rozinante; and then leaping on his ass, he followed the hero, who, without taking leave of those in the coach, put on a good round pace, and rode into a wood that was not far off. Sancho made after him as fast as his ass would trot; but finding Rozinante was like to leave him behind, he was forced to call to his master to stay for him. Don Quixote accordingly checked his horse, and soon gave Sancho leisure to overtake him.

"Methinks, sir," said the fearful squire, as soon as he came up with him, "it won't be amiss for us to betake ourselves to some church, to get out of harm's way; for if that same man whom you have fought with should do otherwise than well, I dare lay my life they will get a warrant from the holy brotherhood, and have us taken up; which if they do, on my word it will go hard with us ere we can get out of their clutches." "Hold thy tongue," cried Don Quixote: where didst thou ever read, or find that a knight-errant was ever brought before any judge for the homicides which he committed?" "I can't tell what you mean by your homilies," replied Sancho; "I do not know that ever I saw one in my born days, not I: but well I wot, that the law lays hold on those that goes to murder one another in the fields; and for your what d'ye call them's, I've nothing to say to them." "Then be not afraid, good Sancho," cried Don Quixote; "for I would deliver thee out of the hands of the Chaldeans, and with much more ease out of those of the holy brotherhood. But come, tell me truly dost thou believe that the whole world can boast of another knight that may pretend to rival me in valor? didst thou ever read in history, that any other ever showed more resolution to undertake, more vigor to attack, more breath to hold out, more dexterity and activity to strike, and more art and force to overthrow his enemies?" " Not I, by my troth," replied Sancho, " I never did meet with any thing like you in history, for I can neither read nor write; but that which I dare wager is, that I never in my life served a bolder master than your worship : pray heaven this same boldness may not bring us to what I bid you beware of. All I have to put you in mind of now is, that you get your ear dressed, for you lose a deal of blood ; and by good luck I have here some lint and a little white salve in my wallet." " How needless would all this have been," cried Don Quixote, " had I but bethought myself of making a small bottle-full of the balsam of Fierabras, a single drop of which would have spared us a great deal of time and medicaments." " What is that same balsam, an't please you?" cried Sancho. "A balsam," answered Don Quixote, " of which I have the receipt in my head. He that has some of it may defy death itself, and dally with all manner of wounds : therefore when I have made some of it, and given it thee, if at any time thou happenest to see my body cut in two by some unlucky back-stroke, as 'tis common among us knights-errant, thou hast no more to do but to take up nicely that half of me which is fallen to the ground, and clap it exactly to the other half on the saddle before the blood is congealed, always taking care to lay it just

in its proper place; then thou shalt give me two
draughts of that balsam, and thou shalt immediately
see me become whole, and sound as an apple." " If
this be true," quoth Sancho, " I will quit you of your
promise about the island this minute of an hour, and
will have nothing of your worship for what service
I have done, and am to do you, but the receipt of
that same balsam; for, I dare say, let me go wherever I will, it will be sure to yield me three good reals
an ounce; and thus I shall make shift to pick a
pretty good livelihood out of it. But stay though,"
continued he, " does the making stand your worship
in much, sir?"   " Three quarts of it," replied Don
Quixote, " may be made for three reals."   " Body
of me," cried Sancho, " why do you not make some
out of hand, and teach me how to make it ?"   " Say
no more, friend Sancho," returned Don Quixote;
" I intend to teach thee much greater secrets, and
design thee nobler rewards; but in the mean time
dress my ear, for it pains me more than I could
wish." Sancho then took his lint and ointment out
of his wallet; but when Don Quixote perceived the
vizor of his helmet was broken, he had like to have
run stark staring mad; straight laying hold on his
sword, and lifting up his eyes to heaven, " By the
great Creator of the universe," cried he, " by every
syllable contained in the four holy evangelists, I
swear to lead a life like the great Marquis of Mantua, when he made a vow to revenge the death
of his cousin Baldwin, which was never to eat
bread on a table-cloth, never to lie with the dear partner of his bed, and other things, which, though they
are now at present slipped out of my memory, I

comprise in my vow no less than if I had now mentioned them; and this I bind myself to, till I have
fully revenged myself on him that has done me
this injury."

" Good your worship," cried Sancho, (amazed to
hear him take such a horrid oath) " think on what
you are doing; for if that same knight has done as
you bid him, and has gone and cast himself before
my lady Dulcinea del Toboso, I do not see but you
and he are quit; and the man deserves no further
punishment, unless he does you some new mischief."
"'Tis well observed," replied Don Quixote; " and
therefore as to the point of revenge, I revoke my
oath; but I renew and confirm the rest, protesting
solemnly to lead the life I mentioned, till I have by
force of arms despoiled some knight of as good a
helmet as mine was. Neither do thou fancy, Sancho, that I make this protestation lightly, or make
a smoke of straw : no, I have a laudable precedent for it, the authority of which will sufficiently
justify my imitation; for the very same thing happened about Mambrino's helmet, which cost Sacri-
pante so dear." " Good sir," quoth Sancho, " let
all such cursing and swearing go to the devil;
there's nothing can be worse for your soul's health,
nay for your bodily health neither. Besides, sup-·
pose we should not this good while meet any one
with a helmet on, what a sad case should we then
be in? will your worship then keep your oath in
spite of so many hardships, such as to lie rough for
a month together, far from any inhabited place, and
a thousand other idle penances which that mad old
Marquis of Mantua punished himself with by his

vow? Do but consider, that we may ride I do not
know how long upon this road without meeting
any armed knight to pick a quarrel with; for here
are none but carriers and wagoners, who are so far
from wearing any helmets, that it is ten to one
whether they ever heard of such a thing in their
lives." "Thou art mistaken, friend Sancho," replied
Don Quixote; "for we shall not be two hours this
way without meeting more men in arms than there
were at the siege of Albraca, to carry off the fair
Angelica." "Well then, let it be so," quoth Sancho; "and may we have the luck to come off well,
and quickly win that island which costs me so dear,
and then I do not matter what befalls me." "I
have already bid thee not trouble thyself about this
business, Sancho," said Don Quixote; "for should
we miss of an island, there is either the kingdom of
Denmark, or that of Sobradisa,* as fit for thy purpose as a ring for thy finger; and, what ought to
be no small comfort to thee, they are both upon
Terra firma.† But we'll talk of this in its proper
season: at this time I would have thee see whether
thou hast any thing to eat in thy wallet, that we
may afterwards seek for some castle, where we may
lodge this night, and make the balsam I told thee;
for I protest my ear smarts extremely." "I have
here an onion," replied the squire, "a piece of cheese,
and a few stale crusts of bread; but sure such coarse
fare is not for such a brave knight as your worship."

---

    * A fictitious kingdom in Amadis de Gaul.
    † In allusion to the famous Firm Island, in Amadis de Gaul,
the land of promise to the faithful squires of knights-errant.

"Thou art grossly mistaken, friend Sancho," answered Don Quixote; "know, that it is the glory of knights-errant to be whole months without eating, and when they do, they fall upon the first thing they meet with, though it be never so homely. Hadst thou but read as many books as I have done, thou hadst been better informed as to that point; for though I think I have read as many histories of chivalry in my time as any other man, I never could find that the knights-errant ever eat, unless it were by mere accident, or when they were invited to great feasts and royal banquets; at other times they indulged themselves with little other food besides their thoughts. Though it is not to be imagined they could live without supplying the exigencies of human nature, as being after all no more than mortal men, yet it is likewise to be supposed, that as they spent the greatest part of their lives in forests and deserts, and always destitute of a cook, consequently their usual food was but such coarse country fare as thou now offerest me. Never then make thyself uneasy about what pleases me, friend Sancho, nor pretend to make a new world, nor to unhinge the very constitution and ancient customs of knight-errantry."

"I beg your worship's pardon," cried Sancho; "for as I was never bred a scholar, I may chance to have missed in some main point of your laws of knighthood; but from this time forward I will be sure to stock my wallet with all sorts of dry fruits for you, because your worship is a knight; as for myself, who am none, I will provide good poultry, and other substantial victuals." "I do not say, Sancho," replied Don Quixote, "that a knight-errant is obliged to feed altogether upon fruit; I only mean, that this was their common food, together with some roots and herbs, which they found up and down the fields, of all which they had a perfect knowledge as I myself have." " 'Tis a good thing to know those herbs," cried Sancho, "for I am much mistaken, or that kind of knowledge will stand us in good stead ere long. In the mean time," continued he, "here's what good heaven has sent us." With that he pulled out the provision he had, and they fell to heartily together. But their impatience to find out a place where they might be harbored that night, made them shorten their sorry meal, and mount again, for fear of being benighted; so away they put on in search of a lodging. But the sun and their hopes failed them at once, as they came to a place where some goat-herds had set up some small huts; and therefore they concluded to take up their lodging there that night. This was a great mortification to Sancho, who was altogether for a good town, as it was a pleasure to his master, who was for sleeping in the open fields, as believing, that as often as he did it, he confirmed his title to knighthood by a new act of possession.

CHAPTER III.

WHAT PASSED BETWEEN DON QUIXOTE AND THE GOAT-HERDS.

THE knight was very courteously received by the goat-herds; and as for Sancho, after he had set up Rozinante and his ass as well as he could, he presently repaired to the attractive smell of some pieces of kid's flesh which stood boiling in a kettle over the fire. The hungry squire would immediately have tried whether they were fit to be removed out of the kettle into the stomach, but was not put to that trouble; for the goat-herds took them off the fire and spread some sheep-skins on the ground, and soon got their rural feast ready; and cheerfully invited his master and him to partake of what they had. Next, with some coarse compliment, after the country way, they desired Don Quixote to sit down on a trough with the bottom upwards; and then six of them, who were all that belonged to that fold, squatted them down round the skins, while ·Sancho stood to wait upon his master, and gave him drink in a horn cup, which the goat-herds used. But he seeing his man stand behind, said to him, " That thou mayest understand, Sancho, the benefits of knight-errantry, and how the meanest retainers to it have a fair prospect of being speedily esteemed and honored by the world, it is my pleasure that thou sit thee down by me, in the company of these good people; and that there be no difference now observed between thee and me, thy natural lord and

master; that thou eat in the same dish, and drink
in the same cup; for it may be said of knight-errantry as of love, that it makes all things equal."
"I thank your worship," cried Sancho; "but yet I
must needs own, had I but a good deal of meat before me, I'd eat it as well, or rather better, standing,
and by myself, than if I sat by an emperor; and, to
deal plainly and truly with you, I had rather munch
a crust of brown bread and an onion in a corner,
without any more ado or ceremony, than feed upon
turkey at another man's table, where one is fain to
sit mincing and chewing his meat an hour together,
drink little, be always wiping his fingers and his
chops, and never dare to cough nor sneeze, though he
has never so much a mind to it, nor do a many things
which a body may do freely by one's self; therefore, good sir, change those tokens of your kindness
which I have a right to by being your worship's
squire, into something that may do me more good.
As for these same honors, I heartily thank you as
much as if I had accepted them, but yet I give up
my right to them from this time to the world's end."
"Talk no more," replied Don Quixote, "but sit
thee down, for the humble shall be exalted;" and
so pulling him by the arms, he forced him to sit by
him.

All this while the goat-herds, who did not understand this jargon of knights-errant, chivalry, and
squires, fed heartily, and said nothing, but stared
upon their guests, who very fairly swallowed whole
luncheons as big as their fists with a mighty appetite. The first course being over, they brought in
the second, consisting of dried acorns, and half a

cheese as hard as a brick; nor was the horn idle all the while, but went merrily round, up and down so many times, sometimes full, and sometimes empty, like the two buckets of a well, that they made shift at last to drink off one of the two skins of wine which they had there. And now Don Quixote having satisfied his appetite, he took a handful of acorns, and looking earnestly upon them, " O happy age," cried he, " which our first parents called the age of gold! not because gold, so much adored in this iron age, was then easily purchased, but because those two fatal words, mine and thine, were distinctions unknown to the people of those fortunate times; for all things were in common in that holy age : men, for their sustenance, needed only to lift their hands, and take it from the sturdy oak, whose spreading arms liberally invited them to gather the wholesome savory fruit; while the clear springs, and silver rivulets, with luxuriant plenty, offered them their pure refreshing water. In hollow trees, and in the clefts of rocks, the laboring and industrious bees erected their little commonwealths, that men might reap with pleasure and with ease the sweet and fertile harvest of their toils. The tough and strenuous cork-trees did of themselves, and without other art than their native liberality, dismiss and impart their broad light bark, which served to cover those lowly huts, propped up with rough-hewn stakes, that were first built as a shelter against the inclemencies of the air: all then was union, all peace, all love and friendship in the world: as yet no rude ploughshare presumed with violence to pry into the pious bowels of our mother Earth, for she,

without compulsion, kindly yielded from every part
of her fruitful and spacious bosom, whatever might
at once satisfy, sustain, and indulge, her frugal
children. Then was the time when innocent, beautiful young shepherdesses went tripping over the
hills and vales : their lovely hair sometimes plaited,
sometimes loose and flowing, clad in no other vestment but what was necessary to cover decently
what modesty would always have concealed: the
Tyrian die, and the rich glossy hue of silk, mar-
tyred and dissembled into every color, which are
now esteemed so fine and magnificent, were unknown to the innocent plainness of that age ; yet,
bedecked with more becoming leaves and flowers,
they may be said to outshine the proudest of the
vain-dressing ladies of our age, arrayed in the most
magnificent garbs and all the most sumptuous
adornings which idleness and luxury have taught
succeeding pride : lovers then expressed the passion
of their souls in the unaffected language of the
heart, with the native plainness and sincerity in
which they were conceived, and divested of all that
artificial contexture which enervates what it labors
to enforce : imposture, deceit, and malice, had not
yet crept in, and imposed themselves unbribed upon
mankind, in the disguise of truth and simplicity :
justice, unbiased either by favor or interest, which
now so fatally pervert it, was equally and impar-
tially dispensed ; nor was the judge's fancy law, for
then there were neither judges, nor causes to be
judged ; the modest maid might walk wherever
she pleased alone, free from the attacks of lewd,
lascivious importuners. But in this degenerate age,

fraud and a legion of ills infecting the world, no
virtue can be safe, no honor be secure; while wanton desires, diffused in the hearts of men, corrupt
the strictest watches, and the closest retreats;
which, though as intricate and unknown as the
labyrinth of Crete, are no security for chastity.
Thus that primitive innocence being vanished, and
oppression daily prevailing, there was a necessity
to oppose the torrent of violence : for which reason
the order of knighthood-errant was instituted, to
defend the honor of virgins, protect widows, relieve
orphans, and assist all the distressed in general.
Now I myself am one of this order, honest friends;
and though all people are obliged, by the law of
nature, to be kind to persons of my order; yet
since you, without knowing any thing of this obligation, have so generously entertained me, I ought
to pay you my utmost acknowledgment; and, accordingly return you my most hearty thanks for the
same."

All this long oration, which might very well have
been spared, was owing to the acorns that recalled
the golden age to our knight's remembrance, and
made him thus hold forth to the goat-herds, who
devoutly listened, but edified little, the discourse
not being suited to their capacities. Sancho, as
well as they, was silent all the while, eating acorns,
and frequently visiting the second skin of wine,
which for coolness sake was hung upon a neighboring cork-tree. As for Don Quixote, he was
longer, and more intent upon his speech, than upon
supper. When he had done, one of the goat-herds
addressing himself to him, " Sir knight," said he,

" that you may be sure you are heartily welcome,
we will get one of our fellows to give us a song;
he is just a-coming; a good notable young lad he
is, I will say that for him, and up to the ears in
love. He is a scholard, and can read and write;
and plays so rarely upon the rebeck,* that it is a
charm but to hear him." No sooner were the words
out of the goat-herd's mouth, but they heard the
sound of the instrument he spoke of, and presently
appeared a good comely young man of about two-
and-twenty years of age. The goat-herds asked
him if he had supped? and he having told them he
had, " Then, dear Antonio," says the first speaker,
" pray thee sing us a song, to let this gentleman, our
guest, see that we have those among us who know
somewhat of music, for all we live amidst woods
and mountains. We have told him of thee already;
therefore, pray thee make our words good, and sing
us the ditty thy uncle the prebendary made of thy
love, that was so liked in our town." " With all
my heart," replied Antonio; and so without any
further entreaty, sitting down on the stump of an
oak, he tuned his fiddle, and very handsomely sung
the following song.

ANTONIO'S AMOROUS COMPLAINT.

Though love ne'er prattles at your eyes,
   (The eyes, those silent tongues of love,)
Yet sure, Olalia, you're my prize:
   For truth, with zeal, even heaven can move.
I think, my love, you only try,
   Even while I fear you've sealed my doom:

---

* A fiddle, with only three strings, used by shepherds.

So, though involved in doubts I lie,
  Hope sometimes glimmers through the gloom.
A flame so fierce, so bright, so pure,
  No scorn can quench, or art improve:
Thus like a martyr I endure;
  For there's a heaven to crown my love.
In dress and dancing I have strove
  My proudest rivals to outvie;
In serenades I've breathed my love,
  When all things slept but love and I.
I need not add, I speak your praise
  Till every nymph's disdain I move;
Though thus a thousand foes I raise,
  'Tis sweet to praise the fair I love.
Teresa once your charms debased,
  But I her rudeness soon reproved:
In vain her friend my anger faced;
  For then I fought for her I loved.
Dear cruel fair, why then so coy?
  How can you so much love withstand?
Alas! I crave no lawless joy,
  But with my heart would give my hand.
Soft, easy, strong is Hymen's tie:
  Oh! then no more the bliss refuse.
Oh! wed me, or I swear to die,
  Or linger wretched and recluse.

Here Antonio ended his song; Don Quixote entreated him to sing another, but Sancho Panza, who had more mind to sleep than to hear the finest singing in the world, told his master, there is enough. "Good sir," quoth he, "your worship had better go and lie down where you are to take your rest this night; besides, these good people are tired with their day's labor, and rather want to go to sleep, than to sit up all night to hear ballads." "I understand thee, Sancho," cried Don Quixote;

" and indeed I thought thy frequent visiting the bottle would make thee fonder of sleep than of music." " Make us thankful," cried Sancho, " we all liked the wine well enough." " I do not deny it," replied Don Quixote; but go thou and lay thee down where thou pleasest : as for me, it better becomes a man of my profession to wake than to sleep: yet stay and dress my ear before thou goest, for it pains me extremely." Thereupon one of the goatherds beholding the wound, as Sancho offered to dress it, desired the knight not to trouble himself, for he had a remedy that would quickly cure him; and then fetching a few rosemary leaves, which grew in great plenty thereabout, he bruised them, and mixed a little salt among them, and having applied the medicine to the ear, he bound it up, assuring him, he needed no other remedy; which in a little time proved very true.

CHAPTER IV.

THE STORY WHICH A YOUNG GOAT-HERD TOLD TO THOSE THAT WERE WITH DON QUIXOTE.

A young fellow, who used to bring them provisions from the next village, happened to come while this was doing, and addressing himself to the goatherds, " Hark, ye, friends," said he, " d'ye hear the news ? " " What news ? " cried one of the company. " That fine shepherd and scholar Chrysostome, died this morning," answered the other; " and they say it was for love of that devilish untoward lass, Mar-

cella, rich William's daughter, that goes up and
down the country in the habit of a shepherdess."
" For Marcella!" cried one of the goat-herds. " I
say for her," replied the fellow, " and what is more,
it is reported, he has ordered by his will, they
should bury him in the fields like any heathen Moor,
just at the foot of the rock, hard by the cork-tree
fountain, where they say he had the first sight of
her. Nay, he has likewise ordered many other
strange things to be done, which the heads of the
parish won't allow of, for they seem to be after the
way of the Pagans. But Ambrose, the other scholar,
who likewise apparelled himself like a shepherd, is
resolved to have his friend Chrysostome's will fulfilled in every thing, just as he has ordered it. All
the village is in an uproar. But after all, it is
thought Ambrose and his friends will carry the day;
and to-morrow morning he is to be buried in great
state where I told you: I fancy it will be worth
seeing; howsoever, be it what it will, I will even go
and see it, even though. I could not get back again
to-morrow." " We will all go," cried the goat-
herds, " and cast lots who shall tarry to look after
the goats." " Well said, Peter," cried one of the
goat-herds; " but as for casting of lots, I will save
you that labor, for I will stay myself, not so much
out of kindness to you neither, or want of curiosity,
as because of the thorn in my toe, that will not let
me go." " Thank you, however," quoth Peter.
Don Quixote, who heard all this, entreated Peter
to tell him who the deceased was, and also to give
him a short account of the shepherdess.

Peter made answer, that all he knew of the matter was, that the deceased was a wealthy gentleman who lived not far off; that he had been several years at the university of Salamanca, and then came home mightily improved in his learning. "But above all," quoth he, "it was said of him, that he had great knowledge in the stars, and whatsoever· the sun and moon do in the skies, for he would tell us to a tittle the clip of the sun and moon." "We call it an eclipse," cried Don Quixote, "and not a clip, when either of those two great luminaries are darkened." "He would also," continued Peter, who did not stand upon such nice distinctions, "foretell when the year would be plentiful or *estil.*" "You would say *steril,*" cried Don Quixote. "*Steril* or *estil,*" replied the fellow, "that is all one to me: but this I say, that his parents and friends, being ruled by him, grew woundy rich in a short time; for he would tell them, This year sow barley, and no wheat: in this you may sow pease, and no barley: next year will be a good year for oil: the three after that, you shan't gather a drop; and whatsoever 'he said would certainly come to pass." "That science," said Don Quixote, "is called astrology." "I do not know what you call it," answered Peter, "but I know he knew all this, and a deal more. But in short, within some few months after he had left the versity, on a certain morning we saw him come dressed for all the world like a shepherd, and driving his flock, having laid down the long gown, which he used to wear as a scholar. At the same time one Ambrose, a great friend of his, who had been his fellow scholar, also took upon him to go like a shepherd, and keep him com-

pany, which we all did not a little marvel at. I
had almost forgot to tell you how he that is dead
was a mighty man for making of verses, insomuch
that he commonly made the carols which we sung
in Christmas Eve, and the plays which the young
lads in our neighborhood enacted on Corpus Christi
day ; and every one would say, that nobody could
mend them. Somewhat before that time, Chrysostome's father died, and left him a deal of wealth,
both in land, money, cattle, and other goods,
whereof the young man remained dissolute master; and in troth he deserved it all, for he was as
good-natured a soul as e'er trod on shoe of leather ;
mighty good to the poor, a main friend to all honest
people, and had a face like a blessing. At last it
came to be known, that the reason of his altering
his garb in that fashion, was only that he might go
up and down after that shepherdess Marcella, whom
our comrade told you of before, for he was fallen
mightily in love with her. And now I will tell you
such a thing you never heard the like in your born
days, and may not chance to hear of such another
while you breathe, though you were to live as long
as Sarnah." " Say Sarah," cried Don Quixote, who
hated to hear him blunder thus. " The Sarna, or
the itch, for that is all one with us," quoth Peter,
"lives long enough too ; but if you go on thus, and
make me break off my tale at every word, we are
not like to have done this twelvemonth." " Pardon me, friend," replied Don Quixote; " I only
spoke to make thee understand that there is a difference between Sarna and Sarah : however, thou
sayest well ; for the Sarna (that is, the itch) lives

longer than Sarah; therefore pray make an end of
thy story, for I will not interrupt thee any more."

"Well then," quoth Peter, "you must know,
good master of mine, that there lived near us one
William, a yeoman, who was richer yet than Chrysostome's father; now he had no child in the versal
world but a daughter; her mother died in child-bed
of her, (rest her soul,) and was as good a woman as
ever went upon two legs: methinks I see her yet,
standing afore me, with that blessed face of her's,
the sun on óne side, and the moon on the t'other.
She was a main housewife, and did a deal of good
among the poor; for which I dare say she is at this
minute in paradise.   Alas! her death broke old
William's heart; he soon went after her, poor man,
and left all to his little daughter, that Marcella by
name, giving charge of her to her uncle, the parson
of our parish.   Well, the girl grew such a fine child,
and so like her mother, that it used to put us in
mind of her every foot: however, 'twas thought
she'd make a finer woman yet: and so it happened
indeed; for, by that time she was fourteen or fifteen
years of age, no man set his eyes on her, that did
not bless heaven for having made her so handsome;
so that most men fell in love with her, and were
ready to run mad for her.   All this while her uncle
kept her up very close: yet the report of her great
beauty and wealth spread far and near, insomuch,
that she had I don't know how many sweethearts,
almost all the young men in our town asked her of
her uncle; nay, from I don't know how many
leagues about us, there flocked whole droves of
suitors, and the very best in the country too, who

all begged, and sued, and teased her uncle to let them have her. But though he'd have been glad to have got fairly rid of her, as soon as she was fit for a husband, yet would not he advise or marry her against her will; for he's a good man, I'll say that for him, and a true Christian every inch of him, and scorns to keep her from marrying to make a benefit of her estate; and, to his praise be it spoken, he has been mainly commended for it more than once, when the people of our parish meet together. For I must tell you, Sir Errant, that here in the country, and in our little towns, there is not the least thing can be said or done, but people will talk and find fault: but let busy-bodies prate as they please, the parson must have a good body indeed, who could bring his whole parish to give him a good word, especially in the country." "Thou art in the right," cried Don Quixote, "and therefore go on, honest Peter, for the story is pleasant, and thou tellest it with a grace." "May I never want God's grace," quoth Peter, "for that is most to the purpose. But for our parson, as I told you before, he was not for keeping his niece from marrying, and therefore he took care to let her know of all those that would have taken her to wife, both what they were, and what they had, and he was at her, to have her pitch upon one of them for a husband; yet would she never answer otherwise, but that she had no mind to wed as yet, as finding herself too young for the burden of wedlock. With these and such like come-offs, she got her uncle to let her alone, and wait till she thought fit to choose for herself: for he was won't to say, that parents are

not to bestow their children where they bear no
liking; and in that he spoke like an honest man.
And thus it happened, that when we least dreamed
of it, that coy lass, finding herself at liberty, would
needs turn shepherdess; and neither her uncle, nor
all those of the village who advised her against it,
could work any thing upon her, but away she went
to the fields to keep her own sheep with the other
young lasses of the town. But then it was ten times
worse; for no sooner was she seen abroad, when I
cannot tell how many spruce gallants, both gentlemen and rich farmers, changed their garb for love
of her, and followed her up and down in shepherd's
guise. One of them, as I have told you, was this
same Chrysostome, who now lies dead, of whom
it is said, he not only loved, but worshipped her.
Howsoever, I would not have you think or surmise,
because Marcella took that course of life, and was
as it were under no manner of keeping, that she
gave the least token of naughtiness or light behavior; for she ever was, and is still so coy, and so
watchful to keep her honor pure and free from evil
tongues, that among so many wooers who suitor
her, there is not one can make his brags of having
the least hope of ever speeding with her. For though
she does not shun the company of shepherds, but
uses them courteously, so far as they behave themselves handsomely; yet whensoever any one of
them does but offer to break his mind to her, be it
never so well meant, and only in order to marry,
she casts him away from her, as with a sling, and
will never have any more to say to him.

" And thus this fair maiden does more harm in

this country, than the plague would do; for her courteousness and fair looks draw on every body to love her; but then her dogged stubborn coyness breaks their hearts, and makes them ready to hang themselves; and all they can do, poor wretches, is to make a heavy complaint, and call her cruel, unkind, ungrateful, and a world of such names, whereby they plainly show what a sad condition they are in : were you but to stay here some time, you'd hear these hills and valleys ring again with the doleful moans of those she has denied, who yet cannot, for the blood of them, give over sneaking after her. We have a place not far off, where there are some two dozen of beech trees, and on them all you may find I don't know how many Marcellas cut in the smooth bark. On some of them there is a crown carved over the name, as much as to say that Marcella bears away the crown, and deserves the garland of beauty. Here sighs one shepherd, there another whines; here is one singing doleful ditties, there another is wringing his hands, and making woful complaints. You shall have one lay him down at night at the foot of a rock, or some oak, and there lie weeping and wailing without a wink of sleep, and talking to himself till the sun finds him the next morning; you shall have another lie stretched upon the hot sandy ground, breathing his sad lamentations to heaven, without heeding the sultry heat of the summer sun. And all this while the hard-hearted Marcella ne'er minds any one of them, and does not seem to be the least concerned for them. We are all mightily at a loss to know what will be the end of all this pride and coyness, who shall be the happy man that shall at last tame her, and bring her to his lure. Now because there is nothing more certain than all this, I am the more apt to give credit to what our comrade has told us, as to the occasion of Chrysostome's death; and therefore I would needs have you go and see him laid in his grave to-morrow; which I believe will be worth your while, for he had many friends, and it is not half a league to the place where it was his will to be buried." "I intend to be there," answered Don Quixote, "and in the mean time I return thee many thanks for the extraordinary satisfaction this story has afforded me." "Alas! Sir Knight," replied the goat-herd, "I have not told you half the mischiefs this proud creature hath done here, but to-morrow mayhap we shall meet some shepherd by the way that will be able to tell you more. Meanwhile it won't be amiss for you to take your rest in one of the huts; for the open air is not good for your wound, though what I've put to it is so special a medicine, that there's not much need to fear but 'twill do well enough." Sancho, who was quite out of patience with the goat-herd's long story, and wished him at the devil for his pains, at last prevailed with him to lie down in Peter's hut, where Don Quixote, in imitation of Marcella's lovers, devoted the remainder of the night to amorous expostulations with his dear Dulcinea. As for Sancho, he laid himself down between Rozinante and his ass, and slept it out, not like a disconsolate lover, but like a man that had been soundly kicked and bruised in the morning.

CHAPTER V.

A CONTINUATION OF THE STORY OF MARCELLA.

SCARCE had day begun to appear from the balconies of the east, when five of the goat-herds got up, and having waked Don Quixote, asked him if he held his resolution of going to the funeral, whither they were ready to bear him company. Thereupon the knight, who desired nothing more, presently arose, and ordered Sancho to get Rozinante and the ass ready immediately; which he did with all expedition, and then they set forwards. They had not gone yet a quarter of a league, before they saw advancing towards them, out of a cross path, six shepherds clad in black skins, their heads crowned with garlands of cypress and bitter rose-bay tree, with long holly-staves in their hands. Two gentlemen on horseback, attended by three young lads on foot, came immediately after them: as they drew near, they saluted one another civilly, and after the usual question, " Which way d'ye travel ? " they found they were all going the same way, to see the funeral ; and so they all joined company. " I fancy, Senior Vivaldo," said one of the gentlemen, addressing himself to the other, " we shall not think our time misspent in going to see this famous funeral, for it must of necessity be very extraordinary, according to the account which these men have given us of the dead shepherd and his murdering mistress." " I am so far of your opinion," answered Vivaldo, "that I would not stay one day, but a whole week, rather than miss the sight." This gave Don Quixote occasion to ask them what they had heard concerning Chrysostome and Marcella? One of the gentlemen made answer, That having met that morning with these shepherds, they could not forbear inquiring of them, why they wore such a mournful dress? whereupon one of them acquainted them with the sad occasion, by relating the story of a certain shepherdess, named Marcella, no less lovely than cruel, whose coyness and disdain had made a world of unfortunate lovers, and caused the death of that Chrysostome, to whose funeral they were going. In short, he repeated to Don Quixote all that Peter had told him the night before. After this, Vivaldo asked the knight why he travelled so completely armed in so peaceable a country? "My profession," answered the champion, "does not permit me to ride otherwise. Luxurious feasts, sumptuous dresses, and downy ease, were invented for effeminate courtiers; but labor, vigilance, and arms, are the portion of those whom the world calls knights-errant, of which number I have the honor to be one, though the most unworthy, and the meanest of the fraternity." He needed to say no more to satisfy them his brains were out of order; however, that they might the better understand the nature of his folly, Vivaldo asked him what he meant by a knight-errant? "Have you not read, then," cried Don Quixote, "the Annals and History of Britain, where are recorded the famous deeds of King Arthur, who, according to an ancient tradition in that kingdom, never died, but was turned into

a crow by enchantment, and shall one day resume
his former shape, and recover his kingdom again?
For which reason, since that time, the people of
Great Britain dare not offer to kill a crow.   In this
good king's time, the most noble order of the
Knights of the Round Table was first instituted,
and then also the amours between Sir Lancelot of
the Lake and Queen Guinever were really trans-
acted, as that history relates; they being managed
and carried on by the mediation of that honorable
matron the Lady Quintaniona.   Which produced
that excellent history in verse so sung and celebrated
here in Spain —

> " There never was on earth a knight
>   So waited on by ladies fair,
> As once was he Sir Lancelot hight,
>   When first he left his country dear."

And the rest, which gives so delightful an account
both of his loves and feats of arms.   From that
time the order of knight-errantry began by degrees
to dilate and extend itself into most parts of the
world.   Then did the great Amadis de Gaul signalize himself by heroic exploits, and so did his
offspring to the fifth generation.   The valorous
Felixmart of Hyrcania then got immortal fame, and
that undaunted knight Tirante the White, who
never can be applauded to his worth.   Nay, had
we but lived a little sooner, we might have been
blessed with the conversation of that invincible
κnight of our modern times, the valorous Don Belianis of Greece.   And this, gentlemen, is that order
of chivalry, which, as much a sinner as I am, I pro-

fess, with a due observance of the laws which those brave knights observed before me; and for that reason I choose to wander through these solitary deserts, seeking adventures, fully resolved to expose my person to the most formidable dangers which fortune can obtrude on me, that by the strength of my arm I may relieve the weak and the distressed."

After all this stuff, you may be sure the travellers were sufficiently convinced of Don Quixote's frenzy. Nor were they less surprised than were all those who had hitherto discovered so unaccountable a distraction in one who seemed a rational creature. However, Vivaldo, who was of a gay disposition, had no sooner made the discovery, but he resolved to make the best advantage of it, that the shortness of the way would allow him.

Therefore, to give him further occasion to divert them with his whimseys, " Methinks, Sir Knight-errant," said he to him, " you have taken up one of the strictest and most mortifying professions in the world. I don't think but that a Carthusian friar has a better time on't than you have." " Perhaps," answered Don Quixote, " the profession of a Car-thusian may be as austere, but I am within two fingers' breadth of doubting, whether it may be as beneficial to the world as ours. For, if we must speak the truth, the soldier, who puts his captain's command in execution, may be said to do as much at least as the captain who commanded him. The application is easy: for, while those religious men have nothing to do, but with all quietness and secu-rity to say their prayers for the prosperity of the world, we knights, like soldiers, execute what they do but pray for, and procure those benefits to mankind, by the strength of our arms, and at the hazard of our lives, for which they only intercede. Nor do we do this sheltered from the injuries of the air, but under no other roof than that of the wide heavens, exposed to summer's scorching heat, and winter's pinching cold. So that we may justly style ourselves the ministers of heaven, and the instruments of its justice upon earth; and as the business of war is not to be compassed without vast toil and labor, so the religious soldier must undoubtedly be preferred before the religious monk, who, living still quiet and at ease, has nothing to do but to pray for the afflicted and distressed. However, gentlemen, do not imagine I would insinuate as if the profession of a knight-errant was a state of perfection equal to that of a holy recluse : I would only infer from what I have said, and what I myself endure, that ours without question is more laborious, more subject to the discipline of heavy blows, to maceration, to the penance of hunger and thirst, and, in a word, to rags, to want, and misery. For if you find that some knights-errant have at last by their valor been raised to thrones and empires, you may be sure it has been still at the expense of much sweat and blood. And had even those happier knights been deprived of those assisting sages and enchanters, who helped them in all emergencies, they would have been strangely disappointed of their mighty expectations." "I am of the same opinion," replied Vivaldo. "But one thing among many others, which I can by no means approve in your profession, is, that when you are just going to engage in some very hazardous adventure, where your lives are evidently to be much endangered, you never once remember to commend yourselves to God, as every good Christian ought to do on such occasions, but only recommend yourselves to your mistresses, and that with as great zeal and devotion as if you worshipped no other deity ; a thing which, in my opinion, strongly relishes of Paganism."

" Sir," replied Don Quixote, " there is no altering that method; for should a knight-errant do otherwise, he would too much deviate from the ancient and established customs of knight-errantry, which inviolably oblige him just in the moment when he is rushing on, and giving birth to some dubious achievement, to have his mistress still before his eyes, still present to his mind, by a strong and lively imagination, and with soft, amorous, and energetic looks, imploring her favor and protection in that perilous circumstance. Nay, if nobody can overhear him, he is obliged to whisper, or speak between his teeth, some short ejaculations, to recommend himself with all the fervency imaginable to the lady of his wishes, and of this we have innumerable examples in history. Nor are you for all this to imagine that knights-errant omit recommending themselves to heaven, for they have leisure enough to do it even in the midst of the combat."

" Sir," replied Vivaldo, " you must give me leave to tell you, I am not yet thoroughly satisfied in this point: for I have often observed in my reading, that two knights-errant, having first talked a little together, have fallen out presently, and been so highly provoked, that, having turned their horses' heads to gain room for the career, they have wheeled about, and then with all speed run full tilt at one another, hastily recommending themselves to their mistresses in the midst of their career; and the next thing has commonly been, that one of them has been thrown to the ground over the crupper of his horse, fairly run through and through with his enemy's lance; and the other forced to catch hold of his horse's mane to keep himself from falling. Now I cannot apprehend how the knight that was slain had any time to recommend himself to heaven, when his business was done so suddenly. Methinks those hasty invocations, which in his career were directed to his mistress, should have been directed to heaven, as every good Christian would have done. Besides, I fancy every knight-errant has not a mistress to invoke, nor is every one of them in love." " Your conjecture is wrong," replied Don Quixote; " a knight-errant cannot be without a mistress; 'tis not more essential for the skies to have stars, than 'tis to us to be in love. Insomuch, that I dare affirm, that no history ever made mention of any knight-errant that was not a lover; for were any knight free from the impulses of that generous passion, he would not be allowed to be a lawful knight; but a misborn intruder, and one who was not admitted within the pale of knighthood at the door, but leaped the fence, and stole in like a robber and a thief." " Yet, sir," replied the other, " I am much mistaken, or I have read that Don Galaor, the brother of Amadis, never had any certain mistress to recommend himself to, and yet for all that he was not the less esteemed."

" One swallow never makes a summer," answered
Don Quixote. " Besides, I know that knight was
privately very much in love; and as for his making
his addresses, wherever he met with beauty, this
was an effect of his natural inclination, which he
could not easily restrain. But after all, 'tis an undeniable truth, that he had a favorite lady, whom he
had crowned empress of his will; and to her he
frequently recommended himself in private, for he
did not a little value himself upon his discretion
and secrecy in love." " Then, sir," said Vivaldo,
" since 'tis so much the being of knight-errantry to
be in love, I presume you, who are of that profession, cannot be without a mistress. And therefore,
if you do not set up for secrecy as much as Don
Galaor did, give me leave to beg of you, in the name
of all the company, that you will be pleased so far
to oblige us, as to let us know the name and quality of your mistress, the place of her birth, and the
charms of her person. For, without doubt, the
lady cannot but esteem herself happy in being
known to all the world to be the object of the wishes
of a knight so accomplished as yourself." With
that Don Quixote, breathing out a deep sigh, " I
cannot tell," said he, " whether this lovely enemy of
my repose, is the least affected with the world's
being informed of her power over my heart; all I
dare say, in compliance with your request, is, that
her name is Dulcinea, her country La Mancha, and
Toboso the happy place which she honors with her
residence. As for her quality, it cannot be less than
princess, seeing she is my mistress and my queen.
Her beauty transcends all the united charms of her

whole sex; even those chimerical perfections, which the hyperbolical imaginations of poets in love have assigned to their mistresses, cease to be incredible descriptions when applied to her, in whom all those miraculous endowments are most divinely centred. The curling locks of her bright flowing hair are purest gold; her smooth forehead the Elysian Plain; her brows are two celestial bows; her eyes two glorious suns; her cheeks two beds of roses; her lips are coral; her teeth are pearl; her neck is alabaster; her breasts marble; her hands ivory; and snow would lose its whiteness near her bosom. Then for the parts which modesty has veiled, my imagination, not to wrong them, chooses to lose itself in silent admiration; for nature boasts nothing that may give an idea of their incomparable worth."

" Pray, sir," cried Vivaldo, " oblige us with an account of her parentage, and the place of her birth, to complete the description." " Sir," replied Don Quixote, " she is not descended from the ancient Curtiuses, Caiuses, nor Scipios of Rome, nor from the more modern Colonas, nor Ursinis; nor from the Moncadas, and Requesenses of Catalonia; nor from the Rebillas, and Villanovas of Valencia; nor from the Palafoxes, Nucas, Rocabertis, Corellas, Lunas, Alagones, Urreas, Fozes, or Gurreas of Arragon; nor from the Cerdas, Manriques, Mendozas, and Gusmans of Castile; nor from the Alencastros, Pallas, and Menezes of Portugal; but she derives her great original from the family of Toboso in La Mancha, a race, which, though it be modern, is sufficient to give a noble beginning to the most illustrious progenies of succeeding ages. And let no man presume to contradict me in this, unless it be upon those conditions, which Zerbin fixed at the foot of Orlando's armor,

> Let none but he these arms displace,
> Who dares Orlando's fury face."

" I draw my pedigree from the Cachopines of Laredo," replied Vivaldo, " yet I dare not make any comparisons with the Tobosos of La Mancha; though, to deal sincerely with you, 'tis a family I never heard of till this moment." " 'Tis strange," said Don Quixote, " you should never have heard of it before."

All the rest of the company gave great attention to this discourse; and even the very goat-herds and shepherds were now fully convinced that Don Quixote's brains were turned topsy-turvy. But Sancho Panza believed every word that dropped from his master's mouth to be truth, as having known him, from his cradle, to be a man of sincerity. Yet that which somewhat staggered his faith, was this story of Dulcinea of Toboso; for he was sure he had never heard before of any such princess, nor even of the name, though he lived hard by Toboso.

As they went on thus discoursing, they saw, upon the hollow road between the neighboring mountains, about twenty shepherds more, all accoutred in black skins, with garlands on their heads, which, as they afterwards perceived, were all of yew or cypress; six of them carried a bier covered with several sorts of boughs and flowers: which one of the goat-herds espying, " Those are they," cried he,

"that are carrying poor Chrysostome to his grave;
and 'twas in yonder bottom that he gave charge
they should bury his corpse." This made them all
double their pace, that they might get thither in
time; and so they arrived just as the bearers had
set down the bier upon the ground, and four of
them had begun to open the ground with their
spades, just at the foot of a rock. They all saluted
each other courteously, and condoled their mutual
loss; and then Don Quixote, with those who came
with him, went to view the bier; where they saw
the dead body of a young man in shepherd's weeds,
all strewed over with flowers. The deceased seemed
to be about thirty years old; and, dead as he was,
it was easily perceived that both his face and shape
were extraordinary handsome. Within the bier
were some few books and several papers, some
open, and the rest folded up. This doleful object so
strangely filled all the company with sadness, that
not only the beholders, but also the grave-makers,
and all the mourning shepherds, remained a long
time silent; till at last one of the bearers, addressing himself to one of the rest, "Look, Ambrose,"
cried he, "whether this be the place which Chrysostome meant, since you must needs have his will so
punctually performed?" "This is the very place,"
answered the other; "there it was that my unhappy friend many times told me the sad story of his
cruel fortune; and there it was that he first saw
that mortal enemy of mankind; there it was that
he made the first discovery of his passion, no less
innocent than violent; there it was that the relentless Marcella last denied, shunned him, and drove

him to that extremity of sorrow and despair that
hastened the sad catastrophe of his tragical and
miserable life; and there it was, that, in token of
so many misfortunes, he desired to be committed
to the bowels of eternal oblivion."

Then addressing himself to Don Quixote and the
rest of the travellers, " This body, gentlemen," said
he, " which here you now behold, was once enli-
vened by a soul which heaven had enriched with
the greatest part of its most valuable graces. This
is the body of that Chrysostome who was unrivalled
in wit, matchless in courteousness, incomparable in
gracefulness, a phœnix in friendship, generous and
magnificent without ostentation, prudent and grave
without pride, modest without affectation, pleasant
and complaisant without meanness; in a word, the
first in every esteemable qualification, and second
to none in misfortune: he loved well, and was
hated; he adored, and was disdained; he begged
pity of cruelty itself; he strove to move obdurate
marble; pursued the wind; made his moans to solitary deserts; was constant to ingratitude; and for
the recompense of his fidelity, became a prey to
death in the flower of his age, through the barbarity
of a shepherdess, whom he strove to immortalize
by his verse; as these papers which are here deposited might testify, had he not commanded me to
sacrifice them to the flames, at the same time that
his body was committed to the earth."

" Should you do so," cried Vivaldo, " you would
appear more cruel to them than their exasperated,
unhappy parent. Consider, sir, 'tis not consistent
with discretion, nor even with justice, so nicely to

perform the request of the dead, when 'tis repug-
nant to reason. Augustus Cæsar himself would
have forfeited his title to wisdom, had he permitted
that to have been effected which the divine Virgil
had ordered by his will. Therefore, sir, now that
you resign your friend's body to the grave, do not
hurry thus the noble and only remains of that dear
unhappy man to a worse fate, the death of oblivion.
What though he has doomed them to perish in the
height of his resentment, you ought not indiscreet-
ly to be their executioner; but rather reprieve and
redeem them from eternal silence, that they may
live, and, flying through the world, transmit to all
ages the dismal story of your friend's virtue and
Marcella's ingratitude, as a warning to others, that
they may avoid such tempting snares and enchant-
ing destructions; for not only to me, but to all here
present, is well known the history of your enamored and desperate friend: we are no strangers
to the friendship that was between you, as also to
Marcella's cruelty, which occasioned his death.
Last night, being informed that he was to be buried
here to-day, moved not so much by curiosity as pity,
we are come to behold with our eyes, that which
gave us so much trouble to hear. Therefore, in the
name of all the company, like me, deeply affected
with a sense of Chrysostome's extraordinary merit,
and his unhappy fate, and desirous to prevent such
deplorable disasters for the future, I beg that you
will permit me to save some of these papers, whatever you resolve to do with the rest." And so,
without expecting an answer, he stretched out his
arm, and took out those papers which lay next to

his hand. "Well, sir," said Ambrose, "you have
found a way to make me submit, and you may
keep those papers, but for the rest, nothing shall
make me alter my resolution of burning them."
Vivaldo said no more; but being impatient to see
what those papers were, which he had rescued from
the flames, he opened one of them immediately,
and read the title of it, which was, The Despairing
Lover. "That," said Ambrose, "was the last piece
my dear friend ever wrote; and therefore, that you
may all hear to what a sad condition his unhappy
passion had reduced him, read it aloud, I beseech
you, sir, while the grave is making." "With all my
heart," replied Vivaldo; and so the company, having the same desire, presently gathered round about
him, and he read the following lines.

CHAPTER VI.

THE UNFORTUNATE SHEPHERD'S VERSES, AND OTHER UN-
EXPECTED MATTERS.

THE DESPAIRING LOVER.

RELENTLESS tyrant of my heart,
Attend, and hear thy slave impart
   The matchless story of his pain.
In vain I labor to conceal
What my extorted groans reveal;
   Who can be rack'd, and not complain?

But oh! who duly can express
Thy cruelty, and my distress?
   No human art, no human tongue.

Then fiends assist, and rage infuse !
A raving fury be my muse,
  And hell inspire the dismal song !

Owls, ravens, terrors of the night,
Wolves, monsters, fiends, with dire affright,
  Join your dread accents to my moans !
Join, howling winds, your sullen noise ;
Thou, grumbling thunder, join thy voice ;
  Mad seas, your roar, and hell thy groans.

Though still I moan in dreary caves,
To desert rocks, and silent graves,
  My loud complaints shall wander far ;
Borne by the winds, they shall survive,
By pitying echoes kept alive,
  And fill the world with my despair.

Love's deadly cure is fierce disdain,
Distracting fear a dreadful pain,
  And jealousy a matchless woe ;
Absence is death, yet while it kills,
I live with all these mortal ills,
  Scorn'd, jealous, loath'd, and absent too.

No dawn of hope e'er cheer'd my heart,
No pitying ray e'er sooth'd my smart,
  All, all the sweets of life are gone ;
Then come despair, and frantic rage,
With instant fate my pain assuage,
  And end a thousand deaths by one.

But even in death let love be crown'd,
My fair destruction guiltless found,
  And I be thought with justice scorn'd :
Thus let me fall unloved, unbless'd,
With all my load of woes oppress'd,
  And even too wretched to be mourn'd.

O ! thou by whose destructive hate,
I'm hurry'd to this doleful fate,
   When I'm no more, thy pity spare !
I dread thy tears; oh, spare them then —
But oh ! I rave, I was too vain,
   My death can never cost a tear.

Tormented souls, on you I call,
Hear one more wretched than you all :
   Come howl as in redoubled flames !
Attend me to th' eternal night,
No other dirge, or fun'ral rite,
   A poor despairing lover claims.

And thou my song, sad child of woe,
When life is gone, and I'm below,
   For thy lost parent cease to grieve.
With life and thee my woes increase,
And should they not by dying cease,
   Hell has no pains like those I leave.

These verses were well approved by all the company; only Vivaldo observed, that the jealousies and fears of which the shepherd complained, did not very well agree with what he had heard of Marcella's unspotted modesty and reservedness. But Ambrose, who had been always privy to the most secret thoughts of his friend, informed him, that the unhappy Chrysostome wrote those verses when he had torn himself from his adored mistress, to try whether absence, the common cure of love, would relieve him, and mitigate his pain. And as every thing disturbs an absent lover, and nothing is more usual than for him to torment himself with a thousand chimeras of his own brain, so did Chrysostome perplex himself with jealousies and suspicions, which had no ground but in his distracted imagination; and therefore, whatever he said in those uneasy circumstances, could never affect, or in the least prejudice Marcella's virtuous character, upon whom, setting aside her cruelty, and her disdainful haughtiness, envy itself could never fix the least reproach. Vivaldo being thus convinced, they were going to read another paper, when they were unexpectedly prevented by a kind of apparition that offered itself to their view. It was Marcella herself, who appeared at the top of the rock, at the foot of which they were digging the grave; but so beautiful, that fame seemed rather to have lessened than to have magnified her charms; those who had never seen her before, gazed on her with silent wonder and delight; nay, those who used to see her every day, seemed no less lost in admiration than the rest. But scarce had Ambrose spied her, when, with anger and indignation in his heart, he cried out, "What makest thou there, thou fierce, thou cruel basilisk of these mountains? comest thou to see whether the wounds of this murdered wretch will bleed afresh at thy presence? or comest thou thus mounted aloft, to glory in the fatal effects of thy native inhumanity, like another Nero at the sight of flaming Rome? or is it to trample on this unfortunate corpse, as Tarquin's ungrateful daughter did her father's? Tell us quickly why thou comest, and what thou yet desirest; for since I know that Chrysostome's whole study was to serve and please thee while he lived, I am willing to dispose all his friends to pay thee the like obedience, now he is dead." "I come not here to any of those

ungrateful ends, Ambrose," replied Marcella; "but
only to clear my innocence, and show the injustice
of all those who lay their misfortunes and Chrysostome's death to my charge: therefore, I entreat you
all who are here at this time to hear me a little, for
I shall not need to use many words to convince
people of sense of an evident truth. Heaven, you
are pleased to say, has made me beautiful, and that
to such a degree, that you are forced, nay, as it
were, compelled to love me, in spite of your endeavors to the contrary; and for the sake of that love,
you say I ought to love you again. Now, though I
am sensible, that whatever is beautiful is lovely, I
cannot conceive, that what is loved for being handsome, should be bound to love that by which it is
loved, merely because it is loved. He that loves a
beautiful object, may happen to be ugly; and as
what is ugly deserves not to be loved, it would be
ridiculous to say, I love you because you are handsome, and therefore you must love me again though
I am ugly. But suppose two persons of different
sexes are equally handsome, it does not follow, that
their desires should be alike and reciprocal; for all
beauties do not kindle love; some only recreate the
sight, and never reach, nor captivate the heart.
Alas! should whatever is beautiful beget love, and
enslave the mind, mankind's desires would ever run
confused and wandering, without being able to fix
their determinate choice; for as there is an infinite
number of beautiful objects, the desires would consequently be also infinite; whereas, on the contrary,
I have heard that true love is still confined to one,
and voluntary and unforced. This being granted,

why would you have me force my inclinations for no other reason but that you say you love me? Tell me, I beseech you, had heaven formed me as ugly as it has made me beautiful, could I justly complain of you for not loving me? Pray consider, also, that I do not possess those charms by choice; such as they are, they were freely bestowed on me by heaven: and as the viper is not to be blamed for the poison with which she kills, seeing it was assigned her by nature, so I ought not to be censured for that beauty which I derive from the same cause; for beauty in a virtuous woman is but like a distant flame, or a sharp-edged sword, and only burns and wounds those who approach too near it. Honor and virtue are the ornaments of the soul, and that body that is destitute of them, cannot be esteemed beautiful, though it be naturally so. If, then, honor be one of those endowments which most adorn the body, why should she that is beloved for her beauty, expose herself to the loss of it, merely to gratify the loose desires of one, who, for his own selfish ends, uses all the means imaginable to make her lose it? I was born free, and, that I might continue so, I retired to these solitary hills and plains, where trees are my companions, and clear fountains my looking-glasses. With the trees and with the waters I communicate my thoughts and my beauty. I am a distant flame, and a sword far off: those whom I have attracted with my sight, I have undeceived with my words; and if hope be the food of desire, as I never gave any encouragement to Chrysostome, nor to any other, it may well be said, it was rather his own

obstinacy than my cruelty that shortened his life.
If you tell me that his intentions were honest, and
therefore ought to have been complied with, I answer, that when, at the very place where his grave
is making, he discovered his passion, I told him I
was resolved to live and die single, and that the
earth alone should reap the fruit of my reservedness, and enjoy the spoils of my beauty; and if, after
all the admonitions I gave him, he would persist in
his obstinate pursuit, and sail against the wind,
what wonder is it he should perish in the waves of
his indiscretion?   Had I ever encouraged him, or
amused him with ambiguous words, then I had
been false; and had I gratified his wishes, I had
acted contrary to my better resolves: he persisted,
though I had given him a due caution, and he de-
spaired without being hated.   Now I leave you to
judge, whether I ought to be blamed for his suffer-
ings?   If I have deceived any one, let him complain; if I have broke my promise to any one, let
him despair; if I encourage any one, let him presume; if I entertain any one, let him boast; but let
no man call me cruel, nor murderer, until I either
deceive, break my promise, encourage, or entertain
him.   Heaven has not yet been pleased to show
whether it is its will I should love by destiny; and
it is vain to think I will ever do it by choice: so let
this general caution serve every one of those who
make their addresses to me for their own ends.
And if any one hereafter dies on my account, let
not their jealousy, nor my scorn or hate, be thought
the cause of their death; for she who never pretended to love, cannot make any one jealous; and

a free and generous declaration of our fixed resolution, ought not to be counted hate or disdain. In
short, let him that calls me a tigress, and a basilisk,
avoid me as a dangerous thing; and let him that
calls me ungrateful, give over serving me : I assure
them I will never seek nor pursue them. Therefore
let none hereafter make it their business to disturb
my ease, nor strive to make me hazard among men
the peace I now enjoy, which I am persuaded is not
to be found with them. I have wealth enough; I
neither love nor hate any one : the innocent conversation of the neighboring shepherdesses, with the
care of my flocks, help me to pass away my time,
without either coquetting with this man, or practis-
ing arts to ensnare that other. My thoughts are
limited by these mountains ; and if they wander
further, it is only to admire the beauty of heaven,
and thus by steps to raise my soul towards her original dwelling."

As soon as she had said this, without expecting
any answer, she left the place, and ran into the
thickest of the adjoining wood, leaving all that
heard her charmed with her discretion, as well as
with her beauty.

However, so prevalent were the charms of the
latter, that some of the company, who were desperately struck, could not forbear offering to follow
her, without being the least deterred by the solemn
protestations which they had heard her make that
very moment. But Don Quixote, perceiving their
design, and believing he had now a fit opportunity
to exert his knight-errantry: " Let no man," cried
he, " of what quality or condition soever, presume

to follow the fair Marcella, under the penalty of incurring my furious displeasure. She has made it
appear, by undeniable reasons, that she was not
guilty of Chrysostome's death; and has positively
declared her firm resolution never to condescend to
the desires of any of her admirers; for which reason, instead of being importuned and persecuted,
she ought to be esteemed and honored by all good
men, as being perhaps the only woman in the world
that ever lived with such a virtuous reservedness."
Now, whether it were that Don Quixote's threats
terrified the amorous shepherds, or that Ambrose's
persuasion prevailed with them to stay and see
their friend interred, none of the shepherds left the
place, till the grave being made, and the papers
burnt, the body was deposited in the bosom of
the earth, not without many tears from all the as-
sistants. They covered the grave with a great
stone, till a monument was made, which Ambrose
said he designed to have set up there, with the following epitaph upon it.

CHRYSOSTOME'S EPITAPH.

Here of a wretched swain
  The frozen body's laid,
Kill'd by the cold disdain
  Of an ungrateful maid.

Here first love's power he tried,
  Here first his pains express'd;
Here first he was denied,
  Here first he chose to rest.

You who the shepherd mourn,
  From coy Marcella fly;
Who Chrysostome could scorn,
  May all mankind destroy.

The shepherds strewed the grave with many
flowers and boughs; and every one having condoled
a while with his friend Ambrose, they took their
leave of him, and departed. Vivaldo and his companion did the like; as did also Don Quixote, who
was not a person to forget himself on such occasions: he likewise bid adieu to the kind goat-herds
that had entertained him, and to the two travellers
who had desired him to go with them to Seville,
assuring him there was no place in the world more
fertile in adventures, every street and every corner
there producing some. Don Quixote returned them
thanks for their kind information; but told them,
" he neither would nor ought to go to Seville, till
he had cleared all those mountains of the thieves
and robbers which, he heard, very much infested all
those parts." Thereupon the travellers, being unwilling to divert him from so good a design, took
their leaves of him once more, and pursued their
journey, sufficiently supplied with matter to discourse on, from the story of Marcella and Chrysostome, and Don Quixote's follies. As for him, he
resolved to find out the shepherdess Marcella, if
possible, to offer her his service to protect her to
the utmost of his power: but he happened to be
crossed in his designs, as you shall hear in the sequel of this true history; for here ends the Second
Book.

PART I. BOOK III.

CHAPTER I.

GIVING AN ACCOUNT OF DON QUIXOTE'S UNFORTUNATE REN-
COUNTER WITH CERTAIN BLOODY-MINDED AND WICKED
YANGUESIAN* CARRIERS.

THE sage Cid Hamet Benengeli relates, that
when Don Quixote had taken leave of all those
that were at Chrysostome's funeral, he and his
squire went after Marcella into the wood; and having ranged it above two hours without being able
to find her, they came at last to a meadow, whose
springing green, watered with a delightful and refreshing rivulet, invited, or rather pleasantly forced
them, to alight and give way to the heat of the
day, which began to be very violent: so leaving the
ass and Rozinante to graze at large, they ransacked
the wallet; and without ceremony the master and
the man fell to, and fed lovingly on what they
found. Now Sancho had not taken care to tie up
Rozinante, knowing him to be a horse of that so-
briety and chastity, that all the mares in the pastures of Cordova could not have raised him to attempt an indecent thing. But either fortune, or the
devil, who seldom sleeps, so ordered it, that a good

* Carriers of the kingdom of Galicia, commonly so called.

number of Galician mares, belonging to some Yanguesian carriers, were then feeding in the same
valley, it being the custom of those men, about the
hottest time of the day, to stop wherever they met
with grass and water to refresh their cattle; nor
could they have found a fitter place than that where
Don Quixote was. Rozinante, as I said before,
was chaste and modest; however, he was flesh and
blood; so that as soon as he had smelt the mares,
forsaking his natural gravity and reservedness,
without asking his master's leave, away he trots it
briskly to make them sensible of his little necessities: but they, who it seems had more mind to feed
than to be merry, received their gallant so rudely,
with their heels and teeth, that in a trice they broke
his girths and threw down his saddle, and left him
disrobed of all his equipage. And for an addition
to his misery, the carriers, perceiving the violence
that was offered to their mares, flew to their relief
with poles and pack-staves, and so belabored poor
Rozinante, that he soon sunk to the ground under
the weight of their unmerciful blows.

Don Quixote and Sancho, perceiving at a distance the ill-usage of Rozinante, ran with all speed
to his rescue; and, as they came near the place,
panting, and almost out of breath, " Friend Sancho," cried Don Quixote, " I perceive these are no
knights, but only a pack of scoundrels, and fellows
of the lowest rank; I say it, because thou mayest
lawfully help me to revenge the injury they have
done Rozinante before our faces." " What a devil
do you talk of revenge?" quoth Sancho; " we are
• likely to revenge ourselves finely! you see they are

above twenty, and we are but two; nay, perhaps but one and a half." "I alone am worth a hundred," replied Don Quixote; and then, without any more words, he drew his sword, and flew upon the Yanguesians. Sancho, encouraged by his master's example, did the like; and with the first blow which Don Quixote gave one of them, he cut through his leathern doublet, and gave him a deep slash in the shoulder. The Yanguesians, seeing themselves thus rudely handled, betook themselves to their leavers and pack-staves, and then all at once surrounding the valiant knight and his trusty squire, they charged them and laid on with great fury. At the second round, down they settled poor Sancho, and then Don Quixote himself, who, as chance would have it, fell at the feet of Rozinante, that had not yet recovered his legs; neither could the knight's courage nor his skill avail against the fury of a number of rustical fellows armed with pack-staves. The Yanguesians, fearing the ill-consequences of the mischief they had done, made all the haste they could to be gone, leaving our two adventurers in a woful condition. The first that came to himself was Sancho Panza, who, finding himself near his master, called to him thus, with a weak and doleful voice: "Ah master! master! Sir, Sir Knight!" "What is the matter, friend Sancho?" asked the knight, in the same feeble and lamenting tone. "I could wish," replied Sancho, "that your worship would help me to two good draughts of the liquor you talk on, if you have any by you; perhaps it is as good to cure broken bones, as it is to heal outward wounds." "Oh! that I had some of it here now," cried Don Quixote ; " we could not then be said to want any thing : but I swear to thee, honest Sancho, by the faith of a knight-errant, within these two days (if no other disaster prevent me) I will have some of it at my disposal, or it shall hardly escape my hands." " Two days, sir! " replied Sancho : " why, pray how many days do you think it will be before we are able to stir our feet ? " "As for myself," answered the bruised Don Quixote, " I must own I cannot set a term to the days of our recovery ; but it is I who am the fatal cause of all this mischief ; for I ought not to have drawn my sword against a company of fellows, upon whom the honor of knighthood was never conferred ; and I do not doubt but that the Lord of hosts suffered this punishment to befall me for transgressing thus the laws of chivalry. Therefore, friend Sancho, observe what I am going to tell thee, for it is a thing that highly concerns the welfare of us both : it is that for the future, whenever thou perceivest us to be any ways abused by such inferior fellows, thou art not to expect I should offer to draw my sword against them ; for I will not do it in the least : no, do thou then draw and chastise them as thou thinkest fit : but if any knights come to take their parts, then will I be sure to step between thee and danger, and assault them with the utmost vigor and intrepidity. Thou hast already had a thousand proofs of the greatness of my valor, and the prevailing strength of my most dreadful arm ; " (so arrogant the knight was grown since his victory over the bold Biscayan.)

But Sancho was not so well pleased with his

master's admonitions, but that he thought fit to answer him. " Sir," said he, " I am a peaceful man,
a harmless quiet fellow, d'ye see; I can make shift
to pass by an injury as well as any man, as having
a wife to maintain, and children to bring up; and
therefore pray take this from me by the way of advice, (for I will not offer to command my master,) that
I will not in any wise draw my sword neither against
knight nor clown, not I. I freely forgive all mankind, high and low, rich and poor, lords and beggars, whatever wrongs they ever did or may do me,
without the least exception." " Sancho," said his
master, hearing this, " I heartily wish I had breath
enough to answer thee effectually, or that the pain
which I feel in one of my short ribs would leave me
but for so long as might serve to convince thee of
thy error.   Come, suppose, thou silly wretch, that
the gale of fortune, which has hitherto been so contrary to us, should at last turn favorable, swelling
the sails of our desires, so that we might with as
much security as ease arrive at some of those islands which I have promised thee; what would become of thee, if, after I had conquered one of them,
I were to make thee lord of it?   Thou wouldst
certainly be found not duly qualified for that dignity, as having abjured all knighthood, all thoughts
of honor, and all intention to revenge injuries, and
defend thy own dominions.   For thou must understand, that in kingdoms and provinces newly conquered, the hearts and minds of the inhabitants are
never so thoroughly subdued, or wedded to the interests of their new sovereign, but that there is
reason to fear, they will endeavor to raise some

commotions to change the face of affairs, and, as
men say, once more try their fortune. Therefore it
is necessary that the new possessor have not only
understanding to govern, but also valor to attack
his enemies, and defend himself on all occasions."
" I would I had had that understanding and valor
you talk of," quoth Sancho; " but now, sir, I must
be free to tell you, I have more need of a surgeon,
than of a preacher. Pray try whether you can rise,
and we will help Rozinante, though he does not
deserve it; for he is the chief cause of all this beating. For my part, I could never have believed the
like of him before, for I always took him for as
chaste and sober a person as myself. In short, it is
a true saying, that a man must eat a peck of salt
with his friend, before he knows him; and I find
there is nothing sure in this world: for, who would
have thought, after the dreadful slashes you gave to
that knight-errant, such a terrible shower of bastinadoes would so soon have fallen upon our shoulders?" "As for thine," replied Don Quixote, " I
doubt they are used to endure such sort of showers; but mine, that were nursed in soft linen, will
most certainly be longer sensible of this misfortune;
and were it not that I imagine, (but why do I say
imagine?) were it not that I am positively sure,
that all these inconveniences are inseparable from
the profession of chivalry, I would abandon myself
to grief, and die of mere despair on this very spot."
" I beseech you, sir," quoth Sancho, " since these
rubs are the vails of your trade of knighthood, tell
me whether they use to come often, or whether we
may look for them at set times? for, I fancy, if we

meet but with two such harvests more, we shall never be able to reap the third, unless God of his infinite mercy assist us."

"Know, friend Sancho," returned Don Quixote, "that the life of knights-errant is subject to a thousand hazards and misfortunes; but on the other side, they may at any time suddenly become kings and emperors, as experience has demonstrated in many knights, of whose histories I have a perfect knowledge. And I could tell thee now (would my pain suffer me) of some of them who have raised themselves to those high dignities only by the valor of their arm; and those very knights, both before and after their advancement, were involved in many calamities: for the valorous Amadis de Gaul saw himself in the power of his mortal enemy Archelaus the enchanter, of whom it is credibly reported, that when he held him prisoner, he gave him above two hundred stripes with his horse bridle, after he had tied him to a pillar in the court-yard of his house. There is also a secret author of no little credit relates, that the Knight of the Sun, being taken in a trap in a certain castle, was hurried to a deep dungeon, where, after they had bound him hand and foot, they forcibly gave him a clyster of snow-water and sand, which would probably have cost him his life, had he not been assisted in that distress by a wise magician, his particular friend. Thus I may well bear my misfortune patiently, since those which so many greater persons have endured may be said to outdo it: for I would have thee to know, that those wounds that are given with the instruments and tools which a man happens to have in his hand, do not really disgrace the person struck. We read it expressly in the laws of duels, 'That if a shoemaker strikes another man with his last which he held in his hand, though it be of wood, as a cudgel is, yet the party who was struck with it shall not be said to have been cudgelled.' I tell thee this, that thou mayest not think we are in the least dishonored, though we have been horribly beaten in this rencounter; for the weapons which those men used were but instruments of their profession, and not one of them, as I very well remember, had either tuck, or sword, or dagger." "They gave me no leisure," quoth Sancho, "to examine things so narrowly; for I had no sooner laid my hand on my cutlass,* but they crossed my shoulders with such a wooden blessing, as settled me on the ground without sense or motion, where you see me lie, and where I don't trouble my head whether it be a disgrace to be mauled with cudgels or with pack-staves; let them be what they will, I am only vexed to feel them so heavy on my shoulders, where I am afraid they are imprinted as deep as they are on my mind." "For all this," replied Don Quixote, "I must inform thee, friend Sancho, that there is no remembrance which time will not efface, nor no pain to which death will not put a period." "Thank you for nothing!" quoth Sancho; "what worse can befall us, than to have only death to trust to? Were our affliction to be cured with a plaster or two, a man might have some patience;

---

* *Tizona:* The romantic name of the sword, which the Spanish general, Roderick Diaz de Bivar, used against the Moors.

but for aught I see, all the salves in an hospital
won't set us on our best legs again." "Come, no
more of this," cried Don Quixote; "take courage,
and make a virtue of necessity; for it is what I am
resolved to do. Let us see how it fares with Rozinante; for if I am not mistaken, the poor creature
has not been the least sufferer in this adventure."
" No wonder at that," quoth Sancho, " seeing he's
a knight-errant, too; I rather wonder how my ass
has escaped so well, while we have fared so ill."
" In our disasters," returned Don Quixote, " fortune
leaves always some door open to come at a remedy.
I say it, Sancho, because that little beast may now
supply the want of Rozinante, to carry me to some
castle, where I may get cured of my wounds. Nor
do I esteem this kind of riding dishonorable, for I
remember that the good old Silenus, tutor and governor to the jovial god of wine, rode very fairly on
a goodly ass, when he made his entry into the city
with a hundred gates." "Ay," quoth Sancho, " It
will do well enough, could you ride as fairly on
your ass as he did on his; but there is a deal of
difference between riding, and being laid cross the
pannel like a pack of rubbish." " The wounds
which are received in combat," said Don Quixote,
"rather add to our honor, than deprive us of it;
therefore, good Sancho, trouble me with no more
replies, but, as I said, endeavor to get up, and lay
me as thou pleasest upon thy ass, that we may
leave this place ere night steal upon us." " But,
sir," cried Sancho, " I have heard you say, that it is
a common thing among you knight-errants to sleep
in the fields and deserts the best part of the year,

and that you look upon it to be a very happy kind of life." "That is to say," replied Don Quixote, "when we can do no better, or when we are in love; and this is so true, that there have been knights who have dwelt on rocks, exposed to the sun, and other inclemencies of the sky, for the space of two years, without their lady's knowledge: one of those was Amadis, when, assuming the name of The Lovely Obscure, he inhabited the bare rock, either eight years or eight months, I can't now punctually tell which of the two, for I don't thoroughly remember the passage. Let it suffice that there he dwelt, doing penance, for I don't know what unkindness his lady, Oriana, had showed him. But setting these discourses aside, pr'ythee despatch, lest some mischief befall the ass, as it has done Rozinante." "That would be the devil, indeed," replied Sancho; and so breathing out some thirty lamentations, threescore sighs, and a hundred and twenty plagues and poxes on those that had decoyed him thither, he at last got upon his legs, yet not so but that he went stooping, with his body bent like a Turk's bow, not being able to stand upright. Yet in this crooked posture, he made a shift to harness his ass, who had not forgot to take his share of licentiousness that day. After this, he helped up Rozinante, who, could his tongue have expressed his sorrows, would certainly not have been behind-hand with Sancho and his master. After many bitter oh's, and screwed faces, Sancho laid Don Quixote on the ass, tied Rozinante to its tail, and then, leading the ass by the halter, he took the nearest way that he could guess to the high road;

to which he luckily came, before he had travelled a short league, and then he discovered an inn; which, in spite of all he could say, Don Quixote was pleased to mistake for a castle. Sancho swore bloodily it was an inn, and his master was as positive of the contrary. In short, their dispute lasted so long, that before they could decide it, they reached the inn door, where Sancho straight went in, with all his train, without troubling himself any farther about the matter.

CHAPTER II.

WHAT HAPPENED TO DON QUIXOTE IN THE INN WHICH HE TOOK FOR A CASTLE.

THE innkeeper, seeing Don Quixote lying quite athwart the ass, asked Sancho what ailed him? Sancho answered it was nothing, only his master had got a fall from the top of a rock to the bottom, and had bruised his sides a little. The innkeeper had a wife, very different from the common sort of hostesses, for she was of a charitable nature, and very compassionate of her neighbor's affliction; which made her immediately take care of Don Quixote, and call her daughter (a good handsome girl) to set her helping hand to his cure. One of the servants in the inn was an Asturian wench, a broad-faced, flat-headed, saddle-nosed dowdy; blind of one eye, and the other almost out: however, the activity of her body supplied all other defects. She was not above three feet high from her heels to her head; and her shoulders, which somewhat loaded her, as having too much flesh upon them, made her look downwards oftener than she could have wished. This charming original likewise assisted the mistress and the daughter; and, with the latter, helped to make the knight's bed, and a sorry one it was; the room where it stood was an old gambling cock-loft, which by manifold signs seemed to have been, in the days of yore, a repository for chopped straw. Somewhat farther, in a corner of that garret, a carrier had his lodging; and though his bed was nothing but the pannels and coverings of his mules, it was much better than that of Don Quixote, which only consisted of four rough-hewn boards laid upon two uneven tressels, a flock-bed, that, for thinness, might well have passed for a quilt, and was full of knobs and bunches, which, had they not peeped out through many a hole, and shown themselves to be of wool, might well have been taken for stones : the rest of that extraordinary bed's furniture was a pair of sheets, which rather seemed to be of leather, than of linen cloth, and a coverlet whose every individual thread you might have told, and never have missed one in the tale.

In this ungracious bed was the knight laid, to rest his belabored carcass, and presently the hostess and her daughter anointed and plastered him all over, while Maritornes (for that was the name of the Asturian wench) held the candle. The hostess, while she greased him, wondering to see him so bruised all over, " I fancy," said she, " those bumps look much more like a dry beating than a fall." " It was no dry beating, mistress, I promise you,"

quoth Sancho, " but the rock had, I know not how,
many cragged ends and knobs, whereof every one
gave my master a token of his kindness. And by
the way, forsooth," continued he, " I beseech you
save a little of that same tow and ointment for me
too, for I don't know what is the matter with my
back, but I fancy I stand mainly in want of a little
greasing too." " What, I suppose you fell too ? "
quoth the landlady. " Not I," quoth Sancho, " but
the very fright that I took to see my master tumble
down the rock, has so wrought upon my body, that
I am as sore as if I had been sadly mauled." " It
may well be as you say," cried the innkeeper's
daughter; " for I have dreamed several times that
I have been falling from the top of a high tower
without ever coming to the ground; and when I
waked, I have found myself as out of order, and as
bruised, as if I had fallen in good earnest." " That
is e'en my case, mistress," quoth Sancho; " only ill
luck would have it so, that I should find myself e'en
almost as battered and bruised as my lord Don
Quixote, and yet all the while be as broad awake as
I am now." " How do you call this same gentleman ? " quoth Maritornes. " He is Don Quixote de
la Mancha," replied Sancho ; " and he is a knight-
errant, and one of the primest and stoutest that ever
the sun shined on." "A knight-errant," cried the
wench, " pray what is that ? " " Heigh-day ! " cried
Sancho, " does the wench know no more of the
world than that comes to ? Why, a knight-errant
is a thing which in two words you see well cudgelled, and then an emperor. To-day there is not a
more wretched thing upon the earth, and yet to-

morrow he'll have you two or three kingdoms to give away to his squire." "How comes it to pass, then," quoth the landlady, "that thou, who art this great person's squire, hast not yet got thee at least an earldom?" "Fair and softly goes far," replied Sancho. "Why, we have not been a month in our gears, so that we have not yet encountered any adventure worth the naming: besides, many a time we look for one thing, and light on another. But if my lord Don Quixote happens to get well again, and I escape remaining a cripple, I'll not take the best title in the land for what I am sure will fall to my share."

Here Don Quixote, who had listened with great attention to all these discourses, raised himself up in his bed with much ado, and taking the hostess in a most obliging manner by the hand, "Believe me," said he, "beautiful lady, you may well esteem it a happiness that you have now the opportunity to entertain my person in your castle. Self-praise is unworthy a man of honor, and therefore I shall say no more of myself, but my squire will inform you who I am; only thus much let me add, that I will eternally preserve your kindness in the treasury of my remembrance, and study all occasions to testify my gratitude. And I wish," continued he, "the powers above had so disposed my fate, that I were not already love's devoted slave, and captivated by the charms of the disdainful beauty who engrosses all my softer thoughts! for then would I be proud to sacrifice my liberty to this beautiful damsel." The hostess, her daughter, and the kind-hearted Maritornes, stared at one another, quite at a loss for the meaning of this high-flown language, which they understood full as well as if it had been Greek. Yet conceiving these were words of compliment and courtship, they looked upon him and admired him as a man of another world : and so, having made him such returns as innkeeper's breeding could afford, they left him to his rest; only Maritornes staid to rub down Sancho, who wanted her help no less than his master.

Now you must know that the carrier and she had agreed to pass the night together; and she had given him her word, that as soon as all the people in the inn were in bed, she would be sure to come to him, and be at his service. And it is said of this good-natured thing, that whenever she had passed her word in such cases, she was sure to make it good, though she had made the promise in the midst of a wood, and without any witness at all: for she stood much upon her gentility, though she undervalued herself so far as to serve in an inn; often saying, that nothing but crosses and necessity could have made her stoop to it.

Don Quixote's hard, scanty, beggarly, miserable bed was the first of the four in that wretched apartment; next to that was Sancho's kennel, which consisted of nothing but a bed-mat and a coverlet, that rather seemed shorn canvas than a rug. Beyond these two beds was that of the carrier, made, as we have said, of the pannels and furniture of two of the best of twelve mules which he kept, every one of them goodly beasts, and in special good case; for he was one of the richest muleteers of Arevalo, as the Moorish author of this history relates, who makes particular mention of him, as having been acquainted with him; nay, some do not stick to say he was somewhat akin to him. However it be, it appears that Cid Hamet Benengeli was a very exact historian, since he takes care to give us an account of things that seem so inconsiderable and trivial. A laudable example, which those historians should follow, who usually relate matters so concisely, that we have scarce a smack of them, leaving the most essential part of the story drowned in the ink-horn, either through neglect, malice, or ignorance. A thousand blessings then be given to the curious author of Tablante of Ricamonte, and to that other indefatigable sage who recorded the achievements of Count Tomillas! for they have described even the most minute and trifling circumstances with a singular preciseness. But to return to our story : you must know, that after the carrier had visited his mules, and given them their second course,* he laid himself down upon his pannels, in expectation of the most punctual Maritornes's kind visit. By this time Sancho, duly greased and anointed, was crept into his sty, where he did all he could to sleep, but his aching ribs did all they could to prevent him. As for the knight, whose sides were in as bad circumstances as the squire's, he lay with both his eyes open like a hare. And now was every soul in the inn gone to bed, nor any light to be seen, except that of a lamp which hung in the middle of the gate-way. This general tranquillity

* In Spain they get up in the night to dress their cattle, and give them their barley and straw, which serve for hay and oats.

setting Don Quixote's thoughts at work, offered to his imagination one of the most absurd follies that ever crept into a distempered brain from the perusal of romantic whimseys.   Now he fancied himself to be in a famous castle, (for, as we have already said, all the inns he lodged in seemed no less than castles to him,) and that the innkeeper's daughter, (consequently daughter to the lord of the castle,) strangely captivated with his graceful presence and gallantry, had promised him the pleasure of her embraces, as soon as her father and mother were gone to rest.   This chimera disturbed him, as if it had been a real truth; so that he began to be mightily perplexed, reflecting on the danger to which his honor was exposed: but at last his virtue overcame the powerful temptation, and he firmly resolved not to be guilty of the least infidelity to his lady Dulcinea del Toboso, though Queen Genever herself, with her trusty matron Quintaniona, should join to decoy him into the alluring snare.

While these wild imaginations worked in his brain, the gentle Maritornes was mindful of her assignation, and with soft and wary steps, barefoot, and in her smock, with her hair gathered up in a fustian coif, stole into the room, and felt about for her beloved carrier's bed: but scarce had she got to the door, when Don Quixote, whose ears were on the scout, was sensible that something was coming in; and therefore having raised himself in his bed, sore and wrapt up in his plasters as he was, he stretched out his arms to receive his fancied damsel, and caught hold of Maritornes by the wrist, as she was, with her arms stretched, groping her way to her paramour; he pulled her to him, and made her sit down by his bedside, she not daring to speak a word all the while. Now, as he imagined her to be the lord of the castle's daughter, her smock, which was of the coarsest canvas, seemed to him of the finest holland; and the glass beads about her wrist, precious oriental pearls; her hair, that was almost as rough as a horse's mane, he took to be soft flowing threads of bright curling gold; and her breath, that had a stronger hogoe than stale venison, was to him a grateful compound of the most fragrant perfumes of Arabia. In short, flattering imagination transformed her into the likeness of those romantic beauties, one of whom, as he remembered to have read, came to pay a private visit to a wounded knight, with whom she was desperately in love; and the poor gentleman's obstinate folly had so infatuated his outward sense, that his feeling and his smell could not in the least undeceive him, and he thought he had no less than a balmy Venus in his arms, while he hugged a fulsome bundle of deformities, that would have turned any man's stomach but a sharp-set carrier's. Therefore, clasping her still closer, with a soft and amorous whisper, " Oh! thou most lovely temptation," cried he, " oh! that I now might but pay a warm acknowledgment for the mighty blessing which your extravagant goodness would lavish on me! yes, most beautiful charmer, I would give an empire to purchase your most desirable embraces; but fortune, madam, fortune, that tyrant of my life, that unrelenting enemy to the truly deserving, has maliciously hurried and riveted me to this bed, where I

lie so bruised and macerated, that, though I were
eager to gratify your desires, I should at this dear
unhappy minute, be doomed to impotence. Nay,
to that unlucky bar fate has added a yet more invincible obstacle; I mean my plighted faith to the
unrivalled Dulcinea del Toboso, the sole mistress
of my wishes, and absolute sovereign of my heart.
Oh! did not this oppose my present happiness, I
could never be so dull and insensible a knight as
to lose the benefit of this extraordinary favor which
you have now condescended to offer me."

Poor Maritornes all this while sweated for fear
and anxiety, to find herself thus locked in the
knight's arms; and without either understanding,
or willing to understand his florid excuses, she did
what she could to get from him, and sheer off, without speaking a word. On the other side, the carrier,
whose lewd thoughts kept him awake, having heard
his trusty lady when she first came in, and listened
ever since to the knight's discourse, began to be
afraid that she had made some other assignation;
and so, without any more ado, he crept softly to
Don Quixote's bed, where he listened awhile to
hear what would be the end of all this talk, which
he could not understand: but perceiving at last by
the struggling of his faithful Maritornes, that it was
none of her fault, and that the knight strove to de-
tain her against her will, he could by no means
bear his familiarity; and therefore taking it in
mighty dudgeon, he up with his fist, and hit the
enamored knight such a swinging blow on the jaws,
that his face was all over blood in a moment. And
not satisfied with this, he got on the top of the

knight, and with his splay feet betrampled him, as
if he had been trampling a hay-mow. With that
the bed, whose foundations were none of the best,
sunk under the additional load of the carrier, and
fell with such a noise, that it waked the innkeeper,
who presently suspects it to be one of Maritornes's
nightly skirmishes ; and therefore having called her
aloud, and finding that she did not answer, he
lighted a lamp and made to the place where he
heard the bustle. The wench, who heard him coming, knowing him to be of a passionate nature, was
scared out of her wits, and fled for shelter to Sancho's sty, where he lay snoring to some tune : there
she pigged in, and slunk under the coverlet, where
she lay snug, and trussed up as round as an egg.
Presently her master came in, in a mighty heat :
" Where's this damned whore ? " cried he ; " I dare
say this is one of her pranks."   By this, Sancho
awaked ; and feeling that unusual lump, which almost overlaid him, he took it to be the nightmare,
and began to lay about him with his fists, and
thumped the wench so unmercifully, that at last
flesh and blood were no longer able to bear it ; and
forgetting the danger she was in, and her dear reputation, she paid him back his thumps as fast as her
fists could lay them on, and soon roused the drowsy
squire out of his sluggishness, whether he would or
no : who, finding himself thus pommelled, by he
did not know who, he bustled up in his nest, and
catching hold of Maritornes, they began the most
pleasant skirmish in the world ; when the carrier
perceiving, by the light of the innkeeper's lamp, the
dismal condition that his dear mistress was in, pre-

sently took her part ; and leaving the knight, whom
he had no more than sufficiently mauled, flew at
the squire and paid him confoundedly. On the
other hand, the innkeeper, who took the wench to
be the cause of all this hurly-burly, cuffed and kicked, and kicked and cuffed her over and over again:
and so there was a strange multiplication of fisticuffs and drubbings. The carrier pommelled Sancho, Sancho mauled the wench, the wench belabored
the squire, and the innkeeper thrashed her again:
and all of them laid on with such expedition, that
you would have thought they had been afraid of
losing time. But the jest was, that in the heat of
the fray, the lamp went out, so that being now in
the dark, they plied one another at a venture ; they
struck and tore, all went to rack, while nails and
fists flew about without mercy.

There happened to lodge that night in the inn
one of the officers belonging to that society which
they call the old holy brotherhood of Toledo, whose
chief office is to look after thieves and robbers. Being
waked with the heavy bustle, he presently jumped
out of his bed, and with his short staff in one hand,
and a tin box with his commission in it in the
other, he groped out his way, and being entered the
room in the dark, cried out, " I charge you all to
keep the peace : I am an officer of the holy brotherhood." The first he popped his hand upon, happened to be the poor battered knight, who lay upon
his back at his full length, without any feeling,
upon the ruins of his bed. The officer having
caught him by the beard, presently cried out, " I
charge you to aid and assist me ;" but finding he

could not stir, though he griped him hard, he presently imagined him to be dead, and murdered by
the rest in the room. With that he bawled out to
have the gates of the inn shut. "Here's a man
murdered," cried he; "look that nobody makes his
escape." These words struck all the combatants
with such a terror, that, as soon as they reached
their ears, they gave over, and left the argument
undecided. Away stole the innkeeper to his own
room, the carrier to his pannels, and the wench to
her kennel; only the unfortunate knight, and his as
unfortunate squire, remained where they lay, not
being able to stir; while the officer, having let go
Don Quixote's beard, went out for a light, in order
to apprehend the supposed murderers : but the innkeeper having wisely put out the lamp in the gate-
way, as he sneaked out of the room, the officer was
obliged to repair to the kitchen chimney, where
with much ado, puffing and blowing a long while
amidst the embers, he at last made shift to get a
light.

CHAPTER III.

A FURTHER ACCOUNT OF THE INNUMERABLE HARDSHIPS
WHICH THE BRAVE DON QUIXOTE, AND HIS WORTHY
SQUIRE SANCHO, UNDERWENT IN THE INN, WHICH THE
KNIGHT UNLUCKILY TOOK FOR A CASTLE.

DON QUIXOTE, who by this time was come to
himself, began to call Sancho with the same lamentable tone as the day before, when he had been
beaten by the carriers in the meadow. "Sancho,"

cried he, "friend Sancho, art thou asleep? art thou
asleep, friend Sancho?" "Sleep!" replied Sancho,
mightily out of humor, "may Old Nick rock my
cradle, then. Why, how the devil should I sleep,
when all the imps of hell have been tormenting me
to-night?" "Nay, thou art in the right," answered
Don Quixote, "for either I have no skill in these
matters, or this castle is enchanted. Hear what I
say to thee, but first swear thou wilt never reveal it
till after my death." "I swear it," quoth Sancho.
"I am thus cautious," said Don Quixote, "because
I hate to take away the reputation of any person."
"Why," quoth Sancho, "I tell you again, I swear
never to speak a word of the matter while you live;
and I hope I may be at liberty to talk on't to-morrow." "Why," cried Don Quixote, "have I done
thee so much wrong, Sancho, that you would have
me die so soon?" "Nay, 'tis not for that neither,"
quoth Sancho, "but because I can't abide to keep
things long, for fear they should grow mouldy."
"Well, let it be as thou pleasest," said Don Quixote, "for I dare trust greater concerns to thy cour-
tesy and affection. In short, know, that this very
night there happened to me one of the strangest
adventures that can be imagined; for the daughter
of the lord of this castle came to me, who is one of
the most engaging and most beautiful damsels that
ever nature has been proud to boast of: what could
I not tell thee of the charms of her shape and face,
and the perfections of her mind! what could I not
add of other hidden beauties, which I condemn to
silence and oblivion, lest I endanger my allegiance
and fidelity to my lady Dulcinea del Toboso! I

will only tell thee, that the heavens envying the in-
estimable happiness which fortune had thrown into
my hand, or rather, because this castle is enchanted, it happened, that in the midst of the most tender and passionate discourses that passed between
us, the profane hand of some mighty giant, which
I could not see, nor imagine whence it came, hit
me such a dreadful blow on the jaws, that they are
still embrued with blood; after which the discourteous wretch, presuming on my present weakness,
did so barbarously bruise me, that I feel myself in
a worse condition now than I did yesterday, after
the carriers had so roughly handled me for Rozinante's incontinency: from which I conjecture, that
the treasure of this damsel's beauty is guarded by
some enchanted Moor, and not reserved for me."

"Nor for me, neither," quoth Sancho; "for I
have been rib-roasted by above four hundred Moors,
who have hammered my bones in such guise, that
I may safely say, the assault and battery made on
my body by the carriers' poles and pack-staves,
were but ticklings and strokings with a feather to
this.* But, sir, pray tell me, d'ye call this such a
pleasant adventure, when we are so lamentably
pounded after it? And yet your hap may well be
accounted better than mine, seeing you've hugged
that fair maiden in your arms. But I, what have I
had, I pray you, but the heaviest blows that ever
fell on a poor man's shoulders? Woe's me, and the
mother that bore me, for I neither am, nor ever

* In the original, were tarts and cheese-cakes to this: *Tortas
y pan pinta.*

mean to be, a knight-errant, and yet of all the mis-
adventures, the greater part falls still to my lot."
" What, hast thou been beaten as well as I ? " said
Don Quixote. " What a plague," cried Sancho,
" han't I been telling you so all this while ! " " Come,
never let it trouble thee, friend Sancho," replied
Don Quixote ; " for I'll immediately make the precious balsam, that will cure thee in the twinkling
of an eye."

By this time the officer, having lighted his lamp,
came into the room, to see who it was that was
murdered.   Sancho seeing him enter in his shirt, a
napkin wrapped about his head like a turban, and
the lamp in his hand, he being also an ugly, ill-
looked fellow, " Sir," quoth the squire to his master,
" pray see whether this be not the enchanted Moor,
that's come again to have t'other bout with me, and
try * whether he has not left some place unbruised,
for him now to maul as much as the rest."   " It
cannot be the Moor," replied Don Quixote : "for
persons enchanted are to be seen by nobody."   " If
they do not suffer themselves to be seen," quoth
Sancho, " at least they suffer themselves to be felt :
if not, let my carcass bear witness."   " So might
mine," cried Don Quixote ; " yet this is no sufficient reason to prove, that what we see is the enchanted Moor."

While they were thus arguing, the officer advanced, and wondered to hear two men talk so
calmly to one another there : yet finding the unfor-

* *Left some place unbruised, &c.*   Literally, left something at
the bottom of the ink-horn ; that is, left the business incomplete.

tunate knight lying in the same deplorable posture
as he left him, stretched out like a corpse, bloody,
bruised, and beplastered, and not able to stir himself; "How is't, honest fellow," quoth he to the
champion, "how do you find yourself?" "Were
I your fellow," replied Don Quixote, "I would have
a little more manners than you have, you blockhead, you ; is that your way of approaching knights-
errant in this country?" The officer could not
bear such a reprimand from one who made so
scurvy a figure, and lifting up the lamp, oil and all,
hit Don Quixote such a blow on the head with it,
that he had reason to fear he had made work for
the surgeon, and therefore stole presently out of the
room, under the protection of the night. "Well,
sir," quoth Sancho, "d'ye think now it was the enchanted Moor, or no? for my part, I think he keeps
the treasure you talk of for others, and reserves
only kicks, cuffs, thumps, and knocks for your worship and myself." "I am now convinced," answered Don Quixote : "therefore let us waive that resentment of these injuries, which we might otherwise
justly show ; for, considering these enchanters can
make themselves invisible when they please, it is
needless to think of revenge. But, pray thee rise,
if thou canst, Sancho, and desire the governor of
the castle to send me some oil, salt, wine, and rosemary, that I may make my healing balsam ; for
truly I want it extremely, so fast the blood flows
out of the wound which the fantasm gave me just
now."

Sancho then got up as fast as his aching bones
would let him, and with much ado made shift. to

crawl out of the room to look for the innkeeper;
and, stumbling by the way on the officer, who stood
hearkening to know what mischief he had done,
" Sir," quoth he to him, " for heaven's sake, do so
much as help us to a little oil, salt, wine, and rosemary, to make a medicine for one of the best
knights-errant that ever trod on shoe of leather,
who lies yonder grievously wounded by the enchanted Moor of this inn."   The officer, hearing
him talk at that rate, took him to be one out of his
wits; and it beginning to be daylight, he opened
the inn door, and told the innkeeper what Sancho
wanted.   The host presently provided the desired
ingredients, and Sancho crept back with them to his
master, whom he found holding his head, and sadly
complaining of the pain which he felt there : though
after all, the lamp had done him no more harm
than only raising of two huge bumps; for that
which he fancied to be blood, was only sweat, and
the oil of the lamp that had liquored his hair and
face.

The knight took all the ingredients, and, having
mixed them together, he had them set over the fire,
and there kept them boiling till he thought they
were enough.   That done, he asked for a vial to
put this precious liquor in : but there being none to
be got, the innkeeper presented him with an old
earthen jug, and Don Quixote was forced to be contented with that.   Then he mumbled over the pot
above fourscore *Paternosters*, and as many *Ave-
marias*, *Salve Reginas*, and *Credos*, making the
sign of the cross at every word by way of benedic-
tion.   At which ceremony, Sancho, the innkeeper,

and the officer were present; for as for the carrier, he was gone to look after his mules, and took no manner of notice of what was passed. This blessed medicine being made, Don Quixote resolved to make an immediate experiment of it on himself; and to that purpose he took off a good draught of the overplus, which the pot would not hold: but he had scarce gulped it down, when it set him a vomiting so violently, that you would have thought he would have cast up his heart, liver, and guts; and his reaching and straining put him into such a sweat, that he desired to be covered up warm, and left to his repose. With that they left him, and he slept three whole hours; and then waking, found himself so wonderfully eased, that he made no question but he had now the right balsam of Fierabras; and therefore he thought he might safely undertake all the most dangerous adventures in the world, without the least hazard of his person.

Sancho, encouraged by the wonderful effect of the balsam on his master, begged that he would be pleased to give him leave to sip up what was left in the pot, which was no small quantity; and the Don having consented, honest Sancho lifted it up with both his hands, and with a strong faith, and better will, poured every drop down his throat. Now the man's stomach not being so nice as his master's, the drench did not set him a vomiting after that manner; but caused such a wambling in his stomach, such a bitter loathing, kecking, and reaching, and such grinding pangs, with cold sweats and swoonings, that he verily believed his last hour was come, and in the midst of his agony,

gave both the balsam and him that made it to the
devil. "Friend," said Don Quixote, seeing him in
that condition, "I begin to think all this pain befalls thee, only because thou hast not received the
order of knighthood; for it is my opinion, this balsam ought to be used by no man that is not a professed knight." "What a plague did you mean
then by letting me drink it?" quoth Sancho; "a
murrain on me, and all my generation, why did not
you tell me this before?" At length the dose began to work to some purpose, and forced its way at
both ends so copiously, that both his bed-mat and
coverlet were soon made unfit for any further use;
and all the while he strained so hard, that not only
himself, but the standers-by, thought he would have
died. This dreadful hurricane lasted about two
hours; and then too, instead of finding himself as
free from pain as his master, he felt himself so feeble, and so far spent, that he was not able to stand.

But Don Quixote, as we have said, found himself
in an excellent temper; and his active soul loathing
an inglorious repose, he presently was impatient to
depart to perform the duties of his adventurous profession: for he thought those moments that were
trifled away in amusements, or other concerns, only
a blank in life; and all delays a depriving distressed persons, and the world in general, of his
needed assistance. The confidence which he re-
posed in his balsam, heightened, if possible, his
resolution; and thus carried away by his eager
thoughts, he saddled Rozinante himself, and then
put the pannel upon the ass, and his squire upon
the pannel, after he had helped him to huddle on

his clothes : that done, he mounted his steed; and
having spied a javelin that stood in a corner, he
seized and appropriated it to himself, to supply the
want of his lance. Above twenty people that were
in the inn stood spectators of all these transactions;
and among the rest the innkeeper's daughter, from
whom Don Quixote had not power to withdraw his
eyes, breathing out at every glance a deep sigh from
the very bottom of his heart; which those who had
seen him so mortified the night before, took to proceed from the pain of his bruises.

And now being ready to set forwards, he called
for the master of the house, and with a grave delivery, " My lord governor," cried he, " the favors I
have received in your castle are so great and extraordinary, that they bind my grateful soul to an
eternal acknowledgment : therefore that I may be
so happy as to discharge part of the obligation,
think if there be ever a proud mortal breathing on
whom you desire to be revenged for some affront or
other injury, and acquaint me with it now; and by
my order of knighthood, which binds me to protect
the weak, relieve the oppressed, and punish the bad,
I promise you I'll take effectual care, that you
shall have ample satisfaction to the utmost of your
wishes." — " Sir Knight," answered the innkeeper,
with an austere gravity, " I shall not need your
assistance to revenge any wrong that may be offered
to my person; for I would have you to .understand,
that I am able to do myself justice, whenever any
man presumes to do me wrong : therefore all the
satisfaction I desire is, that you will pay your
reckoning for horse-meat and man's meat, and all

your expenses in my inn." "How!" cried Don
Quixote, "is this an inn?" "Yes," answered the
host, "and one of the most noted, and of the best
repute upon the road." "How strangely have I
been mistaken then!" cried Don Quixote; "upon
my honor I took it for a castle, and a considerable
one too; but if it be an inn, and not a castle, all I
have to say is, that you must excuse me from paying any thing; for I would by no means break the
laws which we knight-errants are bound to observe;
nor was it ever known, that they ever paid in any
inn whatsoever; for this is the least recompense
that can be allowed them for the intolerable labors
they endure day and night, winter and summer, o'foot
and o'horseback, pinched with hunger, choked with
thirst, and exposed to all the injuries of the air, and
all the inconveniences in the world." "I have
nothing to do with all this," cried the innkeeper:
"pay your reckoning, and don't trouble me with
your foolish stories of a cock and a bull; I can't
afford to keep house at that rate." "Thou art
both a fool and a knave of an innkeeper," replied
Don Quixote; and with that clapping spurs to
Rozinante, and brandishing his javelin at his host,
he rode out of the inn without any opposition, and
got a good way from it, without so much as once
looking behind him to see whether his squire came
after him.

The knight being marched off, there remained
only the squire, who was stopped for the reckoning.
However he swore bloodily he would not pay a
cross; for the self-same law that acquitted the
knight acquitted the squire. This put the innkeeper

into a great passion, and made him threaten Sancho very hard, telling him if he would not pay him
by fair means, he would have him laid by the heels
that moment. Sancho swore by his master's knighthood, he would sooner part with his life than his
money on such an account; nor should the squires
in after ages ever have occasion to upbraid him with
giving so ill a precedent, or breaking their rights.
But as ill luck would have it, there happened to be
in the inn four Segovia clothiers, three Cordova
point-makers, and two Seville hucksters, all brisk,
gamesome, arch fellows; who agreeing all in the
same design, encompassed Sancho, and pulled him
off his ass, while one of them went and got a blanket. Then they put the unfortunate squire into it,
and observing the roof of the place they were in to
be somewhat too low for their purpose, they carried
him into the back yard, which had no limits but the
sky, and there they tossed him for several times
together in the blanket, as they do dogs on Shrove-
Tuesday. Poor Sancho made so grievous an outcry all the while, that his master heard him, and
imagined those lamentations were of some person
in distress, and consequently the occasion of some
adventure: but having at last distinguished the
voice, he made to the inn with a broken gallop;
and finding the gates shut, he rode about to see
whether he might not find some other way to get
in. But he no sooner came to the back-yard wall,
which was none of the highest, when he was an eye-
witness of the scurvy trick that was put upon his
squire. There he saw him ascend and descend, and
frolic and caper in the air with so much nimbleness

and agility, that it is thought the knight himself could not have forborne laughing, had he been any thing less angry. He did his best to get over the wall, but alas! he was so bruised, that he could not so much as alight from his horse. This made him fume and chafe, and vent his passion in a thousand threats and curses, so strange and various that it is impossible to repeat them. But the more he stormed, the more they tossed and laughed; Sancho on his side begging, and howling, and threatening, and damning, to as little purpose as his master, for it was weariness alone could make the tossers give over. Then they charitably put an end to his high dancing, and set him upon his ass again, carefully wrapped in his mantle.

But Maritornes's tender soul made her pity a male creature in such tribulation; and thinking he had danced and tumbled enough to be a-dry, she was so generous as to help him to a draught of water, which she purposely drew from the well that moment, that it might be the cooler. Sancho clapped the pot to his mouth, but his master made him desist: "Hold, hold," cried he, "son Sancho, drink no water, child, it will kill thee: behold I have here the most holy balsam, two drops of which will cure thee effectually." "Ha," replied Sancho, shaking his head, and looking sourly on the knight with a side-face, "have you again forgot that I am no knight? or would you have me cast up the few guts I have left since yesternight's job? Keep your brewings for yourself in the devil's name, and let me alone." With that he lifted up the jug to his nose, but finding it to be mere element, he

spirted out again the little he had tasted, and desired the wench to help him to some better liquor:
so she went and fetched him wine to make him
amends, and paid for it too out of her own pocket;
for, to give the devil his due, it was said of her, that
though she was somewhat too free of her favors,
yet she had something of Christianity in her. As
soon as Sancho had tipped off his wine, he visited
his ass's ribs twice or thrice with his heels, and, free
egress being granted him, he trooped off, mightily
tickled with the thoughts of having had his ends,
and got off shot-free, though at the expense of his
shoulders, his usual sureties. It is true, the innkeeper kept his wallet for the reckoning; but the
poor squire was so dismayed, and in such haste to
be gone, that he never missed it. The host was
for shutting the inn doors after him, for fear of the
worst; but the tossers would not let him, being a
sort of fellows that would not have mattered Don
Quixote a straw, though he had really been one of
the Knights of the Round Table.

CHAPTER IV.

OF THE DISCOURSE BETWEEN THE KNIGHT AND THE SQUIRE,
WITH OTHER MATTERS WORTH RELATING.

SANCHO overtook his master, but so pale, so dead-
hearted, and so mortified, that he was hardly able
to sit his ass. " My dear Sancho," said Don Quixote, seeing him in that condition, " I am now fully

convinced that this castle, or inn, is enchanted; for
what could they be that made themselves such bar-
barous sport with thee but spirits and people of the
other world? and I the rather believe this, seeing,
that, when I looked over the wall, and saw thee thus
abused, I strove to get over it, but could not stir,
nor by any means alight from Rozinante.   For, by
my honor, could I either have got over the wall, or
dismounted, I would have revenged thee so effectually on those discourteous wretches, that they
should never have forgot the severity of their punishment, though for once I had infringed the laws of
chivalry; which, as I have often informed thee, do
not permit any knight to lay hands on one that is
not knighted, unless it be in his own defence, and
in case of great necessity."   " Nay," quoth Sancho, " I would have paid them home myself, whether
knight or no knight, but it was not in my power;
and yet I dare say, those that made themselves so
merry with my carcass were neither spirits nor enchanted folks, as you will have it, but mere flesh
and blood as we be.   I am sure they called one
another by their Christian names and surnames,
while they made me vault and frisk in the air; one
was called Pedro Martinez, the other Tenorio Her-
nàndez; and as for our dog of an host, I heard them
call him Juan Palomeque the left-handed.   Then,
pray don't you fancy, that your not being able to
get over the wall, nor to alight, was some enchanter's trick.   It is a folly to make many words; it is
as plain as the nose in a man's face, that these
same adventures which we hunt for up and down,
are like to bring us at last into a peck of troubles,

and such a plaguy deal of mischief, that we shan't
be able to set one foot afore the other. The short
and the long is, I take it to be the wisest course to
jog home and look after our harvest, and not to
run rambling from Ceca* to Meca, lest we leap
out of the frying-pan into the fire, or, out of God's
blessing into the warm sun."—

"Poor Sancho," cried Don Quixote, "how ignorant thou art in matters of chivalry! Come, say no
more, and have patience: a day will cóme when
thou shalt be convinced how honorable a thing it
is to follow this employment. For, tell me, what
satisfaction in this world, what pleasure can equal
that of vanquishing and triumphing over one's
enemy? None, without doubt." "It may be so
for aught I know," quoth Sancho, "though I know
nothing of the matter. However, this I may venture to say, that ever since we have turned knights-
errant, your worship I mean, for it is not for such
scrubs as myself to be named the same day with
such folk, the devil of any fight you have had the
better in, unless it be that with the Biscayan; and
in that too you came off with the loss of one ear
and the vizor of your helmet. And what have we
got ever since, pray, but blows, and more blows;
bruises, and more bruises? besides this tossing in
a blanket, which fell all to my share, and for which
I cannot be revenged because they were hobgoblins

---

* Ceca was a place of devotion among the Moors, in the city
of Cordova, to which they used to go on pilgrimage from other
places, as Mecca is among the Turks: whence the proverb comes
to signify, sauntering about to no purpose. A banter upon
Popish pilgrimages.

that served me so forsooth, though I hugely long to be even with them, that I may know the pleasure you say there is in vanquishing one's enemy." " I find, Sancho," cried Don Quixote, " thou and I are both sick of the same disease; but I will endeavor with all speed to get me a sword made with so much art, that no sort of enchantment shall be able to hurt whosoever shall wear it; and perhaps fortune may put into my hand that which Amadis de Gaul wore when he styled himself, The Knight of the Burning Sword, which was one of the best blades that ever was drawn by knight: for, besides the virtue I now mentioned, it had an edge like a razor, and would enter the strongest armor that ever was tempered or enchanted." " I will lay any thing," quoth Sancho, " when you have found this sword, it will prove just such another help to me as your balsam; that is to say, it will stand nobody in any stead but your dubbed knights, let the poor devil of a squire shift how he can." " Fear no such thing," replied Don Quixote; " heaven will be more propitious to thee than thou imaginest."

Thus they went on discoursing, when Don Quixote, perceiving a thick cloud of dust arise right before them in the road, " The day is come," said he, turning to his squire, " the day is come, Sancho, that shall usher in the happiness which fortune has reserved for me: this day shall the strength of my arm be signalized by such exploits as shall be transmitted even to the latest posterity. See'st thou that cloud of dust, Sancho? it is raised by a prodigious army marching this way, and composed of an infinite number of nations." " Why then, at this

rate," quoth Sancho, "there should be two armies;
for yonder is as great a dust on the other side."
With that Don Quixote looked, and was transported with joy at the sight, firmly believing that
two vast armies were ready to engage each other
in that plain: for his imagination was so crowded
with those battles, enchantments, surprising adventures, amorous thoughts, and other whimseys which
he had read of in romances, that his strong fancy
changed every thing he saw into what he desired to
see; and thus he could not conceive that the dust
was only raised by two large flocks of sheep that
were going the same road from different parts, and
could not be discerned till they were very near: he
was so positive that they were two armies, that
Sancho firmly believed him at last. "Well, sir,"
quoth the squire, "what are we to do, I beseech
you?" "What shall we do," replied Don Quixote, "but assist the weaker and injured side? for
know, Sancho, that the army which now moves
towards us is commanded by the great Alifanfaron, emperor of the vast island of Taprobana: the
other that advances behind us is his enemy, the
King of the Garamantians, Pentapolin with the
naked arm; so called, because he always enters
into the battle with his right arm bare." "Pray,
sir," quoth Sancho, "why are these two great men
going together by the ears?" "The occasion of
their quarrel is this," answered Don Quixote: "Alifanfaron, a strong Pagan, is in love with Pentapolin's daughter, a very beautiful lady and a Christian:
now her father refuses to give her in marriage to
the heathen prince, unless he abjure his false belief

and embrace the Christian religion." "Burn my beard," said Sancho, "if Pentapolin be not in the right on it; I will stand by him, and help him all I may." "I commend thy resolution," replied Don Quixote, "it is not only lawful, but requisite; for there is no need of being a knight to fight in such battles." "I guessed as much," quoth Sancho; "but where shall we leave my ass in the mean time, that I may be sure to find him again after the battle; for I fancy you never heard of any man that ever charged upon such a beast." "It is true," answered Don Quixote, "and therefore I would have thee turn him loose, though thou wert sure never to find him again; for we shall have so many horses after we have got the day, that even Rozinante himself will be in danger of being changed for another." Then mounting to the top of a hillock, whence they might have seen both the flocks, had not the dust obstructed their sight, "Look yonder, Sancho!" cried Don Quixote; "that knight whom thou see'st in the gilded arms, bearing in his shield a crowned lion couchant at the feet of a lady, is the valiant Laurealco, lord of the silver bridge. He in the armor powdered with flowers of gold, bearing three crows Argent in a field Azure, is the formidable Micocolembo, great duke of Quiracia. That other of a gigantic size that marches on his right, is the undaunted Brandabarbaran of Boliche, sovereign of the three Arabias; he is arrayed in a serpent's skin, and carries instead of a shield a huge gate, which they say belonged to the temple which Samson pulled down at his death, when he revenged himself upon his enemies. But cast thy eyes on

this side, Sancho, and at the head of the other army
see the victorious Timonel of Carcaiona, Prince of
New Biscay, whose armor is quartered Azure, Vert,
Or, and Argent, and who bears in his shield a cat
Or, in a field Gules, with these four letters, MIAU,
for a motto, being the beginning of his mistress's
name, the beautiful Miaulina, daughter to Alpheni-
quen, Duke of Algarva. That other monstrous
load upon the back of yonder wild horse, with arms
as white as snow, and a shield without any device,
is a Frenchman, now created knight, called Pierre
Papin, Baron of Utrique: he whom you see pricking that pyed courser's flanks with his armed heels,
is the mighty Duke of Nervia, Espartafilardo of the
wood, bearing in his shield a field of pure Azure,
powdered with Asparagus (*Esparrago* *) with this
motto in Castilian, *Restrea mi suerte; Thus trails,
or drags my fortune.*" And thus he went on, naming a great number of others in both armies, to
every one of whom his fertile imagination assigned
arms, colors, impresses and mottoes, as readily as
if they had really been that moment extant before
his eyes. And then proceeding without the least

---

* The gingle between the duke's name *Espartafilardo* and
Esparago (his arms) is a ridicule upon the foolish quibbles so
frequent in heraldry; and probably this whole catalogue is a
satire upon several great names and sounding titles in Spain,
whose owners were arrant beggars. The *trailing* of his fortune
may allude to the word *Esparto*, a sort of rush they make ropes
with. Or perhaps he was without a mistress, to which the sparagrass may allude; for in Spain they have a proverb, *Solo comes
el Esparago*: As solitary as sparagrass, because every one of
them springs up by itself.

hesitation : " That vast body," said he, " that is just opposite to us, is composed of several nations. There you see those who drink the pleasant stream of the famous Xanthus : there the mountaineers that till the Massilian fields : those that sift the pure gold of Arabia Felix : those that inhabit the renowned and delightful banks of Thermodoon. Yonder, those who so many ways sluice and drain the golden Pactolus for its precious sand. The Numidians, unsteady and careless of their promises. The Persians, excellent archers. The Medes and Parthians, who fight flying. The Arabs, who have no fixed habitations. The Scythians, cruel and savage, though fair-complexioned. The sooty Ethiopians, that bore their lips ; and a thousand other nations whose countenances I know, though I have forgotten their names. On the other side, come those whose country is watered with the crystal streams of Betis, shaded with olive trees. Those who bathe their limbs in the rich flood of the golden Tagus. Those whose mansions are laved by the profitable stream of the divine Genile. Those who range the verdant Tartesian meadows. Those who indulge their luxurious temper in the delicious pastures of Xerez. The wealthy inhabitants of Mancha, crowned with golden ears of corn. The ancient offspring of the Goths, cased in iron. Those who wanton in the lazy current of Pisverga. Those who feed their numerous flocks in the ample plains where the Guadiana, so celebrated for its hidden course, pursues its wandering race. Those who shiver with extremity of cold, on the woody Pyrenean hills, or on the hoary tops of the snowy Apen-

nine. In a word, all that Europe includes within
its spacious bounds, half a world in an army." It
is scarce to be imagined how many countries he
had ran over, how many nations he enumerated,
distinguishing every one by what is peculiar to them,
with an incredible vivacity of mind, and that still
in the puffy style of his fabulous books.

Sancho listened to all this romantic muster-roll
as mute as a fish, with amazement; all that he
could do was now and then to turn his head on this
side and t'other side, to see if he could discern the
knights and giants whom his master named. But
at length, not being able to discover any, " Why,"
cried he, "you had as good tell me it snows; the
devil of any knight, giant, or man, can I see, of all
those you talk of now; who knows but all this may
be witchcraft and spirits, like yesternight?" " How,"
replied Don Quixote; " dost thou not hear their
horses neigh, their trumpets sound, and their drums
beat?" " Not I," quoth Sancho, " I prick up my
ears like a sow in the beans, and yet I can hear
nothing but the bleating of sheep." Sancho might
justly say so indeed, for by this time the two flocks
were got very near them. " Thy fear disturbs thy
senses," said Don Quixote, " and hinders thee from
hearing and seeing right: but it is no matter ; withdraw to some place of safety, since thou art so terrified ; for I alone am sufficient to give the victory to
that side which I shall favor with my assistance."
With that he couched his lance, clapped spurs to Rozinante, and rushed like a thunder-bolt from the hillock into the plain. Sancho bawled after him as
loud as he could ; "Hold, sir !" cried Sancho ; " for

heaven's sake come back! What do you mean? as
sure as I am a sinner those you are going to maul
are nothing but poor harmless sheep. Come back, I
say. Woe to him that begot me! Are you mad, sir?
there are no giants, no knights, no cats, no aspara-
gus-gardens, no golden quarters nor what d'ye call
thems. Does the devil possess you? you are leaping
over the hedge before you come at the stile. You
are taking the wrong sow by the ear. Oh that I was
ever born to see this day!" But Don Quixote still
riding on, deaf and lost to good advice, out-roared his
expostulating squire. " Courage, brave knights!"
cried he; "march up, fall on, all you who fight under
the standard of the valiant Pentapolin with the naked arm: follow me, and you shall see how easily I
will revenge him on that infidel Alifanfaron of Taprobana;" and so saying, he charged the squadron
of sheep with that gallantry and resolution, that he
pierced, broke, and put it to flight in an instant,
charging through and through, not without a great
slaughter of his mortal enemies, whom he laid at his
feet, biting the ground and wallowing in their blood.
The shepherds, seeing their sheep go to wrack, called
out to him; till finding fair means ineffectual, they
unloosed their slings, and began to ply him with
stones as big as their fists. But the champion disdaining such a distant war, spite of their showers of
stones, rushed among the routed sheep, trampling
both the living and the slain in a most terrible manner, impatient to meet the general of the enemy, and
end the war at once. "Where, where art thou," cried
he, " proud Alifanfaron? Appear! see here a single
knight who seeks thee everywhere, to try now, hand

to hand, the boasted force of thy strenuous arm, and deprive thee of life, as a due punishment for the unjust war which thou hast audaciously waged with the valiant Pentapolin." Just as he had said this, while the stones flew about his ears, one unluckily hit upon his small ribs, and had like to have buried two of the shortest deep in the middle of his body. The knight thought himself slain, or at least desperately wounded; and therefore calling to mind his precious balsam, and pulling out his earthen jug, he clapped it to his mouth : but before he had swallowed a sufficient dose, souse comes another of those bitter almonds, that spoiled his draught, and hit him so pat upon the jug, hand, and teeth, that it broke the first, maimed the second, and struck out three or four of the last. These two blows were so violent, that the boisterous knight, falling from his horse, lay upon the ground as quiet as the slain; so that the shepherds, fearing he was killed, got their flock together with all speed, and carrying away their dead, which were no less than seven sheep, they made what haste they could out of harm's way, without looking any farther into the matter.

All this while Sancho stood upon the hill, where he was mortified upon the sight of this mad adventure. There he stamped and swore, and banned his master to the bottomless pit; he tore his beard for madness, and cursed the moment he first knew him : but seeing him at last knocked down, and settled, the shepherds being scampered, he thought he might venture to come down; and found him in a very ill plight, though not altogether senseless. " Ah! master," quoth he, " this comes of not taking my counsel. Did I not tell you it was a flock of sheep, and no army?" "Friend Sancho," replied Don Quixote, "know, it is an easy matter for necromancers to change the shapes of things as they please: thus that malicious enchanter, who is my inveterate enemy, to deprive me of the glory which he saw me ready to acquire, while I was reaping a full harvest of laurels, transformed in a moment the routed squadrons into sheep. If thou wilt not believe me, Sancho, yet do one thing for my sake; do but take thy ass, and follow those supposed sheep at a distance, and I dare engage thou shalt soon see them resume their former shapes, and appear such as I described them. But stay, do not go yet, for I want thy assistance: draw near, and see how many cheek-teeth and others I want, for by the dreadful pain in my jaws and gums, I fear there is a total dilapidation in my mouth." With that the knight opened his mouth as wide as he could, while the squire gaped to tell his grinders, with his snout almost in his chaps; but, just in that fatal moment, the balsam, that lay wambling and fretting in Don Quixote's stomach, came up with an unlucky hickup; and with the same violence that the powder flies out of a gun, all that he had in his stomach discharged itself upon the beard, face, eyes, and mouth, of the officious squire. " Santa Maria," cried poor Sancho, " what will become of me! my master is a dead man! he is vomiting his very heart's blood!" But he had hardly said this, when the color, smell, and taste, soon undeceived him; and, finding it to be his master's loathsome drench, it caused such a sudden rumbling in his maw, that, before he could turn his

head, he unladed the whole cargo of his stomach full
in his master's face, and put him in as delicate a
pickle as he was himself. Sancho having thus paid
him in his own coin, half blinded as he was, ran to
his ass, to take out something to clean himself and
his master; but when he came to look for his wallet, and found it missing, not remembering till
then that he had unhappily left it in the inn, he was
ready to run quite out of his wits: he stormed and
stamped, and cursed him worse than before, and
resolved with himself to let his master go to the
devil, and e'en trudge home by himself, though he
was sure to lose his wages, and his hopes of being
governor of the promised island.

Thereupon Don Quixote got up with much ado,
and clapping his left hand before his mouth, that
the rest of his loose teeth might not drop out, he
laid his right hand on Rozinante's bridle ; (for such
was the good-nature of the creature, that he had not
budged a foot from his master,) then he crept along
to Squire Sancho, that stood lolling on his ass's
pannel, with his face in the hollow of both his hands,
in a doleful moody melancholy fit. "Friend Sancho," said he, seeing him thus abandoned to sorrow,
"learn of me, that one man is no more than another,
if he do no more than what another does. All these
storms and hurricanes are but arguments of the approaching calm : better success will soon follow our
past calamities : good and bad fortune have their
vicissitudes ; and it is a maxim, that nothing violent
can last long : and therefore we may well promise
ourselves a speedy change in our fortune, since
our afflictions have extended their reign beyond the

usual stint: besides, thou oughtest not to afflict thyself so much for misfortunes, of which thou hast no share, but what friendship and humanity bid thee take." "How!" quoth Sancho, "have I no other share in them! was not he that was tossed in the blanket this morning the son of my father? and did not the wallet, and all that was in it, which I have lost, belong to the son of my mother?" "How," asked Don Quixote, "hast thou lost thy wallet?" "I don't know," said Sancho, "whether it is lost or no, but I am sure I can't tell what is become of it." "Nay then," replied Don Quixote, "I find we must fast to-day." "Ay, marry must we," quoth Sancho, "unless you take care to gather in these fields some of those roots and herbs which I have heard you say you know, and which use to help such unlucky knights-errant as yourself at a dead lift." "For all that," cried Don Quixote, "I would rather have at this time a good luncheon of bread, or a cake and two pilchards heads, than all the roots and simples in Dioscorides's herbal, and Doctor La- guna's supplement and commentary. I pray thee therefore get upon thy ass, good Sancho, and follow me once more; for God's providence, that relieves every creature, will not fail us, especially since we are about a work so much to his service; thou seest he even provides for the little flying insects in the air, the wormlings in the earth, and the spawnlings in the water; and, in his infinite mercy, he makes his sun shine on the righteous, and on the unjust, and rains upon the good and the bad."

"Many words won't fill a bushel," quoth San- cho, interrupting him; "you would make a better

preacher than a knight-errant, or I am plaguily out."
"Knights-errant," replied Don Quixote, "ought to
know all things : there have been such in former
ages, that have delivered as ingenious and learned
a sermon or oration at the head of an army, as if
they had taken their degrees at the university of
Paris : from which we may infer, that the lance
never dulled the pen, nor the pen the lance." —
"Well then," quoth Sancho, "for once let it be as
you would have it; let us even leave this unlucky
place, and seek out a lodging, where, I pray God,
there may be neither blankets, nor blanket-heavers,
nor hobgoblins, nor enchanted Moors; for before I
will be hampered as I have been, may I be cursed
with bell, book, and candle, if I don't give the trade
to the devil." "Leave all things to Providence,"
replied Don Quixote, " and for once lead which way
thou pleasest, for I leave it wholly to thy discretion
to provide us a lodging. But first, I pray thee, feel
a little how many teeth I want in my upper jaw on
the right side, for there I feel most pain." With
that Sancho, feeling with his finger in the knight's
mouth, " Pray, sir," quoth he, " how many grinders
did your worship use to have on that side?"
"Four," answered Don Quixote, " besides the eye-
tooth, all of them whole and sound." " Think well
on what you say," cried Sancho. " I say four," replied Don Quixote, " if there were not five; for I never
in all my life have had a tooth drawn or dropped
out, or rotted by the worm, or loosened by rheum."
" Bless me !" quoth Sancho, " why you have in this
nether jaw on this side but two grinders and a
stump ; and in that part of your upper jaw, never a

stump, and never a grinder; alas! all is levelled
there as smooth as the palm of one's hand." "Oh
unfortunate Don Quixote!" cried the knight; "I had
rather have lost an arm, so it were not my sword-
arm; for a mouth without cheek-teeth is like a mill
without a mill-stone, Sancho; and every tooth in a
man's head is more valuable than a diamond. But
we that profess this strict order of knight-errantry,
are all subject to these calamities; and therefore,
since the loss is irretrievable, mount, my trusty Sancho, and go thy own pace; I will follow thee."

Sancho obeyed, and led the way, still keeping the
road they were in; which being very much beaten,
promised to bring him soonest to a lodging. Thus
pacing along very softly, for Don Quixote's gums
and ribs would not suffer him to go faster, Sancho,
to divert his uneasy thoughts, resolved to talk to
him all the while of one thing or other, as the next
chapter will inform you.

CHAPTER V.

OF THE WISE DISCOURSE BETWEEN SANCHO AND HIS
MASTER; AS ALSO OF THE ADVENTURE OF THE DEAD
CORPSE, AND OTHER FAMOUS OCCURRENCES.

"Now, sir," quoth Sancho, "I can't help thinking, but that all the mishaps that have befallen us
of late, are a just judgment for the grievous sin you
have committed against the order of knighthood, in
not keeping the oath you swore, not to eat bread at
board, nor to have a merry bout with the queen,

and the Lord knows what more, until you had won what d'ye call him, the Moor's helmet, I think you named him." "Truly," answered Don Quixote, "thou art much in the right, Sancho; and to deal ingenuously with thee, I wholly forgot that: and now thou may'st certainly assure thyself, thou wert tost in a blanket for not remembering to put me in mind of it. However, I will take care to make due atonement; for knight-errantry has ways to conciliate all sorts of matters." "Why," quoth Sancho, "did I ever swear to mind you of your vow?" "It is nothing to the purpose," replied Don Quixote, "whether thou sworest or no: let it suffice that I think thou art not very clear from being accessory to the breach of my vow; and therefore to prevent the worst, there will be no harm in providing for a remedy." "Hark you then," cried Sancho, "be sure you don't forget your atonement, as you did your oath, lest those confounded hobgoblins come and maul me, and mayhap you too, for being a stubborn sinner."

Insensibly night overtook them before they could discover any lodging; and, which was worse, they were almost hunger-starved, all their provision being in the wallet which Sancho had unluckily left behind; and to complete their distress, there happened to them an adventure, or something that really looked like one.

While our benighted travellers went on dolefully in the dark, the knight very hungry, and the squire very sharp set, what should they see moving towards them but a great number of lights, that appeared like so many wandering stars. At this strange apparition, down sunk Sancho's heart at once, and even Don Quixote himself was not without some symptoms of surprise. Presently the one pulled to him his ass's halter, the other his horse's bridle, and both made a stop. They soon perceived that the lights made directly towards them, and the nearer they came the bigger they appeared. At the terrible wonder, Sancho shook and shivered every joint like one in a palsy, and Don Quixote's hair stood up on end: however, heroically shaking off the amazement which that sight stamped upon his soul, " Sancho," said he, " this must doubtless be a great and most perilous adventure, where I shall have occasion to exert the whole stock of my courage and strength." " Woe's me," quoth Sancho, " should this happen to be another adventure of ghosts, as I fear it is, where shall I find ribs to endure it ? " " Come all the fiends in hell," cried Don Quixote, " I will not suffer them to touch a hair of thy head. If they insulted thee lately, know there was then between thee and me a wall, over which I could not climb; but now we are in the open field, where I shall have liberty to make use of my sword." "Ay," quoth Sancho, "you may talk ; but should they bewitch you as they did before, what the devil would it avail us to be in the open field ? " " Come, Sancho," replied Don Quixote, " be of good cheer; the event will soon convince thee of the greatness of my valor." " Pray heaven it may," quoth Sancho; " I will do my best."

With that they rode a little out of the way, and, gazing earnestly at the lights, they soon discovered a great number of persons all in white.

At the dreadful sight, all poor Sancho's shuffling
courage basely deserted him; his teeth began to
chatter as if he had been in an ague fit, and as the
objects drew nearer his chattering increased. And
now they could plainly distinguish about twenty
men on horseback, all in white, with torches in their
hands, followed by a hearse covered over with black,
and six men in deep mourning, whose mules were
also in black down to their very heels. Those in
white moved slowly, murmuring from their lips something in a low and lamentable tone. This dismal
spectacle, at such a time of night, in the midst of
such a vast solitude, was enough to have shipwreck-
ed the courage of a stouter squire than Sancho, and
even of his master, had he been any other than Don
Quixote: but as his imagination straight suggested
to him, that this was one of those adventures of
which he had so often read in his books of chivalry,
the hearse appeared to him to be a litter, where lay
the body of some knight either slain or dangerously
wounded, the revenge of whose misfortunes was
reserved for his prevailing arm; and so without any
more ado, couching his lance, and seating himself
firm in the saddle, he posted himself in the middle
of the road, where the company were to pass. As
soon as they came near, " Stand," cried he to them
in a haughty tone, " whoever you be, and tell me
who you are, whence you come, whither you go,
and what you carry in that litter? for there is all the
reason in the world to believe, that you have either
done or received a great deal of harm; and it is requisite I should be informed of the matter, in order
either to punish you for the ill you have committed,

or else to revenge you of the wrong you have suffered." " Sir," answered one of the men in white,
" we are in haste; the inn is a great way off, and
we cannot stay to answer so many questions;" and
with that, spurring his mule, he moved forwards.
But Don Quixote, highly dissatisfied with the reply,
laid hold on the mule's bridle and stopped him:
" Stay," cried he, "proud, discourteous knight! Mend
your behavior, and give me instantly an account of
what I asked of you, or here I defy you all to mortal combat." — Now the mule, that was shy and
skittish, being thus rudely seized by the bridle, was
presently scared, and, rising up on her hinder legs,
threw her rider to the ground. Upon this one of the
footmen that belonged to the company gave Don
Quixote ill language ; which so incensed him, that,
being resolved to be revenged upon them all, in a
mighty rage he flew at the next he met, who happened to be one of the mourners. Him he threw to
the ground very much hurt; and then turning to
the rest with a wonderful agility, he fell upon them
with such fury, that he presently put them all to
flight. You would have thought Rozinante had
wings at that time, so active and so fierce he then
approved himself.

It was not indeed for men unarmed, and naturally
fearful, to maintain the field against such an enemy ;
no wonder then if the gentlemen in white were immediately dispersed. Some ran one way, some an
other, crossing the plain with their lighted torches,
you would now have taken them for a parcel of
frolicsome masqueraders, gambling and scouring on
a carnival night. As for the mourners, they, poor

men, were so muffled up in their long cumbersome
cloaks, that, not being able to make their party
good, nor defend themselves, they were presently
routed, and ran away like the rest, the rather, for
that they thought it was no mortal creature, but the
devil himself, that was come to fetch away the dead
body which they were accompanying to the grave.
All the while Sancho was lost in admiration and
astonishment, charmed with the sight of his master's
valor; and now concluded him to be the formidable
champion he boasted himself.

After this the knight, by the light of a torch that
lay burning upon the ground, perceiving the man
who was thrown by his mule lying near it, he rode
up to him, and, setting his lance to his throat
" Yield," cried he, " and beg thy life, or thou diest."
" Alas, sir," cried the other, " what need you ask
me to yield? I am not able to stir, for one of my
legs is broken; and I beseech you, if you are a
Christian, do not kill me. I am a master of arts,
and in holy orders; it would be a heinous sacrilege
to take away my life." " What a devil brought you
hither then, if you are a clergyman?" cried Don
Quixote. " What else but my ill fortune?" replied
the supplicant. "A worse hovers over thy head,"
cried Don Quixote, " and threatens thee, if thou dost
not answer this moment to every particular question I ask." " I will, I will, sir," replied the other;
" and first I must beg your pardon for saying I was
a master of arts, for I have yet but taken my bachelor's degree. My name is Alonzo Lopez: I am of
Alcovendas, and came now from the town of Baeza,
with eleven other clergymen, the same that now ran

away with the torches. We were going to Segovia
to bury the corpse of a gentleman of that town, who
died at Baeza, and lies now in yonder hearse."
" And who killed him? " asked Don Quixote. —
" Heaven, with a pestilential fever," answered the
other. " If it be so," said Don Quixote, " I am
discharged of revenging his death. Since Heaven
did it, there is no more to be said; had it been its
pleasure to have taken me off so, I too must have
submitted. I would have you informed, reverend
sir, that I am a knight of La Mancha, my name
Don Quixote; my employment is to visit all parts of
the world in quest of adventures, to right and relieve
injured innocence, and punish oppression." " Truly,
sir," replied the clergyman, " I do not understand
how you can call that to right and relieve men,
when you break their legs: you have made that
crooked which was right and straight before; and
heaven knows whether it can ever be set right
as long as I live. Instead of relieving the injured,
I fear you have injured me past relief; and while
you seek adventures, you have made me meet with
a very great misadventure." * "All things," replied
Don Quixote, "are not blessed alike with a prosperous event, good Mr. Bachelor : you should have
taken care not to have thus gone a processioning in
these desolate plains at this suspicious time of night,
with your white surplices, burning torches, and sable
weeds, like ghosts and goblins, that went about to

* The author's making the bachelor quibble so much, under
such improper circumstances, was designed as a ridicule upon
the younger students of the universities, who are apt to indulge
in this species of wit.

scare people out of their wits : for I could not omit doing the duty of my profession, nor would I have forborne attacking you, though you had really been all Lucifer's infernal crew; for such I took you to be, and till this moment could have no better opinion of you."

" Well, sir," said the bachelor, " since my bad fortune has so ordered it, I must desire you, as you are a knight-errant, who have made mine so ill an errand, to help me to get from under my mule, for it lies so heavy upon me, that I cannot get my foot out of the stirrup." " Why did not you acquaint me sooner with your grievance ?" cried Don Quixote; " I might have talked on till to-morrow morning and never have thought on it." With that he called Sancho, who made no great haste, for he was much better employed in rifling a load of choice provisions, which the holy men carried along with them on a sumpter-mule. He had spread his coat on the ground, and having laid on it as much food as it would hold, he wrapped it up like a bag, and laid the booty on his ass; and then away he ran to his master, and helped him to set the bachelor upon his mule: after which he gave him his torch, and Don Quixote bade him follow his company, and excuse him for his mistake, though, all things considered, he could not avoid doing what he had done. "And, sir," quoth Sancho, " if the gentlemen would know who it was that so well threshed their jackets, you may tell them it was the famous Don Quixote de la Mancha, otherwise called the Knight of the Woful Figure."

When the bachelor was gone, Don Quixote ask-

ed Sancho why he called him the Knight of the
Woful Figure? " I'll tell you why," quoth Sancho; " I have been staring upon you this pretty
while by the light of that unlucky priest's torch, and
may I never stir if ever I set eyes on a more dismal
figure in my born days; and I can't tell what should
be the cause on't, unless your being tired after this
fray, or the want of your worship's teeth." " That
is not the reason," cried Don Quixote; " no, Sancho, I rather conjecture that the sage who is com-
missioned by fate to register my achievements,
thought it convenient I should assume a new appel·
lation, as all the knights of yore; for one was called
the Knight of the Burning Sword, another of the
Unicorn, a third of the Phœnix, a fourth the Knight
of the Damsels, another of the Griffin, and another
the Knight of Death; by which by-names and distinctions they were known all over the globe. Therefore, doubtless, that learned sage, my historian, has
inspired thee with the thought of giving me that
additional appellation of the Knight of the Woful
Figure: and accordingly I assume the name, and
intend henceforward to be distinguished by that
denomination. And, that it may seem the more
proper, I will with the first opportunity have a most
woful face painted on my shield." " On my
word," quoth Sancho, " you may even save the
money, and instead of having a woful face painted,
you need no more but only show your own. I am
but in jest, as a body may say; but what with the
want of your teeth, and what with hunger, you look
so queerly and so wofully, that no painter can draw
you a figure so fit for your purpose as your wor-

ship's." This merry conceit of Sancho extorted a
smile from his master's austere countenance: however, he persisted in his resolution about the name
and the picture ; and after a pause, a sudden thought
disturbing his conscience, "Sancho," cried he, " I
am afraid of being excommunicated for having laid
violent hands upon a man in holy orders, *Juxta
illud; si quis suadente diabolo,* &c. But yet, now
I think better on it, I never touched him with my
hands, but only with my lance ; besides, I did not
in the least suspect I had to do with priests, whom
I honor and revere as every good Catholic and
faithful Christian ought to do, but rather took them
to be evil spirits. Well, let the worst come to the
worst, I remember what befell the Cid Ruy-Dias,
when he broke to pieces the chair of a king's ambassador in the pope's presence, for which he was
excommunicated; which did not hinder the worthy
Rodrigo de Vivar from behaving himself that day
like a valorous knight, and a man of honor."

This said, Don Quixote was for visiting the hearse,
to see whether what was in it were only dead bones;
but Sancho would not let him. " Sir," quoth he,
" you are come off now with a whole skin, and
much better than you have done hitherto. Who
knows but these same fellows that are now scampered off, may chance to bethink themselves what a
shame it is for them to have suffered themselves to
be thus routed by a single man, and so come back,
and fall upon us all at once ? Then we shall have
work enough upon our hands. The ass is in good
case ; there's a hill not far off, and our bellies cry
cupboard. Come, let us even get out of harm's

way, and not let the plough stand to catch a mouse, as the saying is; to the grave with the dead, and the living to the bread." With that he put on a dog-trot with his ass; and his master, bethinking himself that he was in the right, put on after him without replying.

After they had rid a little way, they came to a valley that lay skulking between two hills. There they alighted, and Sancho having opened his coat and spread it on the grass, with the provision which he had bundled up in it, our two adventurers fell to; and their stomachs being sharpened with the sauce of hunger, they eat their breakfast, dinner, afternoon's luncheon, and supper, all at the same time, feasting themselves with variety of cold meats, which you may be sure were the best that could be got; the priests who had brought it for their own eating, being like the rest of their coat, none of the worst stewards for their bellies, and knowing how to make much of themselves.

But now they began to grow sensible of a very great misfortune, and such a misfortune as was bemoaned by poor Sancho, as one of the saddest that ever could befall him; for they found they had not one drop of wine or water to wash down their meat and quench their thirst, which now scorched and choaked them worse than hunger had pinched them before. However, Sancho, considering they were in a place where the grass was fresh and green, said to his master —— what you shall find in the following chapter.

CHAPTER VI.

OF A WONDERFUL ADVENTURE ACHIEVED BY THE VALOROUS
DON QUIXOTE DE LA MANCHA; THE LIKE NEVER COM-
PASSED WITH LESS DANGER BY ANY OF THE MOST FAMOUS
KNIGHTS IN THE WORLD.

"The grass is so fresh," quoth Sancho, half
choaked with thirst, "that I dare lay my life we
shall light of some spring or stream hereabouts;
therefore, sir, let us look, I beseech you, that we
may quench this confounded drought, that plagues
our throats ten times worse than hunger did our
guts." Thereupon Don Quixote, leading Rozinante
by the bridle, and Sancho his ass by the halter, after
he had laid up the reversion of their meal, they went
feeling about, only guided by their guess; for it
was so dark they scarce could see their hands.
They had not gone above two hundred paces before
they heard a noise of a great waterfall; which was
to them the most welcome sound in the world: but
then listening with great attention to know on which-
side the grateful murmur came, they on a sudden
heard another kind of noise that strangely allayed
the pleasure of the first, especially in Sancho, who
was naturally fearful, and pusillanimous. They
heard a terrible din of obstreperous blows, struck
regularly, and a more dreadful rattling of chains
and irons, which, together with the roaring of the
waters, might have filled any other heart but Don
Quixote's with terror and amazement. Add to this
the horrors of a dark night and solitude, in an un-

known place, the loud rustling of the leaves of some
lofty trees under which fortune brought them at the
same unlucky moment, the whistling of the wind,
which concurred with the other dismaying sounds ; .
the fall of the waters, the thundering thumps, and
the clanking of chains aforesaid. The worst, too,
was, that the blows were redoubled without ceasing,
the wind blowed on, and daylight was far distant.
But then it was Don Quixote, secured by his intrepidity (his inseparable companion,) mounted his
Rozinante, braced his shield, brandished his lance,
and showed a soul unknowing fear, and superior to
danger and fortune.

"Know, Sancho," cried he, "I was born in this
iron age, to restore the age of gold, or the golden
age, as some choose to call it. I am the man for
whom fate has reserved the most dangerous and
formidable attempts, the most stupendous and glorious adventures, and the most valorous feats of
arms. I am the man who must revive the order of
the Round Table, the twelve peers of France, and
the nine worthies, and efface the memory of your
Platyrs, your Tablantes, your Olivantes, and your
Tirantes. Now must your Knights of the Sun, your
Belianises, and all the numerous throng of famous
heroes, and knights-errant of former ages, see the
glory of all their most dazzling actions eclipsed and
darkened by more illustrious exploits. Do but observe, O thou my faithful squire, what a multifarious
assemblage of terrors surrounds us ! A horrid darkness, a doleful solitude, a confused rustling of
leaves, a dismal rattling of chains, a howling of the
winds, an astonishing noise of cataracts, that seem

to fall with a boisterous rapidity from the steep mountains of the moon, a terrible sound of redoubled blows, still wounding our ears like furious thunderclaps, and a dead and universal silence of those things that might buoy up the sinking courage of frail mortality. In this extremity of danger, Mars himself might tremble with the affright: yet I, in the midst of all these unutterable alarms, still remain undaunted and unshaken. These are but incentives to my valor, and but animate my heart the more; it grows too big and mighty for my breast, and leaps at the approach of this threatening adventure, as formidable as it is like to prove. Come, girt Rozinante straiter, and then Providence protect thee: thou mayest stay for me here; but if I do not return in three days, go back to our village; and from thence, for my sake, to Toboso, where thou shalt say to my incomparable Lady Dulcinea, that her faithful knight fell a sacrifice to love and honor, while he attempted things that might have made him worthy to be called her adorer."

When Sancho heard his master talk thus, he fell a weeping in the most pitiful manner in the world. " Pray, sir," cried he, "why will you thus run yourself into mischief? Why need you go about this rueful misventure? It is main dark, and there is never a living soul sees us; we have nothing to do but to sheer off, and get out of harm's way, though we were not to drink a drop these three days. Who is there to take notice of our flinching? I have heard our parson, whom you very well know, say in his pulpit, that he who seeks danger, perishes therein : and therefore we should not tempt hea-

ven by going about a thing that we cannot compass but by a miracle. Is it not enough, think
you, that it has preserved you from being tossed
in a blanket as I was, and made you come off safe
and sound from among so many goblins that went
with the dead man? If all this won't work upon
that hard heart of yours, do but think of me, and
rest yourself assured, that when once you have left
your poor Sancho, he will be ready to give up the
ghost for very fear, to the next that will come for
it: I left my house and home, my wife, children,
and all to follow you, hoping to be the better for
it, and not the worse; but as covetousness breaks
the sack, so has it broke me and my hopes; for
while I thought myself cocksure of that unlucky
and accursed island, which you so often promised
me, in lieu thereof you drop me here in a strange
place. Dear master, don't be so hardhearted; and
if you won't be persuaded not to meddle with this
ungracious adventure, do but put it off till day-
break, to which, according to the little skill I learned
when a shepherd, it cannot be above three hours;
for the muzzle of the lesser bear is just over our
heads, and makes midnight in the line of the left
arm." "How! canst thou see the muzzle of the
bear?" asked Don Quixote; "there's not a star to
be seen in the sky." "That's true," quoth Sancho;
"but fear is sharp-sighted, and can see things under
ground, and much more in the skies." "Let day
come, or not come, it is all one to me," cried the
champion; "it shall never be recorded of Don
Quixote, that either tears or entreaties could make
him neglect the duty of a knight. Then, Sancho,

say no more; for heaven, that has inspired me with a resolution of attempting this dreadful adventure, will certainly take care of me and thee : come quickly, girt my steed, and stay here for me; for you will shortly hear of me again, either alive or dead."

Sancho, finding his master obstinate, and neither to be moved with tears nor good advice, resolved to try a trick of policy to keep him there till daylight : and accordingly, while he pretended to fasten the girths, he slily tied Rozinante's hinder-legs with his ass's halter, without being so much as suspected : so that when Don Quixote thought to have moved forwards, he found his horse would not go a step without leaping, though he spurred him on smartly. Sancho, perceiving his plot took, " Look you, sir," quoth he, " heaven's on my side, and won't let Rozinante budge a foot forwards; and now if you will still be spurring him, I dare pawn my life, it will be but striving against the stream ; or, as the saying is, but kicking against the pricks." Don Quixote fretted, and chafed, and raved, and was in a desperate fury, to find his horse so stubborn ; but at last, observing that the more he spurred and galled his sides, the more restive he proved, he resolved, though very unwillingly, to have patience until it was light. " Well," said he, " since Rozinante will not leave this place, I must tarry in it until the dawn, though its slowness will cost me some sighs." " You shall not need to sigh nor be melancholy," quoth Sancho, " for I will undertake to tell you stories until it be day; unless your worship had rather get off your horse, and take a nap upon the green grass, as knights-errant are wont, that you may be the fresher, and the better able in the morning to go through that monstrous adventure that waits for you." " What dost thou mean by thus alighting and sleeping?" replied Don Quixote; "thinkest thou I am one of those carpet-knights, that abandon themselves to sleep and lazy ease, when danger is at hand? no, sleep thou, thou art born to sleep; or do what thou wilt. As for myself, I know what I have to do." " Good sir," quoth Sancho, " do not put yourself into a passion; I meant no such thing, not I." Saying this, he clapped one of his hands upon the pommel of Rozinante's saddle, and the other upon the crupper, and thus he stood embracing his master's left thigh, not daring to budge an inch, for fear of the blows that dinned continually in his ears. Don Quixote then thought fit to claim his promise, and desired him to tell some of his stories to help to pass away the time.

" Sir," quoth Sancho, " I am wofully frighted, and have no heart to tell stories; however, I will do my best; and, now I think on it, there is one come into my head, which if I can but hit on it right, and nothing happens to put me out, is the best story you ever heard in your life; therefore listen, for I am going to begin. — In the days of yore, when it was as it was, good betide us all and evil to him that evil seeks. And here, sir, you are to take notice that they of old did not begin their tales in an ordinary way; for it was a saying of a wise man whom they called Cato the Roman Tonsor,* that said, Evil to him that evil seeks, which

* A mistake for Cato, the Roman Censor.

is as pat for your purpose as a ring for the finger,
that you may neither meddle nor make, nor seek
evil and mischief for the nonce, but rather get out
of harm's way, for nobody forces us to run into the
mouth of all the devils in hell that wait for us yonder." " Go on with the story, Sancho," cried Don
Quixote, " and leave the rest to my discretion." — " I
say then," quoth Sancho, " that in a country town
in Estremadura, there lived a certain shepherd,
goat-herd I should have said; which goat-herd, as
the story has it, was called Lope Ruyz; and this
Lope Ruyz was in love with a shepherdess, whose
name was Toralva; the which shepherdess, whose
name was Toralva, was the daughter of a wealthy
grazier; and this wealthy grazier "——" If thou
goest on at this rate," cried Don Quixote, " and
makest so many needless repetitions, thou wilt not
have told thy story these two days. Pray thee tell it
concisely, and like a man of sense, or let it alone."
" I tell it you," quoth Sancho, " as all stories are
told in our country, and I cannot for the blood of
me tell it in any other way, nor is it fit I should
alter the custom." " Why then tell it how thou
wilt," replied Don Quixote, " since my ill fortune
forces me to stay and hear thee."

" Well then, dear sir," quoth Sancho, " as I was
saying, this same shepherd — goat-herd I should
have said — was woundily in love with that same
shepherdess Toralva, who was a well trussed, round,
crummy, strapping wench, coy and foppish and
somewhat like a man, for she had a kind of beard
on her upper lip; methinks I see her now standing
before me." " Then I suppose thou knewest her,"

said Don Quixote. " Not I," answered Sancho, " I never set eyes on her in my life; but he that told me the story said this was so true, that I might vouch it for a real truth, and even swear I had seen it all myself. Well, —— but, as you know, days go and come, and time and straw makes medlars ripe; so it happened, that after several days coming and going, the devil, who seldom lies dead in a ditch, but will have a finger in every pie, so brought it about, that the shepherd set out with his sweetheart, insomuch that the love he bore her turned into dudgeon and ill will; and the cause was, by report of some mischievous tale-carriers that bore no good will to either party, for that the shepherd thought her no better than she should be, a little loose in the hilts, and free of her hips.* Thereupon being grievous in the dumps about it, and now bitterly hating her, he even resolved to leave that country to get out of her sight: for now, as every dog has his day, the wench perceiving he came no longer a suitoring to her, but rather tossed his nose at her, and shunned her, she began to love him and doat upon him like any thing." " That is the nature of women," cried Don Quixote, " not to love when we love them, and to love when we love them not. But go on."

" The shepherd then gave her the slip," continued Sancho, " and driving his goats before him, went

* In the original it runs, She gave him a certain quantity of little jealousies, above measure, and within the prohibited degrees: alluding to certain measures not to be exceeded (in Spain) on pain of forfeiture and corporal punishment, as swords above such a standard, &c.

trudging through Estremadura, in his way to Portugal. But Toralva, having a long nose, soon smelt his design, and then what does she do, think ye, but comes after him barefoot and barelegged, with a pilgrim's staff in her hand, and a wallet at her back, wherein they say she carried a piece of looking-glass, half a comb, a broken pot with paint, and I don't know what other trinkum-trankums to prink herself up. But let her carry what she would, it is no bread and butter of mine; the short and the long is, that they say the shepherd with his goats got at last to the river Guadiana, which happened to be overflowed at that time, and what was worse than ill luck, there was neither boat nor bark to ferry him over; which vexed him the more because he perceived Teralva at his heels, and he feared to be teased and plagued with her weeping and wailing. At last he spied a fisherman, in a little boat, but so little it was, that it would carry but one man and one goat at a time. Well, for all that, he called to the fisherman, and agreed with him to carry him and his three hundred goats over the water. The bargain being struck, the fisherman came with his boat, and carried over one goat; then he rowed back and fetched another goat, and after that another goat. Pray sir," quoth Sancho, "be sure you keep a good account how many goats the fisherman ferries over; for if you happen but to miss one, my tale is at an end, and the devil a word I have more to say. Well then, whereabouts was I? Ho! I ha't — Now the landing-place on the other side was very muddy and slippery, which made the fisherman be a long while in going and coming; yet for all that, he took heart

of grace, and made shift to carry over one goat,
then another, and then another." " Come," said Don
Quixote, "we will suppose he has landed them all
on the other side of the river; for as thou goest on,
one by one, we shall not have done these twelve
months." " Pray, let me go on in my own way,"
quoth Sancho. " How many goats are got over already?" " Nay, how the devil can I tell?" replied
Don Quixote. " There it is!" quoth Sancho; "did
not I bid you keep count? on my word the tale is
at an end, and now you may go whistle for the
rest." " Ridiculous," cried Don Quixote : "pray thee
is there no going on with the story unless I know
exactly how many goats are wafted over?" " No,
marry is there not," quoth Sancho, "for as soon as
you answered, that you could not tell, the rest of
the story quite and clean slipped out of my head;
and in troth it is a thousand pities, for it was a special one." " So then," cried Don Quixote, "the story's
ended?" "Ay, marry is it," quoth Sancho, " it is no
more to be fetched to life than my dead mother."
" Upon my honor," cried Don Quixote, " a most extraordinary story, and told and concluded in as extraordinary a manner! it is a nonsuch, I assure ye;
though truly I expected no less from a man of such
uncommon parts. Alas! poor Sancho, I am afraid
this dreadful noise has turned thy brain." " That
may well be," quoth Sancho; "but as for my story
I am sure there is nothing more to be said, for
where you lose the account of the goats, there it
ends." " Let it be so," replied Don Quixote; "but
now let us try whether Rozinante be in humor to
march. " With that he gave Rozinante two spurs,

and the high-mettled jade answered with one bound, and then stood stock still, not having the command of his hind legs.

Much about this time, whether it were the coolness of the night, or that Sancho had eaten some loosening food at supper, or, which seems more probable, that nature, by a regular impulse, gave him notice of her desire to perform a certain function that follows the third concoction; it seems, honest Sancho found himself urged to do that which nobody could do for him; but such were his fears that he durst not for his life stir the breadth of a straw from his master; yet to think of bearing the intolerable load that pressed him so, was to him as great an impossibility. In this perplexing exigency (with leave be it spoken) he could find no other expedient but to take his right hand from the crupper of the saddle, and softly untying his breeches, let them drop down to his heels; having done this, he as silently took up his shirt, and exposed his posteriors, which were none of the least, to the open air; but the main point was how to ease himself of this terrible burden without making a noise; to which purpose he clutched his teeth close, screwed up his face, shrunk up his shoulders, and held in his breath as much as possible: yet see what misfortunes attend the best projected undertakings! When he had almost compassed his design, he could not hinder an obstreperous sound, very different from those that caused his fear, from unluckily bursting out. "Hark!" cried Don Quixote, who heard it, "what noise is that, Sancho?" "Some new adventures, I warrant you," quoth Sancho, "for ill luck, you know, seldom comes alone." Having passed off the thing thus, he even ventured on another strain, and did it so cleverly, that without the least rumor or noise, his business was done effectually, to the unspeakable ease of his body and mind.

But Don Quixote having the sense of smelling as perfect as that of hearing, and Sancho standing so very near, or rather tacked to him, certain fumes that ascended perpendicularly, began to regale his nostrils with a smell not so grateful as amber. No sooner the unwelcome steams disturbed him, but having recourse to the common remedy, he stopped his nose, and then, with a snuffling voice, "Sancho," said he, "thou art certainly in great bodily fear." "So I am," quoth Sancho; "but what makes your worship perceive it now more than you did before?" "Because," replied Don Quixote, "thou smellest now more unsavorily than thou didst before." "Hoh! that may be," quoth Sancho; "but whose fault is that? you may e'en thank yourself for it. Why do you lead me a wild-goose chase, and bring me at such unseasonable hours to such dangerous places? you know I am not used to it." "Pray thee," said Don Quixote, still holding his nose, "get thee three or four steps from me; and for the future take more care, and know your distance; for I find my familiarity with thee has bred contempt." "I warrant," quoth Sancho, "you think I have been doing something I should not have done." "Come, say no more," cried Don Quixote; "the more thou stir it the worse it will be."

This discourse, such as it was, served them to

pass away the night; and now Sancho, seeing the morning arise, thought it time to untie Rozinante's feet, and do up his breeches; and he did both with so much caution, that his master suspected nothing. As for Rozinante, he no sooner felt himself at liberty, but he seemed to express his joy by pawing the ground; for, with his leave be it spoken, he was a stranger to curvetting and prancing. Don Quixote also took it as a good omen, that his steed was now ready to move, and believed that it was a signal given him by kind fortune, to animate him to give birth to the approaching adventure.

Now had Aurora displayed her rosy mantle over the blushing skies, and dark night withdrawn her sable veil; all objects stood confessed to human eyes, and Don Quixote could now perceive he was under some tall chestnut trees, whose thick-spreading boughs diffused an awful gloom around the place, but he could not yet discover whence proceeded the dismal sound of those incessant strokes. Therefore, being resolved to find it out, once more he took his leave of Sancho, with the same injunctions as before; adding, withal, that he should not trouble himself about the recompense of his services, for he had taken care of that in his will, which he had providently made before he left home; but if he came off victorious from this adventure, he might most certainly expect to be gratified with the promised island. Sancho could not forbear blubbering again to hear these tender expressions of his master, and resolved not to leave him till he had finished this enterprise. And from that deep concern, and this nobler resolution to attend him, the author of

this history infers, that the squire was something
of a gentleman by descent, or at least the offspring
of the old Christians.*   Nor did his good-nature
fail to move his master more than he was willing to
show, at a time when it behooved him to shake off
all softer thoughts; for now he rode towards the
place whence the noise of the blows and the water
seemed to come, while Sancho trudged after him,
leading by the halter the inseparable companion of
his good and bad fortune.

After they had gone a pretty way under a pleasant covert of chestnut-trees, they came into a
meadow adjoining to certain rocks, from whose top
there was a great fall of waters.   At the foot of
those rocks they discovered certain old ill-contrived
buildings, that rather looked like ruins than inhabited houses; and they perceived that the terrifying
noise of the blows, which yet continued, issued out
of that place.   When they came nearer, even pa-
tient Rozinante himself started at the dreadful
sound; but, being heartened and pacified by his
master, he was at last prevailed with to draw nearer
and nearer with wary steps; the knight recommending himself all the way most devoutly to his
Dulcinea, and now and then also to heaven, in
short ejaculations.   As for Sancho, he stuck close
to his master, peeping all the way through Rozinante's legs, to see if he could perceive what he
dreaded to find out.   When, a little farther, at the
doubling of the point of a rock, they plainly dis-

* In contradiction to the Jewish or Moorish families, of which
there were many in Spain.

covered (kind reader, do not take it amiss) six huge fulling-mill hammers, which interchangeably thumping several pieces of cloth, made the terrible noise that caused all Don Quixote's anxieties and Sancho's tribulation that night.

Don Quixote was struck dumb at this unexpected sight, and was ready to drop from his horse with shame and confusion. Sancho stared upon him, and saw him hang down his head, with a desponding dejected countenance, like a man quite dispirited with this cursed disappointment. At the the same time he looked upon Sancho, and seeing by his eyes, and his cheeks swelled with laughter, that he was ready to burst, he could not forbear laughing himself, in spite of all his vexation; so that Sancho, seeing his master begin, immediately gave a loose to his mirth, and broke out into such a fit of laughing, that he was forced to hold his sides with both his knuckles, for fear of bursting his aching paunch. Four times he ceased, and four times renewed his obstreperous laughing; which sauciness Don Quixote began to resent with great indignation; and the more when Sancho, in a jeering tone, presumed to ridicule him with his own words, repeating part of the vain speech he made when first they heard the noise; " Know, Sancho, I was born in this iron age to restore the age of gold. I am the man for whom heaven has reserved the most dangerous and glorious adventures," &c. Thus he went on, till his master, dreadfully enraged at his insolence, hit him two such blows on the shoulders with his lance, that, had they fallen upon his head, they had saved Don Quixote the trouble of paying him his wages, whatever he must have done to his heirs. Thereupon Sancho, finding his jest turn to earnest, begged pardon with all submission : " Mercy, good your worship," cried he, " spare my bones, I beseech you ! I meant no harm, I did but joke a little." "And because you joke, I do not," cried Don Quixote. " Come hither, good Mr. Jester, you who pretend to rally ; tell me, had this been a dangerous adventure, as well as it proves only a false alarm, have I not shown resolution enough to undertake and finish it ? Am I, who am a knight, bound to know the meaning of every mechanic noise, and distinguish between sound and sound ? Besides, it might happen, as really it is, that I had never seen a fulling-mill before, though thou, like a base scoundrel as thou art, wert born and brought up among such mean implements of drudgery. But let the six fulling-hammers be transformed into so many giants, and then set them at me one by one, or all together ; and if I do not lay them all at my feet with their heels upwards, then I will give thee leave to exercise thy ill-bred raillery as much as thou pleasest."

" Good your worship," quoth Sancho, " talk no more on it, I beseech you ; I confess I carried the jest too far. But now all is hushed and well, pray tell me in sober sadness, as you hope to speed in all adventures, and come off safe and sound as from this, don't you think but that the fright we were in, I mean that I was in, would be a good subject for people to make sport with ? " " I grant it," answered Don Quixote, " but I would not have it told ; for all people are not so discreet as to place things, or look upon them, in the position in which they should be considered." "I will say that for you," quoth Sancho, "you have shown you understand how to place things in their right position, when, aiming at my head, you hit my shoulders; had not I ducked a little on one side, I had been in a fine condition! but let that pass, it will wash out in the bucking. I have heard my grannam say, that man loves thee well who makes thee to weep. Good masters may be hasty sometimes with a servant, but presently after a hard word or two they commonly give him a pair of cast breeches : what they give after a basting, heaven knows; all I can tell is, that knights-errant, after bastinadoes, give you some cast island, or some old fashioned kingdom upon the main land."

"Fortune," said Don Quixote, "will perhaps order every thing thou hast said to come to pass; therefore, Sancho, I pray thee, think no more of my severity; thou knowest a man cannot always command the first impulse of his passions. On the other side, let me advise thee not to be so saucy for the future, and not to assume that strange familiarity with me which is so unbecoming in a servant. I protest, in such a vast number of books of knight-errantry as I have read, I never found that any squire was ever allowed so great a freedom of speech with his master as thou takest with me; and truly, I look upon it to be a great fault in us both; in thee for disrespecting me, and in me for not making myself be more respected. Gandalin, Amadis de Gaul's squire, though he was earl of the Firm Island, yet never spoke to his master but with cap

in hand, his head bowed, and his body half bent,
after the Turkish manner.   But what 'shall we say
of Gasabal, Don Galaor's squire, who was such a
strict observer of silence, that, to the honor of his
marvellous taciturnity, he gave the author occasion
to mention his name but once in that voluminous
authentic history?   From all this, Sancho, I would
have thee make this observation, that there ought to
be a distance kept between the master and the man,
the knight and the squire. Therefore, once more I tell
thee, let us live together for the future more according to the due decorum of our respective degrees,
without giving one another any further vexation on
this account; for after all, it will always be the
worse for you, on whatsoever occasion we happen
to disagree.   As for the rewards I promised you,
they will come in due time; and should you be
disappointed that way, you have your salary to
trust to, as I have told you."

" You say very well," quoth Sancho; " but now,
sir, suppose no rewards should come, and I should
be forced to stick to my wages, I would fain know
how much a squire-errant used to earn in the days
of yore? Did they go by the month or by the day,
like our laborers?"   " I do not think," replied Don
Quixote, " they ever went by the hire, but rather
that they trusted to their master's generosity.   And
if I have assigned thee wages in my will, which I
left sealed up at home, it was only to prevent the
worst, because I do not know yet what success I
may have in chivalry in these depraved times; and
I would not have my soul suffer in the other world
for such a trifling matter; for there is no state of

life so subject to dangers as that of a knight-errant."
" Like enough," quoth Sancho, " when merely the
noise of the hammers of a fulling-mill is able to
trouble and disturb the heart of such a valiant knight
as your worship! But you may be sure I will not
hereafter so much as offer to open my lips to jibe
or joke at your doings, but always stand in awe of
you, and honor you as my lord and master." " By
doing so," replied Don Quixote, " thy days shall be
long on the face of the earth ; for next to our parents,
we ought to respect our masters, as if they were
our fathers."

CHAPTER VII.

OF THE HIGH ADVENTURE AND CONQUEST OF MAMBRINO'S
HELMET, WITH OTHER EVENTS RELATING TO OUR INVIN-
CIBLE KNIGHT.

At the same time it began to rain, and Sancho
would fain have taken shelter in the fulling-mills ;
but Don Quixote had conceived such an antipathy
against them for the shame they had put upon him,
that he would by no means be prevailed with to go
in ; and turning to the right hand he struck into a
highway, where they had not gone far before he
discovered a horseman, who wore upon his head
something that glittered like gold. The knight had
no sooner spied him, but, turning to his squire,
" Sancho," cried he, " I believe there is no proverb
but what is true ; they are all so many sentences
and maxims drawn from experience, the universal

mother of sciences : for instance, that saying, That
where one door shuts, another opens : thus fortune,
that last night deceived us with the false prospect
of an adventure, this morning offers us a real one
to make us amends; and such an adventure, Sancho, that if I do not gloriously succeed in it, I shall
have now no pretence to an excuse, no darkness, no
unknown sounds to impute my disappointment to :
in short, in all probability yonder comes the man
who wears on his head Mambrino's helmet,* and
thou knowest the vow I have made." "Good sir,"
quoth Sancho, "mind what you say, and take heed
what you do; for I would willingly keep my carcass and the case of my understanding from being
pounded, mashed, and crushed with fulling-hammers." "Hell take the blockhead!" cried Don
Quixote; "is there no difference between a helmet
and a fulling-mill?" "I don't know," saith Sancho,
"but I am sure, were I suffered to speak my mind
now as I was wont, mayhap I would give you such
main reasons, that yourself should see you are wide
of the matter." "How can I be mistaken, thou
eternal misbeliever?" cried Don Quixote; "dost
thou not see that knight that comes riding up
directly towards us upon a dapple-gray steed, with
a helmet of gold on his head?" "I see what I see,"
replied Sancho, "and the devil of any thing I can
spy but a fellow on such another gray ass as mine
is, with something that glisters o'top of his head."
"I tell thee, that is Mambrino's helmet," replied
Don Quixote : "do thou stand at a distance, and

* See Orlando Furioso, Canto I.

leave me to deal with him; thou shalt see, that
without trifling away so much as a moment in needless talk, I will finish this adventure, and possess
myself of the desired helmet." " I shall stand at a
distance, you may be sure," quoth Sancho; "but
I wish this may not prove another blue bout, and a
worse job than the fulling-mills." " I have warned
you already, fellow," said Don Quixote, "not so
much as to name the fulling-mills; dare but once
more to do it, nay, but to think on it, and I vow to
— I say no more, but I'll full and pound your dog-
ship into jelly." These threats were more than
sufficient to padlock Sancho's lips, for he had no
mind to have his master's vow fulfilled at the expense of his bones.

Now the truth of the story was this : there were
in that part of the country two villages, one of which
was so little that it had not so much as a shop in it,
nor any barber; so that the barber of the greater
village served also the smaller. And thus a person
happening to have occasion to be let blood, and another to be shaved, the barber was going thither
with his brass basin, which he had clapped upon
his head to keep his hat, that chanced to be a new
one, from being spoiled by the rain; and as the
basin was new scoured, it made a glittering show a
great way off. As Sancho had well observed, he
rode upon a gray ass, which Don Quixote as easily
took for a dapple-gray steed, as he took the barber
for a knight, and his brass basin for a golden helmet;
his distracted brain easily applying every object to
his romantic ideas. Therefore, when he saw the
poor imaginary knight draw near, he fixed his lance,

or javelin, to his thigh, and without staying to hold
a parley with his thoughtless adversary, flew at him
as fiercely as Rozinante would gallop, resolved to
pierce him through and through; crying out in the
midst of his career, " Caitiff, wretch, defend thyself,
or immediately surrender that which is so justly my
due." The barber, who, as he peaceably went along,
saw that terrible apparition come thundering upon
him at unawares, had no other way to avoid being
run through with his lance, but to throw himself off
from his ass to the ground; and then as hastily
getting up, he took to his heels, and ran over the
fields swifter than the wind, leaving his ass and his
basin behind him. Don Quixote finding himself
thus master of the field, and of the basin, " The
miscreant," cried he, " who has left this helmet, has
shown himself as prudent as the beaver, who, finding himself hotly pursued by the hunters, to save
his life, tears and cuts off with his teeth that for
which his natural instinct tells him he was followed."
Then he ordered Sancho to take up the helmet.
" On my word," quoth Sancho, having taken it up,
" it is a special basin, and as well worth a piece of
eight as a thief is worth a halter."

With that he gave it to his master, who presently
clapped it on his head, turning it every way to find
out the beaver or vizor; and at last seeing it had
none, " Doubtless," said he, " the pagan for whom
this famous helmet was first made, had a head of a
prodigious size; but the worst is, that there is at
least one half of it wanting." Sancho could not
forbear smiling to hear his master call the barber's
basin a helmet, and, had not his fear dashed his

mirth, he had certainly laughed outright. " What does the fool grin at now?" cried Don Quixote. " I laugh," said he, " to think what a hugeous jolt-head he must needs have had who was the owner of this same helmet, that looks for all the world like a barber's basin." " I fancy," said Don Quixote, " this enchanted helmet has fallen by some strange accident into the hands of some person, who, not knowing the value of it, for the lucre of a little money, finding it to be of pure gold, melted one half, and of the other made this head-piece, which, as thou sayest, has some resemblance of a barber's basin; but to me, who know the worth of it, the metamorphosis signifies little; for as soon as ever I come to some town where there is an armorer, I will have it altered so much for the better, that then even the helmet which the God of Smiths made for the God of War shall not deserve to be compared with it. In the mean time I'll wear it as it is; it is better than nothing, and will serve at least to save part of my head from the violent encounter of a stone." "Ay, that it will," quoth Sancho, " so it is not hurled out of a sling, as were those at the battle between the two armies, when they hit you that confounded dowse o'the chops, that saluted your worship's cheek-teeth, and broke the pot about your ears in which you kept that blessed drench that made me bring up my guts." " True," cried Don Quixote, " there I lost my precious balsam indeed; but I do not much repine at it, for thou knowest I have the receipt in my memory." " So have I too," quoth Sancho, " and shall have while I have breath to draw; but if ever I make any of that stuff, or taste it again, may I give up the ghost with it! Besides, I don't intend ever to do any thing that may give occasion for the use of it: for, my fixed resolution is, with all my five senses, to preserve myself from hurting, and from being hurt by, any body. As to being tossed in a blanket again, I have nothing to say to that, for there is no remedy for accidents but patience it seems: so if it ever be my lot to be served so again, I'll even shrink up my shoulders, hold my breath, and shut my eyes, and then happy be lucky, let the blanket and fortune even toss on to the end of the chapter."

"Truly," said Don Quixote, "I am afraid thou art no good Christian, Sancho, thou never forgettest injuries. Let me tell thee, it is the part of noble and generous spirits to pass by trifles. Where art thou lame? which of thy ribs is broken, or what part of thy skull is bruised, that thou can'st never think on that jest without malice? for, after all, it was nothing but a jest, a harmless piece of pastime: had I looked upon it otherwise, I had returned to that place before this time, and had made more noble mischief in revenge of the abuse, than ever the incensed Grecians did at Troy, for the detention of their Helen, that famed beauty of the ancient world; who, however, had she lived in our age, or had my Dulcinea adorned her's, would have found her charms outrivalled by my mistress's perfections;" and saying this, he heaved up a deep sigh. "Well then," quoth Sancho, "I will not rip up old sores; let it go for a jest, since there is no revenging it in earnest. But what shall we do with this dapple-gray steed, that is so like a gray ass? you

see that same poor devil-errant has left it to shift
for itself, poor thing, and by his haste to rub off, I
don't think he means to come back for it, and, by
my beard, the gray beast is a special one." "It is
not my custom," replied Don Quixote, "to plunder
those whom I overcome; nor is it usual among us
knights, for the victor to take the horse of his vanquished enemy and let him go afoot, unless his own
steed be killed or disabled in the combat: therefore,
Sancho, leave the horse, or the ass, whatever thou
pleasest to call it; the owner will be sure to come
for it as soon as he sees us gone." "I have a huge
mind to take him along with us," quoth Sancho,
"or at least to exchange him for my own, which is
not so good. What, are the laws of knight-errantry
so strict, that a man must not exchange one ass for
another? at least I hope they will give me leave
to swop one harness for another." "Truly, Sancho," replied Don Quixote, "I am not so very certain as to this last particular, and therefore, till I am
better informed, I give thee leave to exchange the
furniture, if thou hast absolutely occasion for it."
"I have so much occasion for it," quoth Sancho,
"that though it were for my own very self I could
not need it more." So without any more ado,
being authorized by his master's leave, he made
mutatio caparum, (a change of caparisons) and
made his own beast three parts in four better *
for his new furniture. This done, they breakfasted
upon what they left at supper, and quenched their

* Literally, leaving him better by a tierce and quint; alluding
to the game of piquet.

thirst at the stream that turned the fulling-mills, towards which they took care not to cast an eye, for they abominated the very thoughts of them. Thus their spleen being eased, their choleric and melancholic humors assuaged, up they got again, and never minding their way, were all guided by Rozinante's discretion, the depositary of his master's will, and also of the ass's that kindly and sociably always followed his steps wherever he went. Their guide soon brought them again into the high road, where they kept on a slow pace, not caring which way they went.

As they jogged on thus, quoth Sancho to his master, " Pray, sir, will you give me leave to talk to you a little? for since you have laid that bitter command upon me, to hold my tongue, I have had four or five quaint conceits that have rotted in my gizzard, and now I have another at my tongue's end that I would not for any thing should miscarry." " Say it," cried Don Quixote, " but be short, for no discourse can please when too long."

" Well, then," quoth Sancho, " I have been thinking to myself of late, how little is to be got by hunting up and down those barren woods and strange places, where, though you compass the hardest and most dangerous jobs of knight-errantry, yet no living soul sees or hears on't, and so it is every bit as good as lost; and therefore methinks it were better (with submission to your worship's better judgment be it spoken) that we e'en went to serve some emperor, or other great prince that is at war; for there you might show how stout, and how wondrous strong and wise you be; which, being perceived by the lord we shall serve, he must needs reward each of us according to his deserts; and there you will not want a learned scholar to set down all your high deeds, that they may never be forgotten: as for mine I say nothing, since they are not to be named the same day with your worship's; and yet I dare avouch, that if any notice be taken in knight-errantry of the feats of squires, mine will be sure to come in for a share." " Truly, Sancho," replied Don Quixote, " there is some reason in what thou sayest; but first of all it is requisite that a knight-errant should spend some time in various parts of the world, as a probationer in quest of adventures, that, by achieving some extraordinary exploits, his renown may diffuse itself through neighboring climes and distant nations: so when he goes to the court of some great monarch, his fame flying before him as his harbinger, secures him such a reception, that the knight has scarcely reached the gates of the metropolis of the kingdom, when he finds himself attended and surrounded by admiring crowds, pointing and crying out, ' There, there rides the Knight of the Sun, or of the Serpent,' or whatever other title the knight takes upon him : ' That is he,' they will cry, ' who vanquished in single combat the huge giant Brocabruno, surnamed of the invincible strength; this is he that freed the great Mamaluco of Persia from the enchantment that had kept him confined for almost nine hundred years together.' Thus, as they relate his achievements with loud acclamations, the spreading rumor at last reaches the king's palace, and the monarch of that country, being desirous to be informed with his own eyes, will not fail to look out of his window. As soon as he sees the knight, knowing him by his arms, or the device on his shield, he will be obliged to say to his attendants, ‘ My lords and gentlemen, haste all of you, as many as are knights, go and receive the flower of chivalry that is coming to our court.’ At the king’s command, away they all run to introduce him ; the king himself meets him half way on the stairs, where he embraces his valorous guest, and kisses his cheek : then taking him by the hand, he leads him directly to the queen’s apartment, where the knight finds her attended by the princess her daughter, who must be one of the most beautiful and most accomplished damsels in the whole compass of the universe. At the same time fate will so dispose of every thing, that the princess shall gaze on the knight, and the knight on the princess, and each shall admire one another as persons rather angelical than human ; and then, by an unaccountable charm, they shall both find themselves caught and entangled in the inextricable net of love, and wondrously perplexed for want of an opportunity to discover their amorous anguish to one another. After this, doubtless, the knight is conducted by the king to one of the richest apartments in the palace ; where, having taken off his armor, they will bring him a rich scarlet vestment lined with ermines ; and if he looked so graceful cased in steel, how lovely will he appear in all the heightening ornaments of courtiers ! Night being come, he shall sup with the king, the queen, and the princess ; and shall all the while be feasting his eyes

with the sight of the charmer, yet so as nobody
shall perceive it; and she will repay him his glances
with as much discretion; for, as I have said, she is
a most accomplished person.   After supper, a surprising scene is unexpectedly to appear: enter first
an ill-favored little dwarf, and after him a fair damsel between two giants, with the offer of a certain
adventure so contrived by an ancient necromancer,
and so difficult to be performed, that he who shall
undertake and end it with success, shall be esteemed the best knight in the world.   Presently it is the
king's pleasure that all his courtiers should attempt
it; which they do, but all of them unsuccessfully;
for the honor is reserved for the valorous stranger,
who effects that with ease which the rest essayed
in vain; and then the princess shall be overjoyed,
and esteem herself the most happy creature in
the world, for having bestowed her affections on
so deserving an object.   Now by the happy appointment of fate, this king, or this emperor, is at
war with one of his neighbors as powerful as himself, and the knight being informed of this, after he
has been some few days at court, offers the king his
service; which is accepted with joy, and the knight
courteously kisses the king's hand in acknowledgment of so great a favor.   That night the lover
takes his leave of the princess at the iron grate before her chamber window looking into the garden,
where he and she have already had several interviews, by means of the princess's confidante, a
damsel who carries on the intrigue between them.
The knight sighs, the princess swoons, the damsel
runs for cold water to bring her to life again, very

uneasy also because the morning light approaches, and she would not have them discovered, lest it should reflect on her lady's honor. At last the princess revives, and gives the knight her lovely hand to kiss through the iron grate; which he does a thousand and a thousand times, bathing it all the while with his tears. Then they agree how to transmit their thoughts with secrecy to each other, with a mutual intercourse of letters during his fatal absence. The princess prays him to return with all the speed of a lover; the knight promises it with repeated vows, and a thousand kind protestations. At last, the fatal moment being come that must tear him from all he loves, and from his very self, he seals once more his love on her soft snowy hand, almost breathing out his soul, which mounts to his lips, and even would leave its body to dwell there; and then he is hurried away by the fearful confidante. After this cruel separation he retires to his chamber, and throws himself on his bed; but grief will not suffer sleep to close his eyes. Then rising with the sun, he goes to take his leave of the king and the queen: he desires to pay his compliment of leave to the princess, but he is told she is indisposed; and as he has reason to believe that his departing is the cause of her disorder, he is so grieved at the news, that he is ready to betray the secret of his heart, which the princess's confidante observing, she goes and acquaints her with it, and finds the lovely mourner bathed in tears, who tells her, that the greatest affliction of her soul is her not knowing whether her charming knight be of royal blood: but the damsel pacifies her, assuring her that so much gallantry, and such noble qualifications, were unquestionably derived from an illustrious and royal original. This comforts the afflicted fair, who does all she can to compose her looks, lest the king or the queen should suspect the cause of their alteration; and so some days after, she appears in public as before. And now the knight, having been absent for some time, meets, fights, and overcomes the king's enemies, takes I do not know how many cities, wins I do not know how many battles, returns to court, and appears before his mistress laden with honor. He visits her privately as before, and they agree that he shall demand her of the king her father in marriage, as the reward of all his services: but the king will not grant his suit, as being unacquainted with his birth: however, whether it be that the princess suffers herself to be privately carried away, or that some other means are used, the knight marries her, and in a little time the king is very well pleased with the match: for now the knight appears to be the son of a mighty king of I cannot tell what country, for I think it is not in the map. Some time after, the father dies, the princess is heiress, and thus in a trice our knight comes to be king. Having thus completed his happiness, his next thoughts are to gratify his squire, and all those who have been instrumental in his advancement to the throne: thus he marries his squire to one of the princess's damsels, and most probably to her favorite, who had been privy to the amours, and who is daughter to one of the most considerable dukes in the kingdom.

" That is what I have been looking for all this

while," quoth Sancho; "give me but that, and let
the world rub, there I'll stick; for every tittle of
this will come to pass, and be your worship's case
as sure as a gun, if you will take upon you that
same nickname of the Knight of the Woful
Figure." "Most certainly, Sancho," replied Don
Quixote; "for by the same steps, and in that very
manner, knights-errant have always proceeded to
ascend to the throne; therefore our chief business
is 'to find out some great potentate, either among
the Christians or the Pagans, that is at war with
his neighbors, and has a fair daughter. But we
shall have time enough to inquire after that; for, as
I have told thee, we must first purchase fame in
other places, before we presume to go to court.
Another thing makes me more uneasy: suppose we
have found out a king and a princess, and I have
filled the world with the fame of my unparalleled
achievements, yet cannot I tell how to find out that
I am of royal blood, though it were but second
cousin to an emperor; for it is not to be expected
that the king will ever consent that I shall wed his
daughter until I have made this out by authentic
proofs, though my service deserve it never so much;
and thus, for want of a punctilio, I am in danger
of losing what my valor so justly merits. It is true,
indeed, I am a gentleman, and of a noted ancient
family, and possessed of an estate of a hundred
and twenty crowns a year; nay, perhaps the learned
historiographer who is to write the history of my
life, will so improve and beautify my genealogy,
that he will find me to be the fifth, or sixth at least,
in descent from a king: for, Sancho, there are two

sorts of originals in the world; some who, sprung from mighty kings and princes, by little and little have been so lessened and obscured, that the estates and titles of the following generations have dwindled to nothing, and ended in a point like a pyramid; others, who, from mean and low beginnings, still rise and rise, till at last they are raised to the very top of human greatness : so vast the difference is, that those who were something, are now nothing, and those that were nothing, are now something. And therefore who knows but that I may be one of those whose original is so illustrious? which being handsomely made out, after due examination, ought undoubtedly to satisfy the king, my father-in-law. But even supposing he were still refractory, the princess is to be so desperately in love with me, that she will marry me without his consent, though I were a son of the meanest watercarrier; and if her tender honor scruples to bless me against her father's will, then it may not be amiss to put a pleasant constraint upon her, by conveying her by force out of the reach of her father, to whose persecutions either time or death will be sure to put a period."

"Ay," quoth Sancho, "your rake-helly fellows have a saying that is pat to your purpose, Never cringe nor creep, for what you by force may reap, though I think it were better said, A leap from a hedge is better than the prayer of a good man.* No more to be said, if the king your father-in-law won't let you have his daughter by fair means,

* Better to rob than to ask charity.

never stand shall I, shall I, but fairly and squarely
run away with her.   All the mischief that I fear, is
only, that while you are making your peace with
him, and waiting after a dead man's shoes, as the
saying is, the poor dog of a squire is like to go long
barefoot, and may go hang himself for any good
you will be able to do him, unless the damsel, Go-
between, who is to be his wife, run away too with
the princess, and he solace himself with her till a
better time comes; for I don't see but that the
knight may clap up the match between us without
any more ado."   " That is most certain," answered
Don Quixote.   " Why then," quoth Sancho, " let
us even take our chance, and let the world rub."
" May fortune crown our wishes," cried Don Quixote, " and let him be a wretch who thinks himself
one!"   "Amen, say I," quoth Sancho; " for I am
one of your old Christians, and that is enough to
qualify me to be an earl."   " And more than
enough," said Don Quixote; " for though thou
wert not so well descended, being a king, I could
bestow nobility on thee, without putting thee to the
trouble of buying it, or doing me the least service ;
and making thee an earl, men must call thee my
lord, though it grieves them never so much."   "And
do you think," quoth Sancho, " I would not become
my equality main well ? "   " Thou shouldst say
quality," said Don Quixote, " and not equality."
" Even as you will," returned Sancho : " but as I
was saying, I should become an earldom rarely ; for
I was once beadle to a brotherhood, and the beadle's gown did so become me, that every body said
I had the presence of a warden.   Then how do you

think I shall look with a duke's robes on my back,
all bedaubed with gold and pearl like any foreign
count? I believe we shall have folks come a hundred leagues to see me." " Thou wilt look well
enough," said Don Quixote; " but then thou must
shave that rough bushy beard of thine at least
every other day, or people will read thy beginning
in thy face as soon as they see thee." " Why then,"
quoth Sancho, " it is but keeping a barber in my
house; and if needs be, he shall trot after me
wherever I go, like a grandee's master of the horse."
" How camest thou to know," said Don Quixote,
" that grandees have their masters of the horse to
ride after them?" " I'll tell you," quoth Sancho :
" some years ago I happened to be about a month
among your court-folks, and there I saw a little
dandiprat riding about, who, they said was a hugeous great lord: there was a man a horseback that
followed him close wherever he went, turning and
stopping as he did, you would have thought he had
been tied to his horse's tail. With that I asked
why that hind-man did not ride by the other, but
still came after him thus? and they told me he was
master of his horses, and that the grandees have
always such kind of men at their tail; and I
marked this so well, that I han't forgot it since."
" Thou art in the right," said Don Quixote; " and
thou mayest as reasonably have thy barber attend
thee in this manner. Customs did not come up all
at once, but rather started up and were improved
by degrees; so thou mayest be the first earl that
rode in state, with his barber behind him; and this
may be said to justify thy conduct, that it is an

office of more trust to shave a man's beard, than to
saddle a horse." "Well," quoth Sancho, "leave
the business of the cut-beard to me, and do but
take care you be a king and I an earl." "Never
doubt it," replied Don Quixote; and with that,
looking about, he discovered — what the next chapter will tell you.

CHAPTER VIII.

HOW DON QUIXOTE SET FREE MANY MISERABLE CREATURES, WHO WERE CARRYING, MUCH AGAINST THEIR WILLS, TO A PLACE THEY DID NOT LIKE.

CID HAMET BENENGELI, an Arabian and Manchegan author, relates in this most grave, high-
sounding, minute, soft, and humorous history, that
after this discourse between the renowned Don Quixote and his squire Sancho Panza, which we have
laid down at the end of the seventh chapter, the
knight lifting up his eyes, saw about twelve men
a-foot, trudging in the road, all in a row, one behind
another, like beads upon a string, being linked together by the neck to a huge iron chain, and mana-
cled besides. They were guarded by two horsemen,
armed with carabines, and two men a-foot, with
swords and javelins. As soon as Sancho spied them,
"Look ye, sir," cried he, "here is a gang of wretches
hurried away by main force to serve the king in the
galleys." "How," replied Don Quixote, "is it possible the king will force any body?" "I don't say
so," answered Sancho; "I mean these are rogues

whom the law has sentenced for their misdeeds, to row in the king's galleys." "However," replied Don Quixote, "they are forced, because they do not go of their own free will." "Sure enough," quoth Sancho. "If it be so," said Don Quixote, "they come within the verge of my office, which is to hinder violence and oppression, and succor all people in misery." "Ay, sir," quoth Sancho, "but neither the king nor law offer any violence to such wicked wretches, they have but their deserts." By this the chain of slaves came up, when Don Quixote, in very civil terms, desired the guards to inform him why these people were led along in that manner? "Sir," answered one of the horsemen, "they are criminals, condemned to serve the king in his galleys: that is all I have to say to you, and you need inquire no farther." "Nevertheless, sir," replied Don Quixote, "I have a great desire to know in few words the cause of their misfortune, and I will esteem it an extraordinary favor, if you will let me have that satisfaction." "We have here the copies and certificates of their several sentences," said the other horseman, "but we can't stand to pull them out and read them now; you may draw near and examine the men yourself: I suppose they themselves will tell you why they are condemned; for they are such honest people, they are not ashamed to boast of their rogueries."

With this permission, which Don Quixote would have taken of himself had they denied it him, he rode up to the chain, and asked the first, for what crimes he was in these miserable circumstances? The galley-slave answered him, that it was for being

in love. "What, only for being in love?" cried Don
Quixote; "were all those that are in love to be used
thus, I myself might have been long since in the
galleys." "Ay, but," replied the slave, "my love was
not of that sort which you conjecture: I was so
desperately in love with a basket of linen, and embraced it so close, that had not the judge taken it
from me by force, I would not have parted with it
willingly. In short, I was taken in the fact, and so
there was no need to put me to the rack, it was proved so plain upon me. So I was committed, tried,
condemned, had the gentle lash; and besides that,
was sent, for three years, to be an element-dasher,
and there is an end of the business." "An element-
dasher," cried Don Quixote, "what do you mean by
that?" "A galley-slave," answered the criminal,
who was a young fellow, about four-and-twenty
years old, and said he was born at Piedra Hita.

Then Don Quixote examined the second, but he
was so sad and desponding, that he would make
no answer; however, the first rogue informed the
knight of his affairs: "Sir," said he, "this canary-
bird keeps us company for having sung too much."
"Is it possible!" cried Don Quixote, "are men sent
to the galleys for singing?" "Ay, marry are they,"
quoth the arch rogue; "for there is nothing worse
than to sing in anguish." "How!" cried Don Quixote; "that contradicts the saying, Sing away sorrow, cast away care." "Ay, but with us the case is
different," replied the slave; "he that sings in disaster,
weeps all his life after." "This is a riddle which I
cannot unfold," cried Don Quixote. "Sir," said one
of the guards, "Singing in anguish, among these jail-

birds, means to confess upon the rack: this fellow was put to the torture, and confessed his crime, which was stealing of cattle; and because he squeaked, or sung, as they call it, he was condemned to the galleys for six years, besides an hundred jirks with a cat of nine tails that have whisked and powdered his shoulders already. Now the reason why he goes thus mopish and out o'sorts, is only because his comrogues jeer and laugh at him continually for not having had the courage to deny; as if it had not been as easy for him to have said no as yes; or as if a fellow, taken up on suspicion, were not a lucky rogue, when there is no positive evidence can come in against him but his own tongue; and in my opinion they are somewhat in the right." "I think so too," said Don Quixote.

Thence addressing himself to the third, "And you," said he, "what have you done?" "Sir," answered the fellow, readily and pleasantly enough, "I must mow the great meadow for five years together, for want of twice five ducats." "I will give twenty with all my heart," said Don Quixote, "to deliver thee from that misery." "Thank you for nothing," quoth the slave; "it is just like the proverb, After meat comes mustard; or, like money to a starving man at sea, when there are no victuals to be bought with it: had I had the twenty ducats you offer me before I was tried, to have greased the clerk's [or recorder's] fist, and have whetted my lawyer's wit, I might have been now at Toledo in the market-place of Zocodover, and not have been thus led along like a dog in a string. But heaven is powerful. Basta; I say no more."

Then passing to the fourth, who was a venerable old Don, with a gray beard that reached to his bosom, he put the same question to him; whereupon the poor creature fell a-weeping, and was not able to give him an answer; so the next behind him lent him a tongue. " Sir," said he, " this honest person goes to the galleys for four years, having taken his progress through the town in state, and rested at the usual stations." " That is," quoth Sancho, " as I take it, after he had been exposed to public shame." *
" Right," replied the slave; " and all this he is condemned to for being a broker of human flesh: for, to tell you the truth, the gentleman is a pimp, and, besides that, he has a smack of conjuring." " If it were not for that addition of conjuring," cried Don Quixote, " he ought not to have been sent to the galleys purely for being a pimp, unless it were to be general of the galleys: for, the profession of a bawd pimp, or messenger of love, is not like other common employments, but an office that requires a great deal of prudence and sagacity; an office of trust and weight, and most highly necessary in a well-regulated commonwealth; nor should it be executed but by civil well-descended persons of good natural parts, and of a liberal education. Nay, 'twere requisite there should be a comptroller and surveyor of the profession, as there are of others; and a certain and settled number of them, as there are of exchange-brokers. This would be a means to prevent an infinite number of mischiefs that happen every day, because

---

* Instead of the pillory, in Spain, they carry malefactors on an ass, and in a particular habit, along the streets, the crier going before, and proclaiming their crime.

the trade or profession is followed by poor ignorant
pretenders, silly waiting women, young giddy-brain-
ed pages, shallow footmen, and such raw inexpe-
rienced sort of people, who in unexpected turns and
emergencies stand with their fingers in their mouths,
know not their right hand from their left, but suffer
themselves to be surprised, and spoil all for want of
quickness of invention either to conceal, carry on,
or bring off a thing artificially. Had I but time I
would point out what sort of persons are best qualified to be chosen professors of this most necessary
employment in the commonwealth; however, at
some future season I will inform those of it who
may remedy this disorder. All I have to say now,
is, that the grief I had to see these venerable gray
hairs in such distress, for having followed that no
less useful than ingenious vocation of pimping, is
now lost in my abhorrence of his additional character of a conjurer; though I very well know that no
sorcery in the world can effect or force the will, as
some ignorant credulous persons fondly imagine:
for our will is a free faculty, and no herb nor charms
can constrain it. As for philters, and such-like compositions, which some silly women and designing
pretenders make, they are nothing but certain mix-
tures and poisonous preparations, that make those
who take them run mad; though the deceivers labor to persuade us they can make one person love
another; which, as I have said, is an impossible
thing, our will being a free, uncontrollable power."
" You say very well, sir," cried the old coupler; " and
upon my honor, I protest I am wholly innocent, as
to the imputation of witchcraft. As for the business

of pimping, I cannot deny it, but I never took it to be a criminal function; for my intention was, that all the world should taste the sweets of love, and enjoy each other's society, living together in friendship and in peace, free from those griefs and jars that unpeople the earth. But my harmless design has not been so happy as to prevent my being sent now to a place whence I never expect to return, stooping as I do under the heavy burden of old age, and being grievously afflicted with the strangury, which scarce affords me a moment's respite from pain." This said, the reverend procurer burst out afresh into tears and lamentations, which melted Sancho's heart so much, that he pulled a piece of money out of his bosom, and gave it to him as an alms.

Then Don Quixote turned to the fifth, who seemed to be nothing at all concerned. " I go to serve his majesty," said he, "for having been somewhat too familiar with two of my cousin-germans, and two other kind-hearted virgins that were sisters ; by which means I have multiplied my kin, and begot so odd and intricate a medley of kindred, that it would puzzle a convocation of casuists to resolve their degrees of consanguinity. All this was proved upon me. I had no friends, and, what was worse, no money, and so was like to have swung for it however, I was only condemned to the galleys for six years, and patiently submitted to it. I feel myself yet young, to my confort; so if my life does but hold out, all will be well in time. If you will be pleased to bestow something upon poor sinners, heaven will reward you: and when we pray, we will be sure to remember you, that your life may be as long and prosperous, as your presence is goodly and noble." This brisk spark appeared to be a student by his habit, and some of the guards said he was a fine speaker, and a good latinist.

After him came a man about thirty years old, a clever, well-set, handsome fellow, only he squinted horribly with one eye : he was strangely loaded with irons ; a heavy chain clogged his leg, and was so long, that he twisted it about his waist like a girdle : he had a couple of collars about his neck, the one to link him to the rest of the slaves, and the other, one of those iron-ruffs which they call a keep-friend, or a friend's foot; from whence two irons went down to his middle, and to their two bars were riveted a pair of manacles that griped him by the fists, and were secured with a large padlock ; so that he could neither lift his hands to his mouth, nor bend down his head towards his hands. Don Quix-ote inquiring why he was worse hampered with irons than the rest, "Because he alone has done more rogueries than all the rest," answered one of the guards. " This is such a reprobate, such a devil of a fellow, that no gaol nor fetters will hold him ; we are not sure he is fast enough, for all he is chained so." " What sort of crimes then has he been guilty of," asked Don Quixote, " that he is only sent to the galleys ? " " Why," answered the keeper, " he is condemned to ten years slavery, which is no better than a civil death: but I need not stand to tell you any more of him, but that he is that notorious rogue, Gines de Passamonte, alias Ginesillo de Parapilla." " Hark you, sir," cried the slave, " fair and softly ; what a pox makes you give

a gentleman more names than he has ? Gines is my
Christian name, and Passamonte my surname, and
not Ginesillo, nor Parapilla, as you say. Blood!
let every man mind what he says, or it may prove
the worse for him." " Don't you be so saucy, Mr.
Crack-rope," cried the officer to him, " or I may
chance to make you keep a better tongue in your
head." " It is a sign," cried the slave, " that a man
is fast, and under the lash; but one day or other
somebody shall know whether I am called Parapilla
or no." " Why, Mr. Slipstring," replied the officer,
" do not people call you by that name ? " " They
do," answered Gines, " but I'll make them call me
otherwise, or I'll fleece and bite them worse than I
care to tell you now. But you, sir, who are so
inquisitive," added he, turning to Don Quixote, " if
you have a mind to give us any thing, pray do it
quickly, and go your ways; for I don't like to stand
here answering questions; broil me! I am Gines
de Passamonte, I am not ashamed of my name.
As for my life and conversation, there is an account
of them in black and white, written with this nu-
merical hand of mine." " There he tells you true,"
said the officer, " for he has written his own history
himself, without omitting a tittle of his roguish
pranks; and he has left the manuscript in pawn in
the prison for two hundred reals." " Ay," said Gines, " and will redeem it, burn me! though it lay
there for as many ducats." " Then it must be an
extraordinary piece," cried Don Quixote. " So
extraordinary," replied Gines, " that it far outdoes
not only Lazarillo de Tormes, but whatever has
been, and shall be written in that kind; for mine is

true every word, and no invented stories can compare with it for variety of tricks and accidents."
" What is the title of the book ? " asked Don Quixote. " The life of Gines de Passamonte," answered
the other. " Is it quite finished ? " asked the knight.
" How the devil can it be finished and I yet living? "
cried the slave. " There is in it every material point
from my cradle, to this my last going to the galleys."
" Then it seems you have been there before," said
Don Quixote. " To serve God and the king, I was
some four years there once before," replied Gines :
" I already know how the biscuit and the bulls-
pizzle agree with my carcass : it does not grieve
me much to go there again, for there I shall have
leisure to give a finishing stroke to my book. I have
the devil knows what to add ; and in our Spanish
galleys there is always leisure and idle time enough
o'conscience : neither shall I want so much for what
I have to insert, for I know it all by heart."

" Thou seemest to be a witty fellow," said Don
Quixote. " You should have said unfortunate too,"
replied the slave ; " for the bitch Fortune is still
unkind to men of wit." " You mean to such wicked wretches as yourself," cried the officer. " Look
you, Mr. Commissary," said Gines, " I have already
desired you to use good language. The law did not
give us to your keeping for you to abuse us, but
only to conduct us where the king has occasion for
us. Let every man mind his own business, and
give good words, or hold his tongue ; for by the
blood — I will say no more, murder will out ; there
will be a time when some people's rogueries may
come to light, as well as those of other folks."

With that the officer, provoked by the slave's threats, held up his staff to strike him; but Don Quixote stepped between them, and desired him not to do it, and to consider, that the slave was the more to be excused for being too free of his tongue, since he had ne'er another member at liberty. Then addressing himself to all the slaves, " My dearest brethren," cried he, " I find, by what I gather from your own words, that though you deserve punishment for the several crimes of which you stand convicted, yet you suffer execution of the sentence by constraint, and merely because you cannot help it. Besides, it is not unlikely but that this man's want of resolution upon the rack, the other's want of money, the third's want of friends and favor, and, in short the judges perverting and wresting the law to your great prejudice, may have been the cause of your misery. Now, as heaven has sent me into the world to relieve the distressed, and free suffering weakness from the tyranny of oppression, according to the duty of my profession of knight-errantry, these considerations induce me to take you under my protection. But because it is the part of a prudent man not to use violence where fair means may be effectual, I desire you, gentlemen of the guard, to release these poor men, there being people enough to serve his majesty in their places; for it is a hard case to make slaves of men whom God and nature made free; and you have the less reason to use these wretches with severity, seeing they never did you any wrong. Let them answer for their sins in the other world; heaven is just, you know, and will be sure to punish the wicked, as it will certainly reward the good.

Consider besides, gentlemen, that it is neither a
Christian-like, nor an honorable action, for men to
be the butchers and tormentors of one another;
principally, when no advantage can arise from it.
I choose to desire this of you, with so much mildness,
and in so peaceable a manner, gentlemen, that I
may have occasion to pay you a thankful acknowledgment, if you will be pleased to grant so reasonable a request : but if you provoke me by refusal, I
must be obliged to tell ye, that this lance, and this
sword, guided by this invincible arm, shall force you
to yield that to my valor which you deny to my
civil entreaties."

"A very good jest, indeed," cried the officer; "what
a devil makes you dote at such a rate? would you
have us set at liberty the king's prisoners, as if we
had authority to do it, or you to command it? Go,
go about your business, good Sir Errant, and set
your basin right upon your empty pate; and pray
do not meddle any further in what does not concern
you, for those who will play with cats must expect
to be scratched."

" Thou art a cat, and rat, and a coward to boot,"
cried Don Quixote; and with that he attacked the
officer with such a sudden and surprising fury, that
before he had any time to put himself into a posture of defence, he struck him down, dangerously
wounded with his lance; and, as fortune had ordered it, this happened to be the horseman who
was armed with a carbine. His companions stood
astonished at such a bold action, but at last fell
upon the bold champion with their swords and
darts, which might have proved fatal to him, had

not the slaves laid hold of this opportunity to break
the chain, in order to regain their liberty; for the
guards, perceiving their endeavors to get loose,
thought it more material to prevent them, than to
be fighting a madman: but, as he pressed them
vigorously on one side, and the slaves were oppos-
ing them and freeing themselves on the other, the
hurly-burly was so great, and the guards so perplexed, that they did nothing to the purpose. In
the mean time, Sancho was helping Gines de Passamonte to get off his gyves, which he did sooner
than can be imagined; and then that active despe-
rado having seized the wounded officer's sword and
carbine, he joined with Don Quixote, and sometimes aiming at one, and sometimes at the other, as
if he had been ready to shoot them, yet still without letting off the piece, the other slaves at the same
time pouring volleys of stone-shot at the guards,
they betook themselves to their heels, leaving Don
Quixote and the criminals masters of the field.
Sancho, who was always for taking care of the main
chance, was not at all pleased with this victory; for
he guessed that the guards who were fled, would
raise a hue and cry, and soon be at their heels with
the whole posse of the holy brotherhood, and lay
them up for a rescue and rebellion. This made
him advise his master to get out of the way as fast
as he could, and hide himself in the neighboring
mountains. "I hear you," answered Don Quixote
to this motion of his squire, "and I know what I
have to do." Then calling to him all the slaves,
who by this time had uncased the keeper to his
skin, they gathered about him to know his pleasure,

and he spoke to them in this manner: " It is the part of generous spirits to have a grateful sense of the benefits they receive, no crime being more odious than ingratitude. You see, gentlemen, what I have done for your sakes, and you cannot but be sensible how highly you are obliged to me. Now all the recompense I require is, only that every one of you, loaden with that chain from which I have freed your necks, do instantly repair to the city of Toboso; and there presenting yourselves before the Lady Dulcinea del Toboso, tell her, that her faithful votary, the Knight of the Woful Countenance, commanded you to wait on her, and assure her of his profound veneration. Then you shall give her an exact account of every particular relating to this famous achievement, by which you once more taste the sweets of liberty; which done, I give you leave to seek your fortunes where you please."

To this the ringleader and master thief, Gines de Passamonte, made answer for all the rest, "What you would have us to do," said he, " our noble deliverer, is absolutely impracticable and impossible; for we dare not be seen all together for the world. We must rather part, and skulk some one way, some another, and lie snug in creeks and corners under ground, for fear of those damned man-hounds that will be after us with a hue and cry; therefore all we can and ought to do in this case, is to change this compliment and homage which you would have us pay to the Lady Dulcinea del Toboso, into a certain number of Ave Maries and Creeds, which we will say for your worship's benefit; and this may be done by night or by day, walking or stand-

ing, and in war as well as in peace : but to imagine
we will return to our flesh-pots of Egypt, that is to
say, take up our chains again, and lug them the
devil knows where, is as unreasonable as to think
it is night now at ten o'clock in the morning.
'Sdeath, to expect this from us, is to expect pears
from an elm-tree." " Now, by my sword," replied
Don Quixote, " sir son of a whore, Sir Ginesello de
Parapilla, or whatever be your name, you yourself,
alone, shall go to Toboso, like a dog that has
scalded his tail, with the whole chain about your
shoulders." Gines, who was naturally very choleric, judging by Don Quixote's extravagance in freeing them, that he was not very wise, winked on his
companions, who, like men that understood signs,
presently fell back to the right and left, and pelted
Don Quixote with such a shower of stones, that all
his dexterity to cover himself with his shield, was
now ineffectual, and poor Rozinante no more obeyed the spur, than if he had been only the statue of
a horse. As for Sancho, he got behind his ass, and
there sheltered himself from the volleys of flints
that threatened his bones, while his master was so
battered, that in a little time he was thrown out of
his saddle to the ground. He was no sooner down,
but the student leaped on him, took off his basin
from his head, gave him three or four thumps on
the shoulders with it, and then gave it so many
knocks against the stones, that he almost broke it
to pieces. After this, they stripped him of his upper
coat, and had robbed him of his hose too, but that
his greaves hindered them. They also eased Sancho of his upper coat, and left him in his doublet ;

then, having divided the spoils, they shifted every
one for himself, thinking more how to avoid being
taken up, and linked again in the chain, than of
trudging with it to my Lady Dulcinea del Toboso.
Thus the ass, Rozinante, Sancho, and Don Quixote, remained indeed masters of the field, but in an
ill condition : the ass hanging his head, and pensive,
shaking his ears now and then, as if the volleys of
stones had still whizzed about them ; Rozinante
lying in a desponding manner, for he had been
knocked down as well as his unhappy rider; Sancho uncased to his doublet, and trembling for fear
of the holy brotherhood : and Don Quixote filled
with sullen regret, to find himself so barbarously
used by those whom he had so highly obliged.

CHAPTER IX.

WHAT BEFELL THE RENOWNED DON QUIXOTE IN THE SIERRA
MORENA, (BLACK MOUNTAIN,) BEING ONE OF THE RAREST
ADVENTURES IN THIS AUTHENTIC HISTORY.

DON QUIXOTE, finding himself so ill treated, said
to his squire : " Sancho, I have always heard it said,
that to do a kindness to clowns, is like throwing
water into the sea.* Had I given ear to thy advice,
I had prevented this misfortune ; but since the thing
is done it is needless to repine ; this shall be a
warning to me for the future." " That is," quoth
Sancho, " when the devil is blind : but since you

* It is labor lost, because they are ungrateful.

say, you had escaped this mischief had you believed
me, good sir, believe me now, and you will escape
a greater; for I must tell you, that those of the holy
brotherhood do not stand in awe of your chivalry,
nor do they care a straw for all the knights-errant
in the world. Methinks I already hear their arrows
whizzing about my ears." * " Thou art naturally
a coward, Sancho," cried Don Quixote; "nevertheless, that thou mayest not say I am obstinate, and
never follow thy advice, I will take thy counsel, and
for once convey myself out of the reach of this
dreadful brotherhood, that so strangely alarms thee;
but upon this condition, that thou never tell any
mortal creature, neither while I live, nor after my
death, that I withdrew myself from this danger
through fear, but merely to comply with thy entreaties: for if thou ever presume to say otherwise,
thou wilt belie me; and from this time to that time,
and from that time to the world's end, I give thee
the lie, and thou liest, and shalt lie in thy throat, as
often as thou sayest, or but thinkest to the contrary.
Therefore do not offer to reply; for shouldest thou
but surmise, that I would avoid any danger, and
especially this which seems to give some occasion
or color for fear, I would certainly stay here, though
unattended and alone, and expect and face not only
the holy brotherhood, which thou dreadest so much,
but also the fraternity or twelve heads of the tribes
of Israel, the seven Maccabees, Castor and Pollux,
and all the brothers and brotherhoods in the universe." "An't please your worship," quoth Sancho,

---

* The troopers of the holy brotherhood used cross-bows.

" to withdraw is not to run away, and to stay is no wise action, when there is more reason to fear than to hope ; it is the part of a wise man to keep himself to-day for to-morrow, and not venture all his eggs in one basket. And for all I am but a clown, or a bumpkin, as you may say, yet I would have you to know I know what's what, and have always taken care of the main chance ; therefore do not be ashamed of being ruled by me, but even get on horseback an you are able : come, I will help you, and then follow me ; for my mind plaguily misgives me, that now one pair of heels will stand us in more stead than two pair of hands."

Don Quixote, without any reply, made shift to mount Rozinante, and Sancho on his ass led the way to the neighboring mountainous desert called Sierra Morena,* which the crafty squire had a design to cross over, and get out at the farthest end, either at Viso, or Almadovar del Campo, and in the mean time to lurk in the craggy and almost inaccessible retreats of that vast mountain, for fear of falling into the hands of the holy brotherhood. He was the more eager to steer this course, finding that the provision which he had laid on his ass had escaped plundering, which was a kind of miracle, considering how narrowly the galley-slaves had searched everywhere for booty. It was night before our two travellers got to the middle and most desert part of

* Sierra, though Spanish for a mountain, properly means (not a chain, but) a saw, from the Latin Serra, because of its ridges rising and falling like the teeth of a saw. This mountain (called Morena from its Moorish or swarthy color) parts the kingdom of Castile from the province of Andalusia.

the mountain; where Sancho advised his master to
stay some days, at least as long as their provisions
lasted; and accordingly that night they took up
their lodging between two rocks, among a great
number of cork-trees: but fortune, which, according to the opinion of those that have not the light
of true faith, guides, appoints, and contrives all
things as it pleases, directed Gines de Passamonte
(that master-rogue, who, thanks be to Don Quixote's force and folly, had been put in a condition
to do him a mischief) to this very part of the mountain, in order to hide himself till the heat of the
pursuit, which he had just cause to fear, were over.
He discovered our adventurers much about the time
that they fell asleep; and as wicked men are always
ungrateful, and urgent necessity prompts many to
do things, at the very thoughts of which they perhaps would start at other times, Gines, who was a
stranger both to gratitude and humanity, resolved
to ride away with Sancho's ass; for as for Rozinante, he looked upon him as a thing that would
neither sell nor pawn: so while poor Sancho lay
snoring, he spirited away his darling beast, and
made such haste, that before day he thought himself and his prize secure from the unhappy owner's
pursuit.

Now Aurora with her smiling face returned to
enliven and cheer the earth, but alas! to grieve and
affright Sancho with a dismal discovery: for he had
no sooner opened his eyes, but he missed his ass,
and finding himself deprived of that dear partner of
his fortunes, and best comfort in his peregrinations,
he broke out into the most pitiful and sad lamenta-

tions in the world; insomuch that he waked Don
Quixote with his moans. "O dear child of my
bowels," cried he, "born and bred under my roof,
my children's playfellow, the comfort of my wife,
the envy of my neighbors, the ease of my burdens,
the staff of my life, and in a word, half my main-
tenance; for with six-and-twenty maravedis, which
were daily earned by thee, I made shift to keep half
my family." Don Quixote, who easily guessed the
cause of these complaints, strove to comfort him
with kind condoling words, and learned discourses
upon the uncertainty of human happiness: but nothing proved so effectual to assuage his sorrow, as
the promise which his master made him of drawing
a bill of exchange on his niece for three asses out of
five which he had at home, payable to Sancho
Panza, or his order; which prevailing argument
soon dried up his tears, hushed his sighs and moans,
and turned his complaints into thanks to his generous master for so unexpected a favor.

And now, as they wandered further in these
mountains, Don Quixote was transported with joy
to find himself where he might flatter his ambition
with the hopes of fresh adventures to signalize his
valor; for these vast deserts made him call to mind
the wonderful exploits of other knights-errant, performed in such solitudes. Filled with those airy
notions, he thought on nothing else: but Sancho
was for more substantial food; and now, thinking
himself quite out of the reach of the holy brotherhood, his only care was to fill his belly with the
relics of the clerical booty; and thus sitting sideling, as women do, upon his beast, he slily took out

now one piece of meat, then another, and kept his
grinders going faster than his feet. Thus plodding
on, he would not have given a rush to have met
with any other adventure.

While he was thus employed, he observed, that
his master endeavored to take up something that
lay on the ground with the end of his lance: this
made him run to help him to lift up the bundle,
which proved to be a portmanteau, and the seat of
a saddle, that were half, or rather quite rotted with
lying exposed to the weather. The portmanteau
was somewhat heavy, and Don Quixote having ordered Sancho to see what it contained, though it
was shut with a chain and a padlock, he easily saw
what was in it through the crack, and pulled out
four fine holland shirts, and other clean and fashionable linen, besides a considerable quantity of gold
tied up in a handkerchief. " Bless my eye-sight,"
quoth Sancho; " and now, heaven, I thank thee for
sending us such a lucky adventure once in our
lives;" with that, groping further in the portmanteau, he found a table-book richly bound. " Give me
that," said Don Quixote, " and do thou keep the
gold," " Heaven reward your worship," quoth Sancho, kissing his master's hand, and at the same time
clapping up the linen and the other things into the
bag where he kept the victuals. " I fancy," said
Don Quixote, " that some person, having lost his
way in these mountains, has been met by robbers,
who have murdered him, and buried his body somewhere hereabouts." " Sure your worship's mistaken," answered Sancho, " for, had they been high-
waymen, they would never have left such a booty

behind them." "Thou art in the right," replied
Don Quixote; "and therefore I cannot imagine
what it must be. But stay, I will examine the table-book, perhaps we shall find something written
in that, which will help us to discover what I would
know." With that he opened it, and the first thing
he found was the following rough draught of a sonnet, fairly enough written to be read with ease; so
he read it aloud, that Sancho might know what was
in it as well as himself:

THE RESOLVE.

A SONNET.

Love is a god ne'er knows our pain,
　Or cruelty's his darling attribute;
Else he'd ne'er force me to complain,
　And to his spite my raging pain impute.

But sure if Love's a god, he must
　Have knowledge equal to his power;
And 'tis a crime to think a god unjust:
　Whence then the pains that now my heart devour?

From Phyllis? No: why do I pause?
　Such cruel ills ne'er boast so sweet a cause;
Nor from the gods such torments we do bear.
　Let death then quickly be my cure:
When thus we ills unknown endure,
　'Tis shortest to despair.

"The devil of any thing can be picked out of
this," quoth Sancho, "unless you can tell who that
same Phyll is." "I did not read Phyll, but Phyllis,"
said Don Quixote. "O then, mayhap, the man has
lost his filly-foal." "Phyllis," said Don Quixote,

" is the name of a lady that is beloved by the author of this sonnet, who truly seems to be a tolerable poet,* or I have but little judgment." "Why then," quoth Sancho, " belike your worship understands how to make verses too ? " " That I do," answered Don Quixote, " and better than thou imaginest; as thou shalt see when I shall give thee a letter written all in verse to carry to my Lady Dulcinea del Toboso: for, I must tell thee, friend Sancho, all the knights-errant, or at least the greatest part of them, in former times, were great poets, and as great musicians; those qualifications, or, to speak better, those two gifts, or accomplishments, being almost inseparable from amorous adventures : though I must confess the verses of the knights in former ages are not altogether so polite, nor so adorned with words, as with thoughts and inventions."

" Good sir," quoth Sancho, " look again into the pocket-book, mayhap you will find somewhat that will inform you of what you would know." With that Don Quixote turning over the leaf, " Here's some prose," cried he, " and I think it is the sketch of a love-letter." " O! good your worship," quoth Sancho, " read it out by all means, for I delight mightily in hearing of love-stories."

Don Quixote read it aloud, and found what follows :

" The falsehood of your promises, and my despair, hurry me from you for ever; and you shall sooner hear the news of my death, than the cause

---

* Cervantes himself.

of my complaints. You have forsaken me, ungrateful fair, for one more wealthy indeed, but not more deserving than your abandoned slave. Were virtue esteemed a treasure equal to its worth by your unthinking sex, I must presume to say, I should have no reason to envy the wealth of others, and no misfortune to bewail. What your beauty has raised, your actions have destroyed; the first made me mistake you for an angel, but the last convince me you are a very woman. However, O! too lovely disturber of my peace, may uninterrupted rest and downy ease engross your happy hours; and may forgiving heaven still keep your husband's perfidiousness concealed, lest it should cost your repenting heart a sigh for the injustice you have done to so faithful a lover, and so I should be prompted to a revenge which I do not desire to take. Farewell."

" This letter," quoth Don Quixote, " does not give us any further insight into the things we would know; all I can infer from it is, that the person who wrote it was a betrayed lover." And so turning over the remaining leaves, he found several other letters and verses, some of which were legible, and some so scribbled, that he could make nothing of them. As for those he read, he could meet with nothing in them but accusations, complaints and expostulations, distrusts and jealousies, pleasures and discontents, favors and disdain, the one highly valued, the other as mournfully resented. And while the knight was poring on the table-book, Sancho was rummaging the portmanteau, and the seat of the saddle, with that exactness, that he did not leave a corner unsearched, nor a seam unripped, nor a single lock of wool unpicked; for the gold he had found, which was above an hundred ducats, had but whetted his greedy appetite, and made him wild for more. Yet though this was all he could find, he thought himself well paid for the more than Herculean labors he had undergone; nor could he now repine at his being tossed in a blanket, the straining and griping operation of the balsam, the benedictions of the pack-staves and leavers, the fisticuffs of the lewd carrier, the loss of his cloak, his dear wallet, and of his dearer ass, and all the hunger, thirst, and fatigue, which he had suffered in his kind master's service. On the other side, the Knight of the Woful Figure strangely desired to know who was the owner of the portmanteau, guessing by the verses, the letter, the linen, and the gold, that he was a person of worth, whom the disdain and unkindness of his mistress had driven to despair. At length, however, he gave over the thoughts of it, discovering nobody through that vast desert; and so he rode on, wholly guided by Rozinante's discretion, which always made the grave, sagacious creature choose the plainest and smoothest way; the master still firmly believing, that in those woody uncultivated forests he should infallibly start some wonderful adventure.

And indeed, while these hopes possessed him, he spied upon the top of a stony crag just before him a man that skipped from rock to rock, over briars and bushes, with wonderful agility. He seemed to him naked from the waist upwards, with a thick black beard, his hair long, and strangely tangled,

his head, legs, and feet bare ; on his hips a pair of
breeches, that appeared to be of sad-colored velvet,
but so tattered and torn, that they discovered his
skin in many places. These particulars were observed by Don Quixote while he passed by, and he
followed him, endeavoring to overtake him, for he
presently guessed this was the owner of the portmanteau. But Rozinante, who was naturally slow
and phlegmatic, was in too weak a case besides to
run races with so swift an apparition : yet the
Knight of the Woful Figure resolved to find out
that unhappy creature, though he were to bestow a
whole year in the search ; and to that intent he ordered Sancho to beat one side of the mountain,
while he hunted the other. " In good sooth," quoth
Sancho, " your worship must excuse me as to that ;
for if I but offer to stir an inch from you, I am almost frighted out of my seven senses : and let this
serve you hereafter for a warning, that you may not
send me a nail's breadth from your presence."
" Well," said the knight, " I will take thy case into
consideration ; and it does not displease me, Sancho, to see thee thus rely upon my valor, which, I
dare assure thee, shall never fail thee, though thy
very soul should be scared out of thy body. Follow me, therefore, step by step, with as much haste
as is consistent with good speed ; and let thy eyes
pry everywhere while we search every part of this
rock, where, it is probable, we may meet with that
wretched mortal, who doubtless is the owner of the
portmanteau."

" Odsnigs, sir," quoth Sancho, " I had rather get
out of his way ; for, should we chance to meet him,

and he lay claim to the portmanteau, it is a plain case I shall be forced to part with the money: and therefore I think it much better, without making so much ado, to let me keep it *bonâ fide*, till we can light on the right owner some more easy way, and without dancing after him; which may not happen till we have spent all the money; and in that case I am free from the law, and he may go whistle for it." "Thou art mistaken, Sancho," cried Don Quixote; "for seeing we have some reason to think that we know who is the owner, we are bound in conscience to endeavor to find him out, and restore it to him; the rather, because should we not now strive to meet him, yet the strong presumption we have that the goods belong to him, would make us possessors of them *malâ fide*, and render us as guilty as if the party whom we suspect to have lost the things, were really the right owner; therefore, friend Sancho, do not think much of searching for him, since, if we find him out, it will extremely ease my mind."

With that he spurred Rozinante; and Sancho, not very well pleased, followed him, comforting himself, however, with the hopes of the three asses which his master had promised him. So when they had rode over the greatest part of the mountain, they came to a brook, where they found a mule lying dead, with her saddle and bridle about her, and herself half devoured by beasts and birds of prey; which discovery further confirmed them in their suspicion, that the man who fled so nimbly from them was the owner of the mule and portmanteau. Now as they paused and pondered upon

this, they heard a whistling like that of some shepherd keeping his flocks; and presently after, upon
their left hand, they spied a great number of goats
with an old herdsman after them, on the top of the
mountain. Don Quixote called out to him, and
desired him to come down; but the goat-herd, instead of answering him, asked them in as loud a
tone, how they came thither in those deserts, where
scarce any living creature resorted except goats,
wolves, and other wild beasts? Sancho told him
they would satisfy him as to that point, if he would
come where they were. With that the goat-herd
came down to them; and seeing them look upon
the dead mule, "That dead mule," said the old fellow, "has lain in that very place this six months;
but pray tell me, good people, have you not met the
master of it by the way?" "We have met nobody," answered Don Quixote; "but we found a
portmanteau and a saddle-cushion not far from this
place." "I have seen it, too," quoth the goat-herd,
"but I never durst meddle with it, nor so much as
come near it, for fear of some misdemeanor, lest I
should be charged with having stolen somewhat out
of it: for who knows what might happen? the
devil is subtle, and sometimes lays baits in our way
to tempt us, or blocks to make us stumble." "It
is just so with me, gaffer," quoth Sancho; "for I
saw the portmanteau too, d'ye see, but the devil a
bit would I come within a stone's throw of it; no,
there I found it, and there I left it; i'faith, it shall
e'en lie there still for me. He that steals a bell-
wether, shall be discovered by the bell." "Tell
me, honest friend," asked Don Quixote, "dost thou

know who is the owner of those things?" "All I
know of the matter," answered the goat-herd, " is,
that it is now six months, little more or less, since
to a certain sheep-fold, some three leagues off, there
came a young, well-featured, proper gentleman in
good clothes, and under him this same mule that
now lies dead here, with the cushion and cloak-bag,
which you say you met, but touched not. He
asked us which was the most desert and least frequented part of these mountains? and we told him
this where we are now; and in that we spoke the
plain truth, for should you venture to go but half a
league further, you would hardly be able to get
back again in haste; and I marvel how you could
get even thus far; for there is neither highway nor
foot-path that may direct a man this way. Now,
as soon as the young gentleman had heard our answer, he turned about his mule, and made to the
place we showed him, leaving us all with a hugeous
liking to his comeliness, and strangely marvelling at
his demand, and the haste he made towards the middle of the mountain.   After that we heard no more
of him in a great while, till one day by chance one
of the shepherds coming by, he fell upon him without saying why or wherefore, and beat him without
mercy: after that he went to the ass that carried
our victuals, and, taking away all the bread and
cheese that was there, he tripped back again to the
mountain with wondrous speed.   Hearing this, a
good number of us together resolved to find him
out; and when we had spent the best part of two
days in the thickest of the forest, we found him at
last lurking in the hollow of a huge cork-tree, from

whence he came forth to meet us as mild as could
be. But then he was so altered, his face was so disfigured, wan, and sun-burnt, that, had it not been
for his attire, which we made shift to know again,
though it was all in rags and tatters, we could not
have thought it had been the same man. He saluted us courteously, and told us in few words,
mighty handsomely put together, that we were not
to marvel to see him in that manner, for that it behooved him so to be, that he might fulfil a certain
penance enjoined him for the great sins he had committed. We prayed him to tell us who he was, but he
would by no means do it : we likewise desired him
to let us know where we might find him, that whensoever he wanted victuals we might bring him some,
which we told him we would be sure to do, for
otherwise he would be starved in that barren place :
requesting him, that if he did not like that motion
neither, he would at leastwise come and ask us for
what he wanted, and not take it by force as he had
done. He thanked us heartily for our offer, and
begged pardon for that injury, and promised to ask
it henceforwards as an alms, without setting upon
any one. As for his place of abode, he told us he
had none certain, but wherever night caught him,
there he lay : and he ended his discourse with such
bitter moans, that we must have had hearts of flint
had we not had a feeling of them, and kept him
company therein ; chiefly considering we beheld him
so strangely altered from what we had seen him before : for, as I said, he was a very fine comely young
man, and by his speech and behaviour we could
guess him to be well born, and a courtlike sort of

a body: for though we were but clowns, yet such was his genteel behavior, that we could not help being taken with it. Now as he was talking to us, he stopped of a sudden, as if he had been struck dumb, fixing his eyes steadfastly on the ground; whereat we all stood in amaze. After he had thus stared a good while, he shut his eyes, then opened them again, bit his lips, knit his brows, clutched his fists; and then rising from the ground, whereon he had thrown himself a little before, he flew at the man that stood next to him with such a fury, that if we had not pulled him off by main force, he would have bit and thumped him to death; and all the while he cried out, "Ah! traitor Ferdinand, here, here thou shalt pay for the wrong thou hast done me; I must rip up that false heart of thine;" and a deal more he added, all in dispraise of that same Ferdinand. After that he flung from us without saying a word, leaping over the bushes and brambles at such a strange rate, that it was impossible for us to come at him; from which we gathered, that his madness comes on him by fits, and that some one called Ferdinand had done him an ill turn, that hath brought the poor young man to this pass. And this hath been confirmed since that many and many times: for when he is in his right senses, he will come and beg for victuals, and thank us for it with tears: but when he is in his mad fit, he will beat us though we proffer him meat civilly: and to tell you the truth, sirs," added the goat-herd, " I and four others, of whom two are my men, and the other two my friends, yesterday agreed to look for him till we should find him out, either by fair means or by force to carry him to Almodover town, that is but eight leagues off; and there we will have him cured, if possible, or at least we shall learn what he is when he comes to his wits, and whether he has any friends to whom he may be sent back. This is all I know of the matter; and I dare assure you, that the owner of those things which you saw in the way, is the self-same body that went so nimbly by you;" for Don Quixote had by this time acquainted the goat-herd of his having seen that man skipping among the rocks.

The knight was wonderfully concerned when he had heard the goat-herd's story, and renewed his resolution of finding out that distracted wretch, whatever time and pains it might cost him. But fortune was more propitious to his desires than he could reasonably have expected: for just as they were speaking they spied him right against the place where they stood, coming towards them out of the cleft of a rock, muttering somewhat to himself, which they could not well have understood had they stood close by him, much less could they guess his meaning at that distance. His apparel was such as has already been said, only Don Quixote observed when he drew nearer, that he had on a chamois waistcoat, torn in many places, which yet the knight found to be perfumed with amber; and by this, as also by the rest of his clothes, and other conjectures, he judged him to be a man of some quality. As soon as the unhappy creature came near them, he saluted them very civilly, but with a hoarse voice. Don Quixote returned his civilities, and, alighting from Rozinante, accosted him in a very graceful manner, and hugged him close in his arms, as if he had been one of his intimate acquaintance. The other, whom we may venture to call the Knight of the Ragged Figure, as well as Don Quixote, the Knight of the Woful Figure, having got loose from that embrace, could not forbear stepping back a little, and laying his hands on the companion's shoulders, he stood staring in his face, as if he had been striving to call to mind whether he had known him before, probably wondering as much to behold Don Quixote's countenance, armor, and strange figure, as Don Quixote did to see his tattered condition: but the first that opened his mouth after this pause was the Ragged Knight, as you shall find by the sequel of the story.

CHAPTER X.

THE ADVENTURE IN THE SIERRA-MORENA CONTINUED.

THE history relates, that Don Quixote listened with great attention to the disastrous Knight of the Mountain, who made him the following compliment, " Truly, sir, whoever you be, (for I have not the honor to know you,) I am much obliged to you for your expressions of civility and friendship; and I could wish I were in a condition to convince you otherwise than by words of the deep sense I have of them : but my bad fortune leaves me nothing to return for so many favors, but unprofitable wishes." " Sir," answered Don Quixote, "I have so hearty a desire to serve you, that I was fully resolved not to depart these mountains till I had found you out, that I might know from yourself, whether the discontents that have urged you to make choice of this unusual course of life, might not admit of a remedy; for if they do, assure yourself I will leave no means untried, till I have purchased you that ease which I heartily wish you : or if your disasters are of that fatal kind that exclude you for ever from the hopes of comfort or relief, then will I mingle sorrows with you, and, by sharing your load of grief, help you to bear the oppressing weight of affliction; for it is the only comfort of the miserable to have partners in their woes. If, then, good intentions may plead merit, or a grateful requital, let me entreat you, sir, by that generous nature that shoots through the gloom with which adversity has clouded your graceful outside; nay, let me conjure you by the darling object of your wishes, to let me know who you are, and what strange misfortunes have urged you to withdraw from the converse of your fellow-creatures, to bury yourself alive in this horrid solitude, where you linger out a wretched being, a stranger to ease, to all mankind, and even to your very self. "And I solemnly swear," added Don Quixote, "by the order of knighthood, of which I am an unworthy professor, that if you so far gratify my desires, I will assist you to the utmost of my capacity, either by remedying your disaster, if it is not past redress; or at least I will become your partner in sorrow, and strive to ease it by a society in sadness."

The Knight of the Wood, hearing the Knight of the Woful Figure talk at that rate, looked upon him,

steadfastly for a long time, and viewed, and reviewed
him from head to foot; and when he had gazed a
great while upon him, " Sir," cried he, " if you have
any thing to eat, for heaven's sake give it me, and
when my hunger is abated, I shall be better able to
comply with your desires, which your great civilities and undeserved offers oblige me to satisfy."
Sancho and the goat-herd, hearing this, presently
took out some victuals, the one out of his bag, the
other out of his scrip, and gave it to the ragged
knight to allay his hunger, who immediately fell on
with that greedy haste, that he seemed rather to devour than feed; for he used no intermission between
bit and bit, so greedily he chopped them up; and
all the time he was eating, neither he, nor the by-
standers, spoke the least word. When he had assuaged his voracious appetite, he beckoned to Don
Quixote and the rest to follow him; and after he
had brought them to a neighboring meadow, he
laid himself at his ease on the grass, where the rest
of the company sitting down by him, neither he nor
they having yet spoke a word since he fell to eating,
he began in this manner:

" Gentlemen," said he, "if you intend to be informed of my misfortunes, you must promise me
beforehand not to cut off the thread of my doleful
narration with any questions, or any other interruption; for in the very instant that any of you does it,
I shall leave off abruptly, and will not afterwards
go on with the story." This preamble put Don
Quixote in mind of Sancho's ridiculous tale, which
by his neglect in not telling the goats, was brought
to an untimely conclusion. " I only use this pre-

caution," added the ragged knight, "because I would be quick in my relation; for the very remembrance of my former misfortune proves a new one to me, and yet I promise you, will endeavor to omit nothing that is material, that you may have as full an account of my disasters as I am sensible you desire." Thereupon Don Quixote, for himself and the rest, having promised him uninterrupted attention, he proceeded in this manner:

"My name is Cardenio, the place of my birth one of the best cities in Andalusia; my descent noble, my parents wealthy, but my misfortunes are so great, that they have doubtless filled my relations with the deepest of sorrows; nor are they to be remedied with wealth, for goods of fortune avail but little against the anger of heaven. In the same town dwelt the charming Lucinda, the most beautiful creature that ever nature framed, equal in descent and fortune to myself, but more happy and less constant. I loved, nay adored her almost from her infancy; and from her tender years she blessed me with as kind a return as is suitable with the innocent freedom of that age. Our parents were conscious of that early friendship; nor did they oppose the growth of this inoffensive passion, which they perceived could have no other consequences than a happy union of our families by marriage; a thing which the equality of our births and fortunes did indeed of itself almost invite us to. Afterwards our loves so grew up with our years, that Lucinda's father, either judging our usual familiarity prejudicial to his daughter's honor, or for some other reasons, sent to desire me to discontinue my frequent visits to his house : but this restraint proved but like that which was used by the parents of that loving Thisbe, so celebrated by the poets, and but added flames to flames, and impatience to desires. As our tongues were now debarred their former privilege, we had recourse to our pens, which assumed the greater freedom to disclose the most hidden secrets of our hearts; for the presence of the beloved object often heightens a certain awe and bashfulness, that disorders, confounds, and strikes dumb, even the most passionate lover. How many letters have I wrote to that lovely charmer! how many soft moving verses have I addressed to her! what kind, yet honorable returns have I received from her! the mutual pledges of our secret love, and the innocent consolations of a violent passion. At length, languishing and wasting with desire, deprived of that reviving comfort of my soul, I resolved to remove those bars with which her father's care and decent caution obstructed my only happiness, by demanding her of him in marriage : he very civilly told me, that he thanked me for the honor I did him, but that I had a father alive, whose consent was to be obtained as well as his, and who was the most proper person to make such a proposal. I thanked him for his civil answer, and thought it carried some show of reason, not doubting but my father would readily consent to the proposal. I therefore immediately went to wait on him, with a design to beg his approbation and assistance. I found him in his chamber with a letter opened before him, which, as soon as he saw me, he put into my hand, before I could have time to acquaint him with my business.

' Cardenio,' said he, ' you will see by this letter the extraordinary kindness that Duke Ricardo has for you.' I suppose I need not tell you, gentlemen, that this Duke Ricardo is a grandee of Spain, most of whose estate lies in the best part of Andalusia. I read the letter, and found it contained so kind and advantageous an offer, that my father could not but accept of it with thankfulness; for the duke entreated him to send me to him with all speed, that I might be the companion of his eldest son, promising withal to advance me to a post answerable to the good opinion he had of me.

" This unexpected news struck me dumb; but my surprise and disappointment were much greater, when I heard my father say to me, ' Cardenio, you must get ready to be gone in two days : in the mean time give heaven thanks for opening you a way to that preferment which I am so sensible you deserve.' After this he gave me several wise admonitions both as father and a man of business, and then he left me. The day fixed for my journey quickly came ; however, the night that preceded it, I spoke to Lucinda at her window, and told her what had happened. I also gave her father a visit, and informed him of it too, beseeching him to preserve his good opinion of me, and defer the bestowing of his daughter till I had been with Duke Ricardo, which he kindly promised me : and then, Lucinda and I, after an exchange of vows and protestations of eternal fidelity, took our leaves of each other with all the grief which two tender and passionate lovers can feel at a separation.

" I left the town, and went to wait upon the

duke, who received and entertained me with that
extraordinary kindness and civility that soon raised
the envy of his greatest favorities. But he that
most endearingly caressed me, was Don Ferdinand,
the duke's second son, a young, airy, handsome,
generous gentleman, and of a very amorous disposition ; he seemed to be overjoyed at my coming,
and in a most obliging manner told me, he would
have me one of his most intimate friends. In short,
he so really convinced me of his affection, that though
his elder brother gave me many testimonies of love
and esteem, yet could I easily distinguish between
their favors.   Now, as it is common for bosom
friends to keep nothing secret from each other, Don
Ferdinand, relying as much on my fidelity, as I had
reason to depend on his, revealed to me his most
private thoughts ; and among the rest, his being in
love with the daughter of a very rich farmer, who
was his father's vassal.   The beauty of that lovely
country maid, her virtue, her discretion, and the
other graces of her mind, gained her the admiration of all those who approached her : and those
uncommon endowments had so charmed the soul
of Don Ferdinand, that, finding it absolutely impossible to corrupt her chastity, since she would not
yield to his embraces as a mistress, he resolved to
marry her.   I thought myself obliged by all the ties
of gratitude and friendship, to dissuade him from
so unsuitable a match ; and therefore I made use
of such arguments as might have diverted any one
but so confirmed a lover from such an unequal
choice.   At last, finding them all ineffectual, I resolved to inform the duke his father with his inten-

tions: but Don Ferdinand was too clear-sighted
not to read my design in my great dislike of his
resolutions, and dreading such a discovery, which
he knew my duty to his father might well warrant,
in spite of our intimacy, since I looked upon such
a marriage as highly prejudicial to them both, he
made it his business to hinder me from betraying
his passion to his father, assuring me, there would
be no need to reveal it to him. To blind me the
more effectually, he told me he was willing to try
the power of absence, that common cure of love,
thereby to wear out and lose his unhappy passion;
and that in order to this, he would take a journey
with me to my father's house, pretending to buy
horses in our town, where the best in the world are
bred. No sooner had I heard this plausible proposal but I approved it, swayed by the interest of my
own love, that made me fond of an opportunity to
see my absent Lucinda.

"I have heard since, that Don Ferdinand had
already been blessed by his mistress, with all the
liberty of boundless love, upon a promise of marriage, and that he only waited an opportunity to
discover it with safety, being afraid of incurring
his father's indignation. But as what we call love
in young men, is too often only an irregular passion, and boiling desire, that has no other object
than sensual pleasure, and vanishes with enjoy-
ment, while real love, fixing itself on the perfections of the mind, is still improving and permanent; as soon as Don Ferdinand had accomplished
his lawless desires, his strong affection slackened,
and his hot love grew cold: so that if at first his

proposing to try the power of absence was only a
pretence, that he might get rid of his passion, there
was nothing now which he more heartily coveted,
that he might thereby avoid fulfilling his promise.
And therefore having obtained the duke's leave,
away we posted to my father's house, where Don
Ferdinand was entertained according to his quality; and I went to visit my Lucinda, who, by a
thousand innocent endearments, made me sensible,
that her love, like mine, was rather heightened than
weakened by absence, if any thing could heighten
a love so great and so perfect. I then thought
myself obliged by the laws of friendship, not to
conceal the secrets of my heart from so kind and
intimate a friend, who had so generously intrusted
me with his; and therefore, to my eternal ruin, I
unhappily discovered to him my passion. I praised Lucinda's beauty, her wit, her virtue, and praised them so like a lover, so often, and so highly,
that I raised in him a great desire to see so accomplished a lady; and, to gratify his curiosity, I
showed her to him by the help of a light, one evening, at a low window, where we used to have our
amorous interviews. She proved but too charming,
and too strong a temptation to Don Ferdinand;
and her prevailing image made so deep an impression on his soul, that it was sufficient to blot out
of his mind all those beauties that had till then
employed his wanton thoughts. He was struck
dumb with wonder and delight, at the sight of the
ravishing apparition; and, in short, to see her, and
to love her, proved with him the same thing: and
when I say to love her, I need not add, to despera-

tion, for there is no loving her but to an extreme. If her face made him so soon take fire, her wit quickly set him all in a flame. He often importuned me to communicate to him some of her letters, which I indeed would never expose to any eyes but my own; but unhappily one day he found one, wherein she desired me to demand her of her father, and to hasten the marriage. It was penned with that tenderness and discretion, that, when he had read it, he presently cried out, that the amorous charms which were scattered and divided among other beauties, were all divinely centred in Lucinda, and in Lucinda alone. Shall I confess a shameful truth? Lucinda's praises, though never so deserved, did not sound pleasantly to my ears out of Don Ferdinand's mouth. I began to entertain I know not what distrusts and jealous fears, the rather, because he would be still improving the least opportunity of talking of her, and insensibly turning the discourse he held of other matters, to make her the subject, though never so far-fetched, of our constant talk. Not that I was apprehensive of the least infidelity from, Lucinda: far from it; she gave me daily fresh assurances of her inviolable affection; but I feared every thing from my malignant stars, and lovers are commonly industrious to make themselves uneasy.

"It happened, one day, that Lucinda, who took great delight in reading books of knight-errantry, desired me to lend her the romance of Amadis de Gaul"——

Scarce had Cardenio mentioned knight-errantry, when Don Quixote interrupted him: "Sir," said

he, " had you but told me, when you first mentioned
the Lady Lucinda, that she was an admirer of
books of knight-errantry, there had been no need
of using any amplification to convince me of her
being a person of uncommon sense; yet, sir, had
she not used those mighty helps, those infallible
guides to sense, though indulgent nature had strove
to bless her with the richest gifts she can bestow, I
might justly enough have doubted whether her perfections could have gained her the love of a person
of your merit; but now you need not employ your
eloquence to set forth the greatness of her beauty,
the excellence of her worth, or the depth of her
sense, for, from this account which I have of her
taking great delight in reading books of chivalry, I
dare pronounce her to be the most beautiful, nay,
the most accomplished lady in the universe; and I
heartily could have wished, that with Amadis de
Gaul, you had sent her the worthy Don Rugel of
Greece; for I am certain the Lady Lucinda would
have been extremely delighted with Daryda and
Garaya, as also with the discreet shepherd Darinel,
and those admirable verses of his bucolics, which
he sung and repeated with so good a grace. But a
time may yet be found to give her the satisfaction
of reading those masterpieces, if you will do me
the honor to come to my house, for there I may
supply you with above three hundred volumes,
which are my soul's greatest delight, and the darling comfort of my life; though now I remember
myself, I have just reason to fear there is not one
of them left in my study, thanks to the malicious
envy of wicked enchanters. I beg your pardon for

giving you this interruption, contrary to my promise; but when I hear the least mention made of knight-errantry, it is no more in my power to forbear speaking, than it is in the sunbeams not to warm, or in those of the moon not to impart her natural humidity; and therefore, sir, I beseech you to go on."

While Don Quixote was running on with this impertinent digression, Cardenio hung down his head on his breast with all the signs of a man lost in sorrow; nor could Don Quixote, with repeated entreaties, persuade him to look up, or answer a word. At last, after he had stood thus a considerable while, he raised his head, and, suddenly breaking silence, "I am positively convinced," cried he, "nor shall any man in the world ever persuade me to the contrary; and he's a blockhead who says, that great villain, Master Elisabat,* never lay with Queen Madasima."

"It is false!" cried Don Quixote, in a mighty heat; "by all the powers above, it is all scandal and base detraction to say this of Queen Madasima! She was a most noble and virtuous lady; nor is it to be presumed that so great a princess would ever debase herself so far as to fall in love with a quack. Whoever dares to say she did, lies like an arrant villain; and I'll make him acknowledge it either a-foot or a-horseback, armed, or unarmed, by night or by day, or how he pleases."

* Elisabat is a skilful surgeon in Amadis de Gaul, who performs wonderful cures; and Queen Madasima is wife to Gantasis, and makes a great figure in the aforesaid romance; they travel and lie together in woods and deserts, without any imputation on her honor.

Cardenio very earnestly fixed his eyes on Don Quixote, while he was thus defying him, and taking Queen Madasima's part, as if she had been his true and lawful princess ; and being provoked by these abuses into one of his mad fits, he took up a great stone that lay by him, and hit Don Quixote such a blow on his breast with it, that it beat him down backwards. Sancho, seeing his lord and master so roughly handled, fell upon the mad knight with his clenched fists ; but he beat him off at the first onset, and laid him at his feet with a single blow, and then fell a trampling on his guts, like a baker in a dough-trough. Nay, the goat-herd, who was offering to take Sancho's part, had like to have been served in the same manner. So the Ragged Knight, having tumbled them one over another, and beaten them handsomely, left them, and ran into the wood without the least opposition.

Sancho got up when he saw him gone; and being very much out of humor to find himself so roughly handled without any manner of reason, began to pick a quarrel with the goat-herd, railing at him for not forewarning them of the Ragged Knight's mad fits, that they might have stood upon their guard. The goat-herd answered, he had given them warning at first, and if he could not hear, it was no fault of his. To this Sancho replied, and the goat-herd made a rejoinder, till from *Pros* and *Cons* they fell to a warmer way of disputing, and went to fisticuffs together, catching one another by the beards, and tugging, hauling, and belaboring one another so unmercifully, that, had not Don Quixote parted them, they would have pulled one another's chins off. Sancho, in great warmth, still keeping his hold, cried to his master, " Let me alone, Sir Knight of the Woful Figure : this is no dubbed knight, but an ordinary fellow like myself; I may be revenged on him for the wrong he has done me ; let me box it out, and fight him fairly hand to fist like a man." " Thou mayest fight him as he is thy equal," answered Don Quixote ; "but thou oughtest not to do it, since he has done us no wrong." After this he pacified them, and then addressing himself to the goat-herd, he asked him whether it was possible to find out Cardenio again, that he might hear the end of his story ? The goat-herd answered, that, as he had already told him, he knew of no settled place he used, but that if they made any stay thereabouts, he might be sure to meet with him, mad or sober, some time or other.

NOTES

DON QUIXOTE.

NOTE I. p. 13.

At a certain village in La Mancha, of which I cannot remember the name. — It is clear that the author meant to assign no special locality to the Aldea, or village of the renowned Hidalgo. But in this, as in other cases, commentators became desirous of seeing farther into the mill-stone, and have assigned to Argasamilla de Alba the honor of being Don Quixote's habitation. Avellenada first named it as such, in his Continuation of Don Quixote.

NOTE II. p. 13.

A lance upon a rack. — In Spain, as in the other parts of Europe, the country gentlemen, when called on to discharge military duty, used the lance, which was usually deposited upon a rack, in the hall or porch of their habitations.

NOTE III. p. 13.

Griefs and groans. — *Duelos y quebrantos.* — This dish has puzzled the critics, having been termed by Stevens, eggs and collops, by Audin, eggs and beer; by Jervis, an omelet; by others, fried hams; by others, pease, herbs, or such other windy diet, as was like to engender cholic; while Ozell hints, it means a dish of nothing at all. Pelicer explains the dish to be composed of sausages, made of sheep which had died of disease, or otherwise, without the butcher's assistance — taking its name, therefore, from the sentiment which the loss excited in the farmer or owner.

NOTE IV. p. 14.

Feliciano de Sylva. — This learned and eloquent Castilian composed (or, according to the title page, amended and edited from the ancient version of Zerfea, Queen of the Argines) the history of the two valiant knights, Don Florisel de Niquea, and the brave Anaxartes, printed at Saragossa in 1584. The author was the son of Tristan de Sylva, the historian of Charles V.

NOTE V. p. 15.

Don Belianis of Greece. — A romance of chivalry, formed on the model of the Amadis, but with infinitely less art and interest, and on a much coarser plan. It seems to have had a great share of popularity, however, in its day ; and made its appearance in all the languages in which romances were written. There is, among others, an English abridgment, (in quarto,) entitled " The Honour of Chivalry, or the Famous and Delectable History of Don Belianis of Greece, containing the valiant Exploits of that magnanimous and heroic Prince, son unto the Emperor Don Belianis of Greece, wherein are described the strange and dangerous adventures that befell him, with his love towards the Princess Florisbella, daughter to the Suldan of Babyloun, &c. &c. London, at the three Bibles, in London Bridge, 1683."

The allusion in the text is to these words, at the end of the original Don Belianis, " Suplir yo con fingimientos historia tan estimada seria aggravio, &c. &c.

NOTE VI. p. 15.

Had taken his degrees at Siguenza. — A Spanish university of minor note.

NOTE VII. p. 15.

Palmerin of England, or Amadis de Gaul. — These knights have been made so well known to the British public, by the excellent abridgments, which Mr. Southey has made of their adventures, that it is only necessary to refer to books in the hands of every lover of ancient literature. It is no small debt we owe to the author of Thalaba, Kehama, and Don Roderick, that he could stoop from his own lofty sphere of original composition, to the task of presenting to us, in an intelligible and pleasing form, whatever was characteristic and interesting in the ancient romance.

NOTE VIII. p. 16.

The Cid Ruydiaz. — A romantic champion, well known by Corneille's tragedy of the Cid, as well as by Southey's curious version of the Chronicle of his exploits. He was, like most popular heroes, an ill requited chief, banished from Castile by his sovereign, and reduced to live the life of an outlaw, and support himself and his followers by warring upon the Moors on his own account. The real history of this remarkable personage is lost in a cloud of romantic fiction. He is said to have conquered Valentia from the Moors.

A distinguished German critic speaks thus of the old Spanish poem on the exploits of the Cid — a production of which some curious specimens are admirably translated by Mr. Frere, at the end of Mr. Southey's Chronicle.

" The literature of Spain possesses a high advantage over that of most other nations, in its historical heroic romance of the Cid. This is exactly that species of poetry which exerts the nearest and most powerful influence over the national feelings and character of a people. A single work, such as the Cid, is of more real value to a nation than a whole library of books, however abounding in wit or intellect, which are destitute of the spirit of nationality. Although in the shape in which it now appears, the work was probably produced about the 11th century, yet the whole body of its inventions belongs to the older period antecedent to the Crusades. There is here no trace of that oriental taste for the wonderful and the fabulous, which afterwards became so predominant. It breathes the pure, true-hearted, noble old Castilian spirit, and is in fact the true history of the Cid, first arranged and extended into a poetical form, very shortly, it is probable, after the age of that hero himself. I have already taken notice that the heroic poetry and mythology of almost all nations is in its essence tragical and elegiac. But there is another less serious view of the heroic life, which was often represented even by the ancients themselves. Hercules and his bodily strength, and his eating, are drawn in the true colors of comedy, and the wandering adventures and lying stories of Ulysses, have been the original of all amusing romances. But, in truth, specimens of this sort of representation are to be found in the histories of almost all great heroes. However powerfully history may represent the hero's superiority in magnanimity, in bravery, and in corporeal strength, it effects its purpose by depicting him not among the poetical obscurities of a world of wonders, but surrounded by the realities of life; and it is then that we receive the strongest impression of his power, when we see it exerted in opposition, not to imaginary evils of which we have little conception, but to the every day difficulties and troubles of the world, to which we ourselves feel that ordinary men are incapable of offering any resistance. We have many instances of this comic sort of writing in the Spanish Cid; for example, there is the description of his rather unfair method of raising money to support his war against the Moors, by borrowing from a Jewish usurer, and leaving a chest of old stones and lumber as his pledge; and the account of the insult offered to his dead body by another of that race, and the terror into which he was thrown by the Cid starting up on his bier, and drawing his sword a span's length out of the scabbard. These are touches of popular humor by no means out of place in a romance founded on popular traditions. But there is a spirit of more delicate irony in those sorrowful lamentations with which Donna Ximena is made to address the King on account of the protracted absence of her husband, as well as in the reply of the monarch."— *See Schlegel on the History of Literature*, vol. i. p. 343.

NOTE IX. p. 16.

Bernardo del Carpio. — Of this personage, we find little or nothing in the French romances of Charlemagne. He belongs exclusively to Spanish History, or rather to Spanish Romance; in which the honor is claimed for him of slaying the famous Orlando, or Roland, the nephew of Charlemagne, in the fatal field of Roncesvalles. · His history is as follows:—

The continence which procured for Alonzo, who succeeded to the precarious throne of the Christians, in the Asturias, about 795, the epithet of The Chaste, was not universal in his family. By an intrigue with Sancho, Count of Saldenha, Donna Ximena, sister of this virtuous prince, bore a son. Some historians attempt to gloss over this incident by alleging that a private marriage had taken place betwixt the lovers; but King Alphonso, who was wellnigh sainted for living only in platonic union with his own wife Bertha, took the scandal greatly to heart. He shut the peccant princess up in a cloister, and imprisoned her gallant in the castle of Luna, where he caused him to be deprived of sight. Fortunately, his wrath did not extend to the offspring of their stolen affections, the famous Bernardo del Carpio. When the youth had grown up to manhood, Alphonso, according to the Spanish historians, invited the Emperor Charlemagne into Spain, and having neglected to raise up heirs for the kingdom of the Goths in the ordinary manner, he proposed the inheritance of his throne as the price of the alliance of Charles. But the nobility, headed by Bernardo del Carpio, remonstrated against the king's choice of a successor, and would on no account consent to receive a Frenchman as heir of their crown. Alphonso himself repented of the invitation he had given to Charlemagne, and when that champion of Christendom came to expel the Moors from Spain, he found the conscientious and chaste Alphonso had united with the infidels against him. An engagement took place in the renowned pass of Roncesvalles, in which the French were defeated, and the celebrated Roland, or Orlando, was slain. The victory was ascribed chiefly to the prowess of Bernardo del Carpio.

In several of the old ballads, which record the real or imaginary feats of Bernardo, his royal uncle is represented as having shown but little gratitude for the great champion's services, in the campaign against Charlemagne. It appears that the king had not relented in favor of Don Sancho, although he had come under some promise of that sort to his son, at the period when his (the son's) services were most necessary. The following is a translation of one of the oldest of the Spanish ballads in which this part of Carpio's story is told.

BERNARDO AND ALPHONSO.

I.

With some good ten of his chosen men, Bernardo hath appear'd
Before them all in the palace hall, the lying King to beard;
With cap in hand and eye on ground, he came in reverend guise,
But ever and anon he frown'd, and flame broke from his eyes.

II.

"A curse upon thee," cries the King, " who comest unbid to me;
But what from traitor's blood should spring, save traitors like to thee?
His sire, Lords, had a traitor's heart; perchance our Champion brave
May think it were a pious part to share Don Sancho's grave."

III.

" Whoever told this tale the King, hath rashness to repeat,"
Cries Bernard, " here my gage I fling before THE LIAR'S feet!
No treason was in Sancho's blood, no stain in mine doth lie —
Below the throne what knight will own the coward calumny?

IV.

" The blood that I like water shed, when Roland did advance,
By secret traitors bought and led, to make us slaves of France;
The life of King Alphonso I saved at Ronseval,—
Your words, Lord King, are recompense abundant for it all.

V.

" Your horse was down — your hope was flown — ye saw the faulchion
            shine,
That soon had drunk your royal blood, had I not ventured mine;
But memory soon of service done deserteth the ingrate,
And ye've thank'd the son for life and crown by the father's bloody fate.

VI.

" Ye swore upon your kingly faith, to set Don Sancho free,
But curse upon your paultring breath, the light he ne'er did see;
He died in dungeon cold and dim, by Alphonso's base decree.
And visage blind, and mangled limb, were all they gave to me.

VII.

" The King that swerveth from his word, hath stain'd his purple black,
No Spanish Lord will draw the sword behind a liar's back;
But noble vengeance shall be mine. and open hate I'll show—
The King hath injured Carpio's line, and Bernard is his foe."

VIII.

"Seize — seize him! "—loud the King doth scream — " There are a
    thousand here —
Let his foul blood this instant stream,—What! Caitiffs, do ye fear?
Seize — seize the traitor! " But not one to move a finger dareth, —
Bernardo standeth by the throne, and calm his sword he bareth.

IX.

He drew the faulchion from the sheath, and held it up on high,
And all the hall was still as death — cries Bernard, " Here am I,
And here is the sword that owns no lord, excepting heaven and me;
Fain would I know who dares his point — King, Conde, or Grandee."

X.

Then to his mouth the horn he drew — (it hung below his cloak)
His ten true men the signal knew, and through the ring they broke;
With helm on head, and blade in hand, the knights the circle brake,
And back the lordlings 'gan to stand, and the false King to quake.

XI.

" Ha! Bernard," quoth Alphonso, " what means this warlike guise?
Ye know full well I jested — ye know your worth I prize."
But Bernard turn'd upon his heel, and smiling pass'd away —
Long rued Alphonso and Castile the jesting of that day.

I shall venture on inserting a translation of part of another
of the many ballads founded on the story of this champion. It
describes the enthusiasm excited among the Leonese, when Bernard first reared his standard, to oppose the progress of Charlemagne. This ballad was, as might have been expected, extremely
popular in Spain during the late war. It was sung frequently
by the Guerillas, while on their march.

BERNARDO'S MARCH.

I.

With three thousand men of Leon, from the city Bernard goes,
To protect the soil Hispanian from the spear of Frankish foes:
From the city which is planted in the midst between the seas,
To preserve the name and glory of old Pelayo's victories.

II.

The peasant hears upon his field the trumpet of the knight,
He quits his team for spear and shield, and garniture of might;

The shepherd hears it mid the mist — he flingeth down his crook,
And rushes from the mountain like a tempest-troubled brook.

III.

The youth who shews a maiden's chin, whose brows have ne'er been
      bound
The helmet's brazen ring within, gains manhood from the sound;
The hoary sire beside the fire forgets his feebleness,
Once more to feel the cap of steel a warrior's ringlets press.

IV.

As through the glen his spears did gleam, these soldiers from the hills,
They swell'd his host, as mountain-stream receives the roaring rills;
They round his banner flock'd, in scorn of haughty Charlemagne,
And thus upon their swords are sworn the faithful sons of Spain.

V.

" Free were we born," 'tis thus they cry, " though to our King we owe
The homage and the fealty behind his crest to go;
By God's behest our aid he shares, but God did ne'er command,
That we should leave our children heirs of an enslaved land.

VI.

" Our breasts are not so timorous, nor are our arms so weak,
Nor are our veins so bloodless, that we our vow should break,
To sell our freedom for the fear of Prince or Paladin, —
At least we'll sell our birthright dear, no bloodless prize they'll win.

VII.

" At least King Charles, if God decrees he must be lord of Spain,
Shall witness that the Leonese were not aroused in vain;
He shall bear witness that we died, as lived our sires of old,
Nor only of Numantium's pride shall minstrel tales be told.

VIII.

" The LION * that hath bathed his paws in seas of Lybian gore,
Shall he not battle for the laws and liberties of yore?
Anointed cravens may give gold to whom it likes them well,
But steadfast heart and spirit bold Alphonso ne'er shall sell."

NOTE X. p. 16.

The giant Morgante. —This giant was for some time Esquire
to Orlando.

* The arms of Leon.

Dimmi a Carlo diceva ancora Orlando
Io pel mondo vo peregrinando
E di ch'i'ho con meco un gigante
Ch'e battezzato, appellato Morgante.

PULCI, M. M. C. C. 48–9.

NOTE XI. p. 17.

Rinaldo of Montalban.— The name of this redoubted knight, son of the Great Duke Aymon, is familiar to all readers of romance, as being one of the most renowned Paladins, as they were called, who were alleged to compose the cycle of heroes around the throne of Charlemagne. He was bold, stout, and gallant; but although one of the most redoubted champions of Christendom, he was as frequently at war as in league with his liege lord Charlemagne. When he was in disgrace with the emperor, he was wont to retreat to his strong fortress of Montalban, where, with his three brothers, he maintained himself by pillage. Orlando and he were cousins-german, but often fought together, divided either by Rinaldo's quarrels with the Emperor Charles, to whom his nephew Orlando was dutifully attached, or, as represented in Ariosto, by their rivalry for the love of the fair Angelica. In the *Espejo de Cavallerias*, these two famous cavaliers are introduced as holding the following somewhat rough colloquy: The names by which they address each other, are pretty much in the same taste with those which Homer puts into the mouths of Agamemnon and Achilles, at the opening of the Iliad.

"*El conde Roldan dixo, sus falso cavaliero, &c. No le responde el buen Renaldo corteses palabras, antes con bravo semblante le dixo.* O Bastardo, hijo de mala Hembra *mientes* en todo lo que has dicho, que robar a los paganos de Espana no es robo, pues yo solo, a pesar de quarenta mil Moros, y mas, les quite *un Mahomet de oro que ove menester para pagar mis Soldados.* — P. 1. C. 46.

NOTE XII. p. 17.

Idol of Mahomet. — "Est Lapis antiquus altissimus super quem elevatur *Imago illa de auro optimo* in Effigiem hominis fusa, super pedes suos."— TURPINUS, L. 1. C. 28.

Note XIII. p. 17.

That traitor Galalon.— Galalon or Ganalon, of Mayence, was one of the best soldiers Charlemagne had, but he afterwards became a practised traitor, and being at length convicted of betraying Orlando to his fate at Roncesvalles, was condemned to be torn in pieces by " four most fierce horses."—Turpin, Book 1. C. 26. There is a ballad in the *Silva de Ronces*, upon another base trick which this Galalon played off against Rinaldo de Montalban.

> No passaron muchos dias,
> Quel traydor de Galalon
> Aquel traydor desleal
> Embio Cartas a Aliarde:
>
> Cartas para le avisar
> Que en su corte tenia
> A Renaldos de Montalban, &c.
>
> Sylva, F. 66.

Pulci frequently mentions him : as for example,

> Aldinghier grido: s'io ben ti squadro
> Non se tu *Ganelon, traditor Ladro;*
> Traditor doloroso, can ribaldo,
> Traditor nato per tradir Rinaldo.
>
> M. M. C. 22. 127.

Note XIV. p. 18.

A worse jade than Gonila's.— Gonnella was an Italian buffoon of great celebrity. Several of his jokes are recorded in Poggio's *Facetiæ;* but they were thought worthy of occupying a separate volume; viz. the "*Buffonerie di Gonnella;*" published at Florence in the year 1568. He was domestic jester to a nobleman of Ferrara, the Marchese Borso; and boasted one day, in his master's presence, of a miserable horse he commonly rode upon. The Marquis inspected the animal, and quoted the line from Plautus, which is here requoted by Cervantes: *Ossa atque pellis totus est, &c.* (Aulularia, *Act* 3. *Sc.* 6.) The jester, nothing dismayed, wagered his steed would take a leap which no horse in the Marquis's own stud would venture upon; viz. from a certain balcony many feet high, to the pavement; and he won his wager.

Note XV. p. 18.

Alexander's Bucephalus, and the Cid's Bavieca. — Montaigne, in his curious Essay, entitled " Des Destriers," says that all the world knows every thing about Bucephalus. The name of the favorite charger of the Cid Ruy Diaz, is scarcely less celebrated. Notice is taken of him in almost every one of the hundred ballads concerning the history of his master, — and there are one or two of these, of which the horse is more truly the hero than his rider. The following contains some very characteristic traits. " *El Rey aguardava al Cid*," &c.— (Deppings Sammlung Spanischer romanzen, p. 182.)

BAVIECA.

I.

The king look'd on him kindly, as on a vassal true;
Then to the king Ruy Diaz spake after reverence due,
" O king, the thing is shameful, that any man beside
The liege lord of Castile himself should Bavieca ride:

II.

" For neither Spain nor Araby could another charger bring
So good as he, and, certes, the best befits my king.
But that you may behold him, and know him to the core,
I'll make him go as he was wont when his nostrils smelt the Moor."

III.

With that, the Cid, clad as he was in mantle furr'd and wide,
On Bavieca vaulting, put the rowels in his side;
And up and down, and round and round, so fierce was his career,
Stream'd like a pennon on the wind Ruy Diaz' minivere.

IV.

And all that saw them praised them — they lauded man and horse,
As matched well, and rivalless for gallantry and force;
Ne'er had they look'd on horseman might to this knight come near,
Nor on other charger worthy of such a cavalier.

V.

Thus, to and fro a-rushing, the fierce and furious steed,
He snapt in twain his hither rein: — " God pity now the Cid,"
" God pity Diaz," cried the Lords, — but when they look'd again,
They saw Ruy Diaz ruling him with the fragment of his rein;

They saw him proudly ruling with gesture firm and calm,
Like a true Lord commanding, — and obeyed as by a lamb.

VI.

And so he led him foaming and panting to the king,
But "No," said Don Alphonso, "it were a shameful thing
That peerless Bavieca should ever be bestrid
By any mortal but Bivar — mount, mount again, my Cid," &c.

In one of these ballads, the Cid is giving directions about his funeral; he desires that they shall place his body "in full armor upon Bavieca," and so conduct him to the church of San Pedro de Cardena. This was done accordingly; and says another ballad —

> Truxeron pues a Babieca ;
> Y en mirandole se puso
> Tan triste como si fuera
> Mas rasonable que bruto.

In the Cid's last will, mention is also made of this noble charger. "When ye bury Bavieca, dig deep," says Ruy Diaz, "for shameful thing were it, that he should be eat by curs, who hath trampled down so much currish flesh of Moors."

NOTE XVI. p. 20.

A knight-errant without a Mistress.

> Hora ti prego
> Se mai fosti anchora inamorato
> Perche *ogni cavalier ch'e senza amore*
> *Sen vista e vivo e vivo senza cuore.*
> Rispose il conte "quel' Orlando sono,
> "Amor m'ha posto tutto in abandono;
> "Voglio che sappi che'l mio cor e in mano
> "De la figliola del Re Galafrone
> "Che ad Albracca dimore nel girone."
>
> BOIARDO, L. 1. 18. 467.

NOTE XVII. p. 20.

Lady, I am the giant Caraculiambro, &c. — Speeches of this kind occur *passim* in the Romances; *e. g.* in *Perceforest*, chapter 46, the title of which runs thus: "Comment le roy Perceforest envoya deux chevaliers prisonniers devers la Royne d'Angleterre sa femme. A la qual un de ceux dit, Il me conquit par force d'armes et me fit jurer que je viendroye en vostre prison de par luy que est mon Seigneur." And again in the text, " Quant il eut ce dit prent son espee per la poynte et saginouille devant la Royne et dist. Dame je me presente de mon cher seigneur le Roy d'Angleterre vostre prisonnier, *ainsi que le vouldrez ordonner* soit de mort on de vie," &c. Perhaps the name *Caraculiambro,* may be in allusion to that of *Calaucolocon,* one of the many huge men who figure in the Merlin.

NOTE XVIII. p. 23.

The ancient and celebrated plain of Montiel. — The celebrity of the plain of Montiel arose from its having been the scene of one of the darkest tragedies in the early history of Spain.

The death of Don Pedro, called the Cruel, by the hands of his brother, Henry of Transtamara, is an incident more than once alluded to by Cervantes. The English reader will probably remember, that Don Pedro, King of Castile, deposed by his subjects on account of his excessive cruelty, was replaced on the throne by the assistance of our Black Prince, who, in 1366, at the battle of Nejara, defeated Henry of Transtamara, the natural brother of Pedro, who had been called to the throne by the insurgents. In 1368, when this formidable ally of Don Pedro had retired into Gascony, Henry, in his turn, came back from exile at the head of a small but gallant army, most of whom were French auxiliaries, commanded by the celebrated Bertram Du Gleaquin, or, as he is more commonly called, Du Guesclin. He encountered Don Pedro, at the head of an army six times more numerous than that which he commanded, but which consisted partly of Jews, Saracens, and Portuguese, miscellaneous auxiliaries, who gave way before the ardor of the French chivalry, so that Henry remained victorious, and Pedro was compelled to take refuge in the neighboring castle of Montiel. The fortress was so strictly blockaded by the victorious enemy, that the king was compelled to attempt his escape by night, with only twelve persons in his retinue, Ferdinand de Castro being the person of most note among them. As they wandered in the dark, they were encountered by a body of French cavalry making the rounds, commanded by an adventurous knight, called Le Begue of Villaines. Compelled to surrender, Don Pedro put himself under the safeguard of this officer, promising him a rich ransom, if he would conceal him from the knowledge of his brother Henry. The knight, according to Froissart, promised him concealment, and conveyed him to his own quarters. But in the course of an hour, Henry was apprised that he was taken, and came with some of his followers, to the tent of Allan de la Houssaye, where his unfortunate brother had been placed. In entering the chamber, he exclaimed, " Where is that whore-son and Jew, who calls himself King of Castile ? " Pedro, as proud and fearless as he was cruel, stepped instantly forward and replied, " Here I stand, the lawful son and heir of Don Alphonso, and it is thou that art but a false bastard." The rival brethren instantly grappled like lions, the French knights and Du Guesclin himself looking on. Henry drew his poniard and wounded Pedro in the face, but his body was defended by a coat of mail; and in the struggle which ensued, Henry fell across a bench, and his brother being uppermost, had wellnigh mastered him, when one of Henry's followers seizing Don Pedro by the leg, turned him over, and his master gaining the upper hand, instantly poniarded him. Froissart calls this man the Vicompte de Roquebetyn, and others the Bastard d'Anisse. Menard, in his History of Du Guesclin, says, that while all around gazed like statues on the furious struggle of the brothers, Du Guesclin exclaimed to this attendant of Henry, " What! will you stand by and see your master placed at such a pass by a false renegade — Make forward and aid him, for well you may."

Pedro's head was cut off, and his remains were meanly buried. They were afterwards disinterred by his daughter, the wife of John of Gaunt, and deposited in Seville, with the honors due to his rank. His memory was regarded with a strange mixture of horror and compassion, which recommended him as a subject for legend and for romance. He had caused his wife Blanche de Bourbon to be assassinated — had murdered three of his brothers — banished his mother, and committed numberless cruelties upon his subjects. He had, which the age held equally scandalous, held a close intimacy with the Jews and Saracens, and had enriched him at the expense of the church. Yet, in spite of all these crimes, his undaunted bravery and energy of character, together with the strange circumstances of his death, excited milder feelings towards his memory. There are many ballads founded on Dou Pedro's history. That which Sancho afterwards quotes more than once, giving an account of his death, may be thus translated:

THE DEATH OF DON PEDRO.

I.

Henry and King Pedro clasping,
   Hold in straining arms each other;
Tugging hard, and closely grasping,
   Brother proves his strength with brother

II.

Harmless pastime, sport fraternal,
   Blends not thus their limbs in strife;
Either aims with rage infernal,
   Naked dagger, sharpened knife.

III.

Close Don Henry grapples Pedro,
   Pedro holds Don Henry strait,
Breathing this triumphant fury,
   That despair and mortal hate.

IV.

Sole spectator of the struggle,
   Stands Don Henry's page afar,
In the chase who bore his bugle,
   And who bore his sword in war.

V.

Down they go in deadly wrestle,
   Down upon the earth they go,
Fierce King Pedro has the vantage,
   Stout Don Henry falls below.

VI.

Marking then the fatal crisis,
   Up the page of Henry ran,
By the waist he caught Don Pedro,
   Aiding thus the fallen man.

VII.

"King to place, or to depose him,
　Dwelleth not in my desire,
But the duty which he owes him,
　To his master pays the squire."

VIII.

Now Don Henry has the upmost,
　Now King Pedro lies beneath,
In his heart his brother's poniard
　Instant finds its bloody sheath.

IX.

Thus with mortal gasp and quiver,
　While the blood in bubbles well'd,
Fled the fiercest soul that ever
　In a Christian bosom dwell'd.

There is another old Spanish ballad on the death of Pedro,
of which Depping, the German collector, speaks in terms of
high commendation. As Pedro's story is so frequently alluded
to by Cervantes, I shall insert a translation of this also.

THE PROCLAMATION OF KING HENRY.

I.

At the feet of Don Henrique now King Pedro dead is lying,
Not that Henry's might was greater, but that blood to heaven was crying.
Though deep the dagger had its sheath within his brother's breast,
Firm on the frozen throat beneath Don Henry's foot is prest.

II.

So dark and sullen is the glare of Pedro's lifeless eyes,
Still half he fears what slumbers there, to vengeance may arise.
So stands the brother; on his brow the mark of blood is seen,
Yet had he not been Pedro's Cain, his Cain had Pedro been.

III.

Close round the scene of cursed strife, the armed knights appear
Of either band, with silent thoughts of joyfulness or fear;
All for a space, in silence, the fratricide survey,
Then sudden bursts the mingling voice of triumph and dismay.

IV.

Glad shout on shout from Henry's host, ascends unto the sky;
" God save King Henry — save the King — King Henry! " is their cry.
But Pedro's Barons clasp their brows, in sadness stand they near,
Whate'er to others he had been, their friend lies murdered here.

V.

The deed, say those, was justly done — a tyrant's soul is sped;
These ban and curse the traitorous blow, by which a king is dead.
" Now see," cries one, how heaven's amand asserts the people's rights; "
Another— " God will judge the hand that God's anointed smites."

VI.

" The Lord's vicegerent," quoth a priest, " is sovereign of the land,
And he rebels 'gainst heaven's behest, that slights his king's command."
" Now heaven be witness, if he sinn'd," thus speaks a gallant young,
" The fault was in Padilla's eye, that o'er him magic flung.

VII.

" Or if no magic be her blame, so heavenly fair is she,
The wisest, for so bright a dame, might well a sinner be.
Let none speak ill of Pedro — No Roderick hath he been,
He dearly loved fair Spain, although 'tis true he slew the Queen."

VIII.

The words he spoke they all might hear, yet none vouchsafe reply,
" God save great Henry — save the King — King Henry! " is the cry;
While Pedro's liegemen turn aside, their groans are in your ear,
" Whate'er to others he hath been, our friend lies slaughtered here! "

IX.

Nor paltry souls are wanting among King Pedro's band,
That now their King is dead, draw near to kiss his murderer's hand;
The false cheek clothes it in a smile, and laughs the hollow eye,
And wags the traitor tongue the while with flattery's ready lie.

X.

" The valour of the King that *is* — the justice of his cause —
The blindness and the tyrannies of him the king that *was* —
All — all are doubled in their speech, yet truth enough is there
To sink the spirit shivering near, in darkness of despair.

XI.

The murder of the Master,* the tender Infant's doom,
And blessed Blanche's thread of life snapt short in dungeon's gloom,
With tragedies yet unreveal'd, that stain'd the king's abode,
By lips his bounty should have seal'd, are blazon'd black abroad.

XII.

Whom served he most at others' cost, most loud they rend the sky,
" God save great Henry — save our King — King Henry! " is the cry.
But still, amid too many foes, the grief is in your ear
Of dead King Pedro's faithful few — "Alas! our lord lies here!"

XIII.

But others' tears, and others' groans, what are they, match'd with thine,
Maria de Padilla — star of thine exiled line!
Because she is King Henry's slave, the damsel weepeth sore,
Because she's Pedro's widow'd love, alas! she weepeth more.

XIV.

" O Pedro! Pedro! hear her cry — how often did I say
That wicked counsel and weak trust would haste thy life away;"
She stands upon her turret top, she looks down from on high,
Where mantled in his bloody cloak she sees her lover lie.　　　·

XV.

Low lies King Pedro in his blood, while bending down ye see
Caitiffs that trembled ere he spake, crouch'd at his murderer's knee;
They place the sceptre in his hand, and on his head the crown,
And trumpets clear are blown, and bells are merry through the town.

XVI.

The sun shines bright, and the gay rout with clamors rend the sky,
" God save great Henry — save the King — King Henry! " is the cry;
But the pale Jewess weeps above, with many a bitter tear,
Whate'er he was, he was her love, and he lies slaughtered here.

XVII.

At first, in silence down her cheek the drops of sadness roll,
But rage and anger come to break the sorrow of her soul;
The triumph of her haters — the gladness of their cries,
Enkindle flames of ire and scorn within her tearful eyes.

* The Master of the order of Calatrava, who was treacherously invited
to a banquet, and slain by Pedro shortly before.

XVIII.

In her hot cheek the blood mounts high, as she stands gazing down,
Now on proud Henry's royal state, his robe and golden crown,
And now upon the trampled cloak that hides not from her view
The slaughter'd Pedro's marble brow, and lips of livid hue.

XIX.

With furious grief she twists her hands among her long black hairs,
And all from off her lovely brow the blameless locks she tears:
She tears the ringlets from her front, and scatters all the pearls
King Pedro's hand had planted among the raven curls.

XX.

" Stop, caitiff tongues ! " — they hear her not—" King Pedro's love
   am I."
They heed her not —" God save the King — great Henry ! " still they cry.
She rends her hair, she wrings her hands, but none to help is near,
" God look in vengeance on their deed, my lord lies murdered here ! "

XXI.

Away she flings her garments, her broider'd veil and vest,
As if they should behold her love within her lovely breast —
As if to call upon her foes the constant heart to see,
Where Pedro's form is still enshrined, and evermore shall be.

XXII.

But none on fair Maria looks, by none her breast is seen,
Save angry Heaven, remembering well the murder of the Queen,
The wounds of jealous harlot rage, which virgin blood must staunch,
And all the scorn that mingled in the bitter cup of Blanche.

XXIII.

The utter coldness of neglect that haughty spirit stings,
As if a thousand fiends were there, with all their flapping wings;
She wraps the veil about her head, as if 'twere all a dream —
The love — the murder — and the wrath — and that rebellious scream;

XXIV.

For still there's shouting on the plain, and spurring far and nigh,
" God save the King —Amen ! amen ! — King Henry ! " is the cry;
While Pedro all alone is left upon his bloody bier,
Not one remains to cry to God, " Our lord lies murder'd here ! "

The story of Blanche of Bourbon has been alluded to so frequently, that I shall venture on inserting a translation of another of these ballads, in which her murder is described.

THE DEATH OF QUEEN BLANCHE.

Maria de Padilla, be not thus of dismal mood,
For if I twice have wedded me, it all was for thy good,
But if upon Queen Blanche ye will that I some scorn should show,
For a banner to Medina my messenger shall go;
The work shall be of Blanche's tears, of Blanche's blood the ground;
Such pennon shall they weave for thee, such sacrifice be found.
Then to the Lord of Ortis, that excellent baron,
He said, "Now hear me, Ynigo, forthwith for this begone."
Then answer made Don Ynigo, "Such gift I ne'er will bring,
For he that harmeth Lady Blanche, doth harm my lord the King."
Then Pedro to his chamber went, his cheek was burning red,
And to a bowman of his guard the dark command he said.
The bowman to Medina pass'd; when the queen beheld him near,
"Alas!" she said, "my maidens, he brings my death I fear."
Then said the archer, bending low, " The king's commandment take,
And see thy soul be ordered well with God that did it make, ˙
For lo! thine hour is come, therefrom no refuge may there be."
Then gently spoke the Lady Blanche, " My friend, I pardon thee;
Do what thou wilt, so be the king hath his commandment given,
Deny me not confession — if so, forgive ye heaven."
Much grieved the bowman for her tears, and for her beauty's sake,
While thus Queen Blanche of Bourbon her last complaint did make: —
" Oh France! my noble country — oh blood of high Bourbon,
Not eighteen years have I seen out before my life is gone.
The king hath never known me. A virgin true I die.
Whate'er I've done, to proud Castille no treason e'er did I.
The crown they put upon my head was a crown of blood and sighs,
God grant me soon another crown more precious in the skies."
These words she spake, then down she knelt, and took the bowman's
    blow —
Her tender neck was cut in twain, and out her blood did flow.

NOTE XIX. p. 25.

Expecting that some Dwarf would appear on the battlements.—
The DWARF is a personage familiar to every reader of romance ;
and without doubt the writers of romances took him from their
own observation of actual manners. In the natural deformity,
which is contemplated in these days with no feelings but those

of pain and pity, it seems undeniable that even the "delicatis-simo donzelle" of the elder time had found much store of such mirth as suited their fancy. The readers of Ariosto, and the other wits of the old Italian school, do not need to be reminded of the more enviable parts sometimes ascribed to these "Sgrin-uti monstri e contrafatti." It is only within these few years that the Dwarf has ceased to be a regular piece of furniture in the saloons of the great ladies of Poland and Russia.

The expectation under which the Don approaches the ima-gined castle, is quite in character. In the *Espejo*, p. 1. c. 86, we find that, "A un lado de la fuerte casa estava *un Enano per avisar la venida* del ladron Minapreso, *el qual sonó el cuerno;*" and in Boiardo, (L. 1. c. 29. v. 41,) the arrival of a noble per-sonage is announced in the same manner.

> " Orlando verso el Pino se n'andava,
> Ecco sopra una torre appare un Nano,
> Che incontinente un gran corno sonava."

Again in the *Gyrone*, L. 15. 89.

> "Ne molte stan che della torre un corno
> Con horribil romor nell' aria suona,
> Ecco apparir sopra un cavallo adorno
> Un cavalier con lucide arme intorno."

And in our own old Romance :

> A dwarf shall wend by her side,
> Such was Launcelot's commandement;
> So were the manners in that tide,
> When a maid on message went.

See also Ariosto, C. 2. 48. C. 4. 15. &c.

NOTE XX. p. 28.

There never was on earth a knight
So waited on by ladies fair.

The lines which the Don here applies to himself, form the opening of one of the innumerable ballads, with which the ro-mantic story of Launcelot of the Lake has furnished the Spanish minstrels. The tone of the ballad is considerably different from

that which English readers have been accustomed to meet with
in the narratives of the loves of Queen Ginevra and her knight.
See Depping's Sammlung, p. 308.

NUNCA FUERA CAVALLERO, &c.

Ne'er was cavalier attended
     So by damsel and by dame,
As Sir Launcelot the worthy,
     When from Brittany he came.

Ladies fair attended on him,
     Highborn damsels dress'd his steed,
She, the courteous Quintanona,
     Pour'd herself the wine and mead.

Tell, I pray, the reason wherefore,
     So to him they minister'd —
Sure of lovely Queen Ginevra,
     Ne'er the story have you heard.

     *   *   *   *   *

Once, when dark was all the valley,
     To Ginevra came her knight,
By her lonely lamp he saw her —
     " Ha! " quoth he, " your cheek is white! "

" If I'm pale," quoth Queen Ginevra,
     " 'Tis for anger, not for fear.
But yon knight had never said so,
     Had my Launcelot been near.

" Words he spake might well enrage me,
     Scornful words the false knight spake."
" Ha! " quoth Launcelot, " securely
     Sleeps he that to death shall wake."

Forth, ere yet the day is dawning,
     Gaily rides Sir Launcelot,
Soon he meets the ribald scorner,
     Yonder pine-trees mark the spot.

Underneath the verdant pine-trees,
     Launcelot his charger reining,
Dares the knight to mortal combat,
     For his words of foul disdaining.

In the first career their lances
  Both are shiver'd at the thrust,
They have drawn their battle-axes,
  Blood-drops rain upon the dust.

Ha! within the ribald's bosom
  Quakes and droops his conscious soul.
Soon the blow of rightful vengeance
  Gives him in the dust to roll.

Fair Ginevra's smile was sweet,
  Balmy were the words she said,
When her true-love at her feet,
  Toss'd that night the caitiff's head.

The story of this ballad seems to be merely a different version of Sir Launcelot's famous battle with Sir Mador, by which Queen Ginevra was saved from expiating at the stake her supposed guilt in relation to the death of " the Scottish knight that Queen Ganore by poison slough."

But those who are read in the old romances, know how frequently gifts of "caitiffs' heads" were received with delight, by fair hands, from the peerless Sir Launcelot du Lake. They know also how irresistible were the personal attractions of the cavalier to whom Don Quixote, in the text, compares himself. There is, for example, the whole adventure of the amorous young lady of the Castle of Ascalot, which is detailed with infinite naiveté in the Morte Arthur.

Launcelot wist what was her will,
  Well he knew by other mo,
Her brother cleped he him till,
  And to her chamber gonne they go.

He set him downe for the maiden's sake,
  Upon her bed there she lay;
Courteously to her he spake,
  For to comfort that fair May.

In her arms she gan him take,
  And these words gan she say,
" Sir, but gif that ye it make,
  Save my life no leech may."

* * * *

> " Sir, gif that your will it were,
>   Sith I of thee ne may have mair,
>   Something ye would leave me here,
>   To look on when me langeth sair," &c.

There is no agreement among the critics of romance as to the
parentage of the first history of the Achievements of Launcelot
of the Lake. Mr. Ellis says, that of all the versions of that
strange history, the most meritorious is that written in verse by
Chretien de Troyes in the 12th century, and entitled, " La Cha-
rette." The general outline cannot be better told than in Mr.
Ellis's own words.

" King Ban, whose acts of prowess we have so often witnessed,
having returned in his old age to Britany, was again attacked
by his inveterate enemy Claudas ; and, after a long war, saw
himself reduced to the possession of a single fortress, the impreg-
nable castle of Trible, where he was besieged by the enemy. In
this extremity, he determined to solicit the assistance of Arthur,
and escaped in a dark night with his infant son Lancelot and his
queen Helen, leaving the castle of Trible in the hands of his
seneschal, who immediately betrayed the place to Claudas. The
flames of his burning citadel reached the eyes of the unfortunate monarch during his flight, and he expired with grief. The
wretched Helen, abandoning for a moment the care of her infant son, flew to the assistance of her husband, and, returning
after the fruitless attempt to restore his life, discovered the little
Lancelot in the arms of a nymph, who, on her approach, suddenly sprung with the child into a deep lake, and instantly dis-
appeared. This nymph was the beautiful Vivian, the mistress
of the enchanter Merlin, who thought fit to undertake the education of the infant hero at her court, which was situated within
this imaginary lake ; and hence her pupil was afterwards distinguished by the name of Lancelot du Lac.

" The queen, after this double loss, retired to a convent, where
she was soon joined by the widow of Bohort ; for this good king,
on learning the death of his brother, died also of grief, leaving
two infant sons, Lyonel and Bohort ; who, having been for some
time secreted by a faithful knight, named Farien, from the fury

of Claudas, were afterwards carried off by the lady of the lake, and educated in company with their cousin Lancelot.

" The fairy, when her pupil had attained the age of eighteen, conveyed him to the court of Arthur, for the purpose of demanding his admission to the honor of knighthood; and at the first appearance of the youthful candidate, the graces of his person, which were not inferior to his courage and activity, made an instantaneous and indelible impression on the heart of Guenever, while her charms inspired him with an equally ardent and constant passion. The amours of these lovers threw a very singular coloring over the whole history of Arthur. It is for the sake of Guenever that the amorous Lancelot achieves the conquest of Northumberland; that he defeats Gallchaut, King of the Marches, who afterwards becomes his secret and most attached confidant; that he cleaves down numberless giants, and lays whole cargoes of tributary crowns at the feet of his suzerain, finding, in his stolen interviews with the queen, an ample indemnification for his various hardships and labors. But this is not all. Arthur, deceived by the artifices of the false Guenever, who was, as we have seen, the illegitimate daughter of Leodegan, declares her the partner of his throne, and dismisses his queen to a distant province; where she is immediately joined by her lover, and follows without restraint the natural bent of her inclinations. Yet Lancelot is dissatisfied; it is necessary to the dignity of his mistress, that she should still share the bed of Arthur, and that, protected in her reputation by the sword of her lover, she should lead a life of ceremonious and splendid adultery. This point is accomplished, and their intercourse continues as usual."

But the same learned and elegant critic who followed Sir Walter Scott in believing, that many of the romantic legends received their first shape from the minstrels of " the North Countrie," finds strong confirmation of his theory in the scenery amongst which the achievements of Sir Launcelot and his companions are represented to have taken place: For example, upon the authority of Knighton, he fixes the " Chateau de la joyeuse Garde," the favorite residence of Sir Launcelot, at Berwick-upon-Tweed; and adds, that at Meigle in Angus, tradition still points out the tomb of " Dame Ganore," the beautiful and lascivious Queen Guenever. For all manner of information

concerning the Knight of the Lake, see Mr. Southey's Edition
of the Morte Arthur, Ellis's Specimens of the Metrical Romances, Vol. I., and the Notes to Marmion and Sir Tristrem.

This note has run out to an unreasonable length, but it would
be wrong to conclude it without quoting one of the most beautiful passages that is to be found either in romance or in poetry —
the speech of Sir Bohart, delivered over the dead body of Sir
Launcelot du Lake: — "And now, I dare say, that Sir Launcelot, there thou liest, thou were never matched of none earthly
knight's hands. And thou were the courtliest knight that ever
bare shielde —And thou were the truest friend to thy lover that
ever bestrode horse —And thou were the truest lover of a syn-
ful man that ever loved woman —And thou were the kindest
man that ever stroke with swerde —And thou were the goodliest
person that ever came among prece of knyghtes —And thou
were the meekest man, and the gentillest, that ever eate in hall
among ladies —And thou were the sternest knyghte to thy mortal foe that ever put speare in rest." — MALORY.

Long after the old romances had past into oblivion, the name
of Launcelot was kept alive among our common people by ballads of the same class with those Spanish ones of which a specimen has been given above. The most popular was that which
begins: —

> When Arthur first in court began,
> And was approved king, &c.

NOTE XXI. p. 31.

This night I will watch my armor in the chapel of yon castle.—
This was invariably a part of the ceremonial described on all
such occasions in the romances; thus, "aveys de saber," &c.
Santiago, 49. — " You must know that antiently it was after this
fashion the order of knighthood was conferred; the night before
any one was to assume the spurs, it behoved him to be armed
cap-a-pee, and so armed, to repair unto the church, and to stand
there on his feet all that night in prayer."

" Venuta la *vigilia* tutti quei Giovani che intendeano di *esser
cavalier novelli* tornavano alla chiesa ove devotamente vigliavano
infino che di buon mattino fusse la mésse celébrata." *Gyrone*,
ded.

The posture seems, however, to have been indifferently either that of standing or kneeling. Thus, in the Amadis, c. 4, " Oriana came before the king, and said, now dub me this young man knight; and in so saying, he pointed towards Amadis, where (armed at all points, save only the head and the hands) he was kneeling before the altar."

St. Ignatius of Loyola conformed, on a very different occasion, to the same ceremonial. Ribadeneira, in his life of the saint, says, that " Ignatius, as he had read in his books of chivalry, how the knights were accustomed to watch their arms; so, to imitate, as a new knight of Christ this knightly fashion, he also watched the whole of that night before the image of Our Lady, sometimes standing on foot, and sometimes kneeling on the marble." *Vida* l. 1. c. 5. The reader must remember the very coarse caricature of all this adventure, in Smollett's Sir Launcelot Greaves, where Captain Crowe's noviciate is described.

NOTE XXII. p. 32.

The Percheles of Malaga, &c. — These were all places noted for rogueries and disorderly doings. The Percheles of Malaga form a sort of suburb of that town, where the fish-market is held. Don Louis Zapata, in treating of the great plague which raged in the city of Malaga, in the year 1582, says, " it was supposed to have been brought thither by a stranger, who died of his illness, and whose foul linen was forthwith sold to some of those of the Percheles." The " Isles of Riaran " are not to be found in any map; but the place where the custom-house stands, still goes by that name. See Carter's Journey from Gibraltar to Malaga, London, 1780. It would appear that there had been a few small islets of sand close to the shore, some of which had shifted their station, while the space between others of them and the mainland had gradually become filled up. " The compass of Seville " was (or is) the name of an open space before one of the churches of that city, the scene of fairs, shows, auctions, &c. The "Azozuejo de Segovia," translated in the text, " Quicksilver house," is said by Bowles to mean nothing but a certain small *place*, or square, — at once the Monmouth Street and Exeter-Change of Segovia. The " Potro " of Cordova — so called from a fountain, the water of which gushes from a horse's mouth —

was another place of the same species. They had all become proverbial before the days of Cervantes; thus, "I say not that I was born in the Potro of Cordova, nor refined in the Quicksilver house of Segovia," &c. — *Rojas*, 282 – 3.

Note XXIII. p. 33.

Sending them some damsel or dwarf through the air in a cloud, &c. — An instance of this species of cure may be found in Amadis de Grecia. "Now Amadis felt from the sword such heat, that it seemed to him he was burning with living flames. But forthwith there appeared a cloud, which covered both him, and Urganda, and Lisuarte, which in an instant opened, and they perceived themselves to be surrounded with a company of four-and-twenty damsels, and in the midst of them was that honored old Alquife, who held in his hand a large glass phial of water; with which when he had smitten upon the helmet, the phial broke, and the water rushing down immediately, there passed from him all that burning glow' of the sword." — P. 2. c. 62.

The fair Jewess in Ivanhoe, has her medical skill in common with almost all the damsels of romance; thus,

"Bernardo de su Elaga, fue curado,
Per manos de la ya libra Donzella."
Garrido, C. 7. 78.

"Una fanciulla che il lor oste aveva,
Medicava Rinaldo."
Pulci, M. M. C. 20. 79, &c. &c.

I need scarcely refer the reader to the story of the pretty *Beguine*, in Tristram Shandy, for the best account of this species of clinical practice.

Note XXIV. p. 36.

"*Thou Queen of Beauty*," *said he, bracing on his shield, &c.* — This invocation to Dulcinea, is copied almost literatim from one in Olivante. "*Ay, soberana Senora*," &c. " O, sovereign lady, grant me thy favor in this battle. Help me, fairest lady, and desert me not utterly." See l. 2. c. 4. The efficacy of this spe-

cies of prayer is thus noticed in Amadis of Gaul. See l. 2. c. 55.
" Beltenebros descended against the giant, and, before he came
close to him, looking towards the place where Miraflores was,
' O, my lady Oriana,' said he, 'never do I begin any deed of
arms, trusting in any strength of mine own, whatsoever it may
be, but in thee only; therefore, oh now, my dear lady, succor
me, seeing how great is the necessity.' And with this, it seemed
that there came to him so much Vigour, that all Fear was forthwith fain to fly away."

NOTE XXV. p. 37.

*He was mad, and consequently the law would acquit him, al-
though he should kill them, &c.*—The technical description, in the
civil law, of " the madman not to be punished," viz. "Absurda et
tristia sibi dicens atque fingens," could most certainly fit no one
more exactly than the guest of whom the good innkeeper spoke
thus. In the tragical story of Lord Ferrers, (see the State
Trials,) we have the very striking example of a man proceeding
deliberately and calmly to the perpetration of an atrocious murder, under the belief, that the plea of hereditary insanity would
be available to save himself from the last severity of the law.
Hence, the obvious propriety of limiting, as narrowly as possible,
the application of the doctrine laid down by the innkeeper.

NOTE XXVI. p. 38.

*He lifted up his sword, and gave him a good blow on the neck,
&c.* —This practical joke seems to have occurred to other con-
ferrers of knighthood, besides mine host of the castle.

Thus, " Franc chevalier donnez moi la collee de chevalerie.
Certes Passellion, dit Lionnel, je le feray voulontiers, a tant il
haulse la main dextre et l'enfant baisse le col, et le chevalier
ferit dessus *complement* en disant. Certes, Gentil Passellion,
Chevalier Soyes. Quand Passellion, eut receu la collée *que luy
fit douloir le col par sa grandeur,*" &c. — *Perceforest*, V. 4. C. 14.

Queen Elizabeth is introduced in Kenilworth, as giving a
collée of malicious sincerity on a similar occasion.— See Du-
cange sub voce *Alapa Militaris.*

NOTE XXVII. p. 43.

Every man is the son of his own works, &c.—There is no

country in the world that has suffered more from the excessive
respect allowed to the pretension of birth, than Spain; and none
by whose authors the same pretension is more severely ridiculed.
There is something of amusement in the gravity with which
Villa Diego speaks: " *Hidalgo* igitur ille solus dicetur qui Chris-
tiana virtute pollet. *Fidalgo*, id est filius bonorom operum et
virtutum; et inde vulgo dicitur *cada uno es hijo de sus obras.*"—
VILL. F. 25.

NOTE XXVIII. p. 46.

*Confess that there is not in the universe a more beautiful damsel
than the empress of La Mancha, &c.*—The terms here proposed
by Don Quixote are, after all, modest, compared with what we
find in some of the romances by whose light he walked. In the
Amadis de Grecia, (p. 1. c. 64.) there is the following passage,
which may serve for an example. " The Duke said, Sir Knight,
it is now time you should be made to know that the beauty of
Infaliana *surpasses* in worth that which so greatly you prize.
Brimartes made answer, Sir Knight, for certain no such knowledge can I possess, for in those who have never seen nor known
Infaliana, how can knowledge of such a thing be found? But
what are arguments, since we stand here at the proof? The
proof fain would I see, quoth the Duke. And when he had said
so, they couched their lances, and at the full career of their
horses, they encountered, being well covered with their shields.
* * * * * * The Duke fell so heavily, that he could stir
neither foot nor hand. Brimartes stooped and unlaced his vizor.
The Duke slowly recovered himself; and then said Brimartes,
Sir Knight, you are a dead knight, if you do not on the instant
acknowledge that your lady in nothing equals the beauty of Ho-
noria. The Duke said not a word," &c. &c.

If the reader wishes to be amused with an excellent account
of a more splendid and authentic specimen of the *Combats pour
l'honneur des dames*, I refer him to the fifth volume of the
"Melanges tirees d'une Grand Bibliotheque," where, among
other French MSS. of the 15th century, a very singular one is
described, containing the history of a famous festival of gallantry,
celebrated A. D. 1493, at the castle, and by the Lord of Sandricourt, near Pontoise, and therefore known by the name of *Le
pas de Sandricourt*. It appears, that the scheme was first started

by some young lords of the court of Charles VIII., and that their plan was put into execution under the immediate patronage of the Duke of Orleans. After mentioning the names of the young knights who were " to defend against all comers, for the honour of their ladies, the Castle of Sandricourt," (among whom we find those of the Sire de Saint-Vallier, father to the famous Diana de Poitiers — of Bernardin de Clermont, Viscount of Tallard — of Louis de Hedouille — of Georges de Sully, &c. &c.) — the author proceeds to his chivalrous relation at great length. Vide *Melanges*, Vol. V. p. 33.

NOTE XXIX. p. 50.

His folly brought to his remembrance the story of Baldwin and the Marquis of Mantua, &c. — Cervantes is here evidently amusing himself at the expense of one Geronimo Trevino, whose ballad or romance of Baldwin (in three parts) had been printed in Alcala, anno 1598. The story of the romance is, that Charlot, (or Carloto,) son of Charlemagne, came unawares upon Baldwin (or Baldovinos) in the *Floresta Sin Ventura* ; his purpose being no other than to kill Baldwin, and then marry his widow. He gave him, it appears, no less than two-and-twenty mortal wounds, (we can scarcely imagine the Don to have made as exact a computation of the blows he himself had just received from the muleteer,) and then left him for dead in the forest. By good fortune, however, Baldwin's uncle, the Marquis of Mantua, happened to be passing at the moment through the wood, and hearing the wounded knight's lamentations, was soon drawn to the spot where he lay. He sent a message to the emperor, who resided at Paris, by the " Count Dirlos, Viceroy beyond the Sea," demanding justice ; and Charlemagne immediately pronounced sentence of death upon his son Charlot. Such is the story. The passage of the romance, which Cervantes alludes to, is that which contains the lamentations of the wounded man, after he had received all his wounds. It would be too much to quote the whole of the verses which Cervantes says the Don applied to his own case ; but these may serve as a sufficient specimen of a very flat and unprofitable composition.

' O my princely Infant Marian ! O my cousin Montesin !
O my Reynold ! and Orlando ! O thou knightly Paladin !

*   *   *   *   *

" O my noble Lord of Mantua, thy soldier true, and sister's son
Lies here wounded in the forest — hears nor helps him never one!
Baldwin was my christen'd name — " The Frank" they call'd me too;
I am the king of Dacia's son, from him my blood I drew.
He was my father and my lord, and I was belted knight,
To eat bread at his table, and for his banner fight.

*   *   *   *   *

" The beautiful Sevilla, she pledged her troth to me ;
She was my wedded wife, but my widow soon she'll be.
Charlot, it was no other, this wicked deed hath done;
I lie here slain by Charlot, the good King Charles's son.
He coveted my wife, and full well I know that I
Lie here, that with my widow my murderer may lie."

Note XXX. p. 52.

He bethought himself of the Moor Abindarraez, &c. —The
loves of the Moor Abindarraez, and of the beautiful Xarifa,
were a favorite subject of song amongst the Moorish, as well as
the Christian minstrels of Spain ; and Montemayor has introduced them into his celebrated pastoral called Diana. The tale
runs briefly thus —

During the reign of King Ferdinand of Arragon, while the
Moorish kingdom of Grenada was nodding to its fall, a gallant
Spanish knight, Rodrigo de Narvaez, was named constable or
governor of the Castle of Alhora, near the boundaries of the
Moorish territory. As he was, according to his custom, one
night making a reconnoissance at the head of several of his followers, to prevent a surprise from the enemy, he met a young
Moorish cavalier splendidly armed and accoutred, who for some
time defended himself valiantly against the superior force of his
enemies ; but was at length severely wounded, and made prisoner. The Castilian endeavored to comfort his noble captive, and
treated him so generously, that he extracted from him his story.
The Moor Abindarraez had been bred up with Xarifa, daughter
of the Alcayde of Coyn, under the belief that she was his sister,
until he learned by chance that he was not of her blood, but descended from the renowned, but unfortunate family of the Aben-
cerrages. Fraternal affection then gave place to a stronger
passion, which Xarifa repaid with equal warmth. The meeting
of the lovers could only be by night, and by stealth ; for Abin-

darraez, after the discovery of his birth, resided no longer in her father's castle. Xarifa had assigned her lover a rendezvous upon the unfortunate night when he fell into the power of Don Rodrigo, and he was on the road to Coyn, when he encountered the Castilian knight. Don Rodrigo de Narvaez was affected by the captive's story; and on his promise to return within three days, and surrender himself to his captor at the Castle of Alhora, he gave him liberty to keep his appointment. He arrives there in safety, and Xarifa, reunited to her lover, refuses again to part with him. She returns with him to the castle of Don Rodrigo, who, charmed with their mutual love, the constancy of Xarifa, and the gallantry and faith of Abindarraez, restores them to liberty, and obtains the consent of the Alcayde of Coyn to their union. There are many ballads on this romantic story, of which the following may serve as a specimen.

ABINDARRAEZ AND XARIFA.

I.

The bold Moor, young Abindarraez,
   Nigh the castle checks his rein,
Where his love, the fair Xarifa,
   Long had watch'd, and wept in vain.

II.

" Do I live to hope that coldness,
   Or some brighter maiden's charms,
Keep the faithless Abindarraez
   From the fond Xarifa's arms?

III.

" Yes, I hope neglect or falsehood,
   Aught but perils, cause him stay;
Aught, save that the prowling Christians
   Met him on his midnight way.

IV.

" 'Gainst their numbers, small assistance
   Sabre, lance, or targe could give;
Gone is gallant Abindarraez,
   And Xarifa will not live.

V.

" Who that loves would live forsaken,
   When her valiant lover fell?
Ne'er such tale of Moorish maiden
   Shall a Moorish minstrel tell."

VI.

With such plaints she toss'd at midnight
   On her couch that knew not rest;
With such plaints by day lamented,
   Gazing from the turret's crest.

VII.

Bold in love, the night she fear'd not,
   Nor the solitude so drear;
And the voice of tempest heard not,
   Howling in the mountains near.

VIII.

Long, long, she kept her lofty station,
   Gazed in vain on earth and sky;
And at length, her hopes renouncing,
   Left it with a heavy sigh.

IX.

Then the Moorish lance gave signal,
   Striking thrice upon the gate;
And Xarifa's trusty maiden,
   Open'd to her lover straight.

X.

O how gay and gallant shew'd he,
   When he sought her chamber door,
In his tunic, loop'd with silver,
   Like a brave and noble Moor.

XI.

With the plumage on his turban,
   Gather'd with a golden check;
And his golden handled sabre,
   Hilted with an eagle's neck.

XII.

Thus stood gallant Abindarraez,
   But for rapture naught could speak,
Till in broken exclamations,
   Love and joy a passage seek.

Note XXXI. p. 53.

The twelve peers of France, nay the nine worthies, &c. — Who the twelve peers of France were, every body knows. It is not quite so well known, that the nine worthies in the language of romance (los nueve de la fama) were, three of them Hebrews, viz. Joshua, David, and Judas Maccabeus; three Gentiles, viz. Hector of Troy, Alexander of Macedon, and Julius Cæsar; and three Christians, King Arthur, Charlemagne, and Godfrey of Bouillon. — See *Carranza*, F. 255.

Note XXXII. p. 54.

He had killed four giants as big as any steeples, &c. — "The beautiful Brandamante, and Aquilante, and Grifon, and Malgesi, encountered then those four fierce giants, who stood like four towers waiting for them," &c. — *Espejo*, L. II. C. 9.

Note XXXIII. p. 54, 55.

The sage Esquife, — the enchantress Urganda. — These personages occur in almost all the books of the lineage of Amadis. We have had occasion already to observe one wonderful cure performed by Alquife (corrupted into *Esquife* by the niece of Don Quixote) in the Amadis de Grecia. Urganda, witch, enchantress, prophetess, &c., &c., appears in the original Amadis sometimes in the likeness of a young damsel, sometimes as the most venerable of crones; but in the later volumes of Esplandian, &c., she is invested with all the more serious terrors of a Medea. Her final departure is very mysterious; whence her appellation of *la desconoscida.*

Note XXXIV. p. 58.

The Exploits of Esplandian. — "El Ramo que de los quatre libros de Amadis de Gaula sale llamado las Sergas del muy esforzado Cavallero Esplandian hijo del exelente Rey Amadis de Gaula," Alcala, 1588. Such is the title-page of a continuation of the Amadis, by one Garci Ordonez de Montalvo, who, having edited the original romance, thought it necessary, it would seem, *invita Minerva,* to try his hand at something original. In the preface, he pretends that the "deeds" (ɛργα) of Esplandian had been originally narrated in Greek "del Mano del Maestro Helizabad." Helizabad is frequently mentioned by Cervantes. He was the well-employed surgeon who commonly cured the wounds of Amadis de Gaul &c.

Note XXXV. p. 58.

This is Amadis of Greece, and I'm of opinion that all those that stand on this side, are of the same family, &c. — The first four books of Amadis of Gaul alone are considered by Cervantes as worthy of being preserved from the flames. The other twenty books, filled with the exploits of the Amadis family, were for the most part composed originally, not in Spanish or Portuguese, (like those which Cervantes preserves,) but by French imitators of very inferior genius. Vicente Placcio, in his *Theatrum Anonymorum et Pseudonymorum*, characterises the whole collection as " a most pernicious library, engendered or composed by Spanish fathers, although mightily augmented by the French," p. 673, § 2731. Amadis of Greece occupies the ninth book of the collection. He was the son of Lisuarte of Greece, who was the son of Amadis of Gaul. The huge folio which Cervantes places in his hero's library, was printed at Lisbon in 1596. The title runs thus : " Chronica del muy valiente y esforzado Principe y Cavallero de la ardienta Espada Amadis de Grecia." The history is divided into two parts, and at the beginning of the second there is a notice, that " Esta Cronica fue sacada de Grieco en Latin y de Latin en Romance segun lo escrivio el gran sabio Alquife en las Magicas." The whole ends with these words : "Aqui hace fin el noveno libro de Amadis de Gaula : que es la chronica del cavalliero de la ardiente Espada Amadis de Grecia hijo de Lisuarte de Grecia." The Queen Pintiquiniestra, and the shepherd Darinel, are both of them personages that figure in the Amadis de Grecia. The former is a giantess of most formidable appearance.

Note XXXVI. p. 59.

Olivante de Laura, and the Garden of Flowers. — Both the stupid romance of *Olivante* and the *Jardin de flores*, were productions of one *Antonio de Torquemada*. The title of the second of them conveys no very perfect notion of its character ; for, in fact, it is nothing but one fearful mass of *diablerie*, interspersed with a few, probably more authentic, *blossoms* of murder, rape, &c. Torquemada was a popular author in his day; but his popularity was not so much founded on either of the works satirized by Cervantes, as on his HEXAMERON, which was translated into French, soon after it was written, by Chapius. This very curious work consists of six dialogues, professedly on subjects of natural history and physics; but Torquemada takes occasion to introduce in the course of his discussions, an infinity of curious stories and anecdotes, which no doubt the readers of his time must have found much more interesting than his philosophy : For example, he fills a great many pages with the natural history of giants, and, among other things, tells us, he had frequently seen with his own eyes a well authenticated tooth of St. Christopher, in the cathedral of Coria ; and a fragment of his jawbone, in the church of Astorga. These must have been tremendous relics ; for the philosophic Torquemada states, that he hàd made an exact computation, and found, that if St. Christopher was formed· in due proportion, he must have stood exactly as tall as the great tower of Segovia. He states also, that the bones of the Paladins, preserved in the abbey of Roncesvalles, were quite of gigantic dimensions. In truth, Torquemada seems to have been a fortunate person, for many are the strange things and persons he gravely tells us he had seen. *Inter alia*, he speaks at much length of a certain lady of his acquaintance, abbess of a convent at Monviedra, who, having lived on to the age of a hundred, with all the appearance of other old women, began of a sudden to manifest many grateful symptoms, external and internal, of returning youth ; she became to all men's view, says he, a comely young religieuse of eighteen years ; she was excessively admired, and liked admiration too ; but, he adds, was, after a little reflection, somewhat ashamed both of her looks and her sensations, and was never seen to trip across the cloister without holding a handkerchief to her face. She enjoyed this second bloom for several merry years, and expired with the brownest of curls, and the brightest of eyes, being cut off by a sudden and most unexpected access of fever, at the age of 110. With sorcerers and magicians of the most terrific power, but all of them most amiably communicative, Antonio de Torquemada appears to have cracked many a bottle. From his accounts of these personages, one would imagine them to have been just as fond of telling all the horrors they had ever perpetrated, as the most respectable " Senor soldado de Carlos quinto" could have been of fighting his battles over again.

NOTE XXXVII. p. 59.

Florismart of Hyrcania.—Another dull and affected folio, written by "Melchior de Orteza Caballero de Ubeda;" and printed at Valladolid in the year 1566. The "wonderful birth" of the hero alluded to by the curate in the text, is narrated at great length in the tenth chapter of the romance. His mother was brought to bed in a desert place, and he saw the light under the auspices of a certain *sage femme*, by name *Belsagina*. His father's name being *Florisan*, (of Misia,) and his mother's, *Martedina*, this dame suggested that the boy should take part of both of these fine names, and be called *Florismarte*. The mother, however, preferred *Felixmarte*, for reasons of which Mr. Shandy would have approved.

NOTE XXXVIII. p. 59.

The noble Don Platir, &c.— An edition of " O cronico del muy valiente y esforzado Caballero Platir, hijo del Emperador Primaleon," was printed at Valladolid in 1533. This, like most of the same sort of books, was anonymous.

NOTE XXXIX. p. 60.

The Knight of the Cross.— The "Book of the invincible knight Lepolemo, called from his achievements the Knight of the Cross," forms the twelfth part of the Amadis Library. The " Chronicle of Leandro the Beautiful, as it was composed by the sage King Artidorus, in the Greek tongue," is the thirteenth; they are both from the pen of one Pedro de Luxan. The preliminary fiction concerning the adventures of the Knight of the Cross, is, that they were "originally written in Arabic, by a Moor named Xarton, at the command of the Sultan Zulema, and translated into Castilian by a captive of Tunis." Then follow two dedications, one by Xarton to Zulema, and another by the Tunisian captive, addressed to the Conde de Saldana. Luxan was author of another work equally stupid, entitled " Colloquios Matrimoniales."

Note XL. p. 60.

The mirror of knighthood. —The " Espejo de Caballerias," is frequently alluded to by all the Spanish commentators on Cervantes. It is a huge collection of all manner of romantic stories, in four parts, formed by as many different writers. The first part (which is alluded to in the text) appeared in 1562, and was dedicated by its author, Diego Ordonez de Calahorra, to Martin Cortes, son of the great Hernan Cortes.

Note XLI. p. 60.

The twelve peers of France, and that faithful historian Turpin, &c. —The achievements of the twelve peers fill a mighty proportion of the *Espejo de Caballerias*, and, of course, the venerable Turpin is throughout cited as the most unquestioned of authorities. Thus, in P. 1. C. 1. we are informed, that " En las Historias Antiguas de Francia una mas verdadera por mano de Arzobizbo Don Turpin se halla." Such is the character uniformly given of Turpin by the grateful bards, who, as Cervantes expresses it, "spun their webs" out of his history. In Boiardo, Pulci, Ariosto, one meets at every turn,

> " Turpin che mai non mente in alcun loco "—

The absurd chronicle attributed to Turpin (or Tilpin) seems to have been composed in Latin, about the end of the 11th, or beginning of the 12th century, but owed much of its celebrity to the innumerable versions and paraphrases of it, which soon after began to make their appearance — first in French, and then in Spanish, English, and all the other vulgar dialects. The original work itself was first printed in a collection, entitled " Germanicarum Rerum quatuor chronographi." Frankfort, 1566, *folio*. Stories of miracles, relics, churches founded, conversions, &c., &c., fill the far greater part of the monkish chronicle; but from the absurd thread of fiction concerning Charlemagne, on which these monastic pearls are strung, there can be no doubt that almost the whole web of the second great class of romances was spun. Those who wish to see what are the most plausible conjectures that have been formed, concerning the origin of all these extraordinary falsifications of the splendid *history* of the great Frankish Emperor, may be referred to Warton, Ellis, Leyden, and Schlegel. The opinions of these critics are so different, and the details, without which these opinions would be unintelligible, so extensive, that it would be useless and absurd to attempt giving any account of this "great controversy," in the shape of a note upon Don Quixote. As to the extent of these falsifications themselves, a tolerable guess may be formed from the initiatory lines of ROLAND AND FERRAGUS, a romance extant in the Auchinleck MS., which, so far as it goes, presents a pretty faithful compendium of Turpin's original *Magnum Opus*.

> "*An hundred years it was and three,*
> Sithan God deed upon the tree,
>   That Charles the king
> Had all France in his hand,
> *Denmark and England,*
>   Withouten any lesing:
> Lorraine and Lombardie,
> Gascoyne, Bayonne, and Picardie,
>   Was still his bidding;
> And Emperor he was of Rome,
> And Lord of all Christendom,
>   Then was he a high lording."

NOTE XLII. p. 60.

"*I have him at home in Italian,*" said the barber; "*but I can't understand him.*" "*It is no great matter,*" replied the curate, &c. Jarvis supposes, from the style of the conversation here, that Cervantes had no great relish for Ariosto. But Pellicer very justly laughs at Jarvis for this remark. The curate's contempt is evidently not of Ariosto, (whose "graces" he has just been praising,) but of the poor barber, whom he does not think capable of reading, or at least of relishing, any thing so beautiful as the *Orlando Furioso*. Don Geronimo Ximenes de Urrea is the "good captain," whose Spanish version of the Orlando, Cervantes in the next sentence satirizes. Don Diego de Mendoza is equally severe upon this gallant translator. "He hath gained," quoth Mendoza, "not only fame, but, what is much better, many a good dinner by translating the Orlando Furioso; *i. e.* by having said, "*Cavalleros* for *cavaglieri*, *armas* for *arme*, *amores* for *amori*." He adds, "*Puez de esta arte yo me haria, mas libros que kizo Matuzalen."* But perhaps, after all, even that might be no very laborious undertaking.

Note XLIII. p. 61.

Bernardo de Carpio, &c.—This condemned book is a long and dull poem on the exploits of the Hero, of whom enough has already been said, written in the *rima ottava*, and published at Toledo in 1585. The author's name was Augustin Alonzo.

Note XLIV. p. 61.

Palmerin de Oliva — Palmerin of England.—"Libro del famoso Caballero Palmerin de Oliva que por el mundo grandes hechos en armas hizo, sin saber cuyo hijo fuese. Toledo, 1580." It was probably this edition of this well known romance that figured in Don Quixote's library. The hero, the secretly produced offspring of Angricona, daughter to the emperor of Constantinople, is carried off as soon as he is born, and concealed beneath a palm tree on the Mount of Olives. He is there discovered by a rustic, who names him from the place where he is found. As to the very superior romance of Palmerin of England, the reader is once more referred to Mr. Southey's admirable abridgment. I may mention, however, in passing, that the royal parentage of that fine romance, although Cervantes would seem to have believed in it, is much more than doubtful; and that it is even far from being certain, that Sir Palmerin made his first appearance in the language of Portugal.

Note XLV. p. 62.

Don Belianis, and his castle of fame.— "There appeared a castle as beautiful and as rich as ever mortal beheld. It was so large, that with ease one might imagine two thousand knights to be its garrison, and it was drawn along by forty elephants of incredible hugeness. From this castle there came forth nine knights, each one having painted on his shield the image of Fame, by which device they signified that they were the Knights of Fame." — *Belianis,* l. iii. c. 19.

Note XLVI. p. 62.

Tirante the White.—The hero of this·fine old romance (for

Cervantes is far too severe on its merits) derives his name partly from his father, partly from his mother; the former being " Lord of the Seigniory of Tirania, on the borders of England," the latter, Blanca, daughter of the Duke of Brittany. The common opinion is, that this romance was originally composed in the Valencian dialect about the year 1460. The Dons Kyrie-eleison, (i. e. *Lord have mercy upon us*,) and Thomas of Montalban, the Knight Fonseca, &c., are personages who appear in the story of *Tirant lo Blanch*. The most interesting of them all, are the empress and her lover, the gentleman-usher Hippolyto. To please her swain, the empress sings to him on one occasion, " Un romance de Tristan co se planya de la lancada del Rey March." "A song of Tristram, in which he laments over a blow he had received from the lance of King Mark." This song is represented to have excessively moved the tender-hearted gentleman-usher; insomuch, that "Ab la dolçor del cant destillaren dels seus ulls vives lagremes."—(Cap. 264.) The first edition of *Tirant* was published at Valencia in 1490. A Castilian version appeared at Valladolid in 1511; and from this was executed the Italian translation of Lelio Manfredi, which was printed at Venice in 1538. *Detirante*, a few lines lower in the text, is a misprint for *Tirante*, which seems to have passed from edition to edition, ever since Don Quixote was first published.

Note XLVII. p. 63, 64.

The Dianas of Montemayor — Salmantino, Gil Polo, &c.— Cervantes does not seem to have been aware, that the Diana, who gives name to the celebrated performance of Jorge de Montemayor, was a real personage. Pellicer, however, has collected abundant evidence that such was the fact; *inter alia*, he cites from a MS., in the Royal Library at Madrid, a passage which I shall translate *literatim*, because the story it tells is in itself interesting. [The writer is the same Father Sapolveda, with whose printed works all are acquainted.] " When the sovereigns, Don Philip III. and Donna Margarita, were on their way back from Portugal, in 1602, they halted for a night in the city of Valencia, and their host there was the Marquis de las Navas, and they were also entertained by that famous woman DIANA, whom George de Montemayor so greatly commends and cele-

brates in his history and verses; for, though very old, this
Diana is still alive, and they say, whoever visits her may discover
plainly, that in her youth she must have been exceedingly beautiful. She is the most wealthy and rich person in the town.
But it was on account of her being so famous, and of the praises
of George de Montemayor, that the sovereigns and all their
court repaired to the house of this woman, being desirous to see
her as a thing worthy of wonder and admiration. And, indeed,
she is a very sensible and well-spoken woman." Lope de Vega
also alludes to the real Diana, in his *Dorotea*, p. 52.

Montemayor himself was not distinguished by his writings
alone; for he was both a great musician and a gallant soldier.
His Diana was the most popular work of its day, and gave rise
to as many *Dianas*, as Lord Byron's Harold, in our own time,
has to *Childes*. Gil Polo, whom Cervantes rather commends,
wrote a professed continuation of the original performance of
Montemayor, which has been reprinted in Madrid so lately as
1778. M. Florian ventures, in spite of the authority of Cervantes, to express a great contempt for Gil Polo; but Pellicer, more
likely to be a good judge, talks of him as " Insigne Poeta Valen-
ciano." The second Diana, that of Alonzo Perez, a physician
of Salamanca, (the *Salmantino* of the text,) was published at
Alcala in 1564. For very elegant abstracts of all these pastorals, see Mr. Dunlop's *History of Fiction*.

Note XLVIII. p. 64.

Ten Books of the Fortunes of Love, by Anthony de Lofraco,
&c. — The true name of this author was Antonio de lo Frasso.
He was a native of Llaguer, a town in Sardinia, but wrote good
Castilian. His work, entitled "Los diez libros de Fortuna
d'Amor, donde hallaran los honestos y apacibles amores del pas-
tor Frexano et de la hermosa pastora Fortuna," was published
at Barcelona by one Pedro Malo, in 1573. It is a pastoral, written partly in prose, partly in verse, like its prototype (the Diana.)
There is every reason for thinking that Cervantes by no means
intended to identify himself with the curate as to the opinion
expressed concerning this work. Nevertheless, entirely on the
strength of such an idea, an edition of these wretched "diez libros de fortuna" was actually printed in London, not a great

many years ago, under the auspices of Pineda, the lexicographer, of course without the smallest success. The other pastoral productions mentioned in the text are all utterly contemptible, with the exception of the *Shepherd of Filida*, which Lope de Vega praises in his Dorotea, (p. 52,) asserting, that its author also, like Montemayor, had been inspired by the charms of a real mistress. This book appeared in 1582. It was written by Luis Galvez de Montalvo, who is designed as " Criado de Don Enrique de Mendoza y Aragon, nieto de los Duques del Infantado."

Note XLIX. p. 65.

The treasure of divers poems. —This is a collection of the same class with the *Sylvæ, Deliciæ, &c.*, formed by Don Pedro Padilla, a gentleman who, after spending an active life in military service, assumed in his latter days the garb of a Carmelite Friar, and died in that sanctified, and, as he probably thought, all-atoning garb, at Madrid, in 1595. Gayton, in his " Festive Notes," talks boldly of this book, as if it had been a dictionary, and as if he had himself turned over its leaves. He had evidently not imagined there could be any *Thesauri*, except of the same class with his Stephanus.

Note L. p. 65.

Lopez Maldonado. — " The Concionero, o Coleccion de varias poesias" of this author, was first published by Droy, in Madrid, in 1586, in quarto.

Note LI. p. 65.

The Galatea of Cervantes. — See Life of Cervantes.

Note LII. p. 66.

The Tears of Angelica. —The author so highly commended by Cervantes, is Luis Baratrona de Soto, who, like Cervantes himself, was a soldier as well as a poet. Nay, Baratrona was a physician to boot. His " *Lagremas de Angelica*," in 12 cantos, appeared in 1586.

Note LIII. p. 67.

The Carolea and Leon of Spain. Don Louis de Avila, &c.— The *Carolea* is a poem treating of the victories of Charles V., printed in Valencia in 1560. Its author was *Geronimo de San Pedro*, or *Sempere*. The *Leon de España* is a poem in twenty-nine cantos, treating of the martial glories of the Leoneze. It was written by Pedro de la Vecilla, and published at Salamanca in 1586. Pellicer contends that Cervantes is wrong in attributing "the deeds of the Emperor" to Don Lewis d'Avila; and is at great pains to convince us that he must have meant Don Lewis Zapata. Avila was author of the *Guerra de Almania*, and therefore entitled to be talked of as having celebrated "the deeds of the Emperor;" but Zapata's work, on the other hand, bore the very title of "Hechos del Emperador." The same person published a long *poem* on the same subject, the *Carlo Famoso;* of which he himself relates that it cost him 4000 maravedis to print it, and that he had no return whatever, but what he calls the "alongamiento de mi voluntad"—a species of profit with which Don Lewis Zapata professes himself to have been by no means satisfied.

NOTE LIV. p. 70.

The Enchanter Freston.—This personage figures in many terrible scenes of the Belianis.

NOTE LV. p. 77.

Diego Perez de Vargas.—The name of this Castilian gentleman occurs frequently both in the ballads and other records of the Moorish wars. He acquired, or was said to have acquired, the name of *Machuca* (i. e. Bruiser, or Pounder,) from an incident which I find related as follows in one of the ballads published by Sepulveda.

MACHUCA

I.

The Christians have beleaguer'd the famous walls of Xeres,
Among them are Don Alvar and Don Diego Perez,
And many other gentlemen, who, day succeeding day,
Gave challenge to the Saracen and all his chivalry.

II.

When rages the hot battle before the gates of Xeres,
By trace of gore ye may explore the dauntless path of Perez.

No knight like Don Diego — no sword like his is found
In all the host, to hew the boast of Paynims to the ground.

III.

It fell one day when furiously they battled on the plain,
Diego shivered both his lance and trusty blade in twain;
The Moors that saw it shouted, for esquire none was near,
To serve Diego at his need with faulchion, mace, or spear.

IV.

Loud, loud, he blew his bugle, sore troubled was his eye,
But by God's grace, before his face there stood a tree full nigh,
A comely tree with branches strong, close by the wall of Xeres —
" Yon goodly bough will serve, I trow," quoth Don Diego Perez.

V.

A gnarled branch he soon did wrench down from that olive strong,
Which o'er his head piece brandishing, he spurs among the throng.
God wot! full many a Pagan must in his saddle reel !—
What leech shall cure, what priest shall shrive, if once that weight
　　　ye feel ?

VI.

But when Don Alvar saw him thus bruising down the foe,
Quoth he, " I've seen some flail-arm'd man belabour barley so!
Sure mortal mould did ne'er enfold such mastery of power;
Let's call Diego Perez MACHUCA from this hour."

NOTE LVI. p. 78.

*A knight-errant must never complain of his wounds, although
his bowels were dropping out through them, &c.* —The Don's doctrine is here, as it generally is, quite correct. *Marquez*, in re-
counting the statutes of the order de la Banda, (an order instituted by Alphonzo XI.,) says, its ninth law was " Que ningun
caballero se quexasse de alguna herida que tuviesse." F. 50.

NOTE LVII. p. 81.

They wore riding masks, with glasses at the eyes, &c. —The
Benedictines being the most wealthy order of religious in Spain,
at the period when Cervantes wrote, furnished, of course, the
most common subjects for this species of satire ; but it should

never be forgotten, that, unlike many of their brethren, the Benedictines were, in general, both the followers and the liberal patrons of literature. The princely style of their literary speculations — their edition of the French historians, &c., &c., will be sufficient to preserve their memory in honor, even should they be deprived in Spain, as they have been elsewhere, of all their great possessions. They have still many magnificent establishments of education under their control at Vienna, Ratisbone, and other places of the Austrian dominion.

Note LVIII. p. 84.

Bad Biscayan and worse Spanish.—To understand fully the frequent allusions which Cervantes makes to the provincial dialects in Spain, one must of course be a Spaniard, and a learned Spaniard to boot. In general, it may be sufficient to observe, that the Latin language was gradually corrupted all over the peninsula, after the invasion of the Goths; and that out of this corruption three main dialects were by degrees formed. One of these, the Catalonian, (for the Valencian was nearly the same thing,) partook very much of the character of that spoken all over Provence, and the southern districts of France. In it several books were written, (particularly the fine romance of Tyrant lo Blanch,) but like the sister Provencal, the soft and beautiful language of the Troubadours, it never received the last finish of cultivation. In Portugal and Galicia, a second dialect was formed, which the Castilians complain of as being effeminate in comparison with their own, but which can never perish, since the Lusiad has been written in it. The Castilian, finally, (the third great branch,) is much more near of kin to the Portuguese than to the Catalonian, and bears the same sort of relation to it which the Swedish does to the Danish, or which the English (but for political events) might have done to the Scotch. All the other provinces of the peninsula, except Portugal, being by degrees consolidated into one empire under a Castilian dynasty, the language of the court became the language of Spain — as the modern High-Dutch has supplanted, under somewhat different circumstances, the multifarious dialects of Germany. The Castilian, however, did not assume this preëminence until about the middle of the 16th century.

The language of the original inhabitants of Spain, previous to the Carthaginian and Roman conquests, found early and secure refuge among the Pyrenees, and in the mountainous province of Spanish Biscay. It is undoubtedly a Celtic dialect, of the same parentage with those which still survive in Wales, Brittany, Ireland, and the Highlands of Scotland. It never altered its main characteristics, nor borrowed any thing more than vocables from the language of any of the nations who successively conquered the peninsula. The *Spanish* spoken by the Biscayan in the text of Cervantes, is therefore about the same sort of thing with the *English* spoken by the Highland personages who figure in *Waverley, the Legend of Montrose, &c.*

NOTE LIX. p. 84.

I'll try titles with you, as the man said. — The original is, "*Aora lo veredes dixo Agrajes.*" — Agrajes is one of the champions who figure in the Amadis, and one of the most quarrelsome of them all. This phrase, part of which is always in his mouth at the beginning of a fray, seems to have been passed into a sort of by-word; for it occurs just in the same sort of way in Quevedo's visions, &c.

NOTE LX. p. 89.

A Morisco that understood Spanish, &c. — In the original, "Morisco Aljamiado." *Aljamia* (from Aljama, *a frontier*,) was a term applied by the pure Arabs to denote the corrupted language of the Moors long settled in Spain. In one of the old ballads, a Moor, who communicates to the Cid a certain plot that is going on against him, is styled "Moro Latinado." How much the two languages must have been mingled in the elder times, may easily be imagined, when we remember that there are still extant several papal rescripts directed against the use of the Arabic language by the Spanish Christians; that, in spite of all these, it was found necessary, after some space, to translate the common devotional books of the Christian religion into Arabic for their use; and that, at Cordova, the Gothic laws rendered into Arabic, were appealed to in the courts of justice, whenever the parties were Christians. (See MURPHY's *Moors in Spain*, and BONTERWECK's *Geschichte der Spanisches Literatur.*) Cer-

vantes adheres closely to the romances which he designs to satir-
ize in all this fiction about the discovery and translation of the
history of this Don. The Amadis de Gaul, the Belianis, &c., &c.,
are all represented as having been originally composed in the
Greek tongue by "the Saga Alquife," Friston, Artemidorus,
Lirgandeus, and the like learned personages. The origin of all
romantic adventures was, in the eye of Cervantes' contemporaries, Moorish, and therefore he takes a Moor in place of a
Greek. The Spanish commentators, finally, have discovered
that *Cid Hamet Ben Engeli*, is, after all, no more than an Arabian version of the name of Cervantes himself. *Cid*, as all the
world knows, means lord or signior. *Hamet* is a common Moorish prefix. *Ben Engeli* signifies the *son of a stag*, which, being
expressed in Spanish, is *hijo del ciervo, cerval*, or *cervanteno*. It
is said in p. 91, that this Morisco translated the whole of Ben
Engeli's MS. in less than six weeks; but this is nothing to Shelton, the first English translator of Cervantes, (and perhaps in
some respects the best,) who says, in his preface, that he finished
his version in forty successive days.

NOTE LXI. p. 96.

The holy brotherhood. —The reader of modern romances may
at first sight imagine that the Inquisition is meant, but it is not
so. The terror with which the words, "holy office," on all occasions inspire honest Sancho, was indeed felt, at the time of his
supposed existence, by every man, woman, and child, within the
Spanish dominions. Under Ferdinand and Isabella, the injunctions of the papal bulls for the establishment of inquisitions,
were first carried into full effect in Castile, and afterwards in
Arragon. Ximenes, Torquemada, and a long series of artful
bigots, effectually riveted the chain; and the delicacy observed
by Cervantes himself, in all his allusions to the functionaries and
functions of the holy office, is one of the most striking proofs of
the extent to which this spiritual tyranny had, in the course of
less than a century, bowed down all Spanish thought and language beneath its sway. In the most of the Spanish historians,
I find the establishment of the Inquisition spoken of in terms of
most hypocritical adulation. In Mariana, however, although the
jesuit (himself at one time an Inquisitor) by no means says all

he thinks, enough is said to let us understand something of his true sentiments. The plain and obvious arguments against a secret, a bloody, and a bigoted tribunal, are set forth very powerfully, and he has tact enough to manage it so, that the effect of these is not at all done away by the pompous arguments he, as in his own person, is compelled to adduce *per contra.* See Mariana's whole chapter, entitled "Inquisitores Castellæ dati;" and particularly the passage beginning, " Grave provincialibus visum est Parentum Scelera filiorum pœnis lui; occulto accusatore reos fieri; neque cum indice compositos damnari; contra quam olim factum erat peccata in religione vindicari morte; *illud gravissimum adimi per inquisitiones loquendi liberi audiendique commercium dispersis per urbes et oppida et agros observatoribus quod extremum in servitute credebant,*" &c. For a full account of the Spanish Inquisition, see *Llorente's Histoire de l'Inquisition en Espagne;* a masterly and very learned article by Mr. Southey, in the Quarterly Review; and an able essay under the head of INQUISITION, lately published in the Encyclopædia Edinensis, by the Rev. Dr. John Hodgson, of Blantyre. The "Holy Brotherhood," alluded to on the present occasion, was a very necessary and useful association for the prevention of robberies and murders in the less populous districts of Spain. The state in which the country had been left, after a long series of wars and tumults, rendered it necessary for well-disposed individuals to take such steps in aid of the (in such matters) too dilatory arm of the Spanish executive. Shortly afterwards, Cervantes mentions the " Santa Hermandad vieja" of Toledo, which was a particular branch of this institution, having its separate prison, &c.

Note LXII. p. 96.

Out of the hands of the Chaldeans. — So the Moors were frequently called by the early Spaniards, whose archaic phraseology is continually in the mouth of Don Quixote.

Note LXIII. p. 97.

Had I but bethought myself of making a small bottleful of the balsam of Fierabras, &c. — Sir Ferumbras or Fierabras, was one of the greatest heroes of the Round-table of Charlemagne, although he has not the advantage of being commemorated in the original *Magnum Opus* of the Archbishop of Rheims. Mr. Ellis has given an analysis of an English unprinted metrical romance upon his story, which appears to be nothing more than a translation from the French one. According to all these authorities, LABAN, Sovereign of Babylon, possessor of the renowned city of Agramore, on the River Flagote, was a sore enemy of the Christians, and drove them out of the Holy Land. Not contented with this, he sent his son Sir Ferumbras, after the poor Christians into Europe, where Ferumbras demeaned himself like a true son of the terrible Laban, and, among other well-authenticated exploits, took possession of ROME itself. Charlemagne forthwith sends some of his paladins to give knightly combat to this fearful Saracen, and a long series of romantic adventures ensues, in which dwarfs, giants, cavaliers, virgins, Moors, priests, and enchanters, walk through their usual paces, all more or less for the exaltation of the glory of Sir Ferumbras, the Prince-Royal of Babylon. At last, however, OLIVER meets with the hero, and then the tables are turned. The combat is long and doubtful, chiefly in consequence of two bottles of balsam which Ferumbras carries, (in his holsters,) a simple drop of which, taken internally, is sufficient to restore the continuity of the most cruelly mangled skin; of which Sir Ferumbras of course avails himself on the receipt of every blow; and, more wonderful far, of which he constantly offers a few drops to his antagonist, every time he sees his own sword come back bloody from the body on which he is exercising its edge with all the accustomed fury of a Babylonian. In the *Carlo Magno*, we have him introduced upon this occasion as using these expressions, " O Senor Olivero, O vos bolved a curer de vos llagas, o beved del balsamo que commego trago, y luego serez salvo, y assi podreys pelear y defendar vuestra vida," &c. Instead of accepting this polite offer, the fierce Oliver aims a back blow at Sir Ferumbras's saddle, the two bottles tumble into a river, and the pagan is then as easily beaten as Antæus was, when Hercules lifted him off the ground. In a word, the son of Laban, the Emperor of Babylon, gives in. " I am so hurt," says he, (to give the words of the English romance,)

> " I am so hurt, I may not stonde;
> I put me all in thy grace;

> My God's bcene false by water and lond;
> I reng them all here in this place;
> Baptized now will I bene," &c.

The baptized Ferumbras is forthwith created a paladin and a peer, and heads on all occasions the host of Charlemagne. His father hearing of his sudden conversion, immediately brings a huge army to fight Charlemagne and his son ; but, as might be expected, they overcome him, and it is only by the intercession of Ferumbras that the head of the Emperor Laban is permitted to remain upon his royal shoulders. Charlemagne spares him, and on the instant

> "Bade them ordain a great vat,
> To baptize the Sowdan in,
> And look what he shall *hat*, (be called.)

The Sowdan, unfortunately, is afflicted, on sight of this great vat, with a very impious species of hydrophobia ; and after a great many vain attempts to reconcile him to baptism, Charlemagne is compelled to have recourse to immediate decapitation, as the only alternative that had occurred either to him or to any of his company. "It was done," quoth the romancer,—

> "It was done at the king's command;
> His soul was sent to hell,
> To dance in that sorry land,
> With devils that were full fell."

Sir Ferumbras, being invested with one half of the kingdom of Spain, prefers settling there to claiming the allegiance of his father's pagan subjects. He marries, and is crowned in due form; and becomes on the whole a peaceable character, but amuses himself now and then with cutting and carving both his own body and the bodies of his friends, merely for the pleasure of exhibiting the wonderful virtues of the "Balsam of Fierabras "— the receipt for concocting the which, Don Quixote will give us in proper form a few pages farther on.

NOTE LXIV. p. 98.

To lead a life like the Marquis of Mantua, &c. — Of this story

I have already said something. The vow of the Marquis runs
thus in the ballad:

> Juro per dios verdadero
> De nunca peynar mis comas,
> Ni los barbas mi tocare,
> De no vestir otras ropas
> Ni renovar mi calzare,
> Ni las armas mi quitare;
> Sino fuera par un hora;
> De no comer en mantele,
> Ni a mesa mi assentare
> Hasta matar a Don Carloto, &c.

See a preceding note on the story of Baldwin, &c. Sylva de
Romances, F. 38.

Note LXV. p. 99, 100.

Saccrapante—Albracca, &c. &c.—For all these, I refer the
reader to Boiardo and Ariosto.

Note LXVI. p. 105.

*O happy age, he cried, which our first parents call'd the age of
gold.*—This beautiful speech, for it is throughout beautiful and
classical in the highest degree, is little more than a translation of
one of the finest passages in Tasso's *Aminta. "O' bell' eta," &c.*
end of act first.

Note LXVII. p. 112.

His parents being ruled by him, grew rich in a short time, &c.—
Cervantes here has in his eye that passage in Aristotle's politics,
where the story is told of a Cretan sage, who, being reproached
with the unproductiveness of his philosophical pursuits, answered,
he could, if he chose, draw an abundant revenue from his science; and, accordingly, did soon realize a fortune, in consequence of arranging his crops, &c., so as to suit the weather he
foresaw.

Note LXVIII. p. 113.

*The plays which the young lads in our neighborhood enacted on
Corpus Christi day.*—These *plays* were of the same nature with

our own *mysteries,* founded, namely, upon subjects taken from holy writ. Such performances were usual all over Europe at this time on Corpus Christi day, and several other festivals of the church.

NOTE LXIX. p. 120.

King Arthur never died, but was turned into a crow by en-chantment; for which reason the people of Great Britain dare not kill a crow, &c. — It is supposed that the superstition alluded to in the text had, in reality, gone so far, as to have influence at least on the *Welch* legislators ; for in the laws of Hoel the Good, we find a heavy fine appointed to be paid by every person, who kills a raven, (Leges Hoeli Boni, Londini, 1730, p. 334,) and I do not think any origin of such a law could be pointed out either more rational or more probable, than the prevalence of this reverential feeling towards Arthur. The inscription on the tombstone of Arthur was, (according to the monkish chronicles, too often rivals of the romancers,)

Hic jacet Arthurus Rex quondam Rexque Futurus.

NOTE LXX. p. 123.

Some knights have at last by their valor been raised to thrones and empires, &c. — Of such elevations, we have already had occasion to notice several instances. They are as plenty as blackberries, in the romances. Reynaldo de Montalban became Emperor of Trebizond, (according to the Sylva de Romances, p. 76.) In Esplandian, c. 177, we are told, that " El emperador casando a su hija Leonorina con Esplandian les renuncio todo su imperio." Bernard del Carpio " se casa con Olympia haziendole Rey de IRLANDA," (Espinosa, canto 33.) Palmerin d'Oliva became Emperor of Constantinople. Tirant the White became " Principe y Cæsar del Imperio de Grecia," &c. &c.

NOTE LXXI. p. 124.

You never commend yourselves to God, but only to your mistresses. — The same reproach was once made to Tirant the White. His answer was, " El que a muchos sirve no sirve a ninguno." — Lib. iii. cap. 28.

Note LXXII. p. 128.

Let none but he those arms deface,
Who will Orlando's fury face, &c.

See Ariosto, Canto 24.

——— Nessun le muova
Che star non possa con Roldan a pruova, &c.

Note LXXIII. p. 128.

I draw my pedigree from the Cachopines of Loredo. — Bowles, upon the authority of the venerable Sir Isaac Heard, mentions that an old house was pulled down at St. Andrews not very long ago, on a stone in the interior wall of which appeared this inscription:

"Antes falten Robles y Enzinas
Que las casas Cachopinas."

Note LXXIV. p. 143.

Yanguesian carriers. —The people of a certain district in Castile, the principal village of which is *Yanguas.*

Note LXXV. p. 148.

Amadis de Gaul in the power of Archelaus. — See the Amadis, chap. xix. and lxix. For the Knight of the Sun, mentioned immediately after, see Palmerin of Oliva, cap. 43.

Note LXXVI. p. 149.

The laws of duels. — The most complete code of duelling is to be found in Maffei's treatise, *Della Scienza Cavalleresca.* Most minute rules are there laid down concerning more improbable contingencies than that alluded to in the text. *Insults* are classed and subdivided, as accurately as crimes against life and property have ever been in statute-books; and the proper *quantum* of revenge to be exacted in every supposable case, is laid down with all the gravity of a Numa; *e. g.* when you are insulted by a lame man, you must tie up your leg before you take the field against him, &c. &c.

Note LXXVII. p. 151.

The Lovely Obscure. — BELTENEBROS is the name given to

Amadis in all the romances, on occasion of this adventure. This has been often cited as one of the most convincing proofs of the Spanish, or, more properly, the Peninsular origin of the romance; but in the old French Amadis, it is Beltenebreux.

NOTE LXXVIII. p. 153.

Maritornes. — Malitorne is old French for " mechante femme."

NOTE LXXIX. p. 154.

A knight-errant! cried the wench; pray what is that?

Io son nutrito sotto il Santo impero
Del magnanimo Artus real e pio,
E da lui fatto *errante cavaliero,*
Vo *cercando avventure* hor quinci hor quindi.

GYRONE, L. 2. 75.

NOTE LXXX. p. 157.

Nay, some do not stick to say, Cid Hamet Benengeli was somewhat akin to the muleteer. — Cervantes probably means to insinuate, that the muleteer was himself a Moor, one of the many who made outward profession of Christianity, after Mahometanism became a crime in Spain; which, as all the world knows, happened in Cervantes's own day, to the great injury of the commerce and agriculture of the Spanish dominions. Before their total expulsion, it would seem the Moriscos were very much employed as carriers and muleteers; for, says the author of certain " Discourses on the Provision of the Court," (never published, but quoted by Pellicer, and composed in 1616,) " By the expulsion of the Moors, Spain lost about four or five thousand carriers, who were of infinite advantage in transporting all kinds of merchandise. Between 1608 and 1616, the charge of carriage from Seville to Madrid has been more than tripled. In Tiemblo, (a little town fourteen leagues from Madrid,) I remember eighteen carriers, and now there is not one. There used to be not less than five-and-twenty at Talamea, (forty-eight leagues from Madrid,) and now there is only one in the whole place."

NOTE LXXXI. p. 165.

The enchanted Moor of this castle. — The fair Rosaliana, in

Belianis of Greece, uses these words: "Acabad de matar aquellos malos gigantes, por que en el entretanto que alguno dellos fuere vivo no scran deshechos los encantamentos de este castillo." L. 3. c. 9.

NOTE LXXXII. p. 172.

You must excuse me from paying any thing; it was never known that knights-errant paid in any inn whatever. —There is a contrary authority in Pulci. Morg. Magg. C. 21.

> Orlando che sentito ha gia il romore
> Presto s'arma per andare a vedere:
> Ma l'Ostier suo per non pigliar errore,
> Volle che pegno lasciasse il destriro
> Che non ista delli Scotti alla fede.
> Orlando scoppia di duolo e di pena,
> Ma da pagar non aveva moneta:
> *Che solea sempre dar bastioni o spade*
> *All' Oste, quando i danar gli mancavano.*

NOTE LXXXIII. p. 179.

Emperor of the vast island of Taprobana, &c.—The most of the fine-sounding names in this catalogue, are to be found (or, at least, something like them) in the Romances. The

> "—— utmost Indian isle, Taprobane,"

is one of the few places enumerated, which it is worth while to seek for on any map.

> ——" Such forces met not, nor so wide a camp,
> When Agrican, with all his northern powers
> Besieged Albracca, as romances tell,
> The city of Gallaphrone, from whence to win
> The fairest of her sex, Angelica,
> Her daughter sought by many prowest knights,
> Both Paynim and the peers of Charlemagne."

NOTE LXXXIV. p. 198.

Knight of the Woful Figure, &c.—" Caballero de la triste figura," is translated by Shelton, " Knight of the ill-favored face;" but Smollett's " Knight of the Sorrowful Countenance," expresses far better than either of these the sense of Cervantes. At a certain chivalric spectacle given by Queen Mary of Hungary, the Count D'Aremberg jousted under the title of " Knight of the Griphon," with Don Juan de Saavedra, who was arrayed in sable armor, and styled " the Sorrowful Knight."

NOTE LXXXV. p. 199.

Remember what befell the Cid Ruy Diaz, when he broke to pieces the chair in the Pope's presence, for which he was excommunicated. — Don Quixote alludes very inaccurately to one of the most evidently apocryphal of all the Cid's achievements. The ballad in which the story is told, must have been composed at some period when the precedence of France and Spain was matter of courtly dispute; therefore long after the time when the best of the Spanish ballads concerning the Cid were framed. I shall translate, notwithstanding,

THE EXCOMMUNICATION OF THE CID.

I.

It was when from Spain across the main the Cid had come to Rome,
He chanced to see chairs four and three beneath Saint Peter's dome.
" Now tell, I pray, what chairs be they?" " Seven kings do sit thereon,
As well doth suit, all at the foot of the holy father's throne.

II.

" The Pope he sitteth above them all, that they may kiss his toe,
Below the keys the Flower-de-lys doth make a gallant show;
For his great puissance, the King of France next to the Pope may sit,
The rest more low, all in a row, as doth their station fit."

III.

" Ha!" quoth the Cid, " now God forbid! it is a shame, I wiss,
To see the Castle * planted beneath the Flower-de-lys.†
No harm, I hope, good father Pope — although I move thy chair."
—In pieces small he kick'd it all, ('twas of the ivory fair.)

IV.

The Pope's own seat he from his feet did kick it far away,
And the Spanish chair he planted upon its place that day;

* The arms of Castile.   † The arms of France.

Above them all he planted it, and laugh'd right bitterly,
Looks sour and bad I trow he had, as grim as grim might be.

V.

Now when the Pope was aware of this, he was an angry man,
His lips that night, with solemn rite, pronounced the awful ban;
The curse of God, who died on rood, was on that sinner's head —
To hell and woe man's soul must go if once that curse be said.

VI.

I wot, when the Cid was aware of this, a woful man was he,
At dawn of day, he came to pray at the blessed father's knee:
"Absolve me, blessed father, have pity upon me,
Absolve my soul, and penance I for my sin will dree."—

VII.

" Who is this sinner," quoth the Pope, " that at my foot doth kneel?"
—" I am Rodrigo Diaz, a poor Baron of Castile."
Much marvell'd all were in the hall, when that name they heard him say,
—" Rise up, rise up," the Pope he said, " I do thy guilt away."

VIII.

" I do thy guilt away," he said, " and my curse I blot it out—
God save Rodrigo Diaz, my Christian champion stout;
I trow, if I had known thee, my grief it had been sore,
To curse Ruy Diaz de Bivar; God's scourge upon the Moor."

NOTE LXXXVI. p. 209.

The shepherd and his goats got at last to the river Guadiana.—
This story (originally told by Petrus Alphonsus) may be found
in its most perfect form in the *Cento Novello Antiche.*

" Il favolatore incommencio a dire una favola de uno villano
che avea suoi cento bisante; ando a uno Mercato a comperire
berbeci ed ebbene due per bisante. Tornando con le sue pecore
uno fiume che avea passa era molto cresciuto. Stando a la riva
brigossi d'accioire in questo modo che vide uno pescator povero
con uno suo burchiello a dismisura picciolino, sì che non vi capea
se non il villano ed una pecora per volto. Lo villano commen-
cio a passare con una berbice, e comincio a vocare il fuime era
largo. Voga è passa. E lo favolatore non dicea pui: E Messere Azzolino disse; chefai? via oltre. Lo favolatore rispose,
Messere lasciate passare le pecore, poi conteremo lo fatto; che
le pecore no sarebbono passate in uno anno, si che in tanto puote
bene adagio dormire."— Nov. xxx.

Note LXXXVII. p. 220.

Mambrino's Helmet. — I refer to Orlando Furioso *passim*, for the whole history of the enchanted and invulnerable head-piece, originally the property of King Mambrino.

Note LXXXVIII. p. 226.

" *Well, then,*" *quoth Sancho,* "*I have been thinking to myself of late how little is to be gained by hunting up and down,*" *&c.* — The reader of romance does not need to be told how faithfully Don Quixote, in reply to this saying of his squire, has abridged the main story of many a ponderous folio. The imaginary career of glory which he unfolds before the eyes of Sancho, is paralleled almost *ad literatim* in the romance of *Sir Degore*, so admirably analyzed by Mr. Ellis. The conclusion of Belianis is almost exactly the same sort of adventure.

Note LXXXIX. p. 243.

He is that notorious rogue Gines de Passamonte. — Cervantes makes even the galley-slaves play upon Don Quixote's foible; for *Passamonte* is the name of a gigantic brother of the illustrious Giant Morgante, slain by Orlando in the Morgante Maggiore. Gines pretends to have written his own life while in the galleys. The preliminary fiction of Guzman d'Alfarache is of the same species.

Note XC. p. 244.

Lazarillo de Tormes. — About the most popular book in Spain, at the time when Cervantes wrote, was the Life of Lazarillo de Tormes, a work of very extraordinary genius, written at a very early period of his career, by the great Spanish historian, poet, soldier, and statesman, Don Diego de Mendoza. It was the first comic romance that had appeared in the modern world, or at least the first that had ever made any noise in the world. The species of tricks and adventures in which Lazarillo is engaged, had indeed been long in great favor among the Spaniards, but Mendoza first embalmed such materials in the elegancies of diction, and adorned them with the interest of an artificial narrative. The contrast his shrewd and humorous representation of human life affords to the pompous romances of chivalry, which then formed almost the sole reading of the Spaniards, is such, that no one can be surprised with the great success of this first effort of Mendoza's genius. Lazarillo de Tormes was immediately translated into Italian and French, and both abroad and at home gave birth to innumerable imitations. The best of all these is, without doubt, the History of Guzman d'Alfarache, commonly called the Spanish Rogue, which made its appearance a few years before the publication of Don Quixote. Like its prototype, this book became exceedingly popular all over Europe; and there soon appeared (among many others) an excellent version of it in English, which ought, without doubt, to be reprinted in its original shape. From these books, Le Sage derived a great many of the best stories with which we have all been made so familiar by his Gil Blas and Batchelor of Salamanca. Indeed, in Le Sage's own abridgment of Guzman d'Alfarache, many of the best stories in the whole book are omitted, for no other reason but that Le Sage had already appropriated them in his Gil Blas. Mendoza's rich and beautiful style, however, gives a charm to his Lazarillo, which the dry and caustic Aleman (the author of Guzman) could never rival. Mendoza composed poems of many sorts, satires, lyrics, epistles, sonnets, pastorals, and ballads; but, next to his Lazarillo de Tormes, which he wrote before he left college at Salamanca, his most celebrated work is his History of the War of Granada, which he composed towards the decline of his life, and which was not suffered to be printed until thirty years after his death, in consequence of the hardihood of some of the opinions expressed in it. With the exception of Machiavelli and Guicciardini, there is perhaps no modern writer who has produced any thing so nearly approaching to the pure and classical character of the great historical monuments left us by the Greeks and Romans. The life of Mendoza himself was a very extraordinary one. He owed his rise to letters, and he never ceased to cultivate them during the whole of a very long life; and yet he was engaged continually in public business, and even bore the first part in many of the most important transactions of his time. He was taken from college by Charles V., soon after he had published his Lazarillo de Tormes, and sent ambassador to Venice, where he greatly distinguished himself in the management of several very difficult intrigues. He afterwards represented the person of the same monarch at the Council of Trent, and still later at the Court of Rome. In the Italian wars of those days he acquired the character of a skilful and decided commander. He was governor of Sienna ; and from thence, it may almost be said, he administered the whole affairs of Italy during a period of six years. After harmony was restored between the Papal See and his own prince, Mendoza was appointed to the high office of gonfalonier of the church, and in that capacity was commander-in-chief of all the ecclesiastical forces. He retired to Spain on the accession of Philip II., who does not appear to have treated him with the same confidence as his father, inasmuch as, for the most part, the rest of his life was passed in comparative privacy and literary leisure. Nevertheless, he accompanied Philip into France, and was present at the great battle of St. Quintin, in 1557. Nor had old age any power to check the fervor of his spirit, if we may put faith in some of the anecdotes commonly recorded of him: For example, we are told, that " long after his hairs were gray," he quarrelled with a nobleman who was his rival in some amour, and coming to high words one day in the presence-chamber of Philip, expressed himself with so much scorn, that his adversary laid his hand on his poniard. Mendoza, observing this, seized the man, who was far younger than himself, and flung him furiously over the balcony into the street. Altogether, the career of Mendoza was like that of Cervantes himself, a striking example, not only of the versatility of genius, but of the benefit which literature, in many of its finest walks, may derive from being cultivated by the active and energetic spirits of the world.

Note XCI. p. 252.

"Methinks," quoth Sancho, " *I already hear the arrows whizzing about my ears."* — It appears that when the officers of the Holy Brotherhood found any one in the act of guilt, or, as we express it in Scotland, *red-hand*, their custom was to tie him to a stake, and shoot at him with their arrows till he died. " Sic deprehensum," says Munsterus, (in his *Cosmographia*, p. 60,) " vivum palo alligatum sagittis conficiunt." Charles V., by an edict, directed that the man should be hanged first, and then shot at in this manner.

END OF VOL. I.

www.ingramcontent.com/pod-product-compliance
Lightning Source LLC
Chambersburg PA
CBHW051516100726
47898CB00005B/1479